Berkley titles by David E. Meadows

THE SIXTH FLEET
THE SIXTH FLEET: SEAWOLF
THE SIXTH FLEET: TOMCAT
THE SIXTH FLEET: COBRA

JOINT TASK FORCE: LIBERIA
JOINT TASK FORCE: AMERICA
JOINT TASK FORCE: FRANCE
JOINT TASK FORCE: AFRICA

JOINT TASK FORCE
AFRICA

DAVID E. MEADOWS

BERKLEY BOOKS, NEW YORK

THE BERKLEY PUBLISHING GROUP
Published by the Penguin Group
Penguin Group (USA) Inc.
375 Hudson Street, New York, New York 10014, USA
Penguin Group (Canada), 10 Alcorn Avenue, Toronto, Ontario M4V 3B2, Canada
(a division of Pearson Penguin Canada Inc.)
Penguin Books Ltd., 80 Strand, London WC2R 0RL, England
Penguin Group Ireland, 25 St. Stephen's Green, Dublin 2, Ireland (a division of Penguin Books Ltd.)
Penguin Group (Australia), 250 Camberwell Road, Camberwell, Victoria 3124, Australia
(a division of Pearson Australia Group Pty. Ltd.)
Penguin Books India Pvt. Ltd., 11 Community Centre, Panchsheel Park, New Delhi—110 017, India
Penguin Group (NZ), Cnr. Airborne and Rosedale Roads, Albany, Auckland 1310, New Zealand
(a division of Pearson New Zealand Ltd.)
Penguin Books (South Africa) (Pty.) Ltd., 24 Sturdee Avenue, Rosebank, Johannesburg 2196, South
Africa

Penguin Books Ltd., Registered Offices: 80 Strand, London WC2R 0RL, England

This is a work of fiction. Names, characters, places, and incidents either are the product of the author's imagination or are used fictitiously, and any resemblance to actual persons, living or dead, business establishments, events, or locales is entirely coincidental.

Joint Task Force: Africa

A Berkley Book / published by arrangement with the author

PRINTING HISTORY
Berkley mass-market edition / March 2005

Copyright © 2005 by David Meadows.
Cover design by Richard Hasselberger.
Interior text design by Kristin del Rosario.

ISBN: 0-425-20147-3

BERKLEY®
Berkley Books are published by The Berkley Publishing Group,
a division of Penguin Group (USA) Inc.,
375 Hudson Street, New York, New York 10014.
BERKLEY is a registered trademark of Penguin Group (USA) Inc.
The "B" design is a trademark belonging to Penguin Group (USA) Inc.

PRINTED IN THE UNITED STATES OF AMERICA

10 9 8 7 6 5 4 3 2 1

*To the men and women who serve on
the nation's reconnaissance missions*

ACKNOWLEDGMENTS

It is impossible to thank everyone who provided technical advice and support for this and other novels. My thanks for those who visited **www.sixthfleet.com** and provided comments.

I do appreciate the encouragement and the honor from authors, talk-show hosts, and readers who provided reviews on my books—such as former Speaker of the House, Newt Gingrich; Stephen Coonts; W.E.B. Griffin; Joe Buff; Robert Gandt; Tom Wilson; Victoria Taylor-Murray; John Tegler; Milos Stankovic; Christy Tillery-French; John Hemry; and other fellow authors. If I have inadvertently missed someone, I apologize, but I would like to express my individual thanks for their technical assistance to Col(S) Marjorie Davis; Ms. Sharon Reinke (with best wishes in her retirement); Mr. Art Horn; Col(S) Randy Coats, USAF; LCDR Nancy Mendonca; CDR Scott Fish (helicopter warrior); Mr. Ed Brumit; Maj Howard Walton, USMC; a Royal Navy supporter, Stephen Barnett; the dynamic LCDR Kevin "Moose" Missel; and Jeff and Yoko Brown. My respects to Col Gene Tyler and Col Cec Tyler, an Army family that represents what keeps America free; Bob "Mr. IA" Gorrie, retired U.S. Army colonel and leader of the DIAP. And, I can never forget the admin team who kept me organized at work. CWO4-ret Tim Bovill, LT Greg Klitgard, Petty Officer Michelle R. Nagle, Petty Officer Jennifer L. McGowan (our junior sailor for 2003), Petty

Officer Tashira L. Hadley (who is now dodging polar bears and snow birds), Petty Officer Mustafa K. Wilson (and may he get his wish to go to sea ASAP), and Petty Officer Regina E. Mitchem (who is surviving the wilds of West Virginia). My thanks to Ms. Terry Smith, Mr. Vincent M. Widmaier, and Mr. William D. Cross for their security insights. And, as always, my continued thanks to Mr. Tom Colgan for his editorial support, and to his able right-hand person, Ms. Sandy Harding.

Rest assured that any and all technical errors or mistakes in this novel are strictly those of the author, who many times wanders in his own world.

David E. Meadows

CHAPTER 1

"LINE THEM UP, SERGEANT," GENERAL FELA AZIKIWE OJO ordered. For emphasis his finger waved at the boys.

The heavyset Guinean lowered his eyes in Ojo's direction and with a huge stick prodded two young boys so hard that one of them fell. The young lad scrambled to stand. A nearby soldier kicked the lad, sending him tumbling across the dirt. None of the boys in line moved to help.

Ojo saw the tears. There would be more tears before he cleansed Africa of the enslavers. The boy scrambled to regain his footing and ran toward the soldiers aligned in front of Ojo. Ojo leaned back in the chair someone had pulled from one of the huts. He shifted the AK-47 so it lay across the chair arms, his right hand clasping the stock so in one smooth motion he could both swing the weapon and fire it at the same time. Around him, Africans from tribes throughout West Africa hustled, carrying out his orders. It hadn't been much of a battle. But, then again, most of these villages had few men of fighting ages. Africa was truly the continent of child warriors. What he was doing was disarming the future weapons Abu Alhaul and his Jihadists would create in these children. With the exception of a few, most of the lads standing in line were barefoot and wore short pants. Thin reeds emerged from the pant legs, attesting to the paucity of food fed to the students who studied ways to die. None of them wore shirts, the shirts having been torn from their thin frames by his soldiers as they rounded up the frightened lads.

A soldier swung his AK-47, cracking the fleeing boy across the temple. The boy fell, dust rising around him from the bare soil.

"Measure him," Ojo said.

The two soldiers who had chased the boy grabbed the unconscious lad by this hands and feet, stretching him out on his back.

From Ojo's side, the elderly man hobbled over to the prone boy. He lay the stick down alongside the lad, one end of it at the feet. The boy's head was several inches above the other end.

The old man looked at Ojo who nodded at the two soldiers. The elder bent over and picked up the stick as the two soldiers rose, one of them carrying the hands and the other the feet. Ojo watched the boys who were staring intently at the soldiers carrying off their classmate. The soldiers quickly disappeared behind the burning schoolhouse with their burden and Niewu, the old man, shuffled back to his place beside Ojo, and eased himself down onto the dirt, laying the shaft across his knees.

"Nuts to butt!" Ojo shouted.

Single pistol shots, one after the other, broke the noise of the shouting troops running back and forth in front of him, forcing the boys standing in line closer together, so close their chests touched the backs of the person in front of them. *Nuts to butt* was the military command he used to force the boys closer and reduce the chance of another one bolting.

Most of the young students continued to stare at the schoolhouse, now burning a couple of hundred yards away near the edge of the jungle, as if afraid of meeting his eyes. The smell of old wood burning, the thatched roof caving down into the center, drifted across the large open center of the village. Ojo glanced at the schoolhouse while reaching up to remove his khaki cap and wipe the sweat from his forehead. These were the bane of Africa—the dirge of terrorism. Schoolhouses where old evil men carved the weapons of terrorism. Every day mullahs canted religious nonsense to them, teaching them life was but a transition to a better place and the more nonbelievers they took with them, the better their position in the afterlife. Ojo wiggled in his seat, glancing at the setting sun on the horizon. August heat was atrocious. He put his cap back on his head and pulled the brim forward. He could have waited in the shade until the selection process was ready to begin. But it was important that the ones who survived the selection process understood who decided they would live. So, he sat in the center of the open court area between the thatched homes of the villagers, watching the scenario unfold as it had unfolded in African village after village as his forces moved eastward through Guinea.

He would catch Abu Alhaul. The man was on the run, hurrying westward, and soon they would enter the jungles of Guinea to give chase, but first he must disarm this village. Ojo recalled the incursion into Ivory Coast. They had been so close, but the Americans had caused him to retreat. This Egyptian terrorist was forcing an unwanted change in West Africa—changes that offended the beliefs of true

Africans, causing them to withdraw from their ancestors. He lifted a water bottle from beside the chair and drank deeply. There was a time, three years ago, when he was known as Mumar Kabir and served as the head African for Abu Alhaul. It had taken an American—a young American of about twelve years—younger than some of those who cower in the selection line—to nearly kill him to give him the opportunity to break from Abu Alhaul. He smiled, a thin, tight smile. Ojo doubted the Egyptian terrorist even knew who Fela Azikiwe Ojo was. It was better this way, and he hoped to be able to look his former master in the eye to see the recognition before he cut the terrorist's throat.

Eventually, he would take on the Americans and the strong western powers. His encounter at Kingsville against the legendary American general, Daniel Thomaston, had taught him caution. Americans could be defeated in the court of world opinion, but he would be foolish to confront them on the battlefield. The Americans and the British were fierce warriors. You fought one; you fought the other. If he could only build a similar alliance with others, the freedom of West Africa would be assured. Ojo sighed, bent over, and retied the loose lace on his right combat boot. He would never live to see Africa as one country, but maybe one of his wives' children would live to see it and honor him as the catalyst that made it possible.

"Ojo," he said softly, enjoying how the name rolled off his lips. This African name was better than the Arab name bestowed on him at birth. An Arab name he carried until the disastrous defeat at Kingsville two years ago. The African National Army had started small, but as victory after victory piled up, it had grown and every day new recruits appeared. Ahead of him was his former master and nemesis of Africa—Abu Alhaul. During the two years since he vanished into the jungle after the defeat at Kingsville, Ojo had convinced himself he had been a reluctant, brainwashed follower of Abu Alhaul; and that his ancestors had taken him from the terrorist camp and guided him to this place of honor, of power, of destiny.

Two soldiers pulled a taller youth from the line, screaming at the boy who covered his face with both hands. The soldier on the right struck the prisoner across face with the stock of his rifle, sending teeth and blood flying. A low wail rose from those in line. One of the soldiers turned and screamed at the boys to be quiet or he would kill them. The caterwauling increased in tempo. Several soldiers raised their weapons, their fingers tight against the triggers, prepared to fire if the boys ran. It had happened several villages ago. If the prisoners rioted from their fear, most would die, but with a hundred or more lads in front, some would survive. The boy fell to his knees.

Ojo nodded to himself. "Mumar Kabir" served him well in the Islamic concentration of Nigeria where his mother lived, but when he returned to Liberia—home of his father— few appreciated the holy implications of his name. Even he failed to appreciate it. He hated the name, but it plucked him from the crowd during the time he spent with the Islamic radicals bent on chasing Westerners from Africa and imposing a religious dictatorship on Africa. Africa has always been a slave under the mantel of those not African. Arabs weren't Africans, though when it suited them, they would claim kinship based on North Africa. North Africa wasn't really part of the Africa Ojo knew and loved. North Africa was never considered Africa, being separated from the real Africa by the Sahara Desert.

Niewu rose from the dirt beside Ojo's chair, pushing his frail frame up with the rough yew staff. On thin legs, the aged man shuffled to where the two soldiers held the unconscious lad upright by the arms. Niewu placed the staff on the ground. The two soldiers dragged the boy, his feet leaving two trails in the dirt, to stand beside the staff. This boy also was several inches taller than the staff. They looked at Ojo. He raised his hand off the stock of the rifle and motioned toward the building from where the shots were coming. The wailing increased as the two soldiers dragged the boy off, disappearing around the edge of the building. Other soldiers walked the line, using short whips on the boys, shouting for them to be quiet.

General Kabaka was behind the burning building in charge of the squads with their knives and guns. Ojo frowned, his eyebrows scrunching. Whenever he thought of Kabaka, he knew that he would eventually have to kill the mercurial general because the man publicly lusted for Ojo's position. The only thing separating Kabaka from Abu Alhaul was that Kabaka was African. For this phase of the emergence, as Ojo thought of it, he needed the man and the Africans he brought with him. Kabaka was inept at treachery, failing to realize how transparent he was. As long as Kabaka had his victims, his ill-concealed plans would never reach fruition. The evil man was never more happy than when torturing someone. A slow kill would give Kabaka orgasms of pleasure. The lad would suffer more than the adults out of sight because Kabaka had a penchant for belts made from human skin and the younger the donor, the better the belt.

A few soldiers in front of Ojo had fashioned the whips individually with leather ends tipped with bits of metal. As the whips rose and fell, the late afternoon sun reflected off the various metal parts the soldiers had sewed, tied, or weaved into the straps. Bloody strips of skin flecked off as the soldiers moved along the line. Ojo looked at the ground beneath the boys and smiled where numerous wet spots showed where a boy had lost control of his bladder. *Your bladder is your least worry right now, lads,* he thought. What was the use of a young soldier who couldn't keep his water when desperate deeds such as this were necessary if Africa was to live in peace? An Africa where everyone had an opportunity to die peacefully in their sleep surrounded by relatives. Few had that opportunity today.

North Africa was different; separated by the protection of the Sahara Desert. Let them have this protection, for the Sahara also provided true Africans a boundary against those who would enslave them again.

Names are important. The stronger a name, the stronger the spirits that follow and support you; the stronger your link with your ancestors; and, the stronger your influence over those with less powerful names. Mumar Kabir never influenced Africans. Many times the name caused humiliation as other older boys teased him. The name *"Fela Azikiwe Ojo"* was African. It was strong. It was a name composed from different west coast tribes.

A commotion to his right caught his attention. A young boy bolted from the line, his quick feints and swerves narrowly avoiding the outstretched hands of the soldiers as he ran across the dirt of the open court area. A whip hit his back, but he kept running. His thin legs propelled up and down like some small locomotive determined to win against the odds. Even from a hundred yards away, moisture on the boy's cheeks glisten in the afternoon sun. The boy dodged right to avoid a charging soldier, the action caused the fleeing prisoner to run directly toward Ojo. For a fraction of a second, their eyes met. In that second, Ojo saw anger echoing inside the boy. For that brief moment, he mentally cheered the boy and hoped the lad reached the safety of the thick Guinean jungles surrounding this isolated village. The boy's lips moved and though Ojo couldn't hear what the boy was saying, he knew it was some sort of Islamic evil prayer for protection. The boy was shorter than the staff. If he had remained in the queue, he would have lived. What would he bring, if he was allowed to live? The spirit was too strong within this lad. If Ojo allowed him to live, one day in the future, the boy may try to kill Ojo.

His decision took less than a second and was based solely on the quick eye contact, but snap decisions had kept him alive in a world where death was a constant companion.

The boy changed direction, racing to the right of Ojo. *The boy must sense death is not far behind. Maybe he is going to try to kill me before death takes him? With what? Bare hands? Bare hands anchored to a body with protruding ribs and arms that are mere bones with skin stretched tight across them?* Ojo shifted the AK-47 across his knees.

Ojo started to raise his weapon, thought against it, and tried to remain impassive as the boy neared. A couple of soldiers jumped in front of Ojo. The boy's feet dug into the ground ten feet from him, sending up a large cloud of red dust. The boy changed direction, his feet churning the dust behind him, the cloud rolling over Ojo turning his khaki pants redder. The lad had found an opening between the soldiers. The jungle was only yards away.

Fear and anger affected each person different ways. He had seen those who wet themselves and curled into a ball muttering "please, please, please," over and over until someone put a pistol to their head and stopped the whining. Others he had witnessed stand straight and proud until someone put a pistol to their head and stopped the pride.

Two soldiers ran from opposite sides toward the boy. The boy put his head down and dashed between them as they dove to tackle him, missing and knocking their heads against each other. The boy reached the edge of the jungle and stopped. He turned and raised his hand, two fingers extended. Several soldiers shouted at the boy and ran toward him, bullets from their AK-47s peppering the ground around the lad, but missing. The boy turned and leaped into the underbrush, vanishing as it closed behind him like the sea over a diver. The boy was gone. A premonition that he hadn't seen the last of the lad caused a pique of angst to sweep over him. A cheer went up from the young prisoners. The guards raised their decorated whips and started working down the line again. Red dust stirred up by the escape rode the slight, but hot, breeze and Ojo resisted an impulse to wipe sweat from his brow, afraid those watching would interpret it as a sign of weakness. Weakness was an unacceptable trait for a leader in an army of killers.

The cheer quickly changed to wails and cries. The noise of their fear drowned the gunshot executions ongoing behind the burning schoolhouse. Ojo nearly lifted his free hand to cover an ear from the dreadful high-pitched wails. The guards' arms rose and fell rapidly as they beat the boys into submission. Soon the wailing descended more into a low mournful cry that had become the dirge of Africans as he lead this nationalistic movement to clean Africa of foreign influence; the worst of which was religion.

The prisoners were tiring. Some leaned on those in front. A few had passed out, but the pressure of the boy behind against the one in front held them upright. More single shots echoed from behind the burning school. The shots were coming less and less, with minutes between the shots. Suddenly, a scream of such intensity silenced the fearful wails and cries of the prisoners, causing them to stare toward the burning schoolhouse. A wave of goosebumps ran down Ojo's back, drawing his attention to the burning schoolhouse along with everyone else. Even the guards ceased their whippings. The boy had awakened and Kabaka was gathering new skin for his belts. The army may respect and worship Ojo, but they feared Kabaka and fear builds its own form of respect. Ojo shifted his weapon and thought, *Kabaka must go, if I am to live and our goal of a free Africa is to come. I must chose a day—a time and do it. It will be soon.*

The wailing of the prisoners resumed with a newer intensity, and a few more who had thus far managed to keep the soil dry beneath them now joined the others. Ojo looked at Niewu who had rejoined him.

"It is time, my friend."

Niewu nodded. "General Kabaka hasn't sent his runner yet, General Ojo. If we start and send too many back to him, he may not have the men to execute them."

Ojo looked down at Niewu and thought, *So, fear has already captured you, my friend. The man to whom I gave the power of the staff, and now you are willing to confront me for fear of Kabaka.*

Niewu saw the look and quickly said. "They have women back there that the men are enjoying. It is the one pleasure our soldiers have as we take your plan forward, General Ojo. If we send the rejections to them too soon, it would spoil their fun before they place the pistol against their heads and pull the trigger."

"Let's start, Niewu, and we will do it slowly. Those back there will be soon gone." The screams from behind the schoolhouse grew in pitch. "You understand who is the leader of this army?"

Niewu nodded rapidly, his head going up and down. "Yes, General." The old man rose quickly, barely using the staff this time.

To change Africa meant starting with the children. The

Islamic Jihadists understood that, and decades ago across the globe, they began to write on the blank chalkboards of youth the belief of killing oneself in furtherance of a religion earned great honor and immediate access to some fanatical version of heaven.

Two soldiers brought the first boy in line forward. The boy's legs kicked and kicked, trying to free the arms the two soldiers held. The two men jerked the boy upright, holding him so his feet couldn't reach them nor touch the ground. The two men looked toward Ojo, saw him watching them, and immediately looked down at their feet. Respect was a good thing. Respect was best earned through hard work, fairness, and camaraderie. That took time. Another avenue to earn respect was through fear and strength of command. Kabaka had learned that well. Fear took less time, but required relentless and ruthless application.

The soldiers continued walking up and down the line, whipping the children into place. Screams for them to "shut up" and "stand straight" had little effect, but the whips kept the line curling like a snake. The noise from their captives would never stop, but it was enough for Ojo that the wailing was more of a murmur now. Ojo knew the fear in each of these boys' minds was like a parasite eating away at it. The screaming from behind the schoolhouse was feeding their fear to such an extent that it was stifling their own moans and wails. Ojo sighed. If they knew what Kabaka was doing, he would never harvest any future warriors from this meager line.

The boys' bare feet beat an uneven tattoo in the dirt of the village, drawing small puffs of red dust into the air. He may have a bath when this was over.

The sergeant in charge of lining up the students walked to where the two held the first lad who was now kicking and screaming obscenities at them. Without a word, the huge man drew his hand back and with open palm slapped the side of the boy's face, the sound of the slap was accompanied by a pistol shot from behind the school. The boy's head snapped to the side, the head twisted back to the front and fell forward, the chin coming to rest on a heaving, thin chest.

"Bring him here," Ojo commanded, his bass voice riding over the background moans from their small captives. Small moist spots speckled beneath the feet of the boys as the line weaved back and forth, trying to avoid the two lines of soldiers narrowing a gauntlet to keep the boys in a single line.

The sergeant motioned the two soldiers to Ojo. Holding the unconscious body by the armpits, they dragged the boy forward, his toes creating small furrows in the dust behind them.

They respectfully nodded to Ojo when they stopped in front of him. They held the boy by the armpits, the lad's small chin lolling back and forth against the chest. Ojo leaned forward, careful not to drop his AK-47, and grabbed a handful of hair, pulling the boy's head up. Only white showed in the eyes, the pupils having slipped back under the top eyelids. Spittle ran from the boy's mouth, mixed with blood from where the sergeant's slap had broken the skin. The upper lip was already swelling. Ojo nodded toward Niewu. He released the boy's head, the chin bounced off the thin chest. "Bring the stick," he said to the sergeant.

He glanced over his shoulder at the spot in the jungle where the African boy had escaped. Others had probably slipped into the jungles when the battle started, but he allowed it as this kept his name and his army's fame growing across Africa.

Many new recruits had spoken of rumors and the pride Africans felt to have an African army achieving victories against the outsiders.

The sergeant standing before him was Nigerian. Nearly the same height as Ojo, his broad shoulders dovetailed to a muscular waist. He wore a sleeveless khaki shirt that lacked buttons. Old scars decorated the man's hands and arms, revealing a lifetime of hard, menial work—day in and day out. A couple of times, in battle, the performance of this sergeant made him think that the man had had military training before Ojo selected him as an enforcer. The Nigerian was a man of few words.

"Niewu!" the sergeant shouted.

The two soldiers turned to where Niewu stood, the staff anchored in the red dirt. The stick was bare of limbs, about three inches in diameter. It had a natural curve along its length, and where limbs had once grown from it, dark rings of age had sealed the spots. Ojo knew the staff was slightly over a meter long because he personally measured it. A meter was a little over three feet. A child captive in a religious school must be shorter than the staff. A child of that height he was considered malleable—capable of being retrained and recovered from religious lies, the worse of which were those that taught you that taking death through your own was God's way—Allah's way to enter paradise. *There is no paradise but Africa.*

His Pan African would remove whatever the mullahs had taught; remove the lies implanted into the fertile minds of African boys. He didn't care for Christianity either, but the Christians weren't teaching their students that salvation lay by blowing yourself up along with everyone else who happened to be around you at the time.

"Hold the staff," Ojo said.

At arm's length, Niewu placed the broad end of the

stick on the ground, holding the slightly narrower end by
his right hand.

"Measure him," Ojo commanded, pointing at the unconscious boy.

The two soldiers dragged the boy the couple of feet to
the stick and lifted him as straight as possible. The boy's
toes touched the ground.

"No, his feet must touch the ground. The heels and toes
must be level," Niewu said.

"Aiwa," they said together, saying "yes" in Arabic.

Ojo grimaced over the foreign language. Having an
army composed of hundreds who spoke dozens of dialects
and languages made necessary the use of Arabic, French, and
English as the common languages. If he could, he would
have mandated English as the common language for the
army, but that would have isolated hundreds. No, for the
time being, until he achieved his goal of ridding Africa of
foreign influence, they would use the three languages.

The two soldiers lowered the lad slowly until the small
feet touched the ground. The boy's feet turned on their
sides. They lifted him slightly so the feet were flat.

Ojo's eyes narrowed as he compared where the top of
the stick ended near the top of the boy's right ear. The stick
had been his idea. He had seen it used on carnival rides in
Lagos where the operator only allowed lads taller than the
stick to ride the machine. Ojo had learned from the experience, for he was one of those old enough to ride. Those too
short were also too young, and while they complained,
their whines were corrected by adults. The lesson he took
away was that when you were taller than the stick, you had
reached an age where you were entombed with the ways of
those who raised you. Entombed with beliefs, good or bad,
that defined you as a person and to change those beliefs

was hard; too hard; harder than an army on the march could afford.

He blinked. The stick hadn't grown and the boy hadn't shrunk. It still ended at the boy's ears.

"What do you think, Niewu? You are the keeper of the stick."

He saw the slight twinge on Niewu's face. The man preferred to call the "stick" a staff. Niewu leaned forward, holding the staff steady with his hand. He shuffled forward a couple of steps, never moving the staff. Ojo heard the familiar throat noises Niewu made as the man judged the height of the boy. Niewu was very serious in his job. After several seconds, the rich chocolate-dark African straightened and bowed toward Ojo. "General, I regret that another African student of Wahabi has exceeded the height of the staff."

The staff had become almost a religious icon in the army. It walked alongside Ojo when the army marched. Niewu wielded it as if it were a weapon. It afforded Niewu a status equal to a shaman. When Niewu entered or approached, soldiers cleared a path for him and his staff.

Ojo nodded. "I think you're right. It's sad, for the lad looks taller than his age." He started to say more, but three rapid pistol shots interrupted. Another piercing scream stilled the noise for a moment. Kabaka had jerked free another length of skin for his belt.

The line alternated back and forth in a slow swing as the captives weaved. The soldiers eased the whips, their arms growing tired from the exertion. They walked up and down the line, touching the young boys, leaning down and whispering things to scare their captives, murmuring orders mixed with promises. Saying things such as how they were going to cook them, or how the boys were going to be used like girls or castrated and forced to eat their own balls. Some of the boys were so young, they had no idea what the soldiers were talking about. Some of the captives stared at Ojo, their stares alternating between him and the unconscious boy.

Ojo looked at the sergeant. "You know what must be done."

"Yes, Master," Elimu said. He nodded at the two soldiers and motioned them toward the back of the schoolhouse where the executions continued.

"No," Ojo corrected. He pointed at the line. "They must see, so they understand the power of your stick. So those we allow to live understand that there is no way back to where they've been. Do it over there, where everyone can see, and use the sword."

The sergeant touched the huge sword he wore tied to his waist. "Yes, master," he said. He pointed near the spot where the two soldiers had tried to catch the young boy who escaped. Ojo knew the sergeant blamed himself for the escape. This was an opportunity for the soldier to redeem himself. *I like him using the word "master,"* he thought.

Ojo watched for a few moments. Then he turned his attention to the captives. "Sergeant, tell the soldiers to keep quiet and force the boys to watch what happens when you're taller than the stick." *Yes, you can't ride the ride when you're taller than the stick,* he thought.

The sergeant did as ordered. A pall of momentary quietness vanished as a new series of gunshots and another scream from the boy being made into a belt filled the village center. Another scream joined the boy's. *That was female,* Ojo thought to himself.

The sergeant motioned for the soldiers to stop. He looked at Ojo and waited for the command. One of the soldiers held the boy with both of his arms pinned behind his back. The boy rolled his head slowly, moaning, shock overcoming any attempt to escape. The other soldier emerged from a nearby hut with a small table. He set the table in front of the boy. The other soldier threw the boy chest first onto the rough wooden table, drawing a small cry from the captive as the wood dug into his naked chest.

The sergeant pulled the boy's arms tight behind his back, and another soldier grabbed a handful of hair and pulled hard, drawing the head back, exposing a slender neck, tendons sticking out visibly.

Ojo held his hand up, waiting for the captives to focus on the scene. When he believed their attention was on the sergeant and their fellow student, he dropped his hand. Ojo braced himself. Not for what was about to happen to the boy, but the ear splitting wails that would burst forth from the other captives.

The broadsword cut through the summer air and dust, slicing cleanly through the boy's neck, leaving the severed head swinging back and forth in the soldier's hand. The soldier danced lightly back and forth, trying to avoid the blood pouring from the head and from the neck. The eyes in the head looked rapidly right to left, so fast they were a blur. The sergeant immediately released the hands. The boy's body shuddered several times before it went limp and tumbled off the table. The soldier set the head on the boy's chest, facing the line. The sergeant placed the sword, blade flat on the tattered short pants of the dead boy and drew it back, wiping the blood off one side of the sword. Looking at the boys, he smiled at them as he wiped the blood from the other side of the sword before slipping it back into its leather sheath.

The next few in line were shorter than the staff. They

were taken to the other side of the village center where they were corralled in the wooden stockade used for cattle. The cattle had been slaughtered earlier, and in a nearby field his soldiers were cooking the meat for their dinner. His soldiers will be very hungry after such a hard day.

CHAPTER 2

"ROCKDALE, YOU ASSHOLE. YOU THINK THAT PARACHUTE is going to work with those loose straps hanging between your legs?" Chief "Badass" Razi said, reaching forward and grabbing Petty Officer Second Class Rockdale by the right shoulder, startling the young sailor. His other huge hand jerked the two straps dangling between Rockdale's legs, causing the slender petty officer to reach forward and cover his crotch.

"You feel that, boy," Razi said, his Georgia accent rolling the words out like a languid stream. He pushed the sailor away and immediately jerked him back. "You feel that between your legs, Rockdale?" He laughed. "Yeah, you better cover those nuts because . . ." He let go and pointed up. "The moment that canopy snaps open it's gonna jerk those straps tight to stop your headlong rush toward mother earth. And, those two straps you haven't tightened between your legs are going flatten those balls of yours like pancakes." He held up two fingers about a quarter-inch apart. "Thin pancakes aren't as much fun to play with, but you'll have a hell of conversation topic as to why you make a slapping sound whenever you walk."

The young dark-haired sailor reached down and pulled the straps tight, his eyes never leaving Razi. "Sorry, Chief."

Razi took a deep breath as he watched the sailor tighten the straps. He reached up and rubbed his chin, cocking his left eye at the sailor as he watched. Rockdale finished and straightened up. Razi let his eyes roam over the young aviation technician for a few seconds before he said, "Good, Rockdale. You pay attention to the little things, big things like having children will take care of themselves. Now, go take the thing off and store it properly. Don't forget to let the straps back out. You'll need them loose to put it on."

Razi watched for a moment as Rockdale walked around him toward the rear of the aircraft. *Rockdale was going to make a fine chief petty officer if he keeps improving like he is doing. By the time the petty officer is a first class, he'll be a crew chief on one of the mission crews.*

Razi drew his attention to the rest of the crew, all of them in various stages of putting on their parachutes. Bailout training was important for an aircrew to know and understand. Just as you fight like you train, you respond to emergencies just like you train, and as the chief petty officer responsible for conducting these drills, Razi had no intention of letting the officers think he didn't take it seriously. He glanced around the fuselage of the EP-3E Aries II reconnaissance aircraft, focusing on the more junior aircrewmen. Some were fumbling in the aisle with their parachutes, tightening straps, helping each other by pushing the parachutes higher on their buddy's back, and most were making sure the lanyard and survival vest were clear of the straps. All the best parachute packing and tightening of straps were useless if you couldn't pull that lanyard, plus what little bit of survival stuff you have in that vest. Those straps can puncture the small plastic bottle of water or rip open the energy bars, exposing them to the environment. He started moving toward the front of the aircraft, stopping at each crewmember to check their rigging. Once he was sure everything was right, he'd say, "Looks good," and then instruct them to take it off and store it properly.

Every flight, Razi ran the flight crew through the bailout drill. That was his job on each mission. He glanced up as he moved, frowning when he noticed Lieutenant Commander Peeters wasn't watching. This was important, and it was something he did well.

Others had the fire drills and ditching drills, but right after becoming airborne, he always had a bailout drill. Wasn't required for every mission, but with this young crew deployed from Rota, Spain, he wanted to make sure they knew what to do in an emergency. And he wanted to make sure that those who provided input to his performance evaluations were aware how professional he was.

He pushed his way down the fuselage toward the cockpit, checking each and every one of the crew, including the officers. No one had ever bailed out of an EP-3E. Urban legend had it that the antennas stretching from top of the four-engine turboprop would slice you in half as you jumped out the lone entry hatch to the aircraft, but NATOPS—the acronym for Naval Air Training and Operating Procedures Standardization—said you could do it. Therefore, someone somewhere must have tried it. EP-3Es had been around longer than computers, so someone had to have actually bailed out and lived for them to put it in NATOPS. Chief Razi may question others, but *if the "by-God" United States Navy put it in writing, then "by-God" it had to be true.*

Even so, Chief Razi doubted they would ever bail out unless the aircraft was on fire, pieces were falling off of it, and it was nose-down heading toward the ground. He had these "Walter Mitty" moments where he fantasized how he saved fellow shipmates from a burning aircraft, receiving a hero's recognition and fawning attention. He stopped in front of a sailor who was already in the middle of taking off his parachute. The man's helmet was already off, laying on its top along one of the narrow operating shelves. It tittered back and forth to the vibration of the aircraft.

"MacGammon, what in the hell are you doing?"

"Chief, what the hell I am doing is taking off my parachute," the second class petty officer snapped. Sweat-soaked hair hung down, matted across the stocky man's forehead.

"I can see you're taking it off, but if I've told you once, I've told you thousands of times: Wait until I tell you to take it off before you decide you know it all and don't need someone to check."

Razi waited for the smart-ass to say something. One of these days he was going to take MacGammon to Captain's Mast and teach him that the United States Navy wasn't the great liberal state of New Jersey.

"How's it going, Chief?"

Razi glanced up. Lieutenant Commander Peeters stood there. Razi straightened, almost to full-attention stance. "Going very well, sir." He jerked his thumb at MacGammon. "Just giving Petty Officer MacGammon some additional instruction on his rigging so he'd understand why we have these bailout drills."

Peeters nodded. "Keep up the good work, Chief."

Razi thanked the mission commander as the lieutenant commander stepped by them.

"Hey, Chief. Peeters wasn't wearing his parachute. . . ."

"Shut up, MacGammon," Razi said in a low voice. "You ain't an officer, and the way you're going you aren't even going to be a petty officer."

"Look, Chief, I've got nearly three thousand hours in the EP-3E, and I've done more bailout drills than most of these people have time in the Navy."

"Just take the damn thing off, MacGammon, and quit giving me a rough time every time we do this. If you're so damn good, then set a good example."

Razi stepped past MacGammon, feeling good about Peeters acknowledging his great work and feeling pissed-off because MacGammon didn't recognize that he—Chief Petty Officer Razi—was in charge. He cleared the next two aircrewmen quickly, letting them shed the bulky gear. His eyes arched as he stepped in front of the new third class, female, officer. He reached up and jerked the center strap crossing her chest, letting the back of his hand rest for a moment on those huge, beautiful tits.

"Good job, Petty Officer," he said to her, taking his hand away.

"Thanks, Chief," she said.

He smiled. A bubbly reply, one full of promise, he said to himself, but he wore khaki and wearing khaki meant not fooling around with the junior help. Of course, what the Navy doesn't find out—

"Chief, would you bail out, if you had to?" she asked.

"Petty Officer, if they ring that bailout alarm, I'll probably be right after you."

She smiled and blinked her eyelashes. "I think I might like that."

"Um . . . um," he muttered, shaking his head and moving past her.

Well, you may bail out, young lady, he thought, but no way was he going to jump out of a perfectly good aircraft, and with three-backup avionic systems, it would take a lot of damage to knock one of these aging warriors out of the sky. Ditch the plane was his mantra. Halfway down the fuselage, he did a double take.

"Sorry, sir," he said through clenched teeth. "The moment you jump out of the aircraft you're going to be some thirty pounds lighter because that parachute is going to go one way while you go the other."

The young ensign, wide-eyed, ran his hands over his straps and buckles, trying to see what Razi saw. After several seconds, Razi reached over, "Allow me, sir," he said, pulling the two straps running down each side of the chest. "See these, sir?"

"Yes, Chief. They're suppose to run down the chest like this, aren't they?"

"Yes, sir, they are. See this clasp here between the two straps? You're supposed to snap them together, otherwise the wind blast from the bailout is going to whip that parachute off you like a nymphomaniac slams a man into bed. You're not going to have time to react. You ain't gonna have a chance to buckle that clasp once you're out of the hatch." He reached up, grabbed the clasps on the two straps, and buckled them. "Other than that, Ensign, your straps are tight, your lanyard's clear, and your SV-2 is aligned. You'll live until you get to the ground. Then, it's up to terrain, vision, and God."

Razi didn't wait for the man to comment. For most chief petty officers, ensigns were fair game. Ensigns were a blank chalkboard upon which every chief petty officer was mandated to write the rules of leadership upon them. If your junior officer screwed up, the command master chief of VQ-2 always called in the chief petty officer and chewed him or her out for allowing their junior officer to fuck up.

He passed the aviation technicians to his left, stepped

by one of the techs, who with his parachute still on, leaned under a console, probably repairing some glitch before they reached track. The radioman stood beside his console on Razi's left, one arm spread to the right, the other shielding his eyes as he posed looking upward. "What do you think, Chief Razi? Am I going to make a good chief petty officer or what? Damn, you guys are lucky—damn lucky the board choose me for chief. You think this is the right pose for my service record?"

"Devine, if I didn't know better, I'd think you were an arrogant son of a bitch."

"Damn, Chief. You think maybe that's why they call me 'Little Razi?' "

"Eat my shorts, Devine. Get that parachute off and stored properly and bring lots of money for your initiation. You're going to need it."

The first class petty officer straightened, dropping his hands by his sides. His eyes narrowed. "I keep telling them, don't call me 'Little Razi' because you're not my dad and there's not an arrogant bone in my body," he said, then started laughing.

"September fifteenth. That's your day, Devine. That's the day we're gonna initiate you, and we ain't in Rota, Spain. We're deployed to Monrovia, Liberia, so there ain't no holier-than-thou types to tell us what we do at our initiation."

"Ah, Chief. You guys can't do anything I can't take. I've been a chief for several years. It just took the Navy a few years to figure it out."

"Make sure your page two is up-to-date, asshole," Razi said with a smile, referring to the next-of-kin notification sheet every sailor had in their personnel record. He pushed the lanky radioman slightly, nearly knocking him down. "You know what, Devine. I think you just might make a fair

chief petty officer, if someone takes you under their wing
and works really hard for twenty or so years."

"Thanks, Chief. I can't tell you how much that means to
me. Yuk yuk. Shit, Chief. I could even be like you if I gave
up things such as modesty, humor, integrity."

"Bite me, Devine." Razi turned and jerked the curtain
back from the small cubicle where the cryptologic technician communicator, hidden from prying eyes, sat. "Okay,
Johnson. You gonna sit in there and not give me a chance to
see your parachute." He motioned to the passageway. "Get
your ass out here!"

"But, Chief, I still have to raise Naples on the SAT-
COM," the second class whined as he unbuckled his seat
belt and slid sideways, extricating himself from the tight
confines of his communications position.

"Johnson, cut me some slack. Have you managed to get
Naples on satellite communications once in the thirty days
we've been here? Besides, Naples ain't going to be there
much longer. Some flag officer is gonna shovel them out so
he can have an office."

Johnson grabbed the sides of the cubicle and pulled
himself into the passageway. "Once, Chief. Did it the other
day for a few minutes. Remember? I gave you the baseball
results and you won several . . ."

Razi glanced behind him. Devine leaned back against
the radio console, smiling and making a sharpening motion with his fingers.

"Johnson, you gotta lose some weight and learn when to
keep your trap shut." Razi touched the straps and checked
the buckles as Johnson talked.

"I think I'm going to have to go HF to reach Naples."

Razi stepped back. "Now, why doesn't that surprise
me? You're fine, Johnson. You'll live if you bail out, but I'll
be surprised if you don't shit yourself when those straps

compress that big belly. Plus, I can't guarantee you'll survive the landing, but it's not the fall that kills you. It's that sudden stop when you reach the ground."

"Ha, ha, Chief. That joke is as old as you are."

"Thanks, Johnson. Just what I like on a flight. Respect from junior petty officers. Remind me to kick your ass when I have a free second or two."

Johnson turned back to the cubicle. "Can I take this thing off now, Chief?" He drew back and gave Razi a light backhand slap. "And how can a sailor with fifteen years be a junior petty officer—Wait! Don't tell me. Keep his nose clean and quit fucking up."

"You should have been a chief by now, Johnson."

"I know."

"If you keep your nose clean and quit trying to break the noses of everyone you meet who you don't like, then you might even make first class petty officer before the Navy chucks you out."

"One thing I can count on, Chief, and that is your great disposition toward positive counseling. Now, can I?" Johnson asked, holding his hands out by his sides and glancing down at the straps.

"Go ahead."

Razi looked toward the cockpit, but that wasn't his territory. In the cockpit the pilot, copilot, and flight engineer wore their parachutes continuously. If the aircraft reached a point where they might have to hit the silk, those three would be too busy trying to keep the aircraft level so the crew could bail out to spend any time putting on their own parachutes.

He turned and started working his way back down the fuselage toward the rear of the aircraft. Razi unzipped his upper-right-arm pocket and pulled out a pack of gum, slipping a piece into his mouth. He watched the motion of the aircrew slow as everyone watched him move aft. Their lives depended as much on how well those parachutes were packed as with how well they strapped them to their bodies. He pulled his left sleeve back and pressed the timer on his watch. Saw the time and grunted.

"Listen up, my fine fellow sailors!" he shouted as he neared the entrance hatch to the plane. "We don't have these drills when we take off so you can grab your flight book and notch off a bailout drill. We do it so when—or if—the time comes for you to bail out of an aircraft that has decided to land without the discretion of the pilot, you'll do it automatically because you've done it so many times as a drill." He tapped his watch. Looking aft he saw Peeters step out of the rear galley to listen. "Nearly three minutes it took to get ready. That's unsatisfactory. We're going to do it again during this flight and we're going to keep doing it until we get it down to a minute and a half. A minute and a half was what we were doing while we were in Rota and a minute and a half is what we're going to do while we're deployed to Liberia."

"Ah, Chief," MacGammon said, his head bopping and weaving as he pushed the parachute off his back. "We've done these drills so much we can do them in our sleep."

"MacGammon, if you have to bail out, you think this aircraft is going to be flying along nice and level, not on fire, and not trying to fight the force of gravity? You think that? What the hell do you think an engine fire is going to do during those three minutes? I'll tell you since you asked. It's going to burn into the fuel tank. Then, it's gonna cause an explosion that rips the wing off." He put both hands on his hips—his John Wayne pose. "You can no more put on a parachute with the aircraft spinning around and around than you can shit gold."

"Chief—"

"Sailor, stow that parachute properly and quit your backtalk."

MacGammon shook his head.

Chief Razi drew himself up to his full height, turning his head right and left so he could see everyone in the aisle. The officers did their bailout drills with them and while he wasn't adverse to helping the new officers, once they reach lieutenant commander rank, they were on their own. Lieutenant commanders could be a pain in the ass; just senior enough to not think of themselves as junior officers and junior enough to still need some professional guidance that only squared-away chief petty officers such as himself, Cryptologic Technician "R" branch Wilbur "Badass" Razi, could provide. Of course, even his wife didn't call him Wilbur. What in the hell were his parents thinking to name a badass like him Wilbur?

"Take 'em off!" he shouted to those still wearing them. "Pack them and put them in their places. We're going to try it again—"

Groans filled the fuselage.

"—later in the flight."

The groans subsided.

"Sometimes Badass forgets," Rockdale whispered to MacGammon.

"Man, don't let him hear you call him that. Badass will feel he has to make us do two drills instead of just one, and he'll use you and I as examples to the officers on how good he is in straightening us out."

"Yeah, you know how he is," a third aircrewman piped up as he shoved his parachute into the racks above the four lounge seats near the entry hatch to the plane.

"Oh, Stetson," Rockdale grunted, struggling out of the tight straps. "I thought you Texans were mean, tough fighting machines." The parachute eased off his shoulders. "There."

"I prefer the Texan image of a love machine," Tommy "Stetson" Carson replied.

"Yeah, longhorn steers," MacGammon added.

Rockdale placed the parachute on the deck, the side previously against his back faced up. He laid the top straps across it, lifting the bottom straps over them.

"About the only image of a lover I can see of you is one with a fistful of dollars." Rockdale lifted the parachute, leaned over the passenger seats along the rear left side of the EP-3E reconnaissance aircraft, and shoved it on top of another parachute someone had stowed.

"Better than what you've got in your fist."

"You three gonna keep grab-assing," Razi said, "Or, you gonna stow those parachutes and get to your positions?"

"Chief, mine's already up there," Rockdale said, smiling.

"Yeah, and with your aircrew skills, you probably got the straps tied together so they don't fall apart. And, you, Carson. You gonna carry your parachute around with you for the mission or you gonna stow it properly?"

"Chief, I was just waiting for MacGammon to move out of the way."

"Gee, thanks, Stetson," MacGammon moaned.

"MacGammon, hurry it up. Why is it whenever there's a problem, you seem to be nearby or in it?"

MacGammon shrugged. "Lucky?" MacGammon turned and threw his parachute up with the others. Standing on tiptoes for a couple of seconds, the experienced aircrewman shoved the parachute into its rack. When he turned, Chief Razi still stood there. "Hey, Chief, how come I don't have a nickname like Stetson, here, and Rocky Rockdale?" He clinched his fist. "I want a name that sounds *studly*—"

"How about dickhead?" Razi said. "Now, shut your griping, stow that parachute, Carson, and you three get to your positions. We're going to cross the border into Guinea shortly and you can't tell me you three have pre-missioned your positions. You think the mission commander is gonna delay on-track time so you prima donnas can finish telling each other how much you like each other?" He jerked his thumb toward the row of operating consoles. "Get your ass in gear," he ordered. Out of the corner of his eye he saw Peeters watching him. *Damn good thing, too,* he thought.

"Here," Rockdale said, taking the parachute from the shorter Carson. He twisted and shoved the parachute on top of another one above the passenger seats.

"You three are the last in the aircraft. You got FOD walk-down tomorrow. Maybe that'll help you get your acts together."

"Yes, Chief," they all said in unison. Foreign Object Damage—commonly known as FOD—was something everyone did, searching the ground for objects that could be sucked up into the engine intake and cause damage or an explosion.

Razi watched the three hurry to their positions. He pulled the gum out of his mouth, wrapped it in the original paper, and twisted it with his fingers. Razi watched until the aircrewmen slid into their seats . . . waiting— There! They buckled their seatbelts. They'd learn. He turned and walked past the two cryptologic technicians manning the special console near the bulkhead of the small kitchenette at the rear of the aircraft.

"Hey, Badass. How many young sailors you convinced today to get out of the Navy?" Senior Chief Brad Conar asked with a hint of distaste.

"Pits, you shit-bird," Razi said, reaching up and pulling a paper cup from the overhead storage area. "What're you doing back here instead of up front? Fight engineers should be in the cockpit, not back here impressing newbies with their importance."

Razi poured himself a cup of coffee, set it on the table, and slid into the booth alongside the senior chief, using his butt to push the older, lankier man against the bulkhead.

"Got that new trainee on board. Thought I'd takeoff back here with you passengers and see how the less fortunate live. Besides, it gives her a chance to be on her own."

"Passengers hell. If it wasn't for us, you wouldn't have any reason to fly."

"Yeah, and if we didn't fly you, you wouldn't have a way to do your mission."

"Gripe, gripe gripe," Razi said good-naturedly, ignoring the obvious dislike of the senior chief. He took a sip of the coffee. "She any good, Senior Chief Brad 'Pits' Conar, or is she an arrogant asshole like the rest of you flight engineers?"

"That's *Pits* with a capital *P,* Badass, and, yes, she knows her stuff and like the rest of us flight engineers, she is modest to a fault, unlike certain chief petty officers who prance and strut to the officers." Pits put a spread hand against his chest. "I have personally tested her aviation knowledge and without doubt, I know she can run rings around you." Then in a lower voice added, "And, I have third class petty officers who can run rings around your knowledge of this aircraft."

"Ain't no way. No one knows the EP-3 fucking Echo better than me."

"What's the mission today, Badass? You guys going to keep us boring holes in the sky for ten hours, or you going to call it quits sooner than yesterday so we can get a good night's sleep?"

Razi looked at the senior flight engineer, his thick eyebrows bunching as he gave quick consideration on what to tell Conar. Then, he nodded to himself, thinking, *He's got the security tickets to know, and besides we're all in this together. Once you leave mother earth, what happens to one, happens to all. Of course, this is one senior chief I wish it would only happen to.*

He lifted his cup and took a long drink. Coffee lost its heat fast at 22,000-feet altitude, and the paper cups didn't help either. Paper cups, though, didn't become projectiles when the aircraft had to take evasive action. Getting hit upside the head with a paper cup was preferable to the Navy ceramic. The rear of the aircraft was always cooler—colder was a better word—than the front part where the flight crew controlled the heaters.

"You going to tell me or are you going to play this 'need to know' crap? You cryppies are all the same, you know. Walk around like God—"

"I never said I wasn't going to tell you. You flight engineers are a might touchy when you think someone is gonna dis' you." He pulled himself out of the booth, crumbled his cup, and tossed it in the trashcan. "I was just thinking that you being the senior flight engineer on board and all, and knowing how technical-competent you are on mechanical things, how in the hell was I gonna find the simple words necessary so you could understand what we're doing today." Razi shook his head. "It ain't easy explaining this complex stuff to people who barely graduated from high school."

Conar's lips tightened, his mustache twitching slightly. "You know something, Badass, someday someone's going to forget those muscles under that flight suit and whip your ass."

Razi leaned closer to the senior chief, glancing around to make sure they were the only two in the galley. "Pits, it won't be you. If you ever hit me and I found out, it might—just might piss me off."

"Let me out, Razi. I can only tolerate so much of your arrogance."

Razi slid off the padded seat so Conar could move.

Pits was half-out when the aircraft dropped a few feet and trembled as it hit slight turbulence. "Damn, better get back up there. Now, you going to tell me or not?"

Razi nodded. "When you turn southeast—" He motioned to the right "—onto the track running parallel to the north of the Liberian border, we're going to try out this new infrared sensing device from Naval Research Laboratory."

"Oh, yeah," Pits said with mock laughter. "If we have to drop down to look at everything that emits heat in Africa, we might as well stay at fifty feet."

"Supposed to be a little more complex than the normal infrared devices. This one detects a heat signature at high altitude. The heat signature profile bounces against a database of heat signatures to determine size and weight of whatever is emitting the heat. If the thing is moving, the computer calculates speed of motion. When all of those factors are combined, the system—called Dragnet—will provide an opinion as to what generated the heat signature."

Conar listened as he pulled a fresh cup of coffee. "Sounds to me like *Star Trek* stuff, Razi. Even if this Dragnet can do this stuff that you say, out here you're going to run into more than humans." He stirred his coffee for a second and then looked up at Razi. "What about monkeys or gorillas? Wouldn't this system call them human?"

Razi hadn't given consideration to that. He shrugged. "Don't know. This is the first time we've tried the system." He turned and pointed at two operators sitting immediately outside the mess area. "See those two petty officers?" he asked, pointing. "They're from Naval Security Group Activity San Diego. They've been training on the system for the past month, so we'll have to depend on that training to tell us what we're seeing."

Conar took a swallow of the black coffee. "Guess that

means we'll be going down for look-sees every time they spot something, huh?"

Razi nodded. "Guess so."

Conar shook his head. Running his right hand through his hair, he faced Razi. "Just what I said. We might as well stay at fifty feet altitude. You know, it's one thing to go low over the water to do an identification pass against a contact, and quite another to go low over a jungle where trees sometimes reach a hundred feet."

Razi laughed. "Tell you what, Pits. You watch the trees and keep the leaves out of the intakes, and I'll watch my operators. Different subject, shipmate; who's the new officer?"

"Oh, that's Ensign Leggatt, Naval Academy class of one of these recent years. Fine outstanding member of the officer community."

"New?"

Conar nodded. "Yeah, as new as a baby's butt." He set the paper cup on the table and turned to Razi. "Razi, don't pull one of your shitty practical jokes on the new officer. They're only funny to you. For the rest of the chiefs' community, they're embarrassing."

"Well, you know these missions are long. A little fun never hurt anyone, and the only thing embarrassing to the chiefs' community is you, Pits. You need to lighten up and enjoy life a little instead of walking around bad-mouthing everyone. My little 'practical jokes' as you call them are rites of initiation. The other aircrew veterans enjoy them."

"They may, but those on the receiving end don't see the humor. Just don't make him barf, Razi. Last time you caused someone to upchuck, we flew the entire eight-hour mission with the smell trapped inside the fuselage."

"I wouldn't do that, Pits. It's our way—the spooks' way—of welcoming new members to the crew."

"Right! Well, I'm heading back up to the cockpit."

Conar glanced at his watch. "About another thirty minutes to the turn. I wouldn't screw with the mission commander, Badass. Peeters isn't known for his sense of humor."

"I know. This isn't my first flight with him, but he tends to leave us CTs alone."

"That's because he hasn't quite figured out how you do what you do, but once he's got it about eighty percent figured out, you'll find him more than ready to jerk you in and put you in your place."

"Which is more than you can or will do, Pits. You're all talk—"

"Fuck you, Razi. Remember one thing," he said, his voice low and menacing. "I'm a goddamn senior chief petty officer and while I support the integrity of the chief's locker, I haven't forgotten some of the things you've done."

"Goat locker," Razi interrupted.

"Goat locker?"

"Yeah, real sailors don't call the comraderie of chiefdom the 'chief's locker.' It's called the 'goat locker.' Been called that all through history, and it hasn't changed."

"Fuck you, Razi." Pits grabbed his cup, sending some of the coffee splashing over the side. "Your time is coming," he added as he walked around Razi and headed toward the cockpit.

Razi watched Pits as the number-one flight engineer worked his way through the fuselage, his left hand touching the backs of the console seats as he moved. *Asshole,* Razi thought as he sipped his coffee. Sure Peeters was a new mission commander, but Razi was sure the man was impressed with his professionalism. Who couldn't be? *Time to make sure everyone is ready. Probably going to be another dull, deadly mission searching for this terrorist Abu Alhaul, and at the same time trying to develop some intelligence on this African National Army.*

Razi stepped out of the lighted mess into the darkened work area of the aircraft. He glanced at the two Dragnet operators as he stepped by them. It looked as if they were going down a checklist, pressing icons on the computer screen. He stopped behind the five cryptologic technician aircrewmen—some called members of that rating "CTs" and sometimes they were called "cryppies"—sitting in a row, manning the EP-3E normal reconnaissance consoles. Razi reached up and grabbed one of the two hollow steel bars that ran the length of the fuselage. The bars helped aircrewmen move up and down the fuselage when flying in heavy turbulence. Razi listened to the low murmur of Petty Officer First Class Brett Lacey speak into the microphone of the internal communications system as he talked with the other team members. Razi glanced to his right at the lab operator located beside the four excess passenger seats. Then, he looked again at the two temporary crewmen manning Dragnet. The system had been installed in the only spare space the aircraft had, a chart table between the reconnaissance positions and a spare position they seldom manned. The downside was that Dragnet blocked the small round window that allowed some daylight into the dark confines of a working reconnaissance aircraft. The two NRL newbies couldn't hear Lacey prepping the team for the mission. They didn't even have their headsets on. Normally, the squadron would have refused to allow anyone who wasn't a qualified aircrewman to fly with them, but the war on terrorism couldn't wait for every valuable soul to become qualified. Luckily, the issue never arose because these two wore aircrew wings and knew how to assume ditching positions, and it only took a little bit of effort on Razi's part to ensure that they knew how to put on a parachute. Somewhere, they had earned their wings.

Movement from the forward console caught his attention.

Lacey had opened a small black notebook and was running
his finger down a page as he spoke into the microphone, going down a checklist to make sure the computer was working. Everything was done by computers nowadays. Not like
when he first joined the Navy. Sure, they had computers
back then, he wasn't that ancient. But back then, when you
joined they sent you off to "A" school for Basic Cryptology
101. You didn't graduate, you didn't become a CT. Instead,
you were shipped out to sea to learn the fine art of chipping
rust and applying paint. The school taught you what the hell
your rating was about. Nowadays, it seemed most sailors had
some college or even a degree or two.

*Who in the hell was that sailor they were talking about
months ago at the Chief's Club in Rota?* He racked his
mind for the name of the second class petty officer at Naval
Information Warfare Activity in Washington that had a
masters degree in electrical engineering and was working
nights on a doctorate. Now why would someone with that
much education want to be a sailor, when he could be
working for some commercial company drawing big bucks
and pontificating great and wonderful things to make more
money? Something wasn't quite right with that picture. But
the commercial world's loss was the Navy's gain.

"Hey, Chief," Petty Officer Lacey shouted above the
constant din of vibrating engines and humming electronics.

Razi turned his head. "Yeah, Lacey?"

"We're done. Everything is A-OK and we're ready."

"Then why in the hell ain't you turning and burning.
Those systems don't operate themselves."

"Ah, Chief. You know they do operate themselves.
We're along for the ride and make sure they don't quit."

Razi took a couple of steps and bent over Lacey. "We've
got a new guy on board," he whispered followed by a short
chuckle.

Lacey lowered his headset, keeping hold of the earpieces with both hands. The first class petty officer looked up and down the fuselage. "You mean the ensign? The one who doesn't look old enough to shave."

"That's the one. A Naval Academy ensign, no less."

Lacey looked up and smiled. "So, which will it be?"

"Peanut butter."

"Peanut butter," Lacey replied, laughing. "No pity, Chief. You ain't got a pity bone in your body."

"Moi?" Razi said, acting bemused. "I am the most sympathetic guy on board this flying bucket of bolts. Why, people come to me with their problems. I listen attentively. I nod when nodding is called for and agree when they need agreeing."

"And then you tell them how no story has ever touched your heart like this one and for them to go fuck off and die somewhere else and leave you alone."

"Lacey, remind me to kick your butt later when we land."

"Of course, Chief Razi, you never say that when an officer or someone senior can hear."

"Lacey, don't bother reminding me to kick your butt. I'll remind myself."

Lacey laughed. "I just happen to have a tube of peanut butter from yesterday's box lunch. When do you want to do it?"

"Let me have it. Eventually, he's going to have to take a leak and when he comes out, we'll do it then."

"That'll give me time to tell the others." Lacey raised his earpieces and placed them over his ears, laughing. "Peanut butter."

Razi looked forward, searching for the victim. No new member went unpunished was the unwritten rule of reconnaissance flying. Fighter pilots, strapped to their seats like wrapped bacon, would never know the camaraderie of twenty-four Navy men and women crammed inside a four-engine propeller-driven aircraft bouncing across the sky on the hidden hills of turbulence where every fart received its due. The young officer was standing beside Lieutenant Commander Peeters. Razi stroked his chin. *Maybe Pits was right and the officer wasn't impressed with him. Lord, protect me from lieutenant commanders. I've had more trouble with lieutenant commanders than any other group of officers. They resent being called junior officers and can't understand why it's taking so long for the Navy to recognize their greatness with the scrambled-egg hat of a commander.*

"Chief!"

Razi looked toward the mess area. One of the two petty officers operating Dragnet waved at him. *What now?*

REAR ADMIRAL DICK HOLMAN STOOD ON THE BRIDGE wing of the USS *Boxer*. He was going to throw that crypto-logic officer overboard when they arrived in Monrovia. No one on this ship had Cuban cigars but him . . . but, no . . . what did he find last night when he walked to the fantail? That's right. The goddamn cryppie smoking one of his ci-gars. At first, he had thought the lieutenant commander had his own, but when he went to his stateroom, he discovered three missing. The man must think he can get away with taking three of his cigars and him not missing them. This morning when he left his stateroom, he counted his cigars and wrote the number on a piece of paper that he slipped under the large calendar on top of his desk.

The slight sea breeze of the afternoon blew the smoke from his Cuban cigar down the side of the huge amphibi-ous carrier. He watched as it quickly dissipated. Other than knowing someone was swiping his cigars and having the audacity to smoke them in front of him, today had been a great day, so far, he said to himself, wondering what could go wrong. He smiled. He'd catch him . . . and when he did, he'd have his nuts for garters. He nodded to himself and thought, *I'm a nice, squared-away admiral with a love of the sea and my sailors, and am such a congenial asshole everyone argues with me, but no one, and I mean no one, touches my cigars. It isn't as if I have an endless supply of them.*

His thoughts drifted elsewhere. Three months from now, he'd no longer be Commander, Amphibious Group Two; the largest, strongest amphibious force in the world.

He turned and leaned against the railing encircling the bridge wing, his elbows resting on them. He had had a great career in the Navy. He was going to miss it unless Admiral Yalvarez, Chief of Naval Operations, decided there was another job for a pudgy, cigar-smoking, fighter-pilot, one-star admiral. He took another puff as a sailor stepped onto the bridge wing with a cup of coffee.

"Admiral, fresh coffee, sir. Compliments of the Officer of the Deck."

"Thanks, *Navi guesser,*" he said jovially to the quartermaster. Holman looked into the bridge, thanking the OOD by hoisting the cup at her. "You make it, First?" He asked the first class petty officer.

The quartermaster shook his head. "Sorry, Admiral, our new boatswain mate seaman made it, sir. This is his first cup and we thought you should be the first to grade it."

"Uh-huh. Guess I'm the guinea pig, eh?"

"Admiral, nothing can kill you, but just in case—since it is his first cup, here's a couple of antacids," the petty officer said, handing Holman a couple of white chewables.

Dick looked into the bridge. Everyone was smiling and watching him. He noticed the young boatswain mate standing near the helm of the *Boxer*, near the 1MC ship-speaker-system mounted on the aft bulkhead. The seaman wasn't smiling, though Dick could see the young lad was watching him. He smiled, thinking of the stories the others in the bridge had made up to scare the newbie. Probably things along the lines of "the admiral is a screamer and when he really gets angry, he's been known to throw sailors overboard, and . . . most of all, he hates seamen."

Dick took a sip, swished it around his mouth, and swallowed. He stuck his head inside the hatch. "Boats, you make this coffee?"

"Yes, sir," the young seaman answered, his voice shaking. Then, as if just thinking of it, the sailor straighten immediately, his arms falling down by his side as he came to attention.

"Good stuff," Dick said, hoisting the cup at the young sailor. The sailor smiled, looking around at the others in the bridge. They clapped.

"Thank you, Admiral."

Holman hoisted the coffee and turned away. *Christ, how I envy these young men and women. Here I am at the twilight of my tour, and they're starting such a great adventure—an adventure only truly appreciated when they reach my age. So much I want to do and so little time to do it.* The young man had smiled. It is ironic sometimes how a few words of praise can change the whole day for a young person in a new job. Take care of your sailors, and your career will take care of itself.

The hatch on the far starboard side of the bridge opened and his chief of staff, Captain Leo Upmann, ducked as he entered. Seeing Holman, the tall African-American surface-warfare officer weaved around the various systems that decorate every bridge of an American warship and made his way to the port bridge wing. Holman leaned back against the railing with his elbows resting on the top. The quartermaster waited until Captain Upmann stepped onto the bridge wing before returning to his post at the navigation plot table.

Behind Admiral Holman a small dark object rose, about ten feet from the side of the forecastle. Upmann saw it and smiled. "Looks as if the Marines have found you again, Admiral."

Dick looked where Upmann pointed. Hovering was a small, prototype aircraft about two feet wide from wingtip to wingtip. Sunlight reflected off the lens that made up the nose and off the whirling propellers located at each wing tip and behind the camera lens. The single propeller in the rear pointed upward. The tactical mobile spy plane hovered in place.

"Damn Marines," Dick said. "I wish they'd practice their skills on this toy somewhere else instead of trying to sneak up on me all the time. Where's their colonel?"

Leo laughed. "Sir, he's probably on the flight deck with the operators of this contraption. I told them to track the cryppie for a while and find out where he's getting his cigars, but he insisted your orders were for them to practice finding you."

Dick turned slightly, his left eyebrow raised. "That's not exactly what I said. What I said was I doubted these things could keep track of me, much less some unknown terrorist lost in the woods of the world."

"Yes, sir, but I think the colonel intends to prove you wrong."

"Is there something about proving an admiral wrong that gives subordinates an innate amount of pleasure?

Upmann shrugged.

"And quit smiling. It wouldn't surprise me to know that you're encouraging them to keep this shit up."

Upmann shook his head. "No, sir. If I was, I'd've already told them to knock it off as it was pissing you off, but the colonel is typical Marine—knows he's right and since I'm Navy, I must be wrong." Upmann waved at the small, unmanned aerial vehicle—UAV. "I was telling the truth when I suggested he use his 'toys' to track the cryppie, but—" Upmann paused.

"But, what?"

"Well, the colonel had a cigar the same brand of yours. He doesn't want to track the cryppie."

"If that doesn't take the cake. I know where the son of a bitch is getting those cigars, Leo. He's getting them from my stateroom."

"Well, Admiral, you also have a box in your Flag Briefing room."

Dick pulled the cigar out from between his lips and holding it between his fingers, jabbed it toward Upmann. "Don't give me that, Leo. I counted—"

Upmann laughed. "You went and counted your cigars, Admiral?" he asked, spreading the fingers of his left hand against his chest. "You went and counted your cigars to see if any were missing? I hope you weren't so paranoid that you wrote down the number."

Dick put the cigar back between his lips. "Upmann, in three months, you're going to get an admiral that doesn't put up with insubordination. Of that, I am sure," he said softly.

"Admiral, I don't think Lieutenant Commander Springhill would sneak your cigars away, and I can't believe you went and counted them to see if any were missing." Upmann laughed louder. "Wait until I tell—"

"You aren't going to tell anyone, Leo."

"You didn't find any missing, did you, sir?"

"You're wrong. I found three missing."

Upmann shook his head. "Admiral, let's lock them up in your stateroom safe."

"Let's don't and say we did. If I lock them up, my officers and crew will think I don't trust them."

"Well?" Upmann asked.

"I trust them explicitly. It's the cryptologic officer I'm not sure about."

"I can ask him if he took them."

Dick shook his head. "Don't do that. If you do, then he'll know I'm onto him and we'll never catch him."

The noise increased off the port bridge wing. The unmanned miniature vehicle bopped slightly and rose another couple of feet in altitude. The good thing was it didn't pick up audio. It only transmitted television signals from the nose to the receiver. Holman had been briefed on this new "toy" as he called it. The Navy, as he knew it, was going more and more to these damn unmanned flying things. Well, they could kiss his butt. You're not going to control the sky without manned fighter aircraft, manned reconnaissance aircraft, and manned tankers.

"Then, why don't I ask Springhill where he got his cigars?"

"I already have," Dick said.

"And what did he say?"

"Said he got them from the same place I did."

"So, that should solve it."

"Not hardly, Leo. I get my cigars from my humidor."

Upmann laughed louder. "Admiral, let me see. You've got the Silver Star for heroism, you have a Purple Heart and Bronze Star from an earlier Middle East conflict, and you made admiral two years after you were in zone for promotion."

"What are you trying to say, Captain Upmann?"

"Admiral, I wouldn't let a cigar upset you."

"Three cigars, Leo," Dick said, holding up three fingers. "The little twerp took three of my cigars. He told me so. He told me he got them from the same place I do."

Upmann was beginning to upset him. Maybe there was a conspiracy or, worse yet, a practical joke. He blew a puff of smoke at the hovering spycraft. The spycraft slid right and turned so the lens followed the smoke as the soft breeze carried it aft. Then, it turned back to watching Holman and Upmann.

Dick turned, stuck his head inside the bridge, and shouted, "Officer of the Deck, bring me your pistol!" He saw the bemused looks being exchanged by the bridge watch. He looked at Upmann. "Let's see what the survival capability is for one of these flying cameras."

The hovering spycraft wasn't much bigger than some larger remote-controlled aircraft Dick had seen being flown by enthusiasts at the local park in Norfolk, Virginia. According to the Marine briefer at Headquarters Marine Corps, these things were called Combat Reconnaissance Vehicles Remote-controlled—CRVTR, pronounced "critter." These critters were a nuisance. *The first time I catch one of these things hovering outside the porthole to my head, I'm going to have the colonel's ears for garters.*

"Amazing how they do that, isn't it?" Leo asked.

The Officer of the Deck emerged onto the bridge wing. "Sir?" she asked.

Dick and Upmann turned together. The lieutenant stood there with her pistol in her hand. "What would you like me to do with it?"

Upmann glanced at Dick for a moment before turning to the OOD. "Nothing, Lieutenant. The Admiral and I wanted to check to see if you were wearing it as ordered."

She put it back in the huge black leather holster. "Yes, sir. It isn't loaded, in keeping with standard operating procedures, but—" She slapped a leather cartridge pouch on her left side. "—I have the bullets here. And, sir, I am capable of loading it in ten seconds."

"Thank you, Lieutenant," Dick said. "I'm glad to see you are fully prepared. Well done. You may return to your duties."

They both turned away, toward the hovering spycraft. "One of these days, one of these junior officers is going to take you at your word and we'll have missiles flying, torpedoes launching, and machine guns blasting before they realize you were being dramatic."

"Leo, don't I hear someone calling you?"

Upmann laughed and nodded at the hovering spycraft. "I wonder how long they can remain airborne."

"Not too long, if you'd allowed me to take that pistol." Dick pointed with his cigar. "Those critters would be a hell of lot more amazing if they'd go after a tactical target other than the admiral of this Expeditionary Strike Group." As he spoke, two more critters rose to join the original, one on each side of it. "Yeah, you better have a talk with him, Leo. Tell him to go do some real Marine Corps stuff like shooting somebody or, better yet, tracking my cryptologic officer."

The three critters turned in formation, facing the bow of the ship, and suddenly took off together, leaving Dick and Upmann watching the almost science-fiction display disappear. Farther away, only the occasional sunlight reflecting off the CRVTRs made it possible to see them. The three small UAVs were hovering about a hundred feet ahead of the bow of the USS *Boxer.*

"You know, the Marines are really enjoying these toys. Wonder how they'll use them in real action?"

"I think they'll do quite well, Leo. Imagine you're in the jungle, which they're going to be in shortly, and you know that ahead of you is an enemy in unknown territory. All the operator has to do is unfold it from his backpack, slap the propellers on it, toss it into the air, and watch his portable TV screen to see what the critter is seeing. They don't make much noise and even if someone heard them, they'd play hell trying to see them. Meanwhile, with all their head-turning and searching, the camera on the nose will lock on the motion and quickly transmit the picture back to the Marines. They'll have better intel and a more current tactical picture of what they are going up against."

"It is amazing the new technology rolling off the assembly line," Upmann added. "Only a matter of time before some military contractor figures out a military application for it. I just never thought I'd see our ground warriors hiking around with a remote-control airplane in their backpack."

"The one constant in all of this information technology we keep incorporating into our military strategy is that you still need muddy boots on the ground to win the conflict."

Dick reached beneath the railing and lifted the 5"/62 shell casing. He ground out his cigar and let the butt fall into the bottom of the makeshift ashtray the gunners' mates had made for him. "How are we doing?"

"Should still be on track and on time, Admiral. We'll dock in Monrovia tomorrow." Upmann lifted up a sealed envelope and handed it to Dick. "And, this 'personal for' message came for you from Chief of Naval Operations. I haven't read it yet, Admiral, but it's from Flag Matters."

"Personal for" messages were sent from flag officers to others. No other rank in the United States Navy could send a "personal for" message over official channels. You had to have those stars on your collar to do that. The little-known office called Flag Matters, working for Chief of Naval Operations, informed you of where you were being assigned or when you were being asked to retire. He hefted the light envelope, slapping it against his palm. Inside, his future lay. He caught Upmann watching him. "Looks like I'm about to find out my future."

Dick ripped open the envelope and quickly read the message before folding it and slipping it into his shirt pocket. Now he knew what his future in the U.S. Navy held for him. He saw the waiting curiosity on his chief of staff's face, but now wasn't the time to tell him. He had mixed feelings over the message. The news was something he needed to digest, quietly and alone.

"Leo, invite the good colonel to dine with us tonight in my cabin."

"Yes, sir. Any specific reason, Admiral, if I may ask?"

Dick shook his head, allowing a sigh to escape. "No specific reason, Leo, but by this time tomorrow the colonel and his Marines will be departing the ship. Just call it an official acknowledgement of the Navy-Marine Corps team."

"That all, sir."

"No. I want to make sure he takes his toys with him."

"Guess this will be your last trip to Liberia, Admiral?"

"Could be, Leo. It is an opportunity to pay my respects to Lieutenant General Thomaston before I depart Amphibious Group Two. Someday, you and I will sit on steps with our grandchildren and tell them of meeting this man."

Upmann nodded. "Fantastic career."

"You can say that again. Here's a man from the slums—"

"—a black man."

"Leo, you don't have to be black to live in the slums. Slums are equal opportunity."

"Boss, that's something we could argue."

"As I was saying before I was interrupted, Leo; here's a man from the slums who rose through the ranks of the U.S. Army to three-star general, commanded the 82nd Airborne, retired, emigrated to Liberia, and now is the president of this former United States colony." Holman's knee knocked the empty shell ashtray.

Upmann reached down and pushed it back on the shelf. "He wouldn't be the president today if it hadn't been for you, Admiral."

Holman gave a short laugh. "Don't bet on it. Thomaston and his small band were doing a good job of holding off the rebels when we showed up."

"Me thinks thou doest protest too much. I had a long chat with his former sergeant major, Craig Gentle, and from what I gathered, they had already fallen back to the last barrier when our Marines stormed through the back."

Holman squinted. The Marine toys were reversing course and heading back toward the *Boxer*. They should be about out of fuel by now.

"Okay, Leo. Granted, our timely over-the-horizon arrival played a role in defeating Abu Alhaul and his band of merry terrorists, but Thomaston achieved the glory for his stand at Kingsville. A stand that has played well not only in Liberia and Africa, but across America, also." Holman patted his shirt pocket, his eyebrows bunching when he realized he had smoked his last cigar. He didn't need another one anyway—one a day was plenty. Someday, he was going to have to give them up. Maybe sooner if he didn't stop that damn cryptologic officer from raiding his humidor.

"Gentle referred to the battle for the armory at Kingsville as their Alamo."

"You're right. Thomaston said the same thing. He called their stand Liberia's 'Alamo.' "

"President Jefferson, the slain Liberian president whose death set off the riots and mayhem in Liberia, would hardly recognize what his actions to raise some much-needed money for Liberia caused."

Upmann pointed at the miniature UAVs as they crossed the bow of the amphibious carrier. "Looks as if the Marines have decided to call it a day."

"Wish they'd go do some Marine stuff like shoot a whale."

"Now, there's a thought that fails the *Washington Post* test."

"Jefferson's idea of allowing African-Americans to apply for a Liberian passport caught on better than most would have thought."

"I have one."

"You do?" Holman asked, astonished.

"Yes, I do. More as a souvenir than anything else, and I got them for my son and daughter so they'd remember their heritage. Wife being German, she didn't rank one, but when she was naturalized, she did get an American passport."

"Guess we have entered the era of multiple citizenships."

"You could say that, Admiral. Jefferson never expected American blacks to emigrate to Liberia like Thomaston did with a hundred or so families. He even put in the citizenship clauses for these Liberian passports that you had to live in Liberia to vote. I think he expected some Americans of African origin to visit, spend money, and then go home. He didn't expect them to move lock, stock, and barrel to Liberia."

Holman looked up at his balding chief of staff. "You're not thinking of emigrating to Liberia when you retire, are you, Leo?"

Upmann laughed. "Oh, Christ, no. My wife would leave me if I took her away from bingo, Wal-Mart, and the Frances Scott Key mall. No, we're too integrated into the Frederick,

Maryland, social scene to pull roots at our age and head off into the sunset for an adventure that could kill us."

"I would hope so. You know you can't go back to a place you've never been."

Upmann's lower lip pushed against his upper for a moment. "But you know what makes it hard for those of us who are black, Admiral? You can go home, and you can trace your family tree on the Internet—back for generations. For us blacks, we might be lucky to take our heritage back to the end of the Civil War. What Thomaston and his people were doing in Kingsville were analyzing DNA from the various African tribes. You could put your DNA into their program data banks and when, or if, they matched it to a specific tribe, you had a piece of your heritage in which you could take interest."

Holman looked up. Hovering above them with its camera pointing down was one of the Marine Corps' miniature UAVs. "Leo, are we providing the fuel for these damn things?"

CHAPTER 3

ABDO, HIS LARGE FRAME PUSHING ASIDE THE BUSHES blocking the faint jungle path, brought the machete down time after time, as effortlessly as he walked. Each slash sent a wave rippling along loose flaps of fat hanging beneath each arm, hiding the strength buried beneath, and sending waves of small, flying, biting insects into the air. Abdo paused, wiping sweat from his forehead. He tucked the machete beneath one arm while using the free hand to poke loose strands of dirty black hair beneath the yellow-stained turban. Cursing, he slapped at the insects surrounding his head. A four-day growth of gray-speckled hair covered his face. Abdo stepped back, leaving the insects swarming around where he had stood. He glanced behind him.

Abu Alhaul—father of terror, Mohammed's chosen one, Abdo's brother—followed.

Abdo wiped his forehead and thought of how truly

blessed he was to have a brother such as Asim—born again as Abu Alhaul. Behind Abu Alhaul followed less than thirty of the Islamic Front for Purification remaining with the Jihadist leader. Two years ago they numbered in the thousands—Africans, Arabs, Pakistani—so many, and now so few. Success had been great two years ago with them overrunning Guinea and Liberia before Allah decided to test their faithfulness again. The defeat at the hands of the Liberian president, Thomaston, caused the growing dissension between the Africans and Jihadists to burst like rotten fruit. The Africans shoved aside the teachings of Mohammed, and now followed this charismatic African, Fela Azikiwe Ojo, shunning religion in favor of nationalism.

"What is it?" Abu Alhaul asked as he approached Abdo.

Abdo knew Abu Alhaul both loved and hated him; he who was his bigger brother. It frustrated Abdo to know his brother fought his own internal arguments because Abdo failed to appreciate that Abu Alhaul believed Allah had much bigger plans for him.

"The path splits, my brother. One goes north and the other continues west."

"We go west."

Abdo shook his head. He turned and faced his brother. The loyal ones who remained reverently gave the two brothers distance. "It is over, Abu Alhaul. It is time to retreat, reassess, and decide a new direction." He pointed north. "We turn north, toward civilization, and an aircraft ticket to Egypt." He sighed. "Ojo is following, and it is only a matter of time until he catches us—unless we leave. There is no 'if' in this statement, only a 'when.'"

"The children of Islam should be available now." Abu Alhaul motioned to the man immediately behind him. The thin, young man stepped forward pushing the flowing robe of a desert Bedouin out of the way. In many places the robe was torn and stained. A dark red patch showed where someone had bled. A dirty white patch covered a wound on the man's cheek. "They are the weapons we have built through years of prayer and study. Let me see—"

Abu Alhaul snapped his fingers. The man handed his leader a thick notebook. Abu Alhaul took the notebook and as if he had all the time in the world, he thumbed through page after page of Arabic script, stopping every so often to run his finger along a line. Abdo stood silent as his brother, once again, tried to identify the locations of Jihadist schools where his followers took children as students and turned them into future martyrs for Allah.

"So many," Abu Alhaul muttered.

"So few," Abdo corrected. "Everywhere you worked these past five years to turn Africa into a Muslim continent is being eaten by this General Ojo. Religion and politics can never defeat nationalism regardless of how hard we try. Abu Alhaul—Asim, my brother—it is time to leave this dark—" He slapped his fleshy upper arm, glancing to see what had bitten him. "—insect-ridden country to those who want it. We never should—"

Abu Alhaul held his hand up. "Enough. Don't say it. We came here because Allah commanded it."

"Then Allah must have seen the consequences, and His greater plans call for you to fail. Your failure is Allah's victory," Abdo said, his tone sharp. "I'm telling you as one who loves you. Now, let's go home and celebrate His wisdom."

"The problem is not Allah's. It is ours. We who lead the holy jihad expect instantaneous results." He threw his arms apart as if simulating an explosion. "What we needed was to increase our patience to reap a bigger result that takes more time for the enemy to realize he's been attacked. But, I failed Him. Instead of concentrating on the jihad, I allowed personal vengeance in seeking out the American who killed my family to shadow my true purpose. I have failed Him, and to fail Him is to die in his service."

"Do you think He can wait until we're close enough for a proper funeral? Ask Him if it is possible for you to stay because your brother wants you to live because he loves you. Tell Him you are prepared to serve Him another day but right now you'd like to have a hot bath, return to Egypt, sit at the sidewalk café near home, and watch the tourists being fleeced of their dollars. I think He'd understand." He pointed north and sighed. "I have always done what you asked. Now, you will follow me. Your safety is my life, and to live we take the northern trail. For the time, you will have to abandon the dream of an Islamic Africa."

"I can never do that! You make small talk of Allah and His wrath is something to behold, for I am the wielder of His wrath."

Fierce eyes stopped Abdo for a moment before he turned his head away from his brother. "Have you thought that maybe one of your sons is to finish what you started?"

"I have no sons."

He faced his brother again. "And you won't, if we don't turn north and leave the battlefield to the Africans. Let them rid the continent of the Westerners, which will make your son's job easier."

Abu Alhaul weighed his brother's words as if weighing his thoughts.

"Maybe Allah is speaking through your brother, telling you to live to fight another day."

"This is a test by Allah to see if I will follow His word even when my family attempts to sway me in another direction."

Abdo shook his head. He wanted to reach out and slap

his brother, but even he had doubts if being blood kin would stop this man he once chased through the streets of their village when they were young; when they laughed and played. It had been many years since laughter had enveloped them as if the Allah that Abu Alhaul followed demanded stern visages and contemplative thoughts.

"We have time. For four days we've been running from the pursuing Africans. There are no more villages; no more of our schools. Village after village where we set up schools to train the children of Africa have been decimated. No one left alive. Heads shoved atop stakes in the center of the village as a warning to others to remain Africans."

Abu Alhaul jumped as his brother's strong hands grabbed him by the upper arms and shook him. "Do you understand that you may die out here. There are no more villages!"

"Release me!" Abdo's arms dropped to his sides.

"Some will have survived," Abu Alhaul said, his voice soft. "Some always survive."

Abdo turned his back to his brother, unsheathed his machete, and returned to the bushes in front of them.

Abu Alhaul had never known his brother to be this anxious. Sure, they have had their setbacks, but Allah was forever testing His followers. The Africans may be searching and killing His followers, but they aided Allah's words by escorting Western missionaries from the jungles. His sources told him that Ojo had warned them never to return. But for his villages, they killed the teachers and the children. It was the children who were the future of Jihad. It was the children upon whose blank slate of life was written the future, teaching them the honor of martyrdom, making them willing to strap bombs to their chests and die, taking the enemy with them. To build such weapons meant teaching them the purity of such acts while young. As they grew older and more mature, the lure of life outweighed the purity of sacrifice.

Abdo stopped chopping and turned again to face him. "My brother, we can't wait for you to make a decision. Even Allah takes a rest. We are going north to safety and someday you may return, but I think your life here is done."

"Only for a short time, my brother. Only a short time. You are right in that you can never succeed if you are killed." He couldn't believe he was agreeing to flee. It was better to die for Allah than to flee for another day.

"Sometimes you say the right thing."

Abu Alhaul opened his mouth to object, his lips opening and closing several times before he shut them and nodded. For once his younger brother was right. What right did he have to die when his service to Allah remained unfulfilled? Or, was it fulfilled? It was something he and the mullahs could argue, balancing successes and failures against the teachings of the Koran.

"Okay, we go north to see if we can lose those who are following."

Abdo nodded. "We should discard those weapons that are too heavy and too useless, such as those Russian missiles. They are antiquated. We have no aircraft upon which to use them and they are slowing down all of us."

"No! We may need them." They were the only weapons they had other than the automatic AK-47s everyone carried.

"Yes, we may need them, but right now we need to escape more than we need the surface-to-air missiles. Look, my brother, we can hide them along the path and when we return—"

"Abdo, you have told me you think we won't return. Why do you say such things if you think we won't return?"

Abdo shrugged. "Because I want to convince you that all may not be lost. There no longer exists an Islamic Front for Purification. It is dead, and with it the glory of the victory you so desired has died. There will be no Shara in this part of Africa for a long time. Instead, African barbarism will triumph until you return."

Abu Alhaul pushed his brother, barely moving the man, a surge of anger bursting forth. Who was he to argue with Abu Alhaul? "You will shut up and do as I command," he said, his voice low, his tone hard. "We will take what we have with us because we are going to return, and when we return we will need such weapons." He saw the red in his brother's face, and he realized he had both angered and humiliated him in front of others.

Abdo stepped forward, and Abu Alhaul prepared himself for the verbal sparring he expected, but his brother turned abruptly, his face still red with anger, and like a huge clearing machine, his younger brother raised his machete. The arm moved in a blur as Abdo chopped and wracked the bushes apart in front of them, raising huge clouds of insects and filling the air around him with fresh leaves. Abu Alhaul watched as his brother broke the trail ahead, aware the path headed north.

Abu Alhaul handed the notebook to the young man. He told himself he had time to change his decision to flee. Those who followed would stay with him, but would his brother? He followed along the path, his brother farther ahead. First, the Americans chase him out of Liberia. Within two weeks of loading a merchant vessel with a deadly cargo to avenge the death of his family and watching it sail from a little-used port in the Ivory Coast, the French mounted such massive searches for him, searches so intense, he was forced to flee north to Guinea.

Six months in Guinea, Abu Alhaul was reconstituting his army when he encountered this makeshift, ragtag gang of Africans chasing him—*him;* the true savior of

Africa—calling themselves the African National Army. Instead of trying to find and kill him, this African National Army should be focusing on the white men who have ravaged this continent for centuries. His thoughts never equated the origin of enslaving Africans to the Arabs from North Africa and the Arabian Peninsula. *The Africans and Arabs were brothers,* he thought. *Together we could do so much, but if I stop to talk, they'll kill me before we could agree on consolidating our forces. It is hard to discuss logically together the better path when false ideology clouds the true path of Jihad.*

Behind this leader marched remnants of an army that two years ago numbered in the thousands. In the middle of the thick, bush-ridden jungles of Guinea, they fled from an army made up of thousands of native Africans whose only thoughts were to find and kill him. After what he had done for this continent, they treat him as if he was scum. They should be fighting the Americans and the French. Free Liberia and Ivory Coast from the western powers, and the rest of Africa would rise to support you. *Whoever this General Ojo was, the man had no grasp for reality.*

An hour later, the man with the books closed the gap with Abu Alhaul. "Master, the men are tired. Several have the surface-to-air missiles and—"

"Abdo, we'll take a break here!" Abu Alhaul shouted.

The remnants of his army squatted where they were, a few quietly exchanging words. The noise of the jungle could be heard again.

Abdo turned and rejoined his brother, who was still standing. "Sit, my brother," he said softly to Abu Alhaul, reaching up and touching the terrorist leader on the shoulders. "Sit and rest. We are free from our pursuers. They won't follow us out of the jungles because they would run into the Ghanaian Army. We are small—"

"Abdo, I would feel better, if you wouldn't remind me of our size. We used to be so many."

Abdo nodded. "And we used to be feared by so many, but now we must reconstitute ourselves; return to where the fields are ripe for your picking; and, if you so desire in a few years, we can return and pursue your guidance from Allah." He pushed down again on Abu Alhaul's shoulders.

Abu Alhaul nodded and squatted on his haunches. No one sat on the jungle floor where so many things could craw upon you to eat.

Abdo squatted beside him, pulling his backpack off and tossing it in front of them. He opened it and rifled through the stuff crammed into the back, pulling out an American energy bar. "Here, eat this."

Abu Alhaul took it, turned it different ways, looking at the English printed on both sides, and then handed it back. "It is Western. It is not fit for the lips of Allah's prophet."

Abdo handed it back. "All the Allah's prophets in the world are useless if they die."

"We can make Him happy by dying."

"We make our enemies happier, so eat." Abdo unwrapped the bar and shoved it back into Abu Alhaul's hand, forcing his brother's fingers around the bar. A few seconds later Abu Alhaul was eating the energy bar.

Abdo looked at his watch.

"How long?" Abu Alhaul asked.

"Ten minutes."

They had been resting and now even he didn't feel like starting again. Were the Africans still pursuing them or as Abdo said, they have stopped or lost our tracks? Were they truly safe for the time being? He lifted his head, twisting it from side to side. *What is that noise—that buzz?*

Several seconds passed as Abu Alhaul listened to the

noise, trying to separate it from the mix of jungle sounds. Whatever it was, it was growing in sound. He recognized the sound.

"Airplane," he said.

Abdo lifted his head.

Abu Alhaul stood. Abdo followed. "Looks as if you will get your wish, Abdo. Have our warriors with those *obsolete* surface-to-air missiles prepare themselves."

"I did not mean to say they would not work."

"I know, my brother, but you are right sometimes and when you are right, it is hard to admit it."

"We don't know whose aircraft it is."

Abu Alhaul shrugged. "Doesn't matter, does it? If it's flying, it can't be a loyal warrior. We have no aircraft, just the foot soldiers of Allah."

Abdo hurriedly moved past Abu Alhaul, and seconds later he had the four men with the missiles lined up, the barrels pointing upward toward the unbroken canopy of vegetation that covered them from the sky.

"HERE HE COMES, CHIEF," PETTY OFFICER LACEY SAID, slapping Razi on the shoulder.

Coffee spilled over the top of the cup, splashing across Razi's hand and onto the small mess table. "Hey, watch it, clown." He winked at Lacey as he eased by the two sailors from the Naval Research Laboratory. Down the aisle came the new ensign. Razi slipped the half-full cup of coffee into a metal holder attached to the side of the bulkhead, leaned around the edge of the half-wall that separated the operating part of the aircraft from the mess area, and watched the ensign work his way aft. *He's heading to the head or back here.* Razi's fingers slipped into the flight-suit pocket on his right leg and found the peanut-butter packet. He laughed. He couldn't help thinking of the expression on newbies' faces when he did this.

He pulled the peanut-butter packet out, ripped the top off, and with his left boot crossed over his knee, he squeezed the mixture along the edge where the sole met the heel, using the empty packet to smooth the stuff down.

Lieutenant Reed, a mission evaluator, stood near the coffee urn. Razi put his flight shoe down and smiled at the officer.

"New meat," Razi said.

"New meat," the lieutenant acknowledged, turning to watch. The officer sipped his coffee with his free hand while the other held on to the safety bar overhead.

Razi walked forward, eased past the two sailors from the Naval Research Laboratory, and sat down on the arm of one of the passenger seats mounted along the starboard side of the aircraft.

Lacey took his earphones off, pushed himself out of his seat and directly in front of the ensign so that he led the way aft.

Razi lifted his flight boot and crossed it over his right knee. Behind the ensign, the new female flight engineer followed by a few paces. Razi's eyebrows rose and fell several times. *Pits must have given up and taken his seat back. A little fleshy, but she looked scrumptious.*

"Chief," Lacey said, stopping a couple of steps from Razi and causing the ensign to stop behind him. "Someone must have stepped in dog shit." Lacey wrinkled his nose as if trying to trace the smell.

"Lacey, what the hell are you talking about?" Razi said, his mind coming back to what he was doing. "No one steps in dog shit without knowing it." Razi stood and tapped the two aircrew members sitting directly across from him. "Either of you two step in dog shit?"

"Not us, Chief," they said in unison, small smiles crossing their faces.

Out of the corner of his eye, Razi saw the two sailors from Naval Research Laboratory turn to watch.

"I don't believe you. Check your flight boots." He pointed at Lacey. "You too, Lacey."

"Chief, I'm the one who smelled it—"

The ensign stopped, unable to get by because of Razi and Lacey.

"Which means you're the one most likely to have it on your shoe. Quit arguing and check."

Behind Lacey, the ensign leaned forward watching the sailors check their shoes.

"Not me, Chief," one of the operators said.

"Me either, Chief," the other echoed.

"And, as I told you, Chief," Lacey said, drawing out his words. "It ain't me, either."

The new flight engineer bunched up against the ensign and Lacey. She leaned around the two, forced her way to the right near the boarding hatch, stopped, and watched.

Razi noticed her breasts first, but that was his job: Notice the finer details of his fellow chief petty officers and make sure they appreciated it. He glanced up at her face to meet hooded lids over sparkling eyes. She smiled. *Well, at least she knows she got my attention.*

"Chief, you haven't checked your flight boots. You must have stepped in it."

Razi sat back down on the arm of the chair. First, he lifted his right boot, showing everyone there was nothing there.

Then, he slowly lifted his left flight boot, the sole facing toward the Lacey, the ensign, and the female flight engineer.

Lacey burst out. "There! I told you so, Chief. You've got dog poop all over the bottom."

Razi raised his hand and waved Lacey down. "Now, now, now," he said patronizingly. "Just because you say it is doesn't necessary mean it's dog poop."

"I can smell it. Can't you?" Lacey asked the ensign.

The ensign shrugged. "I don't smell anything."

By now, others in the aircraft had gathered to watch.

Razi leaned forward, getting his face as close as he could to the offending boot-bottom. "Well, Lacey, it does look like dog poop."

A chorus of agreements came from the onlookers and Razi smiled when he heard the ensign agree. *Wow! This is going to be the best one this year.*

With great show, Razi raised his right hand, held up his index finger, and ran it through the pasty, brown peanut butter, coming up with a large dab of it on the end of his finger.

"Looks like dog poop."

A chorus of "It is dog poop" and "What the hell did you think it was?" and "Damn it, man, don't put your fingers in it" roared from the growing number of aircrew who were working their way aft. Laughter filled the fuselage.

Razi looked around the aircraft. Lieutenant Reed opened the door to the head, stepped inside, and pulled it shut. Aircrewmen in the back, stretched their necks, trying to watch. Most of the eyes were on the ensign. The ensign stared directly at Razi's finger.

Razi raised the stuff near his nose. "Lacey, you may be right. I'm not wrong often, but it sure smells like dog poop." He looked at the two sailors manning Dragnet. One grinned while the other looked awfully pale. Out of the corner of his eye, he saw the new flight engineer move toward him, easing past Lacey and the ensign, but not blocking the ensign's view.

Razi opened his mouth, moved his finger down with its offending dab, and suddenly the new flight engineer leaned over with her finger, swiped the dab off his, and jammed it into her mouth.

The ensign's eyes widened and "Oh, my God's" filled the air as she rolled the stuff around her mouth a couple of times. Razi turned toward the NRL sailors just as the pale-faced one power-vomited, the mixture hitting Razi in the chest, splattering some on his face. The other sailor dove toward the mess area away from the follow-up heaving erupting from his partner. Aircrewmen pushed and shoved to get away from the sick sailor.

Razi jumped up. "What the hell!" He glanced at Lacey who had tears rolling down his cheeks. The first-class fell to his knees, clutching his stomach and lightly hitting his head against the back of a nearby seat. "Did you see that?" he gasped between laughs to the two sailors sitting in the console seats.

Razi looked down, his hands spread out to the side, staring at the yellow bits of half-eaten food that stained his suit.

The ensign shoved past the kneeling Lacey, knocking the leading petty officer into on opening between the two seats. The ensign reached the door to the head and snatched it open. Lieutenant Reed stood there peeing into the large urine container.

"What the—"

The ensign pushed Reed aside and vomited into the quarter-full container while Reed fought to zip up and mold himself to the backside of the head at the same time.

The flight engineer brought her finger out of her mouth. "Nope, peanut butter, Chief. Nothing but peanut butter." She reached inside a flight-suit pocket on her chest and pulled out a wad of napkins. "Here, Chief. You probably can use this." She smiled, leaving him looking like a wet dishrag as she continued to the mess area, stepping over the heaving sailor. She patted him on the head as she passed. "There's more fun later, sailor," she said.

A series of beeps from the Naval Research Laboratory position sounded over the noise of the crowd dispersing, as they returned to their mission positions. The sailor on the deck pulled himself up and slid back into his seat. The other sailor reached over and handed his shipmate a wet rag from the galley. The recovering sailor wiped his face before placing the wet handkerchief on the console table so he could press the computer-image icons on the data screen.

"Looks good," the other sailor said. "Gotta tweak it a little."

The sickened sailor acknowledged with a slow nod, grabbed the handkerchief, and wiped his face again. "Good God," the man muttered.

"Peanut butter."

"I didn't know it was peanut butter."

Razi watched the two as he wiped the mess off of his flight suit. The beeping continued until the sailor to the left pressed an icon and the beeping stopped. Razi started toward the mess area. He needed more water to get this smell off of him. *This isn't the way I planned it. That sailor wore wings, what in the hell kind of aircrewman is he who gets sick over a little practical joke?* As he crossed into the lighted area of the galley, he realized the laughter was more on him than the sailor and the ensign. *Oh, well, you win some and you lose some.* He wished he had brought along another flight suit. Staying in this one for ten hours wasn't his idea of a good flight.

The new flight engineer turned as Razi entered.

"Good job, Chief," he said to her.

"Couldn't have done it without you," she said, then she

started laughing as she held out her hand. "Anita Jennings, Chief."

"Bad"—He couldn't say Badass to her.—"Will Razi," he said gripping her hand and shaking it.

"Funny, I thought they called you 'Badass'?

"They do," he replied, then, holding his hands out and looking down at the mess on the front of his flight suit, "but after this, I think I'm going to need a new handle for my flying days."

"How about 'vomit man'?" said Lieutenant Reed from behind him.

"Chief!" one of the NRL sailors shouted. "You better come here."

"Good to meet you, Anita. Great job, once again, but if we're going to work together on things like this, we need to coordinate our actions."

She smiled.

She does have a nice smile, Razi thought. It's the dimples in the cheeks that make the smile look wider and friendlier than she probably means.

"Sounds like we will have to get together after the flight, Chief, and develop our coordination."

He felt a slight blush, but didn't understand why— unless it was the quick image of her spreadeagled and moaning that was zipping through his thoughts.

She laughed. "No, not that type of coordination, Chief."

"Chief!" the sailor shouted again. "We've got something."

"Excuse me." Razi hurried toward the prototype system. "What have you got?"

"This." The screen on the CRT display flickered for a moment and then a graphic display of heat signatures appeared. Immediately, small computer-generated figures of men replaced them. "We have just flown over a group of about twenty to thirty humans."

"How you know?"

"The computer knows."

"Chief, I'm sorry for puking on you," the other sailor said.

Razi patted him on the shoulder. "Don't worry about it. If you get hungry later, you know where you can find some food." He turned to the sailor in charge. "How do we know the computer is right?"

The other sailor turned pale again.

The sailor shrugged. "It hasn't been wrong yet when we've tested it."

Razi moved to the other side. "Don't puke again, son. You've done enough damage," he said, frowning. "Lots of difference between testing it in the field and testing it in the laboratory."

"Chief, while we argue here; the aircraft is getting farther and farther away. We need to turn back."

"If we turn back are we going to get anything more than we have people below us?"

"Well, Chief, we also have a magnetometer on board EP-3Es. The magnetometer has a similar database concept as Dragnet. The magnetometer can tell, by the intensity and density of the metal below, what type of weapons may be there. If we consolidate the intelligence from Dragnet and the magnetometer, we might be able to determine what is below us."

Razi stared at the man for moment, his eyes looking at the second-class crow. *How in the hell did he put this together?* Razi slapped the sailor on the shoulder. "Damn, you're good. I was thinking the same thing."

Five minutes later, the aircraft was in a turn heading back to where Dragnet had detected the warm bodies. In the front end of the aircraft, the magnetometer operator, a sailor trained as a cryptologic technician in the technical rating—a former electronic warfare technician—energized the magnetometer database. They hadn't planned on using this system while flying over the jungles of West Africa. It wasn't as if they were searching for tanks or submarines.

"Chief, I have another contact!" the NRL sailor shouted.

Razi leaned over his shoulder. Numerous contacts speckled the 360-degree screen, icons popping up all over it, indicating humans. "What the—"

"Look here, Chief," the sailor said, tapping a readout above the screen. "Over three hundred contacts and growing."

"What does that mean?"

"It means we have a small group—twenty miles away from this group."

"Or, they could be together," the other sailor said, color returning to his face.

Lieutenant Reed appeared beside Razi. "What have you got, Chief?"

Razi pointed at the display screen and the readout. "Looks as if this prototype is picking up a large number of people below the jungle canopy."

"Which way are they heading?" Reed asked.

Razi shrugged.

The lead sailor from NRL replied, "Don't know, sir. We're in a turn and this system has problems determining direction and speed of movement unless we stay straight, level, and keep our speed steady."

"We're already in a turn, Chief, to go back to where the first contact was made. We'll get another chance to look at the large contact." The mission evaluator looked at the two sailors. "You have confidence this system is working—functioning properly."

"Yes, sir," they said in unison. "We have put this system

through rigorous testing, Lieutenant, and it has been one-hundred-percent accurate."

Reed pursed his lips. "Then, I'm going to be hard-pressed to trust it, sailors. Haven't seen anything in the Navy during my short career one-hundred-percent any-thing that wasn't as hosed up as Hogan's goat." He turned and walked back toward the front, disappearing into the dark shadows of the fuselage, lit by the soft green of the various displays on the consoles.

"Chief, we have two groups of people down there," the lead sailor protested. "Not one, but two groups and this system—Dragnet is one-hundred-'by-God'-percent accu-rate, and I don't care what that VQ lieutenant says."

Razi put his hand on his shoulders. "Don't worry about what he thinks, worry that your data is refined, accurate, and there're no problems caused by the electronics in this aircraft. Then, we'll let the system prove itself."

The EP-3E Aries II aircraft leveled itself. Razi glanced at the digital compass on the main console. It showed two-eight-five. They were heading back toward the first contact. He bent his head, the odor from the vomit along the front of his flight suit wafted through his nostrils, nearly causing him to heave. *Serve the sailor right if I puked on him.*

CHAPTER 4

OJO NODDED. "GENERAL EZEJI, THE AMERICANS ARE HERE again," he said, nodding upward. "You hear the airplane?"

"They will never leave us alone, General. One month ago, they sent a team to kill you. And, when they failed, they continued the hunt. It is good that we have friends in Monrovia keeping watch so we are aware of their plans."

Ojo glanced down at the heavyset Nigerian and smiled. "The Americans are never satisfied unless they know everything that is going on around them. They trust no one and verify everything." He reached out and touched General Ezeji. Ezeji was the only general in the African National Army with military experience, experience much broader than his own. Ezeji said he was a former general in the Nigerian Army, but Ojo had never been able to confirm the information. It would be too much to push an inquiry in Nigeria, for if the man is what he says, then his value is so great that to endanger him to the Nigerians would be regrettable.

When the rotund man appeared a year ago at their encampment, Ojo believed him to be a member of Nigerian intelligence. The angry Kabaka warned that Ezeji had been sent to spy on the ANA and report everything to Nigeria, the regional West African power. The months had been kind to Ezeji in Ojo's eyes. Ojo valued the insight and suggestions from the Nigerian, and if Ezeji was a member of Nigerian intelligence, then his worth-for-the-moment outweighed the risk. The sound of the aircraft grew. "Stop the men," Ojo said, raising his hand.

"But, General, they cannot see us through the canopy nor hear us from their aircraft."

"I know, but it gives us an opportunity to reconstitute our forces so that when we reach the Arabs we will be ready. It would be incompetent for us to stumble into them and have them kill our soldiers before we were ready."

Ezeji passed the word to the runners who fanned out in all directions to stop the movement of the army. Cellular telephones were useless in the absence of towers and the fledging army could ill afford satellite telephones, so the poverty of their fighting force hid them from their adversaries who would remotely exploit their activities. Their own human intelligence networks had reported newspaper articles telling of how Western governments had reached the conclusion months ago that only humans interjected into the ANA could provide any real information on this growing, mysterious African army. Intelligence abhors military and political mysteries. The lower the technology capability of an adversary, the more important human intelligence gathering becomes.

Ojo lifted his khaki hat and ran the back of his hand across his forehead. It was a Western misconception that

Africans were unaffected by the high humidity and heat of the jungle—that dark skin and generations of living here protected them. *What a lie!* Heat was heat, and it could kill an African as quickly as it could kill a white man. The interlocking leaves of the jungle canopy hiding them from the reconnaissance aircraft trapped heat, turning the shaded jungle into a sweaty cauldron of fatigue and dehydration. Every night, his generals brought new stories of missing and dead soldiers. The missing, most tired of constant marching and fighting the deadly heat, had simply slipped into the bush to return to dust-ridden patches they called farms. Dead did not necessarily mean *dead.* For the army to keep moving, it was sufficient for a soldier to lie down and refuse to go on or become unresponsive. Ojo had little doubt that many of them waited until the army had moved on before they miraculously recovered and disappeared into the jungles to join the more adventurous "missing" ones.

Ojo overheard Ezeji direct a runner to locate Kabaka and to return with the news. Ezeji's actions had either proved Ojo's surmise that the man was loyal to him, or that the Nigerians wanted the ANA to succeed. Someday, he would figure out why the Nigerians would allow the ANA free reign in West Africa. Even America checked with the Nigerians before they did anything in this part of the world. Could the Americans be afraid of the Nigerians? No, Ojo thought, shaking his head. The Americans needed the Nigerians. Needed them to patrol and pacify this volatile area of Africa. It was an American strategy to use regional powers to promote stability for failed states, and areas of instability provided sanctuary for terrorists such as Abu Alhaul.

"It is hot," Ezeji said, his voice soft.

Ojo acknowledged the comment, slid his hat back on his head, straightening it so the brim rode above the eyebrows.

Ezeji seemed as dedicated to the cause as he did. Maybe he was too paranoid. Then again, sometimes a cause and a person are one in the same. Early causes must be explicitly linked to a personality. He was the personality. Only when the turmoil of birth was over could a cause stand alone. Sometimes he wondered what causes ANA fought, other than to rid Africa of foreign intervention. He must not fall for the trappings of power, but it was a grand feeling to raise one's hand and watch others wait for his words. Ojo had a far-off goal he wanted to achieve. Someday, when he handed over power, a power he hoped would be far-reaching over an independent Africa, he would be allowed to gracefully rock away his older years watching his child grow. Most African futures seemed filled with violence and death.

"General Ojo, we are stopped," Ezeji said. "I have talked with General Darin, and he is aligning his soldiers along our left flank. They will move parallel with us. The scout who returned an hour ago reported finding a fresh trail of our quarry, turning north."

"How old?"

Ezeji shrugged. "One day, possibly two. It is hard to say without stumbling onto a campsite, and it looks as if the Arabs are fleeing. It is easy to say they know we are pursuing them. Our village visits have told us that. What I don't believe they know is how far back we are. As long as they think we are close, they will continue to hurry away, sapping their strength, until we finally catch up."

"They're smaller, they can move faster."

Ezeji nodded. "Yes, but we have groups already surging forward to block the path they may have taken. When the Arabs run into this block, they won't know how many and they will stop to fight. When that happens, then we can surge forward and finish this quest quickly."

Ojo nodded and glanced around him. The constant

noise of hundreds of feet tramping through the virgin jungles had ceased. Everyone stopped moving. Many would be throwing their packs to the side to grab rest, and some even a short sleep.

Ojo nodded to the stake-bearer, Niewu, who had joined them during Ojo's reverie.

Ojo, Ezeji, and Niewu stood together listening to the noise of the aircraft grow, then for an unknown reason the aircraft noise steadied. Ezeji believed the aircraft had found them, and for a short time, Ojo agreed. Then, as slow as it approached, the sound of the aircraft engines began to decrease.

"It is turning around," Ojo offered.

"Why would it turn around, if not to fly over us again?"

"I don't know, General Ezeji. It is hard to say what is happening above the forest without being able to see, and without being inside the minds of the Americans on board. I believe they fly looking for signs of us and signs for the Arabs we chase. All we know is what we hear, and what we hear is that it has turned around. It is leaving our area, and since it is American we are going to take no action against it, right?" Ojo asked. *Where is my comrade Kabaka who marches very much to his own brand of chaos? We don't need him firing at the Americans—*

"Of course. I agree completely. We finish one step at a time—"

"Not engage the world all at once. For the Americans, as well as the French in the Ivory Coast, we will wage our battles with them in the court of world opinion, and to do that we must avoid anything that gives them reason to take action against us."

"Would not you say this aircraft is an action against us, General Ojo?" Niewu asked, his voice betraying the fatigue of old age.

Ojo shook his head. "No, the aircraft is an unarmed reconnaissance aircraft filled with American military men twirling their cameras, staring at their radars, and searching the jungles beneath them with binoculars. What can they see through the jungle blanket that barely lets the sun hit our faces? As long as we stay away from anything electronic, not light campfires, and avoid open areas, we are safe."

"What do you think they will do if they do find us?"

Ojo shrugged. "I think they will just fly more and stay overhead more, orbiting and orbiting, trying to discover who and what we are. I think we are an enigma, and America, like France, and even your home country of Nigeria, dislikes enigmas near their centers of influence and power."

"That would be dangerous," Ezeji said.

"What would be dangerous?" Niewu asked, coming closer.

"Dangerous to have them orbiting overhead all the time. Then, no matter where we moved, we would be tracked and the American presence would tell everyone where we are, like a float above a fishing line.

Ojo nodded and pointed up. "The airplane is leaving. Once the troops are realigned, General Ezeji, we will continue. We will pursue in the three lines of advance, with you in the center and Darin on our left and Kabaka to our right. Somewhere ahead awaits our quarry, and once we are done with Abu Alhaul and have rid Africa of his Jihadist schools and teachings of death, we will move to the next step for an independent and poverty-free Africa. The Americans will be happy when they learn of what we have done. It is the Americans who make me more nervous than the French or the British, so if we convince them we are no threat to their homeland, they will leave us alone."

"They will never leave us alone. They will view what

we have done in the villages as war crimes. They will continue to look for you."

"How can they say it is a war crime to disarm a terrorist? Those boys we killed were already dedicated to dying in a suicide explosion to take themselves and as many innocents as they could with them. I would say we have disarmed the terrorists by killing them."

"They won't see it that way. They will see us killing children and say we are war criminals. They may back away from trying to engage us militarily or through their CIA, but they will forever watch us."

"I prefer them watching to acting."

"If we convince them we are a positive factor in their war against terrorism, they may even provide dollars to help us in our attempt to raise our people out of poverty."

Ezeji exhaled loudly. "Africa will always have its poverty."

"You may be right," Ojo sighed. "But we would be wrong not to try." *Poverty is a great cause for rallying a people,* he thought.

"We can try—"

The cry of a point sentry interrupted Ezeji, drawing both their attention. The noise of weapons being unlimbered and the clicks of safeties switching off reminded Ojo of childhood and witnessing swarms of locusts rolling across the countryside like great waves washing away everything beneath them. The fading sound of the American aircraft was lost in the noise of soldiers preparing for the unexpected, and when the rising noise of the army achieving readiness settled, the sound of the American aircraft had vanished completely. Ojo glanced up at the jungle canopy, wondering where the aircraft had gone. For whatever reason, the aircraft had been overhead and now had left the area. Would it return?

A soldier rushed up to General Ezeji, whispered something, and quickly departed.

"Seems one of our patrols has returned."

A few minutes later, two of Ojo's enforcers—soldiers chosen personally by him with the belief that their loyalty was to him and to him alone—led several young boys through the brush to where Ojo and the other two stood. He guessed the oldest boy to be twelve, but individual age was, at best, a guess in the growing African epoch of orphans. Four, he counted, each carrying an AK-47, the weapon of choice for terrorists and freedom fighters alike. The smallest, and most likely the youngest, had his weapon slung over his shoulder with the barrel pointing down. With each step the AK-47 bounced off the boy's lower leg only a couple of inches above the ankle. AK-47—the weapon of choice for an impoverished army. Ojo nodded in admiration of the boys. All four marched, heads high, lips pursed together. He could see their pride in being soldiers in the African National Army. He doubted that they realized how expendable they were as a fighting element. It was the young ones that were sent forward to reconnoiter the terrain and to be the trailblazers for the main body. The loss of a child warrior was preferred over an adult. Africa was the continent of child warriors. Child warriors so numerous that they were an expendable item for the army, like a basket of corn leaking kernels, many at a time. For a brief moment, Ojo wondered how many had died in his battles. His head dipped for a moment. They never buried their dead, leaving them to the jungle to return to mother earth.

"General Ojo," the enforcer leading the boys said, his hand raised in a British-style salute. "This group has been sent back. They have found our target."

Ojo nodded at the young leader of the four. "You have found the Arabs?"

"Yes, General Ojo," The tallest boy in front said, raising his thin hand in imitation of the salute like the enforcer. "Little Nikku is following them, staying out of sight, and marking the trail. He sent me back with my boys to tell you."

Ojo smiled. "You can drop your hand," he said to the boy, who smiled and dropped the salute.

Ojo glanced at Ezeji. "Little Nikku?"

Ezeji shrugged. The enforcer in the rear of the boys answered. "Nikku is the number-one tracker for General Ezeji," he said, nodding down at the boys standing in front of him. "He leads these fine African warriors for you, General Ojo."

For the next few minutes the leader of the patrol debriefed General Ojo about where Abu Alhaul was located and how there appeared to be only twenty or thirty followers, at the most, with him. The Arabs were fleeing toward the edge of the jungle that opened into the plains of Guinea. Ojo and Ezeji peppered the boys with questions about the weapons and disposition of Abu Alhaul and his forces. Finally satisfied, Ojo stepped back and smiled at the four boys.

"I see. Okay, my soldiers," Ojo said to the leader. "Go have some food and water. When you finish, come see General Ezeji, who will give you instructions." He turned to Ezeji, "So these are yours?"

"I am afraid I don't know everyone who has joined my ranks, General."

"Thank you, General Ojo," the leader of the four boys said, "but we must go see General Kabaka first. He has ordered us to report to him everything we see."

He couldn't help himself. Blood rushed to his face as a wave of anger swept over him. Without the guise of his rich African skin, he would never have hidden how much this knowledge affected him. He stopped in midbreath and forced his breathing to slow, his eyelids and brow to relax.

Hide visible emotion. No one must know of his desire to kill Kabaka. This tall, lithe warrior from some nondescript tribe in Ghana was becoming more than a nuisance, he was breeding discontent and fermenting disloyalty. These boy soldiers couldn't know, but on the blank slate of childhood, others, such as Abu Alhaul, had written their own mantras, sending thousands of innocents to death.

"You are in my command!" Ezeji shouted, stepping forward and with a quicker motion than Ojo thought possible, the Nigerian's hand drew back and slapped the boy. "You will obey only me."

The blow sent the young boy reeling backward into the shorter lad behind him, knocking both of them to the ground. Ojo saw the tears well up in the young soldier's eyes as he lifted his hand and rubbed his cheek. The child warrior had no idea why his general had slapped him. The other lad pushed the boy off him and scurried away to where the others had stepped back.

Ezeji stepped forward. Ojo put his hand on the larger man's arm. "No, let him be. He is still part of your command, General. In a way, it is good that he told us what General Kabaka asked him to do. It affirms that we are teaching our soldiers to obey the orders of those above them. It's part of being a soldier."

"But—"

Ojo shook his head and turned to the boy on the ground. The other three took another step away, no longer wanting to be associated with the boy who was, until moments ago, their leader. Loyalty was a fragile thing in a rebel army and the slap by their general had immediately destroyed any hope this lad had of resuming his role as their leader. It was something the boy on the ground wouldn't discover until much later.

"Get up and go do what you were ordered," Ojo said, unable to hide the sharp tone. He hated the idea of Kabaka's tentacles twisting and churning through the ranks of his army, feeding the ambition of this one person he mistrusted the most. "You are right to tell us what your orders were."

"Kill him," Ezeji whispered. "Kill him before we—"

The young boy on the ground thought Ezeji meant him. He jumped up and took off running. Ojo and Ezeji turned and watched the lad disappear into the jungle.

"Enough, General," Ojo interrupted, raising his hand. "Kabaka is a loyal soldier who follows my orders. We have no cause to worry." Ojo thought, *I lie so easily to keep the army together. Ezeji, you are right: When the time is right, I will kill him. Every action has a time and sometimes that very time calls for no action. Today is not the day for Kabaka. Soon—so very soon. I will know when the time is right. Deaths must help, not shatter, the tender glue of a cause that holds us together. I wonder if my death will ever be required and, if so, who decides such a thing?* He glanced at Ezeji for a moment.

"Of course, General Ojo," Ezeji apologized, looking down at his feet and withdrawing a couple of steps. "With your permission, I will send a company of older soldiers— maybe some in their twenties," he said with what Ojo thought was sarcasm, "to where Abu Alhaul and his hundreds wait."

"There are no more hundreds," Ojo said. "These soldiers tell us their numbers are small. There is only he and his core. We kill them and we will mop up the sleepers he leaves behind. Human weapons trained to kill and die. How stupid are we when we are young, so young to believe everything we are told? We are at a crossroad to jerk Africa away from the self-destruction of Jihad." He paused for a moment, then looked at the Nigerian and smiled. "Go ahead, General. And, while you are sending others forward, send someone for General Kabaka."

"I sent someone earlier to make sure he was in position for when we encounter Abu Alhaul. He sent a reply back saying he knew his job and he was in position."

"That's good, but I still would like him to come see me. Did you ask him to join us?"

Ezeji looked up and shook his head. "I only want to know where he is. The less I am around him, the better. I compare my desire to know where he is to the Americans wanting to know where we are at all times. Who was it that said, 'keep your friends close, but your enemies closer'? I think whoever said it had great insight, so I want to know where Kabaka is at all times. Unlike my esteemed leader and commander, I have little trust in this general."

"I agree it is best to keep our most active general close." Ojo smiled. For Ezeji to feel comfortable to voice his suspicions and fears reassured Ojo of his loyalty.

Ezeji laughed. "Active isn't the word I would use. Sir, here is my proposal for encircling Abu Alhaul, since we know his location."

For the next several minutes the two men talked. Niewu sat down on the ground to rest his old bones, and he listened with his head turned upward. Ezeji's soldiers would vault ahead of Abu Alhaul to block the terrorist's escape route while the ANA would continue its pursuit, spread out so no one could escape. Somewhere ahead, Ezeji's Nigerians would engage the Arabs and hold them—slow them down at worst case—until the main body of the ANA surrounded and crushed the invaders.

*   *   *

"THE AIRPLANE IS RETURNING," ABU ALHAUL SAID.

"We're ready," Abdo said, pointing at the four men squatting twenty meters away, their black turbans torn and dirty.

Each held a surface-to-air missile canister between their knees. Abu Alhaul took a deep breath. Was Allah with him, or had he done something to cause his God to turn His back on him? This would be a sign. If he was successful and blew the Americans from the sky, then it would be Allah showing him—Abu Alhaul, father of terror—he was still blessed. If the missiles missed, and he didn't see how four of them could, then it would be evident that he must go away and restore the holistic link between him and Allah. If only everyone could recognize his Holiness and that Abu Alhaul, like Osama, was His messenger, then the world would bask in the glory of Shara, the law of Islam, as they rid the earth of heretics.

"Up!" Abdo shouted at the men. "Prepare to fire."

"The aircraft is still approaching," Abu Alhaul said, placing his hand on Abdo's arm.

"Yes, my brother, but we want to be ready."

"Allah will provide."

"Then He should hurry, because we are hungry and thirsty, also."

Abu Alhaul jerked his hand off his brother's arm. "You blaspheme. You will bring wrath upon us."

Abdo leaned close to his brother and, in a sharp tone Abu Alhaul had not heard since their childhood, said, "Asim, it is time to quit being foolish. You have to pull yourself out of the vapors of religion long enough to understand that those behind us want to kill us; those above us want to kill us; and, wherever you and I go, there will be stacks of rewards for whoever else wants to kill us—" Abdo stopped, waved his hands about for a few moment. "Damn it, Asim. You're not Abu Alhaul anymore. Abu

Alhaul is dead. He has failed. You're Asim, my brother. Allah has abandoned us." Abdo leaned forward and pointed at the small cadre scattered around them. He whispered, "They can turn us into anyone and be rich the rest of their lives. Turning us in, also saves theirs. Right now, they stand with us, but when they truly realize they are going to die, their loyalty will disappear like water in the desert."

"You are wrong!" Abu Alhaul said sharply. "My disciples will never abandon me, and whatever happens to us will be the will of Allah."

"We just went through that. Let us fire these missiles and hope they at least penetrate the jungle overhead and don't turn and kill us."

"They will hit Great Satan's aircraft and kill everyone on board."

A deep sigh accompanied Abdo's nods. Abu Alhaul saw a couple of tears roll down the cheeks of his brother, clearing away days of caked dirt and dust that had accumulated during their trek. Maybe this flight from the Africans was what Mohammed suffered in his flight from Mecca to Medina. Maybe it was Allah's way to show that he—Abu Alhaul—was the chosen one. His brother's loyalty was something he never doubted, but his brother's loyalty was to him, Asim, instead of Allah and Abu Alhaul, His messenger. He loved Abdo, but Abdo tore his heart apart with his lack of reverence to Allah. Love of one's brother was nothing compared to love of one's God. Would Allah test him against his brother? He hoped not because he did love Abdo, and to have to prove his love for Allah, he would grieve greatly to lose Abdo.

The four men stood, unlimbered the firing mechanism, and removed the stops that protected both ends of the canister. Abu Alhaul watched, his face an impassive mask. It was not in his hands whether the missiles worked and carried out Allah's wishes. It was in the hands of Allah. If they failed, then it was because of his brother's blasphemy. He stepped back as he realized what he would have to do if the missiles missed. The test of his love for his brother was at hand sooner than he expected. He shouldn't be surprised, for Allah demanded tests constantly for it was only the holy who could enter paradise. Abu Alhaul shut his eyes for a moment. The vision of paradise flowed across his thoughts, visions that grew of sweet water, cool breezes, nuts, dates, and a parade of virgins as rewards for the true religion and faith shown in the harsh world of life.

The four men kneeled.

"Wait!" Abdo ordered, moving fast for a big man.

Abu Alhaul opened his eyes. Abdo turned the men so the blasts would be away from them and the other men firing their missiles. What good would it do to shoot down the Americans and kill your selves while doing it? However, Allah expected His servants to die in service to Him.

Abdo stepped back, reached out, and took Abu Alhaul's arm. "We need to move away."

"Why?"

"We're too close to the firing," Abdo said softly. "These are old missiles, carried for decades from one place to another; always never used because they were too important and irreplaceable. When things are too important to use, eventually they become dangerous."

Abu Alhaul allowed his brother to guide him farther from the four kneeling men. He glanced behind him. The four Jihadists stared upward, three of them ignoring the two leaders who opened the distance between them. The fourth stared unabashed, causing Abu Alhaul to wonder what the man was thinking. The man didn't glance down in respect when their eyes met. What will the others think, he asked himself as he broke eye contact and followed Abdo?

The noise of the aircraft engines increased. Suddenly a flicker of a shadow crossed over them. Abdo released him and glanced upward. Abu Alhaul looked also. You could see nothing through the canopy, but the sunlight that brightened it had dipped for a moment as the aircraft passed directly between them and the hot African sun.

"Fire!" his brother shouted at the four men.

Three of the missiles left their canisters. The fourth lit off but remained inside the canister. One of the missiles rose many feet into the air before suddenly cartwheeling away through the top of the trees and then exploding against one over a hundred meters away. The Jihadist with the misfired canister threw it down and started running. Abdo knocked Abu Alhaul to the ground and covered him with his body.

Abu Alhaul pulled his head from under his brother's massive body and continued to watch. The remaining two missiles penetrated the jungle canopy and disappeared. Shouts from the direction of the four men drew his attention. One of the men whose missile had penetrated the canopy picked up the misfired canister and shook it, trying to dislodge whatever held the missile inside. The other two threw their empty canisters down and took off running, shouting as they broke through the bushes, putting as much distance between them and their comrade as they could.

The explosion blinded Abu Alhaul, causing him to instinctively shut his eyes. He felt Abdo's massive hand cover his face in the same instant that the heat and concussion from the explosion rolled over them.

Seconds later, Abu Alhaul mumbled Abdo's name, but no reply came. He opened his eyes, one eye was covered by his brother's hand. Abu Alhaul struggled for a few moments to free himself and when he did, he reached up and moved Abdo's hand. His brother's eyes were shut and trickles of blood ran from his nose and ears. For a moment, Abu Alhaul believed Allah had extracted His retribution for the blasphemy, but then he felt his brother's chest rise as he took a deep breath.

Several others ran to the two of them and pulled Abu Alhaul from beneath Abdo. His brother's back was covered in blood.

Abu Alhaul looked up at the jungle canopy. A large hole where the first missile had exploded let a huge beam of sunlight enter the shadowy underworld of the jungle. He was unable to tell where the two missiles penetrated the canopy. The noise of his followers overrode the aircraft sounds and by the time he quieted them, there were no sounds of the American aircraft.

The moan of his brother caught his attention, but to Abu Alhaul it mattered little whether Abdo survived or not. Allah had failed to answer Abu Alhaul's faith. He had nothing to show that the missiles had hit the aircraft, while at least one more of his shrinking band of followers had died. The two who ran away were probably still running and he realized that the man who threw away the misfired canister was the one who stared so hard at him moments ago. Maybe Abdo was right in that his followers were beginning to realize that they might truly die in the service of Allah. Then why would they flee, for to die for Allah was to immediately enter into paradise? Who would not want such a thing?

He squatted beside Abdo and laid his hand on his brother's shoulder. He watched as the only soldier of the Islamic Front for Purification who had any medical knowledge cut the robe from Abdo. At that moment, Abu Alhaul knew they would leave Africa. He must regain Allah's favor and discover what his God wanted of him. This flight was truly his Hadj and Allah would want him to atone for

Abdo's disbelief. It is a hard thing to take one's kin to task, but what happens here on earth is but a test for the hereafter and here he had failed Allah.

"He will live, Ya Sheik," the medical person said. The robe lay opened, exposing the naked back of the huge man. From numerous small holes, blood flowed.

"He will die," Abu Alhaul said softly.

"No, he will live," the man responded, failing to realize that Abu Alhaul's words were not a question.

CHAPTER 5

THE AGED SA-7 GRAIL, A 1970'S WEAPON, BROKE THROUGH the leafy canopy like a baseball through a window. The second missile followed a few hundred feet farther west, before arching gracefully on path toward the descending EP-3E aircraft for a few seconds. Then, the rocket engine sputtered several times before igniting back to full power twice. The second full-power was too much for the old missile frame. One of the tail fins broke off, sending the missile into a right-handed spiral away from its target. The missile nose turned earthward, and miles from where it was launched, the runaway disappeared back through the canopy, sending leaves and limbs cascading into the air. The other missile—a small metallic spot in the sky with a huge corkscrew contrail marking its flight path—continued toward its target.

* * *

THE PILOT OF THE EP-3E RECONNAISSANCE AIRCRAFT, LIEU-
tenant Paul Gregory, had the yoke pressed forward slightly,
watching the altimeter as he fought the rough air at this
lower altitude. His primary gauge for altitude around this
jungle was his eyes. The altimeter told him the altitude of
the aircraft from the ground, but his eyes watched the approaching canopy of the jungle trees. During daylight, it
wasn't hard to do because you could see the trees. At night,
he'd be damned if he would be doing this. No one, except
maybe Crazy Harry, would bring the aircraft in this low. Of
course, flying with Crazy Harry made you appreciate the
safety consciousness of the other pilots, though it always
surprised him that everyone wanted to fly with Crazy
Harry. It still perplexed him how the man ever made commander, much less the commanding officer, and never had
had an aircraft mishap. Gregory had his check-ride with
Crazy Harry when he came into the squadron, and he was
barely able to control his legs when they landed, the man
so unnerved him. Not from the check-ride, but Crazy Harry
decided he'd try one more time to break the altitude record
for the EP-3E. The aircraft wasn't designed to go higher
than 28,300 feet, but Crazy Harry believed that was some
desk jockey's SWAG—Scientific Wild-Ass Guess. The
commanding officer's goal was to reach 40,000 feet. Problem was the engines tended to sputter and stop at about
35,000 feet, causing the aircraft to nose over, and the pilot
to have to do a hot start as the plane raced toward mother
earth. The EP-3E wasn't the lightest aircraft in the Navy's
inventory. Lieutenant Paul Gregory's mind turned away
from Crazy Harry. At least he had control of the aircraft.

He glanced at the altimeter. Two hundred feet. He'd
level off at one hundred feet. He looked at the approaching
jungle for a moment, glanced at Babs, his copilot, who
was scanning the sky, and then Gregory looked over his

shoulder at Pits Conar, who was strapped into the slightly higher seat than his and Babs's. The senior chief flight engineer was watching the altimeter, his hands on both knees. Gregory turned to the scene filling the cockpit windows. Radar had no return on the leaves that weaved an unbroken blanket across the jungle of Africa, and the last thing he wanted was to share his seat with a tree limb. The image of a surprised monkey screaming and running around the cockpit caused him to smile.

With his thumbs wrapped tightly on the yoke, he wiggled his fingers for a moment, the movement stretching the flight gloves so they fit snug on his fingers. His thoughts moved to another, more pleasant, arena. That of returning to Rota and the Spanish lass with whom he had developed such a fond affection. Deeply in "like" as his fellow aviators would say. "Great showpieces for your tour, but don't get too involved," his mentor from two squadrons ago had told him. "Once you're hooked with a Spanish girl, you're hooked for life, and you might as well buy yourself a house in Rota because she ain't gonna live in the States." *Rosario was—what was the right word? Worldly?* He shook his head. Thought, *No, makes her sound as if she has her own street corner. European? Well, hell yes, that'd be the right word—she is European! No, they'd figure it out.* An image of him marching a slew of Spanish children down the streets of Puerto Santa de Maria, wearing school uniforms, calling him papa, and not a word of English among the bunch was a convincing argument that being deployed might be in his best interests. Maybe Kilburn was right. He should just enjoy the fruits of a girl in every port—or a different girl for every tour of duty, then forget them and move on. He shook his head slightly. Life is really rough for a pilot.

"What the hell!" Senior Chief Pits Conar shouted, reaching forward, slapping Gregory on the shoulder, and pointing to the right. Two contrails tracked back to torn portions of the carpet canopy.

"Shit! Air-to-surface missiles!" the copilot shouted.

"Surface-to-air!" Gregory corrected, instinctively jerking the yoke to the right, toward the missiles.

"What in the hell are you doing?" Pits Conar shouted.

"Trying to get under them," he mumbled back. "Hit the alarm."

"Which one," the young copilot asked.

"Shit, sir!" Pits Conar shouted. "When you want motion, anything will do." He reached up and hit the ditching alarm. A tattoo of rapid beeps filled the aircraft.

The air was clear, almost movie-screen quality, Gregory thought as his eyes shifted from the controls to the two missiles. One of the missiles seemed in trouble. Bad luck for it, good luck for them. It tumbled end-over-end and disappeared from view, blocked by the left wing.

The flight engineer started a steady recitation of the altitude. At one hundred feet, Gregory shouted. "Hard left turn!" He jerked the yoke to the left. Out of the corner of his eye, he saw the missile change its direction slightly. Silently, he estimated a hundred yards—seconds—to impact, and in the time this thought registered, the missile closed the distance and exploded beneath the aircraft.

"Fire, number-four engine!" Pits Conar shouted.

The aircraft started vibrating, picking up in intensity. Gregory pulled back on the yoke, taking the aircraft up. The copilot leaned forward, pressed her face against the right window so she could see the burning engine.

"We got flames coming out the back," Babs said, referring to the exhaust of the number-four engine. "Shit!"

Pits reached up, flipped open the protective Plexiglass cover, and flipped the engine switch. "Engine number-four secured."

"Fire extinguisher?" Gregory asked.

"Number-one initiated. Passing one hundred feet."

Gregory glanced down. The airspeed seemed to be decreasing, but that was to be expected with the loss of an engine at this low of an altitude. The noise of the aircrew securing loose items and strapping themselves into their seats came through the half-opened curtains that separated the cockpit from the operational portion of the aircraft. He knew that in the very rear of the aircraft classified material was being dropped into the urinal where the water-soluble paper would turn to mush. If they had been over water, metal containers filled with classified material would be weighted down and dropped. Every operator would be securing their electronic gear to reduce chances of a fire. Shouts of alarm came from the rear as the aircrew became aware of the burning engine. Fire in flight meant a landing was imminent. The question was whether the pilot got to land it or the aircraft made the decision for you. For the first time, he thought of a bailout.

"Radio says situation report sent. It's in the air."

"Babs!" Gregory shouted to his copilot. "Get on the SAR frequency and broadcast our location."

"I thought our location was supposed to be kept secret," she replied.

"Ma'am, if our location was secret, we wouldn't have been shot!" Pits Conar shouted, his hands above his head, flipping toggle switches to turn off unnecessary electrics.

"Babs, get that mayday out. Senior Chief, the extinguisher?"

"Dropping past forty percent! Engine still burning."

"Look, we've got one more extinguisher in that wing. If we haven't put it out by the time we use that second extinguisher then we're going to—"

"Bail out." Pits Conar finished.

"Bail out." Babs added.

"Two extinguishers should be sufficient. Passing six hundred feet, Lieutenant," Pits offered.

"If the fire isn't out when we've reached twelve thousand feet, then we'll put the nose over. But, first we've got to get the aircraft to that altitude."

"If the second will last until we reach it," Conar said, reaching up and tapping the extinguisher button. "If it'll last that long," he added softly.

"If it doesn't work, then we'll dive it out. We'll push Ranger over on its nose and let the wind-blast extinguish it as we head down."

"Will that work?" Babs asked.

"Of course, it'll work," Gregory said, "At least, NATOPS says it should."

"And, it could," Conar added.

"And, if it don't?"

"Babs, how's the wing?" Gregory asked. *If doesn't work, then the last thing we'll see will be that fine carpet of green as the EP-3E rips through it.*

Gregory glanced at his copilot. Fear is a hard commodity to hide when it grips your insides—the heart rate increases, the bladder shouts at you to hit the bathroom, and the bowels join in hollering "me, too—me, too." "Eyeball sweat" was the term Kilburn used when he told tales of MiG-23s chasing his aircraft to sea level, trying to shoot him down, but flaming out at the lower levels while the old Willy Victor Super Constellation moseyed along, swinging from side to side to confuse the fire-control radars. Kilburn's experience couldn't have been much different from the one Gregory was going through now.

"First bottle gone. Activating second bottle."

"Babs, the engine."

She leaned to the right, putting her face against the

window again. "Still burning. The flames are larger, and we've got a black smoke trail reaching miles behind us."

"Senior Chief, what are you doing with the fuel?"

"Sir, I'm dumping it from the port wing. I've already started pumping the fuel from the starboard wing over to the port tanks. Fifteen minutes. Give me fifteen minutes, sir."

Good job, thought Gregory. Instinct is to dump the fuel from the burning side, but when you do that, the fire leaps onto the air trail of the fuel and can rush back up and ignite inside the tank. Fast way to lose a wing. NATOPS was the bible for aviation safety. Pilots and aircrew were expected to know the NATOPS for their aircraft cover-to-cover because in an emergency such as this, there wasn't time to be looking up what to do. NATOPS says dump fuel on the unaffected wing, the fuel tank that ran across the top of the EP-3E, and then pump fuel from the area of the fire to other wing. Problem was they had been airborne less than four hours, so they still had a little over six hours of fuel in the three main fuel tanks. As long as the extinguisher lasted, the fire wouldn't reach the starboard wing tank. Once the extinguisher was depleted, they had seconds to bailout before— He didn't want to think about it.

"Altitude?"

"Passing two thousand feet and climbing. Speed increasing, sir."

"Babs, tighten my straps," Gregory said. If he had to order bailout, he would be the last to go and, by then, he doubted the situation would give him time to check and make sure his parachute was ready. A set of flat pancakes would not go well with the hot Spanish tortilla waiting for him in Rota. For a fleeting moment, the image of her slapping them together and crying *"Que pasa?"* passed through his mind.

The low vibration caused by the loss of engine number-four started increasing as they gained altitude, shaking the aircraft. Gregory's coffee spilled over the rim of the cup, splattering the lukewarm coffee onto his flight-suit pants leg.

The copilot leaned back into her seat. "Tight enough?"

"Thanks," Gregory muttered, his knuckles white from gripping the yoke. "Senior Chief, increase number-three, reduce power on number-one." Maybe it would offset the pull to the left.

"Extinguisher low, sir. I've got a temperature increasing in starboard fuel tank!" Pits Conar shouted. He reached up and slapped the red extinguisher knob.

Gregory glanced at Babs and then the flight engineer before facing forward.

"Lieutenant, I said the temperature is increasing in starboard fuel tank. It's going to hit critical in the next minute or two unless—"

"Senior Chief, I know!" Gregory snapped. Thought, *What in the hell does he want me to do? Not a damn thing I can—*

"Passing six thousand feet, sir."

"Paul!"

Gregory looked at his copilot. His eyes locked with Babs's.

"Paul, NATOPS says we bail out when the temperature—"

He reached up and ran the back of his hand across his forehead.

"Put on your helmets! We should have had—"

"Lieutenant, we're going to have to bail out, sir."

Gregory looked forward, glancing at the altimeter. Passing six thousand, four hundred. Still climbing. The temperature will start backing down, he told himself. Just three thousand, four hundred more feet and then I'll dive. That'll cool the engine.

"Extinguisher?" Gregory asked. Out of the corner of his eye, he saw the copilot face forward. A slight sigh of relief escaped. He didn't want to answer her and since she turned away he told himself he didn't have to answer.

"We have less than sixty to seventy seconds left before it empties. Lieutenant, when that happens the temperature is going to hit *kaboom* stage and the last thing we're going to see is that tunnel with a light at the far end—"

"Altitude, Senior Chief?" *If it's not her, then it's him.*

"Sir! We're passing seven thousand feet. Extinguisher has fifty seconds remaining."

"Paul, we're going to have to bail out!" Babs shouted. "Jesus Christ, Paul! Give the goddamn order."

Gregory glanced at the altimeter. He looked forward at the slight cloudbank overhead. Thought, *Clouds mark the ten-to-twelve thousand-feet-altitude area. If I can just make that.*

"Lieutenant, she's right. The fire is still burning. First extinguisher is gone. Second nearly kaput. When it goes, we won't have any way of putting out the fire. The time between empty canister and raining pieces of airplane will be seconds, not minutes."

Gregory took a deep breath and released it. *Only a few more minutes and I could have done it. I could have saved the aircraft and brought everyone home safely.* He reached up and hit the bailout alarm.

Senior Chief Conar snatched up his checklist and started going down each item. The copilot shouted "check" at items under her cognizance and Gregory responded in kind when his turn. Behind the curtain that separated the cockpit from the operational section of the aircraft, crewmembers started waddling their way aft, maneuvering the bulky parachutes strapped to their backs and buttocks, toward the hatch where only four hours earlier they had boarded the aircraft.

"GET YOUR ASSES UP OUT OF THOSE SEATS AND LINE UP!" shouted Razi. Involuntarily, he shivered. He glanced toward the front of the aircraft and saw Lieutenant Commander Peeters looking in his direction. Razi intentionally straightened, trying to look taller than five-foot-seven allowed. An aircrewman behind Razi, stumbling as he tightened his parachute straps, bumped into Razi, who turned and pushed the man upright. "Be careful. Take your time," he said.

Razi took a deep breath. Must stay calm. He ran his hands over his straps, checking again to make sure they were tight. How could this happen? Naval Intelligence said no one in this area had SAMs. He glanced at the two Naval Research Lab sailors, the one who had vomited earlier had tears running down his cheeks. The sailor's visor was down on his helmet and the moisture was fogging the shatterproof plastic. *Damn, I know how you feel, shipmate. Good thing I hit the head before that missile hit us or I'd have piss running down my leg.*

"Chief! My parachute!"

Razi turned around, keeping one hand tightly gripping the metal railing that ran the entire length of the aircraft. It was MacGammon. "Damn it, MacGammon. I told you to take these bailout drills seriously."

"Chief, I'm taking it serious now. I know what the hell I'm doing. I just want you to check these damn straps!"

Razi's expert eyes quickly ran down the straps. "Damn it, MacGammon. You've got the damn thing on upside down. How in the—" He said as he let go of the railing, grabbed the latch across MacGammon's chest and snapped it open. The parachute fell onto the deck. Razi jerked it up, flipped it around, and holding the fifty-pound weight with one hand, he shoved MacGammon around, so the sailor's back was to him. The aircraft shook, dropped a couple of feet, throwing MacGammon forward into two sailors who were busily checking each other's rigging.

Razi reached forward, grabbed MacGammon by the flight suit. "Straighten up, shitbird!" Then Razi slammed the parachute against MacGammon's back. "Arms! Arms! Put your goddamn New Jersey arms through the straps."

MacGammon, speechless for a change, shoved his arms through the straps. Razi noticed the shaking, but he couldn't decide whether it was him or MacGammon. Christ's sake, he was as scared as they were, but he was a chief petty officer, and chiefs didn't show how scared they were regardless of how bad the situation was, and the situation must be bad if the bailout alarm was sounded. He should have stayed in Rota, Spain! What the hell was he thinking to volunteer for this deployment? If he didn't make "senior chief" last time off the selection board, why in the hell did he think this would make them select him?

The bailout alarm continued beeping. When the beeping changed to a steady tone, it would be his job to open the hatch and start the aircrew out of the aircraft—shoving them if he had to. "Goddamn it, MacGammon, you got those straps buckled yet?"

"Nearly there, Chief."

His knees felt wobbly, which Razi quickly attributed to the shaking of the aircraft as it climbed at the more-than-usual angle.

"Pull those straps tight and snap them together!" he shouted into MacGammon's ear. Razi pushed the parachute upward on the man's back. Then he held the bottom of the parachute, keeping the upward tension on it so the tightly packed silk rode high on the sailor's back, but not so high the top edge protruded above the shoulders. Sure, this was great on paper, in the schoolhouse, and even practicing while the aircraft was parked on the tarmac, but he never expected to have to bail out of an aircraft. His flight goal had never changed in over 5,000 hours of flight time, and that was to walk on and walk off aircrafts an equal number of times. This was sure as hell going to throw that goal into the odd-number column.

"Got it, Chief. I got it."

Razi continued holding it for a moment, his thoughts on bailing out.

"Chief, I said I got it! Let go!"

Razi released his hold. MacGammon turned around facing Razi. Razi reached forward, grabbed where the two straps running down each side were locked together in the center and jerked them. MacGammon fell forward, and then was pushed backward.

"Damn it, Chief, don't kill me."

"Don't tempt me. If you'd paid attention during the drills. . ."

"I know, Chief, I know. I do pay attention during the drills."

Razi turned away, his ears listening to the bailout alarm while his hands, again, traced his parachute straps, making sure they were in place, still tight, and ready for that sudden jerk when the parachute was released. Damn, he had never bailed out of an aircraft. He heard MacGammon behind him asking Rockdale if he was scared. *Christ yes, you should be scared, MacGammon. If you'd paid attention like a third class petty officer should, you'd have known something like this could happen anytime. But no, you were just one more smart-ass who has to show everyone how to act up when they're practicing putting on a parachute. You think putting on a parachute is easy? Sure, it's easy—when the aircraft is flying nice and level and everyone is laughing and joking. But, it's a whole new world when bullets are flying, engines are burning, and you got nothing between you and the ground but a thin sheet of fabric wavering above your head, capturing air, and hopefully slowing you enough so when you land, you don't break anything. When we land, if you haven't broken anything, I may remedy that situation.*

"TWENTY SECONDS, LIEUTENANT."

"It's still burning," Babs added. "Flames still coming out the rear of the engine."

Gregory pushed forward on the yoke, forcing the aircraft level. "Altitude?"

"Passing seven thousand feet, sir. Should be high enough."

"Okay. Equalize air pressure so they can open the hatch."

"Two thousand more feet would be nice," Babs added.

Senior Chief Pits Conar reached up and pushed another button. Their ears popped as the air pressure inside the aircraft dropped, equalizing with the outside air pressure. Until the air pressure was released, the crew couldn't bail out because they wouldn't be able to open the rear hatch. The air pressure wasn't released until the last minute so no one would decide to leave the plane early.

"We don't have time for another two thousand feet," Gregory replied.

"You're right. Just more air space under us—"

"Air pressure equalized."

"Okay, Senior Chief. Let's do it," Gregory said. "Hit it, and then you two head aft."

Pits Conar reached up and pushed the bailout alarm the

rest of the way. The alarm changed to a steady tone. "Think I'll stay with you, sir. Never can tell about these things."

Gregory opened his mouth to tell him to buzz off, get the hell out of his cockpit, and go bail out, but he didn't. NATOPS might say this was the way it should be, but the flight engineer and copilot were only going to reach the bailout door a few seconds ahead of him. What did it matter if they went now or went together.

Gregory looked down and quickly rechecked the settings of the autopilot. Then he flipped it on. "Autopilot engaged."

"Guess it's that time."

Babs leaned toward the window and looked back at the burning engine. "Oh, God!" she shouted, reaching back with her left hand and waving frantically at Pits Conar. "Turn it off! Turn it off!"

RAZI REACHED FORWARD, TWISTED THE HANDLE, AND heard the suction break as the hatch opened a crack. Wind pushed the hatch into the fuselage. The hatch jerked out of Razi's hands, crashing back, slamming into a catch, and like a metal trap, the catch held it. There was nothing between Razi and the sky except a couple of steps. Razi reached up and pulled the clear visor down on his helmet, protecting his eyes from the wind shooting into the cabin.

Rockdale was first in line. Razi would have commented on this fact if the situation hadn't been so serious. Rockdale was one of his stellar performers; one who Razi believed eventually would be picked up for commission. For a third class petty officer, Rockdale performed at a much higher paygrade, and the sailor listened to him. Razi even saw him jotting down notes once after Razi had given the sailor a lecture on leadership. Their eyes locked for a moment before Rockdale stepped into the doorway, hands on each side of the hatch, and without prompting, jumped. MacGammon was next, hesitated for moment, and as Razi reached forward to shove him, MacGammon jumped, surprising Razi. *Probably surprised MacGammon also,* he thought.

Tommy "Stetson" Carson stepped up. "Senior Chief—" he started.

"No!" Razi shouted. "Don't think, just do it!" No time for talking. He reached forward, turned Carson toward the door, and before the blond-headed young man from Texas could say anything, Razi pushed him through the opening.

A sharp electronic piercing sound, like fingernails down a chalkboard, rode over the relative quiet as others moved toward the opened hatch. "Don't bail out! I say again, don't bail out!" blared the announcement over the internal communications system. The bailout alarm stopped, replaced by the ditching alarm.

"What the hell is going on?" Razi shouted.

Someone nearer the cockpit shouted down the crew line that the engine fire was out.

Razi looked at the open door. Petty Officer First Class Lacey was the next one in line to jump. Razi turned toward the door and positioned himself. Lacey reached forward and grabbed him by the shoulder. Razi glanced toward the front and saw Lieutenant Commander Peeters frantically waving at him.

"Chief—"

"Three of my sailors are down there!" he shouted above the wind, turned, and before Lacey could reply, Razi was gone.

*   *   *

"WELCOME ABOARD, GENERAL—OR SHOULD I CALL YOU Mr. President?" Dick Holman asked as he shook hands with retired U.S. Army Lieutenant General Daniel Thomaston.

"Dan or Daniel would be fine, Dick."

The two years had not been kind to the former commander of the famed 82nd Airborne. The gray hairline Dick remembered encircling Thomaston's head was gone. Two straggly sideburns stopped level with the middle of the ears, military style, and the peppered mustache from two years ago was now permanently gray. Harsh wrinkles covered the forehead, painted permanently across the brow from two years of hard work to restore and reconstitute the Liberian Republic. The dark age spot on Thomaston's right cheek had either been so faint Dick didn't recall it being there, or it was new. He would offer the services of his medical team before Thomaston departed. For all of the facial changes, the man was still razor thin, chest tight, with arms that filled the sleek cotton short sleeves of the white shirt.

"You have done well, Daniel," Dick said, dropping the hand.

Thomaston chuckled. "I don't think many thought we'd still be here this long, Admiral. I want to once again thank you and your Amphibious Group Two forces that helped us in our time of need."

Dick motioned to a chair near the small table that occupied a quarter of his in-port stateroom. Background sounds of boatswain mates shouting politically incorrect orders to each other as they finished tying up the USS *Boxer* to the Monrovia pier brought smiles to both flag officers as they sat down.

"Looks as if you've lost some weight since we last met," Thomaston said.

Weight wasn't something military people discussed with each other. Weight was the one element everyone had control of, but found challenging as they rose in rank and age. Dick blushed slightly. "Could be, but I'm just happy to have maintained the same pants size," he replied, trying to make light of the comment.

"Maybe I should have waited until tomorrow to pay a courtesy visit?" Thomaston asked, seemingly unaware how his compliment uneased Dick Holman.

"Dan, you're welcome anytime," Dick said, happy to change the subject. It wasn't as if he had a choice of what type of body he inherited in life. Dick glanced down at his waistline, sucking in his gut slightly when he realized his belt buckle was hidden by a slight waistline bulge.

"Thanks, appreciate that." Thomaston reached up and straightened the collar on his shirt.

"Besides, what can an admiral do when the sailors are securing the ship? Only get in the way, and if I should, in a moment of pique, suggest something, they'd consider it an order, and later when they unscrewed up whatever I caused, they'd realize I was just another aviator trying to play sailor."

A mess specialist opened the side door to Holman's inport cabin and stepped inside, carrying a tray with a silver-plated coffee urn, a couple of cups, and the usual condiments necessary for a fine Navy coffee. From under a cloth napkin, the aroma of fresh pastries wafted amidst the smell of freshly percolated coffee. Dick jerked his eyes away from the pastries, promising himself he was going to the gym later in the day.

The men waited while the petty officer arrayed the coffee. When the mess specialist departed, they both started to speak, interrupting each other.

"Guess you're wondering—"

"Dan, I would think you—"

They laughed. Dick poured the coffee as he spoke. "I'm sure you have more on your mind than thanking us for our help. After all, you are an American and that's what we do best: rescue our fellow citizens. Plus, you've been the acting president of Liberia for two years."

Thomaston nodded. "True, I am an American and will always be an American first. The opportunity President Jefferson gave us African-Americans before the Jihadists killed him is something that nearly reaches the same level as being an American. I hold a Liberian passport and like the Jewish community in America, we African-Americans are allowed dual citizenship with Liberia."

Dick poured some coffee creamer into his cup and stirred. "I'm aware and have to admit it that has turned this nineteenth-century American colony into a role model for the rest of Africa."

"I appreciate your sentiment, but, unfortunately, I can't agree with you. Not yet, it hasn't. Someday, I hope it will. I've identified some simple goals for my administration so that whoever is elected next summer will inherit a good infrastructure upon which he or she can build." Thomaston held up his right hand. "One, I want to make sure our electric-generating capability is stable" One finger went up. "Two, I want pure water and a secure sanitation system for every Liberian." A second finger rose. "Third and fourth, I hope to make medical services available to each Liberian and give them free education, as we do in America." He lowered his hand. "Not too complicated, just concentrate on the fundamentals and let whatever administration comes in to build on them."

"Sounds simple, but I'm sure you've had more than your share of challenges in meeting even one of those goals."

Thomaston shrugged as he lowered his cup. "What I found surprising was the electric-generating part has been the simplest. Just the opposite with education and medical services. I have rediscovered what I already knew from my active military life. When you're dealing with people, nothing is simple. One man's lie is another man's truth." He lifted the cup and sipped. "And everytime I have to defend education reforms with the people, there is always some faction or other with differing opinions on how that free education is going to be provided. Whether we are going to concentrate solely on the hard sciences, language, and mathematics or incorporate the various social beliefs of each tribe and religion."

"I hadn't thought of it that way." In reaching for his coffee cup, Dick noticed the general's belt buckle was easily visible. He reached over and shoved the fresh pastries toward Thomaston. *There! Eat this calorie-loaded shit and put on some weight.*

"Of course, every time I have to deal with the hundreds of social issues confronting us, I can't help but glance at the calendar on the wall in my office and mentally count the days until I turn over the reins of government to a freely elected president." He pushed his chair away from the table and crossed his legs.

"Rumor has it the people will elect you." Dick lifted the plate and held it toward Thomaston.

Thomaston shook his head—his eyebrows lifting as he reached forward and took one of the frosted raisin breads. "I haven't had anything like this in a long while," he said, biting into it.

"What you don't eat, I'll send with you," Dick said, hoping the mess specialist had made several hundred.

Thomaston took another bite and the pastry disappeared. "Good," he mumbled through a full mouth. He slapped his hands together a couple of times, wiping the sugar off them. Then, he reached down and straightened the crease on his gray slacks.

"What if the people decide they want you to continue on as president?"

"They can't elect you, if you refuse to run."

Dick nodded.

"I'm aware of the mythical position some people have put me in, but the bottom line is I seized the power of government when this fanatic Abu Alhaul and his minions ripped through Monrovia and most of Liberia, killing and destroying the government of President Jefferson. If it hadn't been for own little 'Alamo' in Kingsville and the strength your forces brought into the fray, Liberia today could have become one more sump for the Jihadists to spread death and destruction. A failed state decaying further into chaos—a ripe breeding ground for terrorists."

"I don't think you have to worry about that anymore," Dick offered.

"He's still out there, but I think he is on the run." Thomaston uncrossed his legs and leaned forward. "I'm here for two reasons." He held up one finger. "First, we've about cleared out the Jihadist strongholds in Liberia and believe we have secured our borders sufficiently to keep a resurgence from occurring." He lowered his hand. "We have also won the hearts and minds of the people—something we army types have talked about in every conflict since the Korean War and always found hard to do. Killing is so much easier than talking, and when you're killing the natives, it's hard to win their hearts while their minds are scared shitless. But I like to think we did it here. We won their hearts and minds by improving the quality of life for the citizens— modern roadways, plumbing, free schooling, and a growing health care. All of that supported by a growing electrical base. Another initiative I would like to set on its way before I leave is a better telecommunications structure."

"Sounds like a success story to me."

Thomaston bit his lower lip, pensive for moment. "In a way, it is. What most Americans fail to understand is that we Americo-Liberians make up less than three percent of Liberia's population. Another five percent trace their heritage back to the United States and the Caribbean Islands. The United States and repatriated Africans from the Caribbean Islands made up the bulk of the former slaves transported here in the early eighteen hundreds."

"Eight percent."

"Right. Eight percent of the people of Liberia are our true base. The remaining ninety-two percent are native Liberians, native to the tribes who inhabited this country long before America decided to repatriate slaves to Africa." He leaned forward again. "Did you know the only reason we started this repatriation back in the early eighteen hundreds was because we were following the British in their experiment with Sierra Leone?" He leaned back in the chair.

Dick held the pastry plate toward Thomaston, who took another one. *Good, good.*

"The first trip from America back to Africa offloaded the repatriated slaves in Sierra Leone." He bit into the pastry, much to Dick's enjoyment.

Thomaston reached out and topped off his coffee.

"I'm afraid I don't see what the problem is, Daniel," Dick said. "In setting up a democracy, various factions compete for power, though in a perfect world, it should be programs and positions that carry the day. That's the way America is and was built."

"This isn't America," Thomaston replied as a crumb tumbled down his chin.

Dick detected a slight ire in the response and nodded. "I guess you're going to tell me America doesn't really understand the challenges you are facing here in Liberia. I guess I should add that most Americans aren't engaged on a daily basis with much of what goes on outside their local areas. I think we both know that. So, what is your concern about the different origins of Liberians?"

"My concern is that there has always been an underlying prejudice by the native Liberians against us Americo-Liberians, whom they view as interlopers."

"Kind of like a carpetbagger."

Thomaston nodded. "Good analogy. There will be those who will abuse these new freedoms to throw a wedge between our two groups, instead of working to make us one people."

"I would submit, General, that with the terrorist Abu Al-haul and the African National Army running around, the fact of a common threat will promote unity, even though I agree with you that Liberia has passed the point where it has to be too concerned about a resurgence. Just have to have a sense of alert awareness. You agree?"

"I do," Thomaston replied, wiping his chin with a napkin from the table. "And I am confident that the majority of native Liberians will stand with us Americo-Liberians against a resurrection of the Jihadist movement." He leaned back, resting his elbows on the chair arms, with his hands raised, fingers laced together. "This is the second reason I came here. The Jihadist movement is dead in Liberia. Sure, there are a few simmering sections, but local authorities have them well in hand. What we don't have in hand is the cry for African nationalism being heralded by this so-called General Ojo and his African National Army."

"They're staying out of Liberia, I'm told," Dick replied.

"And they haven't done anything that would cause us to get too excited, though we are watching them."

"For the time being, they are staying out of Liberia. I had an audience with the French ambassador a couple of months ago, who told me of an incident at one of their air bases in the Ivory Coast where the African National Army attacked and destroyed one of their aircraft."

Dick nearly choked on the coffee he had just swallowed. The man was referring to the so-called Joint Task Force France that he authorized and his Seabees in Harper, Liberia, executed. He glanced up, to meet the hard stare of Thomaston.

"Admiral, I think you've just answered a curious itch of mine."

"Itch? Don't know what you mean, General."

"Oh, don't get too proper with me." Before Dick could reply, Thomaston continued. "My intelligence service, which is basically human intelligence—HUMINT, you and I would call it—have discovered that a rogue American element may have been involved. You wouldn't know anything about that, would you?"

Dick set his cup on the table in front of them. "I know nothing about the Africans attacking the French, but I hope they were successful."

Thomaston laughed. "I really have you against the ropes, don't I, Admiral." He unlaced his hands and lifted his cup again.

"What—"

Thomaston shrugged. "You don't have to tell me, Dick. I'm not going to press you for the truth. It's probably something I don't want to know, but eventually my contacts at the American Embassy will fill in the blanks for me. Besides, my issue isn't with your incursion into the Ivory Coast, though the continuing bickering between our country—America—and France impacts the fragile, but growing economy of Liberia. We're like two sibling brothers who can't decide whose turn it is to throw the ball."

"Dan, you know I have no control over the politics of our nation nor those of other nations," Holman said. "Like you when you were on active duty, I fight our nation's wars to win. I don't determine what battlefield on which I will fight nor do I decide who my adversary is; I execute the orders of the President of the United States."

Thomaston drained his coffee. He laughed as he put the cup down. Dick offered him another pastry. "Admiral, I think you're trying to get me fat."

"If I had your metabolism, Dan, I'd eat everyone of them." He put the plate back on the table. "When you leave, I insist you take them with you."

"I couldn't have said it better about our country. When I was commander of the 82nd Airborne, I marched to the drums of the politicians. But I'm not now. I'm retired, my country allows me to draw the pension of a three-star Army general, and also allows me to hold dual citizenship. Liberia is my other nation, a nation I now lead. I probably have more control over America's politics as president of Liberia than you do as a one-star admiral." Thomaston leaned forward. "I sound like one of those checker players on the steps of an old Georgian courthouse, talking about 'way back when I was' stories. I have an important reason for meeting you pierside, Dick, rather than wait for your formal visit tomorrow."

Dick's eyebrows bunched, questioningly.

Thomaston leaned back. "Let me give you some background first. I told you my challenges in Liberia between us Americo-Liberians and those who consider themselves native Liberians. Well, my intelligence service is telling

me that a large portion of the native Liberians are support-
ers of this African National Army. You know the old adage,
Dick: one man's terrorist is another man's freedom fighter.
So far, the ANA have remained out of Liberia. For you to
keep within classified channels, I have a spy that is very
close to this General Ojo. For the time being, the ANA is
on our side because this Ojo is after the same person we
are—Abu Alhaul. This Ojo has a unique way of dealing
with the Jihadists that we, as Americans, could never do."

Dick waited as Thomaston paused. *If a method of dealing with the growing threat of terrorism was out there and
it was effective, then why wouldn't we use it?* he asked
himself.

"I'll satisfy your curiosity on their method shortly,"
Thomaston said in answer to the unasked question. "Right
now, the ANA wants to rid Africa of the Jihadists just as
we do. They then intend to turn their attention to the other
nongovernment agencies in West Africa who are not
African in nature. I'm sure you're aware of the Baptist and
Mormon missionaries, along with several priests and nuns,
whom they've physically escorted out of what they believe
to be their areas. This is only the start." Thomaston uncrossed his legs. "Eventually they will engage the Western
powers—mainly the U.S. and France—but my sources tell
me they will use the United Nations and the world press as
their vehicles for driving you—and those of us with dual
citizenship—out of Africa. The primary reason the ANA
has steered clear of Liberia is you—the growing presence
of American forces. That hasn't stopped them from recruit-
ing Liberians into their forces. It has kept them from conducting operations within this country, but it hasn't kept
their fiery rhetoric out of Liberia."

"What can we do?"

Thomaston shrugged. "You can share your information

with our intelligence services, for one. The other is you can track them better and quicker than we can with your satellites and aircraft."

"We have a VQ-2 EP-3E Aries II bird flying down here now."

"That's true. You also have another arriving tomorrow to relieve this one. We are committed to giving you all the bases you want. Now, I can't say that whoever the people elect to take my place will feel the same."

"So, how does this General Ojo defeat the Jihadists? Win the hearts and minds of the people like you have?"

Before Thomaston could reply, several sharp raps on the door leading into the compartment from the passageway interrupted them. Holman opened his mouth to say, "enter," but it opened abruptly and Captain Leo Upmann stepped inside.

"Admiral, General," he said, nodding slightly at both, before looking directly at Holman. "Admiral, our aircraft has taken a missile hit."

"Which aircraft?" They had two helicopters airborne enroute to the Seabees at Harper and several helicopters off-loading the Marines at their encampment north of Monrovia. Every one of those CH-53 Super Stallions had been launched before they entered the port of Monrovia.

"The EP-3E."

Holman and Thomaston stood.

"And their status?" Dick asked as he headed toward the door. He looked back at Thomaston. "General, my apologies, but duty calls."

"Admiral, if my government can be of any assistance—"

"Thanks, we may need it." Dick said as he stepped through the doorway and hurried quickly down the passageway, heading toward Combat Information Center.

Behind him, Thomaston motioned his aide into the

room. He picked up the remaining two pastries, wrapped them in a napkin, and quickly left. "What's happening?" he asked the younger man.

"Seems a SAM has hit the American reconnaissance aircraft while it was on track north of our border."

Thomaston nodded as they stepped into the passageway and the two of them started toward the exit. "We need to see what we can find out as to whether there are any survivors or not."

"From what I gathered, the aircraft hasn't crashed."

"Yet. Aircraft with missiles through them tend to crash. Where did the missile hit?"

"We don't know yet, Admiral. All we have is their mayday, and last update is they're heading back to homeplate."

"That's Monrovia. Let's hope they make it back. Get me my vehicle. We're going to the airport."

CHAPTER 6

THE WIND WHIPPED HIS FLIGHT SUIT AGAINST HIS BODY,
the cloth beating painlessly against the back of his legs.
Razi spread his arms and legs as far as he could, emulating
the style he had seen on television, but never, ever thought
he'd do it himself. By God, who in their right mind would
jump out of a perfectly good aircraft? Granted, the aircraft
had been on fire. They probably canceled the bailout because the engine fire had been controlled.

A part of his terrified mind was pleased to see the maneuver steady him in midair. Where were the cheering
crowds when he needed them? He was face down hurling
toward the green carpet of African jungle beneath him, a
carpet that stretched as far as he could see. The bright
African sun lit up the green canopy below him. The colors
seemed so vivid to him. Maybe that was because he was
heading—what was the max speed of a falling body? One
hundred and eighteen miles per hour was max speed. No

way he could calculate when he'd hit the trees. Shit! His wife balanced the checkbook. His parachute! Where in the hell was it. The panic hit and vanished in a second. His parachute was on his back, strapped tight, waiting for him to pull the ripcord.

Razi raised his head. To the right and below about a mile away floated the three parachutes of his aircrewmen, descending toward the jungle. They were together. That's one thing in his favor. He didn't relish the idea of being alone in the jungle.

He should have connected the static line to the bailout rail before he jumped like those lucky sons of bitches! Razi pulled his right hand toward the ripcord located top-right on his chest. His body tilted to the right, he quickly pulled the left hand inward to correct the balance. Thought, *This is way too easy.* Razi's right hand gripped the handle just as his body arched forward and sent Razi into a headlong rush toward the earth. Damn! The screaming that was disturbing him was coming from his own throat. He jerked the handle—thirty-five pounds of pressure opened it. The handle end appeared in his hand, startling him for moment before he recalled that was supposed to happen. He dropped the handle, the wire on the end whipping his legs as it fell earthward.

Behind Razi, the parachute opened. The pilot parachute rippled out first, a small caricature of the main parachute. The small pilot anchored itself in the airstream, pulling the main canopy from the parachute assembly. The 28-foot, flat canopy immediately followed the pilot parachute, unfolding rapidly, a snapping blossom as the canopy grabbed and trapped the wind beneath it, jerking the chief petty officer upward at sixty miles an hour and away from his headlong fall. His screams picked up in intensity as he shot upward, and he made several promises to God such as giving up beer, quit wasting prayers on the Washington Redskins, and stop having eyeball-orgies when out with his wife. The parachute fully unfolded. Razi reached the crest of the upward jerk and fell downward; the suspension lines running from his harness to the main canopy brought him up short, and Razi came to a swinging stop beneath the parachute. His breath came in rapid, short gasps while his lips continued to mouth "Thank you, God; thank you, God; thank you, God." Everything was dark. Somewhere in the past few seconds Razi had clamped his eyes so tightly shut, it took another several seconds for him to will them open. When he did, the trees seemed closer.

He forced his attention away from his own fall, looking in the direction where he thought the other parachutes should be. Nothing. He turned his head side to side and Rockdale, MacGammon, and Carson were nowhere to be seen. Where in the hell where they? They couldn't have landed yet. He had a brief feeling of anxiety, wondering how in the hell he was going to land near them if he didn't know where they were?

Razi reached up, pulled the right suspension line, and congratulated himself when he turned. His breathing was slowing as the shock of bailing out was replaced by self-congratulations on how well he was doing. Man, oh man, he was great with this. Wait until happy hours at the Rota chief's club. *Line those drinks up, me laddies, and let me tell you about when I bailed out of Ranger 20.*

A slight movement caught his attention. There they were. During his own fall and riding the opening of his parachute, Razi had came out of the parachute opening with his back to the three other parachutes. His three air-crewmen, as he thought of them, seemed to be the same distance as when he first spotted them. He looked up at the parachute canopy. Now, how did he go about playing with the suspension lines to maneuver his parachute toward them? One thing he did recall from bailout training, which consisted of twenty hours of classroom and jumping off a ten-foot-high ramp to ride a cable down to the ground, was that you could, by manipulating the suspension lines, cause the air inside the parachute to tilt out one side or the other, thereby changing your direction and, with luck, push yourself into a safe landing zone. This was very handy when you violated certain well-known, but unwritten rules such as never bailing out over a place you've just bombed or strafed. In this instance, that specific rule applied here. Someone down below had fired that missile.

Another thing he recalled about bailout, as his stomach muscles started to relax from the mind-numbing, fear-filled worry of whether the parachute was going to open or not, was the warning echoing in his mind that if he pulled the suspension line too hard, it could cause the wind to spill out too fast, collapsing the parachute, and sending him hurling toward the ground and slamming into it like a dull dart off of a brick wall. Only bodies don't bounce when they hit the earth. If they do, Razi was sure it'd be a sloshing sound slapping the earth the second time. His stomach tightened again. He brought his hand down from the suspension cord without pulling it. A second later he gripped it again. The harness may hold you to the line that held you to the parachute, but something in the human psyche made him want to hold on. He glanced down at the leg straps: Those crisscrossed three-inch-wide canvas straps capable of turning him into an alto.

He lifted his head, watching the three parachutes descending together. *Why in the hell did I do this?* he thought. *I know what I said sounded good, and, it's going to sound even better when I have a cigar in one hand and a beer in the other, but I'm not a mutter-frigging SEAL or trained killer. I'm a cryptologic technician. I operate electronic and reconnaissance equipment. I make love, not war. And, I don't bail out of aircraft because— Shit! I did this to myself! Who's leadership book was I believing when I bailed out? My own? Remind me to kick the shit out of myself when—when, hell—if I get back.*

He reached up and without thinking about the dangers, jerked the suspension line downward. His stomach tensed. Damn, his waistline was getting a hell of a workout. At the same instant he jerked the suspension cord, Razi glanced at the three aircrewmen and thought they seemed farther away. *They need me more than I need them right now,* he told himself, *and unless I get to them before—*

Wind spilled out of the parachute spinning Razi farther to the right. Now the three aircrewmen were to his left, but the bearing drift was in the same direction.

—before! Damn, we're going to have more problems when we finish this airborne ride. The NRL bunch said they detected two groups of people down there. The smaller group was probably the terrorist bunch, about twenty, I recall them saying. The other group numbered in the hundreds. That'd be those African National Army wanna-be soldiers. Christ! I hate soldiers.

Razi reached up and pulled the left suspension line. He swung slowly to the left. He squinted his eyes. Was the distance increasing between them? The altitude disparity seemed the same. He shut one eye and tried to get a drift-bearing on the three. If he watched them, in a measuring sort of way, and they weren't moving left or right or up and down as he watched, then they would be on a constant bearing. Constant bearing meant you had a damn good chance of running into each other.

They were drifting slowly to the right. Not much, but enough to add distance between him and them when they landed. He reached up and pulled the right suspension line again. He was getting good at this, he told himself, as he swung to the right. The next sighting showed them drifting to the left. For the next minute or two, Razi alternated pulls on the suspension lines, eventually realizing that each new course turn was causing the bearing-drift to lessen. It wasn't that Razi believed himself out of control of the situation. It wasn't in his character to believe there was anything he wasn't capable of doing. Razi had preached for years the rhetoric of the omnipotence of a chief petty officer; for so long that he believed whatever he did was preordained as correct. When he did something and it turned out right, Razi never got over-excited because as a chief petty officer it was bound to be right. The important thing was to make sure his bosses knew it. He should have been a senior chief petty officer three years ago, but the Navy . . .

When something unexpected panned out good, but differently than what he planned or expected, he reconciled himself with the knowledge it turned out right for no other reason than he was a chief petty officer.

He tugged on the left suspension line. His arms were growing tired from the exertion. He tried a couple of more attempts to fine-tune his direction of fall. Suddenly, after several more back-and-forth attempts to change his direction, he discovered himself lined up with the descent of the others. Razi was neither surprised nor elated. It was just one more proof that there was nothing a chief petty officer couldn't do when he or she decided to do something. Those three young men should fall to the ground, bow down, and thank me when I reach them. Where would sailors and junior officers be, if it wasn't for us chief petty officers? They'd still be changing their diapers.

Razi gripped the two suspension lines running from his parachute harness to the 28-foot nylon canopy above him.

He glanced up, a brief chill raced through him. Such a flimsy piece of cloth between him and death.

He looked toward the three other parachutes and as he watched, they winked out one after the other as the aircrewmen crashed through the jungle green and disappeared from sight.

"SHE'S RIGHT, SIR," PITS CONAR SAID. THE FLIGHT ENGINEER reached up and tapped the extinguisher readout. "The second extinguisher is gone, Lieutenant—kaput! If that engine flames up again, we can't even spit on it."

"Put her in a left-hand turn and let's take Ranger 20 up—quick."

The curtain snapped apart and Lieutenant Commander Chuck Peeters stuck his head inside the cockpit. "We've got crewmen outside!"

"Outside? How can anyone be outside?"

"They bailed out before you turned off the fucking alarm."

Gregory leaned forward and glanced at the altimeter. "We've no choice, Chuck. There's not a damn thing a four-engine aircraft can do to help those who bailed out. Right now, we've a bigger problem than them. They'll be rescued. We need altitude and that's where I'm taking this bucket of bolts." He nodded to the right. "If that engine reflames, the only chance we'll have to put it out is a steep dive. I want as much altitude as possible between us and the ground if we have to do this."

Peeters nodded. "The radioman has already sent Sitrep follow-ups to Sixth Fleet, Amphibious Group Two, and our detachment at Monrovia."

"Rota?"

"VQ-2 was one of the action addees. They should have it at the same time as the others."

"This isn't going to make Crazy Harry happy," Babs said.

"Don't call the skipper 'Crazy Harry,' " Peeters admonished, his voice shaking. "Damn it, Lieutenant Gregory, we've got people below us."

"There's nothing I can do, but what you've done already, Lieutenant Commander Peeters, and that's send a position report and an updated Sitrep. You've done both. My job is to get this aircraft back to Monrovia with the remaining souls onboard." The aircraft shook violently as Gregory and Babs pulled together on the yoke, bringing the nose of the EP-3E up. "Besides, as long as we're gaining altitude, there's little chance of us flying through them."

Several seconds passed as the two pilots fought the aircraft into a spiral ascent. "There is one other thing we can do," Peeters said suddenly.

"What's that?"

"We can drop a life raft."

"What the hell—" Gregory started.

"The radio beacon," Pits Conar interrupted. "The search-and-rescue beacon will start automatically when the life raft inflates. It'll inflate on the way down, giving the beacon longer range."

"Plus," Peeters added as he turned, the curtains closing behind him as he hurried away. "It'll mark the spot where we'll need to start our search when we return!"

"What did he say?" Babs asked.

"He said he was going to mark the bailout spot so we'll know where to start our search when we return."

"If we return," Babs added softly.

"Babs, help me keep the aircraft in a left-hand turn as we ascend. This will keep the right engine on the outside of the spiral where higher wind speeds will hit it."

*   *   *

WHERE THE PARACHUTES DISAPPEARED, A SPRAY OF leaves rose into the air, raining around the holes Rockdale, MacGammon, and Carson made as they penetrated through the leaves, limbs, and vines that reached from the ground of the jungle to a hundred feet above, where the tops of the trees melded together. Razi squinted, trying to see any signs of a parachute. As he watched, he noticed his head was turning to the left. He glanced up at the nylon canopy above him. The wind was pushing him to the right, giving him a right-bearing drift away from the holes where his aircrewmen had disappeared.

Razi gripped the lines tightly and pulled strongly on the left suspension line, looking up to watch the canopy dip in response. He swung to the left as air fell out of the parachute. He looked forward, searching for a few moments for the holes where the three had disappeared. He spotted them. The holes were to his right now. Without looking up, he pulled on the right line, swinging himself around again. Suddenly, his stomach lurched as he fell straight down for several feet before the parachute blossomed out and stopped the fall.

"That's enough of that," he mumbled. He stretched his fingers for a moment before retightening his grip on the lines. He'd just walk to where they landed. He thought, *How in the hell am I going to do that? Once I hit the ground, I'll have no idea where I'm at and in which direction they are.*

He watched where the three sailors had disappeared, wondering how he was going to find them once he was on the ground. Biting his upper lip, Razi looked down at the leaves on the trees below him. He was close enough he could make out individual leaves. *My compass!* he thought. Releasing the lines to the parachute, the fingers on his right hand, encased in flight gloves, fumbled with the chest-high top zipper of his survival vest. He hadn't realized how much he was shaking until then. It seemed an eternity before he finally managed to get a grip on the zipper, unzip the pouch, and grab the military compass. He rezipped the pouch. His small container of water and a power bar was in that pouch and if he left it open and they fell out, it'd be a hungry, thirsty night until rescue helicopters arrived. He held the compass up, steadying it as much as he could from the buffeting of the wind, and lined the needle with true north. It was visual guess, but the bearing from his position and where the other three landed was three-two-zero. He dropped the compass, letting it bob on the yellow nylon cord tying it to the survival vest. He grabbed the two suspension lines and then did what he did badly; he guessed distance. Razi had never had to guess distance while bailing out—he had never bailed out of an aircraft before today. Sure, he talked about it, but like those who can't do it, he taught it. Three miles. No less than two miles, no more than five miles.

He looked down. What would his landing be like? Lots of trees down there. What if there's a limb poking straight up, with a sharp point, waiting to rip through his flight suit and impale him? Involuntarily, his sphincter tightened. Jungles had swamps. Down below these trees could be nothing but swamp and malaria. But he'd taken his malaria pills. A vision of a gigantic crocodile crossed his mind, causing his thoughts to migrate instantly to the croc in *Peter Pan* that constantly chased the notorious Captain Hook. "Tick tock," he said aloud.

He shook his head. The treetops seemed to be whirling as he approached. Razi saw open space to his right between several limbs. Without thinking, he jerked on the right line, swinging his descent to the right. He was pleased with himself as he crashed through the opening. At the last moment, he jerked his legs up, tucked his head down, and crossed his arms across his chest. Though he intended to keep his eyes open once he reached here, he clinched them tightly, so tight he felt the pressure pushing them back into their sockets.

A limb slammed across his left ankle as he crashed through the trees. Leaves and light branches whipped against the visor of his helmet. His fall slowed, and abruptly he jerked to a stop. Razi opened one eye and peered down. The ground was about ten feet below him. Looking up, the parachute had tangled on the stump of a limb. How it became a stump never entered his thoughts. Ten feet was nothing, unless he broke a leg or ruptured his spleen. Razi wasn't really sure what a spleen was, but he knew it was something dangerous to rupture.

"Well, I'm here," he said aloud. He opened his arms, holding his hands out. They shook, and *why in the hell shouldn't they?* he thought to himself. *It's a wonder I didn't piss myself,* he thought. Razi looked around the jungle, amazed how quiet it seemed until he told himself that with the noise he made crashing through the trees, his arrival probably scared everything away. At least, he hoped so. "Looks solid," he said as he scanned the ground below him. "But then, what in the hell do you know?" he replied to his comment.

Brown was the color that came to mind. Jungles were supposed to be lush, wet, and green, filled with man-eating animals. Instead, below him was an open area blanketed with decaying limbs and leaves interspaced with leafy vines that ran from one side to the other as if racing to cross the open area as fast as possible.

He thought, *How to get down is the big question?* Without thinking about it, he bent his knees, released the leg straps, then reached up and released the chest straps. His stomach lurched again as he fell.

"Oh, shit!" he shouted. His feet hit the ground squarely and instinctively, Razi rolled to the right, coming to rest on his back. He lay there for several moments, breathing deeply, and telling himself how stupid he was. He could have broken his legs and laid there, unable to move, until the man-eaters recovered from the fright he dealt them. Then they'd angrily return to show him what they thought about those who disturbed their domain.

He opened his eyes wide as he sat up and swung his head from side to side scanning the jungle. For some reason it reminded him of the forests of North Carolina, only hotter, more humid, and bears weren't the main threat here. He reached up and tapped the survival vest, the SV-2B, the main pouch where the water was, then reminded himself that in survival training the instructors said to wait twenty-four hours before having a drink after an emergency situation. Damn it! Bailing out of an aircraft after they tell you not to is damn well an emergency, and a chief petty officer would never disobey Navy regulations.

He leaned to the side and pushed himself up. His left ankle was tender. Razi took several steps. It didn't seem to be damaged or hurt too bad, just sore along the side where the limb had hit it.

Razi looked in the direction he believed he had to walk to rescue the three aircrewmen. It never dawned on the chief petty officer that his mission was anything but a rescue— Damn, two of the aircrewmen were third class petty officers, and Carson had just put on his second-class crow. What did the three of them know about survival? He had nineteen years in the Navy, nearly five times more than Carson, who was approaching his fourth year. He brushed his gloves together, knocking off the leafy debris stuck to the cloth. Shit! He'd had more time going to the head in the Navy than those three had total Navy service. Petty officers need their chiefs in times such as these he told himself. He glanced in the direction he believed he needed to travel. *And, the sooner I get to them the better for them . . . and for me.*

Razi reached up and unsnapped his helmet, taking it off. Holding it under his arms, Razi surveyed the surrounding landscape. A tight row of bushes blocked his way. He opened the compass, gave it a moment to steady up, and was surprised to see it was pointed in the wrong direction. Razi took a moment to congratulate himself on using his head when he was descending. This would be one great sea tale when those Air Force bubbas pulled the four of them out later today. He just hoped that he didn't have to wait for his zoomie comrades-in-arms to finish their golf game or indulge in crew's rest—the secret, high-five term for taking a nap. *We ought to have something like crew's rest in the Navy,* he thought to himself. He smiled as he imagined the vision of Crazy Harry trying to come to terms with the idea that aircrew needed to rest.

He touched his pouch again, listening to an inner voice arguing with him that if he was going to be rescued tomorrow morning or, better yet, this afternoon, then a small drink wouldn't hurt. He shook off the little devil-thoughts. Devil-thoughts were the bane of ankle-biters. Ignore them or small irritants would overrun bigger concerns, and his biggest concern was to find those three sailors of his. If he was going to be the hero and take credit for rescuing them, then he needed to be with them when the Air Force decided to show up.

He turned right. Nodded when he saw a path nearly fifty feet in this direction, marking it as the clearest from where he stood. Lined up with the compass. He clicked his lips in appreciation, "It is indeed a host of miracles that descends upon you when you make chief petty officer."

OJO OPENED HIS EYES. HIS HEAD HURT. HE WAS FACE DOWN on the jungle floor. The stinging smell of explosives mixed with the decaying odors of the disturbed humus beneath him. His back and thighs hurt. They felt heavy. Whatever happened involved an explosion; he'd been around war long enough to recognize that whatever exploded had been near him. He pushed himself into a sitting position before reaching up and running his hands over his head. Then he started down his body, touching places that hurt—his back, his thighs—then he checked his ribs. A moan, which he quickly stifled, escaped as he touched his right side. Thought, *Cracked, not broken. Stirred, not shaken.* "What happened?" he asked himself. Debris rained from the vegetation overhead. One moment they were standing motionless, listening to the approaching aircraft, and talking about the troops rushing ahead to stop Abu Alhaul, and the next he was lying on the floor of the jungle.

He looked around. His AK-47 lay nearby on the ground, the barrel protruding from beneath a bush. He leaned over and pulled it to him. He blinked, feeling the sting of salt and grit. Ojo wiped his eyes as he turned his head, trying to locate the muffled screams penetrating the ringing in his ears. He saw others crashing through the brush, taking care of the wounded. Some turned toward him. He couldn't hear the noise he knew they had to be making. Only the screams penetrated the fog of his hearing. He removed his hand, bent his head over, and blinked rapidly, feeling tears wash out his eyes. Finished, he lifted his head. His right eye was clear. Ojo blinked several times, until his left eye cleared. Using his free hand for balance, the jet-black

African stood. His dark eyes surveyed the carnage surrounding him. So, the Americans were truly after him. He found it hard to believe since he had calculated so carefully to avoid any offense or action that would give them reason to do what they just did.

A hand touched his shoulder, causing him to jump slightly. The pressure within his ears had hidden the approach of General Darin, the child-warrior from Liberia, now a young man, who was his youngest general. The young man's mouth moved, but Ojo couldn't understand him; the words were garbled. Ojo opened his mouth and wiggled his lower jaw until the air pressure in his ears released with a pop. The screams heralded the cascade of familiar sounds he had come to greet as familiar with the end of combat. They flooded his hearing. Ojo raised his AK-47 and quickly scanned the area. What if the Americans were also on the ground?

"What happened?" he asked Darin as his eyes surveyed the scene, searching for an attack, tilting his head to see if could hear gunfire elsewhere.

"It was a missile, General. An American missile. The aircraft came back. One moment the engine noise was increasing and the next a missile broke through the trees and exploded."

"Ezeji?"

Darin pointed to where a group of men stood. "He is badly shaken." The young man reached forward and touched Ojo's shoulder. "More important; are you okay?"

Shouts and orders for everyone to be quiet drew Ojo's attention before he could answer. Marching through the carnage was General Kabaka, surrounded by his warriors. Here was the mercurial general who wore a belt made of human skin. It was not lost on Ojo that the belt was black. This was not the time to have Kabaka near him. A tree

limb crashed to the ground fifty yards from where they
stood, causing Kabaka to jump aside. A fleeting pleasure
even as Ojo saw the man's eyes never left him. If Kabaka
wanted, he could kill him, Ezeji, and Darin, and seize control of the African National Army. He would do it, if roles
were reversed. On the other hand, Kabaka was more a tactical adversary than one who pondered strategic moves.
Ojo glanced at his AK-47. At this very moment, he was at
his most vulnerable. How stupid of the Americans to try to
kill him!

Kabaka stopped a few feet from Ojo. "I am glad to see
you are alright, General," he said in a tone that made Ojo
doubt its sincerity. He watched the volatile general's head
turn as the lithe killer surveyed the area. Kabaka turned
back to Ojo, their eyes locking for several seconds before
Kabaka looked away and pointed to the top of the trees.
Sunlight broke through a large hole in the canopy. "I hope
you believe me now when I say the Americans want to kill
you."

Ojo glanced over Kabaka's shoulder to the right. Ezeji
was standing, supported by two Nigerians from Ezeji's division. Unseen by Kabaka, the Nigerian general said
something to the two soldiers and they released him, only
to grab him again as his knees buckled. The huge Nigerian
shook their hands off and started toward Ojo. The other
Nigerians followed.

Ojo straightened. His vulnerability was being reduced
every second. He met Kabaka's stare. "Are we sure it was
the Americans and not Abu Alhaul, who we know has missiles?" Ojo asked, knowing it was the Americans, but not
wanting to give Kabaka the pleasure of being right.

Kabaka laughed. "Oh, General Ojo, you do love the
Americans, and they love you so much they keep trying to
kill you. Of course, the terrorists have missiles, but they are

surface-to-air missiles designed to shoot down aircraft." He pointed to the opening overhead. "This missile came from the air. It is indeed a blessing," he said with a trace of derision, "that you are still alive." He turned as Ezeji entered his vision. "Ah, I see even the Nigerian has survived the assassination attempt by the Americans. What a pity you are wounded."

"General Ojo, are you okay?" Ezeji asked.

"Of course, he is okay," Kabaka snapped. "The Americans failed to kill him again." He faced Ojo and ran his eyes up and down the leader of the African National Army. "He is invulnerable. Nothing can kill our leader; not even the Americans with their superior technology."

"Maybe it was the Americans," Ojo admitted. "If it were the Americans—"

"No one else was flying above us!" Kabaka interrupted. "It is time to realize that regardless of what your time schedule and plans are for dealing with the Western powers, they know of them. Why would they try to kill you— and us," he continued, pounding his chest, "When you have taken great pains to avoid antagonizing them?"

"I refuse to believe—"

Ezeji sighed. "For once, as much as I hate to, I must agree with General Kabaka, General Ojo. I can fathom neither reason nor rationale for the unprovoked attack. You have returned their missionaries unharmed. You have avoided intruding into Liberia, though we did chase the Jihadists into the Cote D'Ivoire. Every signal you have sent them has been one of appeasement."

"And we are marching along the northern border of Liberia inside the country of Guinea. Guinea! Another American ally in this so-called war against terrorism!" Kabaka's voice rose and his hands gesticulated dramatically. "It isn't terrorism the Westerners led by the Americans want to see dead. It is any form of resistance against their might." Kabaka pounded his chest several times. "We are a threat to their omnipotence. We present the people with options—"

"I think we should take care of the wounded," Ojo said, raising his hand palm out toward the angry general. Maybe Kabaka was right and he, Ojo, had been blinded by his own arrogance. Arrogance in believing he could outsmart the superpowers that surround Africa. America may be a hyperpower, as the French call it, but for poverty-ridden Africa, any country that could muster a foreign policy was a superpower, and all Ojo wanted, or so he told himself, was to pave a better way of life for his people. Of course, being in charge was always the preferable way of making improvements.

"The wounded are dead," Kabaka said. "All the grace, good manners, and 'oohing and awing' won't save someone with open wounds from the angry, invisible man-eaters that ride the winds in our hot, humid jungles." The angry Kabaka turned sideways and waved an arm in a broad sweep around them. "Look! Look closely. There is an arm there; a leg near that bush; and, that round bushy thing surrounded by wet clay was moment's ago someone's head." He looked at Ezeji. "General Ezeji, you are lucky your head wound is shallow. Mud packed across it may protect you."

"We must do what we must do."

Kabaka turned angrily to Ojo and drew his long machete. "I will take care of the wounded. They will only slow us down."

Ojo nearly took a step back. He drew his right arm closer to his side, slipping his finger onto the trigger of the AK-47. He wondered for a moment if the safety was on or off? He nearly looked down.

"I will deal with the wounded," Kabaka said, waving the

machete back and forth in front of him. "Better a quick, unexpected death than the long, drawn-out pain as they watch the red snake creep upward from their wounds toward their heads and heart."

Ojo's eyes widened. Kill the very men who had followed him throughout the growing campaign?

Ezeji reached forward and touched Ojo for a moment before dropping his hand. "For once Kabaka is right, General. We do not have the medicine or the means to save these men. We only have a man who once worked in a hospital, and I doubt he was more than an orderly."

"How many—"

"It doesn't matter."

"General Kabaka, if we are going to kill our own men, then we should know how many."

Darin, who had stood respectfully a few feet behind Ojo during the entire exchange, stepped up to the three generals. "General Ojo, there are no more than ten who are wounded. Most should be able to have their wounds bandaged and rejoin the army. If we kill these ten, then there are ten dead. If we allow them to live and even one lives, then that is one more soldier for the ANA."

"They would slow us down," Kabaka argued.

"They are my soldiers!" Darin rebutted. "I will take care of them."

"Then they are the walking dead who will slow us down and bring more walking dead into their ranks."

"They will be able to do their jobs."

"You are wrong," Kabaka said, taking a step toward Darin.

Ojo saw Darin glance at the machete.

"And you are too young and inexperienced to recognize when death is a valuable weapon for an army, even when ministered from within."

"Do not mistake my youth for inexperience, General Kabaka, nor my patience for cowardice. I have been fighting since I was five. War is my mother and father. It is the family that has embraced me since I learned not to wet my pants." He nodded toward the machete. "Is that for the wounded? Are you going to be the one who wields it? Do you think those who are wounded, but alert will lay there, stretch their necks, and say thanks?" He turned to Ojo. "General, if we kill our own men, word will filter first through the nearer troops before erupting like a burst dam to flood through the will of the remaining soldiers."

"Kabaka is right. They will slow us down and if they become worse, then we have little choice but to leave them." Ezeji turned to Kabaka. "Rather than killing them, we should make them comfortable and leave them behind to either heal or die."

"Then you would subject them to a slow torture. My men are used to killing—"

"No one should be used to killing," Ezeji objected. "Killing is what we do because we have to do it. Not because we want to do it."

"Enough," Ojo said. "Leave this argument for another time. We will leave the wounded. Ahead of us waits the coming battle with Abu Alhaul, and though the Americans may—I say may—have been the ones who fired on us, we will not allow it to distract us from our plans. We will discuss this later."

OJO SIPPED THE HOT CUP OF TEA. KABAKA HAD FAILED TO return to his command as Ojo had expected; instead the man had remained, even making the tea himself as they reconstituted their forces for the continued march forward. Ezeji had sent a runner to his soldiers telling them of the plans, estimating a couple of hours for them to arrive. With Ojo's blessing he had given the captain leading the soldiers permission to make his own decision to engage the Arabs, if it appeared they might escape the trap.

The thrashing of bushes drew their attention. Child warriors who were the point men for the ANA emerged through the brush. A young warrior, his eyes wide and his breath coming in quick gasps, stopped in front of Ojo. Ojo waited for several seconds, while the lad regained his breath, recognizing the admiration in the young African's eyes.

"What is it?" he asked.

"Parachutes, General Ojo. Three men landed in the trees several kilometers to the north, ahead of us. They are trapped, caught on the limbs. I hurried back—"

"I will go," Kabaka said, stepping toward the young boy. "I will go, and what I bring back will be a lesson to those who stand in our way."

Ojo reached out and touched Kabaka on the arm, causing the angry general to jump. "No, we will move forward toward Abu Alhaul. We will leave whoever is in the parachutes to their fate. I will not allow something else to distract us. Those in the trees are trapped. Leave them. They are out of our path, and we will avoid them as we move forward."

"They are Americans! Americans like the ones sent into Cote D'Ivoire to kill you; only this time they have miscalculated. They are trapped in the trees so we won't have to worry about where they are. We know why they are here. We can kill them from afar. They will never see who killed them or even know the bullets are coming until they enter their bodies."

"Why do you want to kill them, Kabaka?" Ezeji said, his voice tight. "Is it because you like to kill and you want to draw the Americans onto us?"

The cries of the wounded had long ago passed into moans as one casualty after another died, leaving only those who would live and those so seriously wounded that they were unconscious, thereby stifling their screams. Why would the Americans fire on him? If the Americans saw how they dealt with Jihadists, they would embrace the ANA as one of their allies.

"This is another attempt to kill Ojo—General Ojo, just as they tried two months ago in Cote D'Ivoire," Kabaka finally answered. "If it hadn't been for my men routing them and forcing them to flee in their helicopter, they would still be chasing us."

Ojo turned to the forward scout. "Did you leave anyone to watch the men in the parachutes?"

"No, sir, General. The others continued to track the Arabs and sent me back to warn General Ojo."

"Go back and rejoin your group. Tell them to leave the men in the parachutes alone. If they become free and you discover them following you, then lose them."

The boy stood straight, his lower lip pushed against the upper. "If they follow, General, we can kill them. We are not afraid."

Ojo shook his head. "No, if they follow, then you are to avoid them. Don't take them prisoner and don't fight them. Those in the parachutes are professionals. They are what the Americans call Special Forces, but here they are on our ground and we know the jungles; they don't, so we will avoid them until they tire and call for the helicopter to take them out."

"For this, my general," Kabaka said, his voice soft, "you are wrong. Allow me to kill them. I will go with the boy and kill the Americans after we have questioned them. Allowing them to live only endangers ourselves and our soldiers. If these are allowed to leave, they will be back, and they will continue to return until they capture or kill you."

Ojo nodded. "You may be right, but if we kill them, then there will be no negotiating with the Americans. Leaving them alive, we may have a chance to show them our value to their prolonged war on terrorism, and then they will leave us alone."

Ezeji nodded. "That is sage wisdom, General Ojo. You may be right. Dead Americans do not encourage Americans to talk, but it does cause them to commit others to ensure that future Americans will not die. The American Special Forces are smart. They will be able to tell that we knew of their dilemma and didn't take advantage of it. That is a point in our favor."

Kabaka sheaved the machete. "I am returning to my troops." He pointed at Ojo and Ezeji. "In this you are wrong. Patience may not be cowardice, but it can lead to a wrong decision and, in this, you are wrong. Patience isn't called for now. Decisive—" He made chopping motions with his hands. "—death is the answer. A dead person never argues with a live one, but a dead person sends his own message to those who sent him."

"Enough, General Kabaka. Thank you for your insight. Let's hope you are wrong."

"In this, I am not," Kabaka said, his voice shaking with anger. "You are endangering our army by allowing them to live." He turned, motioned his men to follow, and marched back the way he had come.

"He is dangerous," Ezeji mumbled.

"Yes, he is dangerous. I wonder sometimes if that is good or bad, but most times I believe that anger has its own place in combat, and a soldier can't say whether that anger was good or bad until afterwards."

"By then it is too late," Ezeji said.

"By then it is too late," Ojo agreed, nodding.

Ojo turned to the young warrior. "You have your orders, soldier. Return to your unit and tell them of my decision."

KABAKA WAITED UNTIL THE JUNGLE GROWTH HID THEM from Ojo and Ezeji. He turned to one of his lieutenants. "We cannot allow our great leader to imperil himself at the advice of a Nigerian traitor. I want a squad of our young warriors to take the Americans. It matters little to me whether we take them alive or dead. If alive, then they are to hold them for me." He laughed and patted the top of his khaki short pants. "I need a new belt."

CHAPTER 7

"ROCKY! YOU OKAY?" MACGAMMON SHOUTED, HIS VOICE shaking.

Rockdale turned his head left, motion below him causing him to look down. There was MacGammon about twenty feet below swinging from the suspension lines of the tangled parachute.

"I'm okay!" he shouted back. Rockdale ran his hands over his body, feeling through the aches of the landing, making sure nothing was broken. *Where in the hell were they?* Satisfied nothing was broken, he glanced around, assessing their situation. A huge tree limb jutted out directly below—he estimated three feet—running toward the group of limbs of the nearby tree where MacGammon's parachute was entangled. Rockdale craned his head forward, but vegetation hid the ground. Be hell if they had to stay in the trees until rescue arrived because they couldn't get down. *Where are the others?* He wondered. The EP-3E had twenty-four souls on board. He saw three of them drifting close together as they came down. The other person was Carson. You couldn't mistake the Texan's lanky frame for anyone else. *But, where in the hell was Carson?* Rockdale turned his head as far to each side as possible. The helmet hindered a clear view and obstructed peripheral vision. Rockdale knew Carson could be right behind him and he wouldn't be able to see him until he removed his helmet. He looked down. He thought he could see the ground, if that patch of brown was the ground and not a bunch of dead leaves or limbs. Either way, it was too far down to un-snap and drop.

"Hey, you see Stetson?" Rockdale shouted, using Carson's nickname.

"Hell, Rocky! I can barely see me. I'm surrounded by leaves. How far from the ground are we?"

"Too far to drop."

MacGammon had been close enough for Rockdale to recognize as they descended. His descent was right behind MacGammon, and Carson had been slightly off to his right.

"Rocky! What the hell are we going to do?"

"I think," he said, drawing out the reply. "We'll wait here a while and see if we can contact anyone. Stetson has to be around here someplace."

"I didn't see him when we came down."

"He was with us. I was behind you and he was to my right."

"I came through first. Did you see where he hit?"

"I had my eyes shut." A few second later MacGammon added. "I thought we were going to die. I didn't see anyone else bail out. You don't suppose?"

"Blew up?" Rockdale shook his head. Aircraft on which

you flew never blew up. They blew up on other people. "No!" he shouted. "No, I don't think it blew up."

Rockdale released his grip on the suspension lines and let his harness hold him up. If the parachute was going to come loose and send him falling through the maze of inter-twined limbs and vines, it would have already done so. He pulled his flight gloves off and jammed them in the large flight-suit pocket on his right leg. He'd need those later. He unsnapped the pouch on his survival vest, the SV-2, and pulled out the AN/PRC-90 survival beacon. They may call this small radio a survival beacon, but it was a dual-channel rescue transmitter with a two-way voice and Morse-code capability. Every aircrewman had one of these expensive radios in their survival vests. And none of them knew Morse code, though the Navy in its infinite wisdom had embossed the dots and dashes for Morse code on the side of the PRC-90. It was a joke with Rockdale and the others that by the time they could send a Morse message, they would have been rescued. By the time they found someone who could copy Morse code, they'd be retired and drawing Social Security.

He turned the PRC-90 around, making sure it wasn't broken. This little box was the key to them being rescued. Between him and MacGammon, the batteries should last a couple of weeks. *Two weeks!* The thought sent a moment of panic zipping through him. No way they'd be here that long, he told himself, feeling his heart rate subside a bit.

"Hey, Mac!" he called. "I'm going to try to raise some-one on the PRC-90. You keep yours off."

"Why should I keep mine off?"

Rockdale nodded. MacGammon was returning to nor-mal. "Because we don't want both of us using up our bat-teries at the same time."

"Okay, but—"

Rockdale switched on the radio, turned the switch to voice, and hit the press-to-talk button. "Anyone this station, anyone this station, this is Rockdale, aircrewman Ranger 20. Do you read?" He released the button. The PRC-90 couldn't receive when the button was pushed down. Every fifteen minutes, Rockdale thought, as he mentally reviewed the rescue lessons for using the PRC-90. The first few hours, he would transmit every fifteen minutes in the hope of making contact with friendly forces. On the hour; fifteen minutes after the hour; then, on the half-hour and fifteen minutes to the hour. Trained for communications like clockwork. Throughout the U.S. Navy, the fives and zeros of the clock drove rescue time.

He looked upward, not expecting to see anything, but checking each block of what he recalled of Search, Escape, Evasion, and Rescue—SEER training. Know your surroundings; know your location; know which way to friendly forces. Friendly forces, there's a concept he hoped never to have to think about except during briefings. The nearest friendly forces, as far as Rockdale could recall, was somewhere south of them in Liberia and even then, two young white boys stumbling out of the jungles might be seen more as an opportunity than a rescue. Rockdale pushed the button again and repeated the call several times. Somewhere out here in the jungle, the NRL boys had detected two groups of humans running around. They wouldn't be friendly forces.

Rockdale clamped his eyes shut, forcing the tears back. This wasn't why he joined the Navy. He should have listened to his mother and aunt, gone on to the local community college, and hope some college scout saw him playing basketball. But, no . . . he had to do his duty like his father and join the Navy.

He opened his eyes, a sigh escaping at the same time. The scope of survival overwhelmed him. What did Chief Razi say about surviving? Understand the big picture, but concentrate on one thing at a time. The big picture will scare the shit out of you. Razi was partially right. The scope of their situation did scare him, but the scope depressed him by making him realize they might never make it out of here.

Suddenly, the static blared from the PRC-90, followed by a voice. "Rockdale, this is Lieutenant Commander Peeters. Do you read me?"

Rockdale's eyes widened. He nearly dropped the radio when he heard the voice. Gripping the PRC-90 tighter, he took a couple of deep breaths, worrying his voice would betray his momentary lapse of control. Then, he pressed the talk button. "Yes, sir. We do. There is Petty Officer MacGammon and me here. We saw one other with us. It was Petty Officer Carson, sir, but he must have landed nearby. We can't see him. Where are you, Commander? Are the others with you?"

"Rockdale, the rest of us didn't bail out. We're still on Ranger-20. The last gasps of the extinguisher put out the engine fire so we halted bailout, but not before four of you jumped. Lacey is still on board."

"I only saw three parachutes, Commander."

"The fourth person is Chief Razi. He bailed out after we halted bailout. He jumped to help you guys. So, he's somewhere nearby, also."

Rockdale pressed the talk button, shutting off Peeters. "Sir, I didn't see him coming down, so I didn't see the chief land. Right now, we aren't in a situation yet where we can search for anyone. Both our parachutes are snagged in trees."

"Carson, this is Peeters. Do you hear me?"

Rockdale waited, not wanting to miss Carson's reply.

Seconds passed without hearing anything on the radio other than Peeters continuing call to the third member of what Rockdale was beginning to consider as their group.

"Chief Razi, this is Lieutenant Commander Peeters, I have you fivers. Rockdale, did you hear the chief's transmission?"

Rockdale raised the radio and put it against his ear. He hadn't heard Razi reply to Peeters. He pushed the talk button. "No, sir. I didn't hear nothing. I guess you have comms with the chief?"

"That's right. Listen up, Chief; Rockdale and MacGammon are northwest of your position about miles. I have comms with both you and Rockdale, but he can't hear you. Means you're out of range of each other. At three miles, even with the jungle, you two should be able to hear each other. Rockdale and MacGammon are tangled up in some trees. Petty Officer Carson is down somewhere in their vicinity, but his situation is unknown at this time."

"Rocky, what in the hell is going on?" MacGammon shouted.

Rockdale looked down at the very moment MacGammon's parachute ripped free, sending his friend falling another dozen feet before the nylon canopy entangled itself on other limbs.

"Jesus Christ! I have got to get the hell out of this tree!"

"Rockdale, the chief is heading your way, but doesn't know how long it will take. What is your situation?"

"Sir, we're still tangled up in the trees. We can't see the ground. At least, I can't tell if it's the ground I see. MacGammon's parachute just ripped free and he fell—" He stopped. Wasn't much else he could tell the officer who was buzzing holes in the sky above him. Wasn't as if these radios sent photographs or anything. They were just your basic Mach-1 radio designed to guide rescuers to your position.

"Is he okay?"

"Yes, sir. The tree limbs caught his parachute again, but he's farther away. We can still shout at each other, Commander."

"Rockdale, you and MacGammon are going to have to figure out a way to untangle yourselves. You need to get out of the trees. You need to do it soon. Two things; you don't want to be in those trees when rescue comes. The rotors will suck the canopy up into the intakes, so if you're not free of those parachutes, it's going to turn a quicker, easier rescue into a longer, harder one. And two, you don't want to dangle like free meat through the night."

He didn't think anything could reach them this far up in the trees, but Lieutenant Commander Peeters knew more than he did. Rockdale listened as the mission commander gave him more tips. As he listened, he watched MacGammon start to swing back and forth. The shorter, squat man from New Jersey pumped his legs back and forth, building up momentum. Above MacGammon, the man's parachute was edging forward, toward the end of the main limb that held it. The leaves wrapped around it would never hold it when the nylon came free.

". . . Do you copy, Rockdale? First, get out of the trees."

"Yes, sir, we will," Rockdale replied, his eyes switching back and forth between MacGammon and the snag. He released the push to talk button. "Mac! Your parachute is about to come—"

MacGammon's parachute broke free just as MacGammon swung toward the trunk of the huge tree across from Rockdale. The aircrewman tumbled downward toward the trunk. MacGammon bounced onto a huge limb, his hands and legs scrambling to hold on. The 28-foot nylon canopy drifted down and rolled over the top of the prone aircrewman.

"Mac! You alright?"

"I'm alright!" a muffled scream came back, followed by a tattoo of cursing and swearing. "I may have shit myself, but I'm all right."

"Rockdale, you hear me?"

Rockdale pushed the talk button. "Yes, sir, Commander. MacGammon is free. He's up against the trunk of the tree across from mine. I don't suppose you'd have any idea how far from the ground we are, would you, sir?" Rockdale asked, mentally kicking himself for the dumb question. How in the hell would Commander Peeters know how far he was from the ground? He waited for the derisive reply.

"Sorry, Rocky, I don't," Peeters replied solemnly. "I know the height of the trees where you landed sometimes reach a hundred feet."

"That's great news!" came another muffled shout.

"You hear that?" Rockdale shouted.

A hand snaked out from beneath the nylon, holding up a PRC-90. MacGammon had turned on his survival radio. He might as well save the batteries on his, if MacGammon wasn't going to listen. It wasn't as if he was senior to the other third class petty officer or something. Carson was, but neither of them had any idea where Carson had landed. Carson might be badly—

"Rockdale, listen to me. Your location and situation has been broadcast to homeplate and to Commander, Amphibious Group Two, who sailed into Monrovia this morning as we were taking off. Everyone knows where you are and they're working on a rescue team."

"Thanks, Commander—"

"Commander, this is Petty Officer MacGammon. How long are we going to be out here? It ain't exactly Kansas, you know."

"Rockdale, your comms were blocked by MacGammon.

MacGammon, you and Rockdale are probably going to be there at least overnight."

The nylon rippled back, uncovering MacGammon's head. MacGammon turned his head to the side and looked up at Rockdale. "Overnight! Did you hear that, Rocky? They make us bail out, and they're going to go back, sip beer, and watch CNN, while we stay out, getting eaten alive by mosqui—"

Rockale pushed the talk button. "Commander, what is the aircraft situation?"

Two clicks acknowledged his question. It seemed to Rockdale that a few minutes passed, with the sound of MacGammon griping in the background before the radio blazed to life. "Rockdale, we are heading back to Monrovia. The fire is out, but if we have reflash, we have no way of stopping it. If it blazes back up or if another casualty on that wing causes a fire, then we will have to either ditch or bail out. On the bright side for you, there is another EP-3 heading into homeplate from mother, due to arrive shortly. We're not forgetting our shipmates on the ground. Rockdale, MacGammon, I know this is hard on you two, but you're going have to have faith that rescue is on the way. Tomorrow morning at first light, either us or the new aircrew will be orbiting overhead, and by tomorrow afternoon, there'll be cold beer and hot food waiting for you."

"Roger, sir. We'll try."

"You two need to work your way down and search for Carson. But don't wander too far from where you're at now. We have you pinpointed. If you drift away, then we'll have to search anew tomorrow. As for Carson, something's wrong and let's hope it's just his radio, but you two don't split up and get lost hunting for him. We are leaving the area now. I'll stay in contact as long as I can. We pushed out a life raft right after the chief bailed out. Should be supplies and a larger radio in it, if you can find it."

Rockdale's brow bunched. Thought, *How in the hell are we going to find a life raft in the middle of this jungle? We can't even find the ground.* He sighed. When the talk is finished, you're always on your own, even when those who do foolish things to help surround you.

"Yes, Chief," Peeters broadcast. "Rockdale and MacGammon are alright, but they're going to have to get themselves out of the trees."

A few second later, Peeters returned to the airwaves. "Yes, Chief, I'll tell them."

Rockdale looked up at his parachute. A long rip he hadn't noticed earlier ran from where the suspension lines connected to the canopy to where the nylon had become knotted in numerous places, wrapped about the entwined limbs of two trees. No way his parachute was going to come free like MacGammon's. He wasn't sure if that was good news or bad.

"Rockdale," Peeters broadcast. "Chief Razi is working his way to you, but I wouldn't count on him getting there anytime soon. You two are going to have to free yourselves, find Carson, and wait where you are for rescue."

Rockdale lifted his radio to reply.

"We copy you, sir," MacGammon answered before Rockdale hit the talk button.

"Hey, Mac, you watch the radio for a while. I'm turning mine off and putting it away while I try to free myself."

MacGammon looked up and nodded.

Rockdale could release the straps and fall the three feet to the limb beneath him. He craned his head forward. It didn't look rotten or anything. It should hold him, but he'd have to hit it squarely. There were no limbs or vines he could grab. If he didn't land squarely, he could roll off, and though he couldn't see the ground, it wouldn't surprise him to find it on the way down. From MacGammon's radio, he could hear Peeters talking to Chief Razi, but he couldn't make out what they were saying.

Rockdale released the two leg straps. Decisions are best made when enough information becomes available and before you worry yourself out of making one. He took a deep breath, let it out, and then took another one. Only the chest straps held him to the parachute.

He glanced at MacGammon, who had dragged himself out from under the parachute and was resting with his back against the trunk of the tree. MacGammon was watching, even as he pulled the parachute toward him, rolling it up as it came forward. Rockdale took MacGammon's unfamiliar silence as knowing what he was about to do.

The volume of the radio increased. Rockdale glanced down and saw that MacGammon had moved it away from against his ear.

"Okay, Chief," Peeters said. "Don't worry about what I said and concentrate on closing in on the others who bailed out. I have radio communications with you, Rockdale, and MacGammon. I have not heard anything from Carson and that gives me cause to worry. He might be injured. Rockdale, you copy?"

Looking down, Rockdale released the two chest straps. He didn't hear Peeters's question as he fell the three feet to the limb. His right leg slid off the limb. Rockdale scrambled to the left, his hands and legs thrashing about, searching for something to grab, anything—only the limb was smooth. His body slid farther to the right. His left leg slid off the limb and the next thing he knew he was falling. He heard MacGammon screaming at him as branches and leaves beat his body and slapped against his helmet. Something slammed him upside the head and the last thing he remembered before blackness encased him was a dry coppery taste.

"Got to go, Commander. We're free, but Rockdale fell and I gotta go find him."

CHIEF RAZI TURNED THE VOLUME ON HIS RADIO DOWN. HE should turn it off, but with no one to notice, he kept it on against Navy survival instructions. After all, he wasn't going to be out here long. If everything goes right, the Air Force might even get their helicopter out here before dark, so Razi didn't see how the batteries would run out. He slipped it back into his survival-vest pocket, leaving the pocket unsnapped so he could grab it if Peeters called again. The EP-3E may be wounded and heading back to homeplate, but as long as he was in reception range of the EP-3E, the radio gave him the feeling that he was not alone. Alone was something he was not used to. A loud screech from somewhere to his left caused Razi to jump. "Jesus Christ!" he shouted. *Stay calm, you twit. Jungles are supposed to be filled with strange noises and animals. Animals!* He turned, searching the area as thoughts of lions, tigers, and gorillas filled his mind. He checked his compass to make sure he was still heading in the general direction of where Rockdale, MacGammon, and Carson had come down, weaving around bushes and brambles that blocked his way. He figured it was an animal trail, but in a sense he was just another animal using it for a while and then those maneaters could have it back.

An hour later he realized he hadn't heard anything else from Peeters and thought about using the radio to check and see if they were still within reception range, but he stumbled, cursed himself for being clumsy, and fought his way through a light section of brush, forgetting about making contact. He always had people around him. In the air, he was surrounded by twenty-four of the greatest Americans in the armed forces. At work, he had the entire squadron and Rota, Spain, Naval Base. The club at happy hour, he was surrounded by his fellow chiefs. Of course, there was his wife and children at home. Virginia, Nelson, John Paul, and Cleopatra. He smiled. The other chiefs could eat their hearts out. Each of his kids had been named for famous commanders who fought wars at sea. The daughter, and youngest, had been a surprise to him and Virginia, of which he blamed the squadron picnic of five years ago, the abundance of sangria, and that cute little seaman who played softball in a mini-skirt. He barely got his wife inside the door . . .

A series of screeches interrupted his thoughts. What in the heck was he doing thinking about his family at a time like this?

The two of them expected another boy, so he had chosen the names of Farragut and Horatio for Virginia to choose from. When little Cleo emerged, he surprised his wife by already having a navy name picked for their daughter. Cleopatra—the first woman to command a fleet in combat. On the negative side was that Cleopatra and Mark Anthony lost the battle, but his daughter was definitely a navy child. Only four and already she knew her bells. What more could a chief petty officer dad ask for?

Razi stopped for a moment and leaned against a nearby tree. He shifted his helmet to the other armpit, lifted the compass, and checked his heading. The screeches continued, but other jungle sounds joined whatever was making the noise, and Razi shoved them to back of his mind. What he couldn't shove away were the images of what he considered man-eaters flickering through his thoughts and causing him to glance over his shoulders periodically.

He knew he needed to concentrate on the matter at hand and not think about his family or allow his thoughts to be distracted, but they never told him in survival training that sometimes your mind refuses to function like you want it to when you're coming down off an adrenaline high. Here, in the middle of the jungle in the middle of the afternoon, Razi was as alone as he had ever been. Damn good thing I am a chief petty officer, he kept telling himself. A lesser person would be a basket case by now—alone in a place where you couldn't see fifty feet in front of you and surrounded by animals who wanted nothing more than to eat you. Well, by God, if one of those animals wanted to eat him, it would know real quick it was messing with a goddamn U.S. Navy chief petty officer. When he finished with it, it'd think twice the next time it messed with one. The bushes to his right shook and from beneath them a wild boar shot out, grunting, and quickly disappeared across the open space. Razi jumped, slamming his back hard against a tree. "Shit, shit, shit!"

"Damn," he finally said, moving away from the tree. "Scared the shit out of me." He bent over, trying to see where the animal disappeared and tripped, the radio falling out of the pocket, hitting the ground, and tumbling a few times before coming to rest right-side up. Razi quickly picked it up, muttering obscenities to himself as he dusted the vegetation from it. He pushed the button, his eyes searching for anything else that might attack him. "Commander, you still there?" he asked, heard the high pitch sound of his voice, and immediately stopped.

Nothing. Christ, if it's broke, he'd have to walk out of here and no telling how many years that would take. His daughter would be married with kids by the time he emerged. "Chief Razi, I presume," they'd say. A slight chill washed over him at the thought. He pressed the button again, and with his voice in a slightly calmer tone, called for Lieutenant Commander Peeters again. "Ranger 20, this is Chief Razi. You still out there?" How could he check it, if no one answered?

Static emerged from the small speaker on the side. Someone was answering him. He breathed a sigh of relief. "Not for much longer, Chief. We're about thirty miles from you and starting to descend back to Monrovia. We'll be back tomorrow. Stay safe, shipmate." The voice faded as Razi listened.

"Well, at least it still works," he said, smiling. He knew they'd be back tomorrow. It went without saying that when your shipmate was down, your duty was to go get him. Razi turned the volume down and slipped the radio back into his survival-vest pocket. The radio pocket was near the center of his chest, so Razi would easily hear any further transmissions it picked up. He warned himself to turn the radio off and conserve the batteries. Nearly an hour later and he estimated a half-mile farther, he heeded his own advice, slipped his hand into the pouch, and flipped the radio off. He buckled the top of the pouch so the radio wouldn't fall out again.

Razi kept moving, his thirst growing. He had expected moving through the jungle to be like the dreams where he was running and no matter how fast he ran, his legs moved as if wading through molasses. Instead, this was more like a stroll in a North Carolina woods, except the shade was thicker, trapping the heat and humidity and shutting out the sunlight. He pulled back the Velcro holding the sleeve of the flight suit tight, slid the sleeve back, and checked his watch. A little after 1600 in the afternoon—even in his thoughts, time was military. *What in the hell was a sailor doing in the middle of the jungle?* If someone had asked him prior to this morning if he would ever bail out of an aircraft, he would have laughed. He had always told people, and himself, that if he ever had to ditch an aircraft, it would be over water, and he'd be with others leaning back against the bright orange sides of a life raft, waiting for rescue. Jungles were for Marines and soldiers. He shouldn't even be here. If Peeters hadn't been looking at him, he wouldn't have bailed out.

For the first time, he started to worry about where he was going to sleep. He couldn't sleep on the ground. The man-eaters were everywhere. Look at the one that shot out from under the bushes, missed him, and took off running. Lieutenant Commander Peeters's attempt to make him feel better was admirable, but Razi knew better than to trust everything a lieutenant commander said. They were good for your career, but if you hung around too long, they'd crucify you. Lieutenant commanders were "wanna-be" commanders. He even knew one who had gone to the Navy uniform shop and bought every shoulder device, all the way up to four-star admiral. Sure, they could argue he was self-promoting, but every chief should own the devices all the way up to master chief petty officer. He wasn't always going to be a chief. One of these days, the Bureau of Naval Personnel, in their infinite reasoning, would recognize that he was a senior chief wearing the chief petty officer device, and then they would promote him. He smiled. Damn, this bailout would force them to promote him. *He ought to be thanking Peeters instead of blaming him.*

Chief petty officers had more problems with lieutenant commanders than any other officer rank. "Give me an ensign any day," Razi said aloud. "One would be good right now." Man-eaters probably prefer younger meat to tough, sinewy chief petty officers.

Most lieutenant commanders were a pain in the ass. Senior enough they didn't believe they were junior officers and junior enough they didn't have much real authority. Some were all right, Razi guessed, but Christ, they were hard to train.

Razi pushed aside some limbs to find a fallen tree blocking his path. Razi stopped and rubbed his chin as he looked at it. So far, he hadn't had to make any decisions other than to keep moving in the same direction. The tree posed a problem as it disappeared on both ends into deep bushes. Clambering through the bushes to go around this thing didn't appeal to him. He took the two steps needed so he could touch it. The top of the fallen tree was slightly higher than his chest. He couldn't see over it because of the vegetation that blocked his view. In the woods of North Carolina, you never stepped over a fallen tree. Snakes like to take refuge beneath fallen trees.

Razi jumped back quickly, leaned, and looked along the base of the tree. They definitely had snakes here. Those that weren't poisonous could swallow you whole. What he wouldn't give to have another chief here. "Ummmm what was the name of that new flight engineer? She'd be a welcome distraction."

A rustle from the bushes near to his left caught Razi's attention. Adrenaline pulsed through his veins. Images of lions, tigers, gorillas, and a lost race of Amazons raced through his mind. Without taking his eyes off the rustling bushes, Razi opened his survival vest and pulled his survival knife out of its sleeve. He turned slightly, facing the rustling bushes. With the back of his hand, he wiped the sweat from his forehead, realizing at the same time his breath was rapid and quick. Damn straight, he was scared, but whatever was in that bush would easily chase him down and in a couple of bites, he'd be a memory.

The bushes quieted and after a couple of minutes, Razi told himself whatever had been there had left. He lowered the knife, straightened, and laughed aloud. Something small and furry shot from under the bushes and dashed across the top of the fallen tree. The laughter stopped abruptly as Razi slashed back and forth in the air with the survival knife. He stumbled back, tripping over a vine. The knife flew into the air as the small creature jumped off the tree and disappeared into the bushes on the other side. The knife came down on the tree trunk, the blade sticking into it.

Razi laughed again, his head going back and forth. He stepped forward and pulled the knife out of the trunk. *Good thing I didn't have another chief petty officer here. I'd never live this down.*

"You stupid shit," he said. "Letting a small thing like that scare you. Some sort of rabbit, I guess" He placed his hand against his chest, feeling rapid heartbeats. "Damn glad no one saw that," he mumbled.

A loud roar filled the jungle, causing Razi to jump. He looked back the way he had come, half-expecting to see whatever caused the roar bounding down the trail at him. The roar lingered through the jungle. Razi turned back to the fallen tree and leaped. Two steps and he was in the middle of the limbs, clawing his way over the top of the trunk, scrambling for the other side. A second roar, closer and louder, emerged from his right, sent his heart racing anew. There was a pack of them out there, and years from now when chiefs sat around the winter fire asking each other whatever happened to poor Razi, he'd be part of some lion's DNA somewhere. Not the way he wanted to go. He stopped for moment, at the far edge of the tree trunk. The way seemed clear, but he couldn't see what was beneath it. There was still the risk of snakes, and what if the lions had dug out a den under the fallen tree. It'd be like home delivery if he jumped into the middle of a lion's den.

He raised his knife and bent his knees. Then, he

straightened again. Maybe he should jump backward, he told himself, turning so he faced the way he had just come. This way, when he landed, he'd be facing whatever was beneath the trunk. Another loud roar rattled the trees. He raised his knife. On the other hand, if he landed facing the way he wanted to go, he could land running. He bent his knees and jumped. He stumbled when he landed, falling onto his back. He looked at the tree trunk expecting to see feral eyes staring at him, but there was nothing but trunk and vines. He laughed. His own imagination was going to kill him. More roars echoed through the trees, rising in tempo to only stop suddenly. Starting low, rising in intensity each time; and each time it seemed to him the roars were getting closer. The chattering of animals in the trees drew his attention as he stood up, brushing himself off with his free hand. Whatever was out there was scaring the monkeys, also.

The trees above him disappeared from view as a second later, rain showered Razi, soaking him and sending water penetrating into his flight suit. One moment the jungle was hot, humid, but dry; and the next, Razi couldn't see ten feet because of the heavy, thick, summer rain pelting the jungle, the noise of it hitting the surrounding vegetation drowning out the rustling of the wind. Several roars echoed in tandem and Razi breathed a sigh of relief. The roars that had sent him crashing across the fallen tree he recognized now. They had been no more than thunder, muffled by the jungle in which he marched. That was what the monkeys were fleeing; thunder. He pushed himself up, laughing aloud as he turned forward and continued to push through the overlapping bushes paralleling the faint trail he followed. He gripped the knife tight, not wanting to drop it, but not completely convinced he could put it away. What if it wasn't thunder he had heard? What if lions, tigers, and such were out there, tracking him, waiting for him to relax his alertness so they could rush in and finish him off. No, the knife remained in his hand in the event those roars had not been thunder. It wasn't as if he'd spent a lot of time in the jungles, but the knife was a comfort.

ROCKDALE OPENED HIS EYES. HE RAISED HIS HAND AND touched his head. His body tilted to the right. He quickly lowered his hand. He raised his head. A crisscross of limbs had stopped his fall. The sound of a limb cracking behind him drew his attention. He turned his head slowly. The main limb holding him was bent forward, broken nearly in half, the inside white of the limb easily visible and easily fresh. The creaking continued, so Rockdale laid his head back against the leaves. The cracking sound stopped. As long as he lay in this position, he should be all right, but eventually he was going to have to move. He could not stay there until rescue arrived. Lieutenant Commander Peeters had told him and MacGammon to find Carson.

"Rockdale, you all right?" MacGammon shouted from below him.

Rockdale turned his head to the right. A parting of the leaves showed MacGammon standing a few feet below him without his helmet on. "I'm okay. Where are we?"

"I'm standing on the ground. You are laying in a bed of limbs about eight feet off the ground."

"Eight feet?"

"Well, it could be more, but you're not going to kill yourself if you sit up and jump down here with me." MacGammon held up his parachute. "I saved my parachute, so we can build some shelter for tonight."

Rockdale raised his head again. The creaking of the breaking limb started anew. He searched with his hands until both found small limbs to hold onto, and then he pushed himself up. The crack was sharp.

"Damn, Rocky!"

Rockdale went sliding forward, riding the breaking limb down like a chute on a playground. The ground was coming toward him—fast. Rockdale bent his knees as the tree delivered him to the ground in a standing position. When he stepped away, the limbs bounced back up, hitting him in the back and shoving him forward a few steps.

"Well, you got down a little easier than I did, Rocky."

Rockdale touched his helmet gingerly on the left side. He unbuckled the chin strap and lifted the clear visor before pulling it off and laying it on the ground beside him. Then, he reached up and touched his head, bringing away blood on his hand.

"Looks as if you've bumped your head. Damn good thing you had your helmet on." MacGammon unzipped his survival vest and pulled out the small first-aid kit each of them had. "Here, sit down so I can bandage you."

Rockdale eased himself onto the brown jungle floor.

"You okay, Rocky? You haven't said a word."

"My head hurts."

"Of course it hurts. Why wouldn't it hurt? You banged yourself upside the head, and you're bleeding like a—"

"Stuck pig. Don't say it."

"Now you've done it," MacGammon said as he held the square gauze over the cut."

"I haven't done anything."

"You know what I mean." MacGammon fell onto his knees, pulling the tape out with one hand and using his teeth to rip it. A couple of minutes later the third class petty officer had spread anti-bacteria cream on the cut and a bandage was across the cut.

"This ain't going to stay on long, you know? The cut

isn't that deep, but it's bleeding. Head wounds do that, you know?" He leaned away from Rockdale. "You know what your problem is?" MacGammon asked as he stood. "You got too much hair. If you had gotten a haircut like Badass told you—"

"How long have I been out?" Rockdale asked, reaching up and gently patting the bandage.

MacGammon shrugged. "Not too long. I watched you fall, but there wasn't much I could do. We needed the parachute; that's what they taught us in SEER training. I hurried as fast as I could, but I finished rolling the parachute before I worked my way down the trunk to check on you. I figured there wasn't much I could do for you. Either you were going to still be alive or you were going to be dead. Either way, I'd need the parachute." MacGammon held up the parachute. "You know, Rocky, it was amazing, really amazing. Did you know that nearer the trunk of the trees, there's fewer leaves, so it was kinda like climbing down a weird ladder—know what I mean?"

Rockdale shook his head. It hurt. "No, I don't know what you mean. Just tell me how long have I been out?" Rockdale asked, irritation with MacGammon showing in his voice.

"Don't get angry with me, boyo. You're the one who fell, not me." MacGammon turned and walked away, his head turning as if searching for something.

"You could have come down and checked on me before taking your time with the parachute."

MacGammon shrugged. "Look, asshole, I've already told you. Either you were going to be alive or you were going to be dead. Wasn't gonna help either of us if I hurried down, found you dead, and didn't bring my parachute. Now, would it?"

"You could have gone back up for it."

MacGammon laughed. "And what if I'd gotten down and couldn't climb back up. Wow, Rocky! You mental geniuses bug the shit out of me."

Rockdale ignored MacGammon. Thought, *MacGammon, you're a pain in the ass.* Rockdale pushed himself up on his elbows. How would he explain to the rescuers why he throttled his shipmate minutes after they landed? He smiled at the irony of being stranded with a dumb-shit like MacGammon.

"What are you smiling at?"

Rockdale shook his head once, causing a rush of pain across his scalp. "Nothing," he said, reaching up and holding his head for moment. "We need to find Carson."

MacGammon shrugged. "Just because the commander told us to find him doesn't mean we have to."

"Mac, you wanna leave Stetson out here to die?" Rockdale asked incredulously.

MacGammon opened his mouth for a moment, shut it, and then said softly, "No, guess I don't, but I don't want to wander too far from here. The aircraft commander did say they had us located. So, if we're going to find him, we need to do it soon and we need to bring him back here. I don't want us getting lost and discovering that when the rescue helos show up, they can't find us. Won't help us, nor help Stetson." MacGammon looked around the area again. "You have any ideas on how we're gonna go about it? It ain't as if this jungle ain't a jungle."

Rockdale reached out, braced himself against the trunk of a nearby tree, and stood. Little white dots danced around his vision. First a few, then growing in such number that they hurt his eyes, forcing him to shut them. Must have been a hell of a blow to cause this. A feeling of nausea rushed over him and for a few seconds, Rockdale believed he was going to throw up. He was afraid to lean forward, afraid he'd pass out and fall, but if he threw up in this position, the vomit would run down his flight suit. He opened his eyes. And into his helmet, the way he was standing. He turned his head. Rockdale didn't want to spend the short time they were going to be on the ground walking around in a barf-covered flight suit, and he'd need the helmet when they rescued them.

"You'd better sit down, Rocky, before you fall. That must have been some blow to stagger you like that." MacGammon reached out and took him by the arm. "Probably hit several limbs coming down."

Rockdale felt the man's hands on his arm and meekly allowed himself to be led away. He opened his eyes. The white spots were still there, but he could see the jungle surrounding them—varying shades of green intermixed with browns. Sharp odors of decaying humus assailed his nostrils. He stumbled, causing pain to shoot up his leg where his foot had tangled with a thick vine.

"Whoa, boy. Don't go falling on me. You weigh too much for this New Jersey lad to have to carry you."

Another arm enveloped his shoulders and, involuntarily, he leaned on the shorter sailor's shoulder.

"Here, sit here and let me get you some water. You must have a concussion or something."

Rockdale bent his knees, reaching out with his free hand to ease himself down onto the moist ground. MacGammon had moved them nearer the other man's tree where the limbs and leaves above shaded the area, keeping other plants from taking root. The clearing was about ten feet across, running downhill to where a wall of bushes, bramble, and vines wove an impenetrable wall of vegetation.

They both looked up as the noise of rolling thunder rode through the jungle.

"I don't like the sound of that," MacGammon said,

tossing the rolled up parachute onto the ground beside Rockdale. "We may need that, and to think, I just tied it together a few minutes ago."

Rockdale lifted the bound parachute. Not only did MacGammon watch him fall and continue to roll the parachute, but the man took time to tie line around it before climbing down to find him!

The sound of rain hitting the jungle canopy drew their attention.

"Here, let me have the parachute," MacGammon said, reaching out and taking it from Rockdale. With several quick flicks, the sailor untied the parachute. "Too late to build a lean-to, I think." He held his hand out, watching the raindrops bounce off it. "Yep, too late."

Several seconds later, a deluge broke through the jungle canopy and soaked the men. Rockdale sat in the rain, listening to MacGammon curse as he snapped open the parachute as if laying a blanket across a bed.

"The parachute!" MacGammon shouted, reminding Rockdale of a small child claiming his toy.

A moment later the nylon of the parachute enveloped him, and seconds after that MacGammon crawled beneath the makeshift shelter and held him against his side.

"You'd better never, ever tell anyone about this," MacGammon said, his words fading as Rockdale passed out again.

CHAPTER 8

A CHIEF NEVER DRINKS; BUT IF A CHIEF DRINKS, A CHIEF never gets drunk. But, in the unlikely event a chief gets drunk, a chief never falls down. But, if the chief falls down, he will fall in such a fashion as to hide his rank insignia so others seeing him will think he is an officer. Razi leaned against the tree, the sound of the rain echoing inside his flight helmet from the heavy drops bouncing off it. Why did that initiation phrase pass through his mind? It was a ditty learned when he was initiated into the chief-petty-officer ranks years ago. Where in the hell did that come from? It was one with little relevance or reverence in today's Navy where alcohol could cost you your career, and Razi had no intention of anything stopping him from making master chief. "It's a legacy thing," he mumbled aloud, eyebrows rising slightly. What would they say if they knew he had been in the jungle two hours and was already talking to himself? It wasn't as if he could hear himself talk. He couldn't even hear himself think, with the rain pounding on his helmet like tiny hammers—never stopping. How would he remember any interesting tidbits of his conversation if he couldn't hear himself talking? Razi smiled and pressed closer against the rough bark of the tree. The water-soaked fabric of the flight suit matched closely the bark of the tree. He blinked a couple of times as he strained to tell where the flight suit left off and the bark began. The manufacturer never intended for the flight suit to be a camouflage—or did they? Maybe the color was a Vietnam-holdover thing? He glanced up for a moment, only to quickly shut his eyes as the rain blinded him across his down visor. He looked down again, thinking at least the lions wouldn't find him, if they were out looking for him. As long as this rain continued and he stayed where he was, nothing could find him.

Minutes passed without any sign of letup. Razi wondered how long this rain was going to last. Africa was the land of many things, but experiencing them wasn't in his list of things to do. They could have their monsoons and monstrous rains that flooded everything one season, only to vanish and be replaced by desert the next. Like most Westerners who visited the Dark Continent, when the rains fell, Razi retreated to his hotel and the lounge until it lifted. Sure, he had been here long enough to know about them; to see them; and, to the best of his ability, avoid them. What he hadn't done was try to assess how long they averaged because you never knew if they were going to be a short burst, over with by the time he drank his first beer; or a longer one lasting throughout the afternoon, into the evening, and continuing when you woke the next morning with a throbbing headache. This one wasn't a short one, and he couldn't stay in place forever waiting for it to end. Everything about Africa he wanted to know could be found on *National Geographic*. Let those who enjoy mud, rain, insects, man-eating— He turned his head back and forth. He had to stop thinking about lions.

He stuck his tongue out, letting the rain run onto it. Razi curled his tongue, catching the rain, and letting the water trickle into his mouth. He was proud of himself. The plastic jar of water was still full and tucked away in his survival vest. He was drinking from the sky. Razi congratulated himself. He tilted his head up slightly, even so, rivulets of rain blocked his vision, but he wasn't trying to see this time. He was satisfied with being walled in by the rain, hiding everything behind it. He doubted he could see more than twenty feet in any direction. The giant leaves of the bushes bounced from the impact, and the trail where he had been walking was covered with a couple of inches of water. He opened his mouth and was pleasantly surprised to discover the rain quickly filled it. So, for the next several minutes, Razi kept his mouth opened long enough to get a mouthful of rain, and then he swallowed.

The rain poured through the jungle canopy, hitting the trees hard and fast. Clouds, hidden by the jungle canopy, made Razi think of the rains he had once seen inside an old dirigible hanger near Elizabeth City, North Carolina. The hanger had been so huge, moisture collected near the ceiling, forming clouds, and then it would rain. That's the way it seemed here—of course, the small showers inside the dirigible hanger were nothing like this. Maybe the clouds were trapped inside the canopy; maybe they were outside. All he knew was that the rain was torrential, pounding, drowning out any noise, washing the jungle clean. Razi swallowed. His thirst was disappearing, and he was proud of thinking of this. Something else to share with them at the club as they insisted on buying him his beer. His mouth began to fill again. Here he was, drinking rain water. Rain

water pouring down so fast, washing the leaves as it . . .
Monkey shit!

His mouth slammed shut. He swallowed the water before his mind told him to spit it out. Every animal that lived
in those trees defecated in them, and here he was drinking
water that had hit every leaf above him. No telling what
diseases he was going to get. *Worms.* That would be least
of his problems. Already hatching in his stomach, giving
each other "high-fives" over having them an American. He
had heard stories of humans shitting worms over five feet
long—the scene in one of the *Alien* movies of those alien
babies eating their way out of their human hosts caused
him to jerk his head back, his helmet slamming into the
tree. "Damn, Razi," he said.

Razi stayed in that position for minutes, different sce-
narios of what could happen to him before he was rescued
dashing across his mind, no one set of thoughts overriding
the others, but not one thought had him getting out of the
jungle with all four limbs attached. After a while, he leaned
forward. For just a moment it seemed that the rain was
slackening, but it must have been his imagination, for the
bushes he could see a few moments ago on the other side
of the trail were covered by a curtain of rain. Razi sighed
as he leaned back against the trunk. He couldn't stay here
and wait for the rain to stop.

If he stayed here, Rockdale, MacGammon, and Carson
might do something dumb like decide to march out of the
jungle. If a hike through the North Carolina–like jungle of
Guinea was going to be like this, then he'd "by God" handle it. It wasn't as if he was a newbie seaman with no experience. He was a chief petty officer, and chief petty officers
never showed their insignia when they fell. Besides, Razi
had decided this being-alone crap was for someone else,
not him.

He tensed, putting his left hand flat against the tree behind him, feeling his glove snag slightly on the rough back. Razi would shove himself away from the tree and get back on the trail. The rain was more like a waterfall than rain, and it didn't look as if it was going to stop soon. When he was stationed at the old Bureau of Naval Personnel at Arlington, he drove I-95 between Washington and his hometown of Raleigh many times. Only once could he recall pulling off the expressway to shelter under a bridge because of a summer thunderstorm. Even then, he could see a quarter mile down the road. Here, he couldn't see twenty feet.

He took one last look around him. Here, he was safe from anything sneaking up on him, but once back to walking toward the others, if something didn't leap out at him, he could unexpectedly walk into them. Razi's eyes widened and his head twisted back and forth a couple of times with thoughts of man-eating lions racing toward him. He raised the survival knife in his hands, twisting it slightly, as he imaged how he'd fight the lions. As long as he had the knife, it gave him comfort, though he knew he'd have to be lucky to take one of those huge man-eaters with him. Several seconds later, he dropped the hand with the knife alongside his leg as well as the other hand. He leaned motionless against the tree. *If I get out of this alive, there are parts of this tale that no one will ever know.* Even now, those lions could be sneaking up on him, hunched forward as their rear legs tensed for the leap. Lions don't need to see their prey. They could smell him and right now, if fear could be smelled, they wouldn't even have to sniff to smell him. They could be in Rota and smell him here in Guinea. Lions were big cats, he told himself. They hated water more than he did. Those lions, if there were any, were holed up someplace such as a cave or somewhere dry, he argued to his fear. *National Geographic* only showed lions hunting when it wasn't raining.

Razi took a deep breath, looking down to change the direction of the water running off his helmet and the tempo of the pounding. His flight suit was soaked. He wiggled his toes. His socks were soaked. That was all he needed. A vision of fungus growing up his foot, wrapping around his ankle and, like runaway ivy, wrapping around his leg—and up his ass to choke that five-foot worm growing inside him filled his mind. They'd better rescue him as soon as he found his sailors. Green feet and legs were another part of this tale he promised himself he would never tell his fellow chief petty officers. Fat chance of keeping it a secret if the squadron hospital corpsman chief treated him. His underwear was matted to his body. So much for the fungus vine stopping at his legs. By God, if he had to stay here a week, he'd look like the Swamp Thing when they rescued him.

A new stream of warm rain rolled down his back. The water had sneaked under the back collar of his flight suit when he had leaned forward. He brought his head upright.

He never thought there was anything that would ever scare him, and even though he knew it was his own imagination, it was as real to him as if it was fact. He shut his eyes for a moment, taking deep, slow breaths to slow down his heartbeat, forcing himself to keep control of his thoughts. It was just that he never expected to be alone. No one expects to be alone. Most survival training had to do with two- and three-man parties, evading and escaping from pursuers. The single escape always had you in the snow-covered mountains or the woods near San Diego. Not one time did they teach him what to do against man-eating lions during survival training. He took a deep breath and let it out slowly. *Imagination.* That's all it was, he told himself, and he concentrated on his breathing in an attempt to bring his fears under control.

Too many times in his career, he had been in life-threatening situations to believe anything new could un-nerve him. He'd flown reconnaissance missions over Somalia. He'd been shot at by Iranian fighter aircraft. During Operation Enduring Freedom, he flew the first mission over Afghanistan—everyone likes to say they're unarmed and unafraid. Even when artillery bursts were exploding around the aircraft and missile contrails stretched upward from the ground reaching toward them, marking the paths of angry weapons hell-bent on destroying them, he hadn't been as unnerved as he was now. Being apprehensive over something you're familiar with is a hell of a lot different than being scared—*no, unnerved was a better word,* he thought—over something you have no knowledge of how it works or thinks. But he had seen it eat on television.

All you know is what *National Geographic* shows you on television, and the last time Razi watched a show about Africa, he recalled how the lions seemed to run on their two hind legs; their paws outstretched—humongous paws with razor-sharp claws—ripping the spinal cord right out of those buffaloes even as its front legs kept on running. His teeth grinded together. Well, maybe not that graphic, but they sure brought it down, and what did he do? He sat there in his Lazy Boy rocker, drinking his third beer, and scaring the "bejesus" out of the kids with talks about lions being loose inside the naval base at Rota, Spain. He even laughed when their youngest refused to sleep in her bed be-cause "Daddy told her lions were beneath her bed." Virginia had not been amused.

Bad joke, he thought. One he would never do again. *Damn, Cleo, I'm sorry Daddy scared you.*

Razi raised his eyes, looking through the lowered visor of the helmet. He froze. Several feet away squatted a small boy wearing short pants. He blinked several times, but the boy was still there. The boy's rib cage was molded to a tattered colorless shirt matted by the rain to the boy's body. Razi remained perfectly still, barely breathing, his back pressing hard against the tree as if trying to crawl inside it. The apparition carried an automatic weapon, a strap across his thin shoulder, and the barrel pointing downward. Water running down the stock of the automatic and off the barrel gave the weapon its own miniature waterfall. Razi had been in enough war zones to recognize an automatic weapon. He wasn't a soldier or Marine who had to know which was which. All he knew was it fired bullets and could kill him. He knew enough about handheld weapons that it wasn't a M-16. It looked like an AK-47, but Razi wasn't an expert on hand weapons. He was an aircrewman who took off, flew ten hours, landed, and went home to the missus, kids, and a cold beer.

If those sailors of his hadn't bailed out, he wouldn't be here now, facing death a few feet away. If he'd been thinking when the command to cease bailout had been given, he wouldn't be here. He'd be aboard Ranger 20 heading toward Monrovia, nursing a feathered engine, and sharing sea tales about the action over beers in the hotel lounge.

The rain bounced off the boy's small back—so thin, Razi could see the outline of the boy's spine and it didn't appear to him the boy had any meat on those arms. *How did such a reed of a boy carry such a huge weapon?* The armed lad's head moved up and down as he scanned intently the water-covered trail beneath his feet. *This is the land of boy warriors; too many boys without parents—bad combination,* thought Razi as he watched, remaining motionless except for his eyes. *No one to beat their butts when they got out of line. No one to teach them right from wrong. No time to play.*

This boy, less than ten feet from him, was one of those

heat spots the sailors from Naval Research Laboratories had detected. *Why couldn't those sailors tell from the heat signatures whether the image was an adult or a child?* Here Razi tensed, motionless, off balanced, against a tree, quickly realizing man-eating lions had become the least of his problems. This armed child was tracking him. *Him—Razi!* A few seconds passed with Razi expecting any moment for the boy to look his way. *Whatever they do in the future, don't change the color of these flight suits.* The boy stood up and quickly disappeared through the curtain of rain, heading off in the direction Razi had been heading before the rain forced him to take shelter near this tree.

He took a deep breath, relaxed slightly, when a shout from the direction of where the boy soldier had disappeared caused him to jump. *Time to go,* he told himself. Razi raised his right leg, taking a step toward a nearby bush. As he put his foot down, four other lads raced out of the rain on one side and disappeared into the rain on the other side. All of them running where Razi should have been going. No, this jungle was nothing like the woods of North Carolina.

Razi figured the tracker would eventually figure he hadn't continued onward. They'd come back. He had seconds before they started retracing their tracks. He took a deep breath, expecting to hear bullets ripping into him at any time, and quickly eased around the tree, trying to keep his back against it. This time, the heavy brush growing close to his path didn't play on his imagination. False fears fell away against real ones. Razi stumbled, thankful the rain hid the noise. If he could put something along with distance between him and those armed kids, he'd be okay.

They were looking for him. He didn't need the cryptologic skills of his rating to figure that out. It wasn't as if they were young boys trouncing off to a 7-Eleven for their ma and pa. He may not understand this mumbo-jumbo language of theirs, but he figured rightly that the shouting was to tell the others that Razi had disappeared. Disappear was just what he intended to do. The rain should hide his tracks. He discovered himself praying for the rain to continue, when only minutes ago he was wishing for it to stop. *Lord, keep the rain coming; the harder, the better.*

The first row of brush closed behind him, but when he took his second step, a limb whipped back, causing him to shut his eyes as it slapped across his visor. That would have hurt, if the rain hadn't forced him to put the helmet back on. He may have disliked the monsoon rainstorm that caused him to take refuge against the tree, but the Almighty must have been looking over him, for this rain saved his life.

Razi pushed his foot through a tangle of vines and when he leaned forward to put his weight on it, something gave, and in the next instant he was sliding down a steep hill, his helmet *rat-a-tat-tating* off the roots and rocks along the way. His helmet bounced off something huge, rattling his teeth, and bringing tears to his eyes, but Razi didn't have time to think about it, and he sure as hell wasn't going to run his tongue between his teeth and have it bit off. The incline dipped sharply, and Razi screamed once as he picked up speed. A moment later, his butt slammed into the bottom of the muddy incline where momentum catapulted him forward to where the ground abruptly ended, sending him tumbling into the air as if he had reached the end of a slide in some godforsaken playground. His stomach dropped as his forward momentum stopped, and he started rolling head-over-heels on his way down.

"Christ!" he shouted, the word both a prayer and a cry, the rain muffling the shout.

His body twisted in midair. Over and over, he kept

repeating the word, "Christ" as he fell. There was nothing beneath him. It was as if he was in the middle of a water tunnel. Water above him, water below him, water beside him, and he couldn't see a damn thing but water. Was he dead, and this was his hell?

At the last second, when his tumble brought him face down for a moment, he saw a body of water below him before he rolled over, hitting the surface on his back, splashing through, thrashing beneath the water. Crocodiles replaced the boy soldiers who had replaced the *lions. A chief petty officer never drinks* . . .

Razi's head popped through the surface of the water. His mouth open wide, and he gasped deep breaths—the rain churning the water around him. *God, if you're trying to scare to me to death, you're doing a damn fine job.*

He was in a river or stream or something that moved because the water pulled him along with a steady flow. There were lots of rivers in Africa. Some stayed wet year round. His head bobbed on the surface, fighting for air against the water that choked him with each breath. The current slowed, giving Razi time to check his aches, satisfying himself in a few seconds that he had no broken bones. He had a lot of sore ones and tomorrow was going to be one painful—

Piranhas flashed into his mind for a moment before he recalled they lived in South America, not Africa. *National Geographic* was becoming invaluable to his well-being. A flash of green to his right caught his attention, and the waterlogged Razi turned and swam toward it, kicking his boot-laden feet to stay afloat. As he neared, a flat area devoid of vegetation emerged from the cover of rain. He changed direction and swam toward it. Better to walk out of the river than have to fight the bush. In North Carolina, water moccasins preferred the waters beneath vegetation that overlapped the waters. He didn't see any reason snakes in Africa would be any different. Other than that they had one that could swallow you whole. He picked up the pace.

A couple of minutes later, his hand touched bottom, the flight glove sinking into the mud. Razi pulled his hand free and stood, his flight boots sinking, nearly causing him to splash forward, but they only sunk into the mud a couple of inches. Struggling against the sucking mud, the current, and the rain, he walked the remaining few feet to the natural ramp leading up out of the water. When his last step took him out of the water, Razi stopped, leaned forward, and put both hands on his knees, taking time to catch his breath. The rain seemed to be slackening. Around the area, several rough-hewed fallen trees and limbs lay scattered, probably washed ashore by floods. He glanced ahead. A steep incline led up to where a six-foot-high embankment waited. He would have to climb it. *Shouldn't be too hard.* He clawed his way up the churned and muddy incline to a flat area just below the embankment.

Razi straightened and unzipped his survival vest, removing the compass. He let the needle settle on north and then glanced in the direction he needed to go. He was sure he had come out on the right side of the river so it wasn't between him and his sailors. All he had to do was get on higher ground away from the river. He had to be on the same side, because if he wasn't, then Razi would never find Rockdale, MacGammon, or Carson. He could wander forever until something happened to him. No one would ever know what became of Chief Petty Officer Razi.

The rain picked up in tempo again. Razi accepted it as fate—a sign that he was meant to find his sailors and bring them home safely. Of course, if he didn't, then who was going to find and bring *him* home safely. He zipped the compass back in the survival vest, realizing for the first time as he zipped up the pouch that he no longer held the survival knife in his right hand. Instinctively, he glanced behind him at the water, knowing somewhere between the tree he had been hugging and the mud where he stood, he had lost the only weapon he had. The knife wasn't designed for fighting, but it did provide a small measure of security. No way he could have moved the knife fast enough to stop AK-47 bullets.

He looked at the embankment facing him and walked toward it. He had to move. That six-foot embankment might mark where the river crested when the rains came, and he didn't want to be here when a flash flood raced down this valley. He thought, *How far did I fall? It could have been tens of feet or hundreds for all I know. I was too busy praying, breathing, and trying not to ruin my underwear to keep track.*

Stepping up to the embankment, Razi reached his hand out and touched it. Rotten humus and wet leaves covered the six-foot-high barrier. This wasn't going to be easy— too slippery. He looked for a vine, a root, anything to hold onto to help him climb. A thin tree grew at the very edge of the embankment. Razi could probably jump and grab it at the bottom of the trunk, but he wasn't sure it would hold his weight. He lifted one foot and then the other, watching the water and mud swirl around them. Then again, the worst that could happen was it could come loose, and he'd fall back onto the gray-brown muck beneath him. He would have to jump, grab it, and kind of crab walk up the embankment. If it didn't hold him, then it'd be a dirty but soft landing.

Razi took a deep breath, his hands resting on his hips, as he surveyed the embankment, looking for an easier solution. Looking left, a slight motion drew his attention toward the river. He turned his head for a better look. Didn't

see anything. Realized the number of logs and old trees
were more numerous than he thought. Maybe he could
shove one of them over here and use it like a step or a ladder. He turned back to the problem of the embankment
when several of the logs rose from the ground and moved
toward him. The motion caught his attention. They weren't
logs. They were African crocodiles. A second later, Razi was
on top of the embankment; unaware of how he climbed it.
The slim tree was on the mud below. Four crocodiles looked
up at him, their mouths opening and closing. *Yes, Virginia,
there is a Santa Claus and there be monsters under your
bed, too.*

Razi took a deep breath, threw his head back, and
roared at the top of his voice, pounding his chest. Tears ran
down his cheeks, but damn it, he wasn't scared any longer.
Screw you, Africa. Bring it on!

"THIS IS WHERE I LEAVE YOU, DICK," THOMASTON SAID,
looking down at Admiral Holman. The rain pelted the
awning above them, forcing them to raise their voices as
they talked.

Admiral Dick Holman reached out and shook the hand
of the interim president of Liberia. "I hope you understand
that I have little choice but to rescue those downed aircrewman, General."

Behind retired General Thomaston, Dick saw his chief
of staff, Captain Leo Upmann, step out of the small building across the open area that separated the two buildings.
Upmann was returning from Airport Operations, a floor
down from the airport tower on top of the building. Holman and Thomaston had commandeered the only waiting
room at Monrovia International Airport, only to have Holman step outside for a cigar.

Thomaston nodded. "I would probably do the same if I was still active-duty Army, but as the head of the Republic of Liberia, I have to think of the political side of it."

Dick politely smiled. Politics, politics, politics. Now, there's a profession that could use a rise in unemployment. He dropped the cigar and ground it out in the mud. "Definitely makes you appreciate the small amount of politics we have in the military when you jump into the career field of politics. Domestic, national, international . . . worries within worries within categories." He shook his head. "Can't say I envy you this job you've taken."

Thomaston nodded without smiling. "It is different, which is why I have to formally forbid you from landing inside Guinea. The bilateral agreement between your country and Guinea for flying reconnaissance missions was predicated on Liberia ensuring that no Americans would violate their territorial sovereignty by putting troops on the ground."

Holman nodded. He had a lot of respect for Thomaston, but he found it hard to reconcile this apparent double standard of loyalty the retired general had developed. "I understand completely, Dan, but that agreement is open to interpretation. I don't think a rescue party can be construed as putting troops on the ground. Just as surely, the Guineans can't put four men bailing out of an aircraft struck by a missile over their territory in the same category."

Thomaston shrugged. "I wish I knew, but my people tell me the Guinean ambassador has scheduled an urgent appointment with me later tonight. I will put him off until tomorrow afternoon, Dick. That may give you time to extract those sailors. After that, I may have little choice but to ban flights that cross Liberia's northern border area."

"Admiral, General," Captain Upmann said as he approached the two.

Dick returned his chief of staff's salute. "What'd you find out?"

"Thirty minutes out, Admiral. Number-four engine feathered. Temperatures are within acceptable range. Low-oil light flickering on number-three engine. Hydraulics seems to be holding. They're dumping fuel and want to make a straight-in approach for landing."

"If they have to feather the number-three engine, that's going to complicate them making Monrovia. It will leave the aircraft flying on the two engines on their port side only."

"Feather? Port? Dumping fuel, I can understand," said Thomaston.

"Feather is when you shut down an engine while in flight and lock it in place. Port is—"

"Port is to the sailor as left is to us old soldiers," Thomaston answered. "I remembered what port is after I asked the question. Feather is a new term for me."

Upmann continued, "They may have to feather number-three before they reach here. The VQ-2 pilot has reduced airspeed, trying to keep number-three engine on line and reduce the resistance against the airframe."

"If they have to feather the engine, does that mean they'll crash?" Thomaston asked.

Upmann shrugged. "I'm a surface-warfare officer."

"It could. Right now, the aircraft is dumping fuel— reducing weight to reduce drag. There are a lot of factors that go into making that determination, and the best people to make it are on board that aircraft." Holman pointed at the sky. "Yeah, the best to make that determination are up there."

"Yes, sir. They are dumping excess fuel. That fuel will evaporate—"

A couple of buildings away, sirens drowned out Upmann, causing the three men to cover their ears. A second later, two fire trucks roared out of the airport fire station, heading toward the runway to join other trucks already in position. The three stood watching, unable to talk while the sirens blared so closely. A couple of minutes later as the decibel level from the sirens lowered, the two fire trucks reached the landing end of the runway, and joined the two other fire trucks already there. Holman glanced up at the sky. The rain must be easing for them to be able to see the end of the runway. On the tops of the two trucks already at the end of the runway stood firemen dressed in silver-colored reflective fire suits, manning foam hoses. Foam was the fire-fighting weapon of choice for any gasoline or petrol fire. All water did was spread the fire as burning petrol rode atop of it like an unpaid passenger, enjoying the ride while wreaking havoc for everything around it.

"That would be the Liberian volunteers," Thomaston said loudly, above the fading sirens. "Thankfully, the U.S. Air Force is still providing civilian firemen, but eventually that will go away. We have been training Liberians to replace them. Gave a contract to a nonprofit company out of Savannah, Georgia-Southside or something like that—to teach our firefighters and medical first-responders how to do their jobs. Another year, and I expect Liberians to be able to do for themselves what we need America to help us do today. We need to be fully independent before the unforeseen developments of tomorrow jerk the cornucopia of American aid and support we're enjoying today out from under us. It isn't as if Liberia can expect America to be there everytime we need it."

Holman's brows wrinkled at Thomaston's words.

The *chop-chop* of rotors on approaching helicopters grew as the fire trucks cut their sirens. Holman shielded his eyes as he searched the skies. That would be the Marine Corps Company that the colonel promised. The Air Force helicopters were gearing up for the search-and-rescue down at the other end of the runway. The Air Force was trained to do this, but in the event something happened and they failed to make the mission, Holman wanted a backup. He did not intend to leave his sailors in the jungles longer than he had to.

The Air Force commander, Colonel Hightower, said his two birds would be airborne at dawn to bring back the Navy aircrewman. He had tried to convince the Air Force to go this afternoon, but Hightower was insistent that they needed to reconfigure their birds, and if they got to the bailout site and were unable to find the flyers, they'd have less time to search. He didn't agree with the argument, but the four-star general at United States Air Force European command did.

Thomaston lowered his hand from his eyes. "I'm going now, Dick. I do not want to know what your plans are, but officially, I must ask you not to attempt to rescue your downed aircrew. We will formally ask the Guineans to do it. It is one thing to fly over another country's land, and another when you put boots on the ground without their permission. Good day." Without waiting for a reply, Lieutenant General, retired, Thomaston walked toward the long black Mercedes-Benz waiting to take him to the palace.

"What was that about?" Upmann asked.

"He's caught between the rock of politics, the hard place of being an American, and unable to decide where his loyalties lie. If we go into Guinea without his knowledge and bring out our sailors, then he can bluster truthfully that he told us not to and he never knew our intentions."

"I would think he knows."

"If he doesn't, then he never deserved to be a three-star general in our armed forces."

Upmann handed Dick a soda. "From how he talks, I'm not sure he did deserve it."

"I try not to prejudge people, Captain Upmann."

Upmann drew back in mock shock and then leaned close to Holman. "Sorry, Admiral. Just wanted to make sure it was you."

"Thanks. How much longer until they land?"

"Twenty-five minutes, Admiral. I would suggest we go over to the American Liaison Office and wait. When the aircraft lands, that's where Naval Intelligence has asked the crew be brought."

The two walked along the front edges of the small white buildings lining the runway, keeping close to them as shelter from the rain, and running from one to the other. Someone at one time had slapped white paint over the buildings, but years of weather and neglect had left them with holes, broken windows, and cracked floors, giving each building a unique appearance. Otherwise, the buildings, one after the other, would have been almost identical.

Across the two runways and taxiways, several helicopters and small jet trainers sat idle, their sides painted with Liberian marks. One bomb would take out the entire Liberian Air Force, but why would you take out something that was no threat to you? Upmann kept up a running dialogue as the two moved, apprising Admiral Dick Holman of the conditions of the aircrew; the aircraft; and the four men who were on the ground in Guinea.

The idea that a chief petty officer jumped for no other reason than loyalty to his sailors—Holman took a deep breath. Things like that made him proud to be an American warrior. No greater value can a leader have than to risk his or her own life for the lives of their troops. He and Admiral Duncan James, head of the Navy's SEALs, were talking once about people moving through their careers, climbing that ladder behind them. People who would one day stand where they stood today, making life-and-death decisions. You reach the twilight of a military career wondering about the caliber of the folks following you, and you're proud when you reach the conclusion that they are the best of the best. Both of them had reached this same conclusion—before their third mile. The military, not just the Navy, was filled with stories such as this, lending confidence that when the old-timers of today were relieved by the newcomers of tomorrow, the military was being passed into great, confident hands to defend the Constitution of the United States of America. Next year, when Rear Admiral–lower-half Xavier Bennett relieved him, Dick Holman would leave a navy manned by some of the greatest people America had to offer. People such as this chief petty officer, Wilbur Razi. Holman stepped in a puddle, the water cascading above the top of and pouring into his shoe. He should have worn his flight suit and boots.

Somewhere out there in the jungle was this chief petty officer, hurrying toward his sailors, unafraid—doing his duty, and risking his life for his sailors. Dick promised himself to see that the man received recognition for this act of heroism. Chief Razi must be one brave soul to leap out of an aircraft when he didn't have to do it. Dick shook his head slightly. The idea of being alone in the jungle would be terrifying to him, but he had no doubt this chief petty officer was a lot braver than he'd be in the same situation.

The rain picked up again as they dashed between buildings. Stopping briefly beneath an eave, Upmann and Holman could barely see the next building. Dick heard Upmann talking, but he couldn't make out what his chief of staff was saying. The noise of the rain pelting the tin roof of the building drowned out everything around them. His hand hit against his pants. Dick looked. His khakis

were soaked, but he consoled himself with the understanding that in Africa, what is wet one moment is steam
dried the next.

They kept moving, walking under the eaves, then running between the buildings, until they reached the last
building, where a couple of petty officers stood under the
far end of the long eave, smoking cigarettes, and leaning
against the outside wall in protection against the rain. They
snapped to attention and saluted when they recognized the
Commander, Amphibious Squadron Two, emerge through
the curtain of rain. Dick nodded as he ducked through the
doorway. Inside would be Captain Mary Davidson, his intelligence officer, arranging for the debriefs. She had wanted
them trucked back to the USS *Boxer* for the debriefing, but
Dick knew what would be going through the minds of the
flight crew once they landed.

The first thing they'd want to know would be what rescue efforts were being mounted and how soon could they
join the search. *So it has ever been and so it shall ever be.*
Leaving a shipmate in harm's way was not the Navy way.

ROCKDALE OPENED HIS EYES. AN EXPANSE OF WHITENESS
blinded him. Shocked, he involuntarily sucked in a
deep breath, coming up short, as something covered his
mouth; blocking off the air. Just as quickly it was gone
and he could breath again.

"Christ, Rocky, what the hell you trying to do? Drown
and suffocate yourself?

Rolling his eyes upward, he saw a hand holding the
parachute away from his face.

"About time you woke up."

Rockdale turned toward the voice. MacGammon was
squatting beside him, one hand holding the parachute away

from Rockdale's face so he could breath and the other hand stretched overhead like a tent pole.

"How long have I been out?"

"That's getting to be a common question," MacGammon griped, shaking his head. "About forty minutes, if you must know, and my arms are getting tired, so it would help if you would sit up and push the parachute away from your own face instead of me having to do it."

Rockdale reached up and pushed the parachute away from his face, keeping one hand up to hold the parachute. MacGammon's hand disappeared.

"Whew! That feels great," MacGammon said. "You don't know how hard it is to hold your hands up over your head for a long time."

"Thanks," Rockdale said. He looked down. Water ran around his legs. It reached the top of MacGammon's steel-toed flight boots.

"You don't have to thank me," MacGammon protested. "If you hadn't woke up when you did, I was going to have to throw the parachute off, and we'd gotten soaked."

Rockdale touched his chest, his legs, and arms. "Seems like we're soaked already, Mac."

"What are you talking about? Oh, you! Well, you were laying down in it, and there wasn't much I could do to get you out of it."

Rockdale looked up at the parachute. Nylon parachutes weren't waterproof, but they could shelter you from the bulk of the water. The saturated parachute was folding around their hands.

"I don't think this is going to work much longer," Rockdale said. "Maybe we should move nearer the tree."

MacGammon shook his head. "Listen, shipmate," he said, his voice sharp. "I've been doing this for over forty minutes while you slept. Don't come awake and start telling me what I should or shouldn't do. This is keeping us dry—keeping me dry somewhat and, besides, these monsoons don't last long."

Rockdale opened his mouth to reply at the same time the rain stopped. "I guess that settles it, doesn't it."

MacGammon's eyes narrowed and without replying, the stocky sailor from New Jersey pulled the parachute off, hand over hand.

Freed of the soaked parachute, the two stood. Rockdale was relieved to find the white spots of earlier didn't return, though a slight nausea still persisted. He probably had a slight concussion, but this wasn't the time to throw up his hands and give up. It wasn't as if he could call 911 from here in the middle of nowhere.

"We've got to find Stetson," Rockdale said above the sound of the rain, which had started falling again.

MacGammon began to gather up the parachute. "Let's roll the parachute first. We'll want to take it with us."

Rockdale shook his head. "It needs to dry out, Mac. Why don't we stretch it across the clearing so that when the rain stops, the heat can dry it? It'll serve as a marker as we try to find—"

MacGammon continued rolling the wet nylon. "Right! We leave it here to mark a spot that we won't even be able to see once we've gone twenty yards in any direction." He stopped and with raised arm, rotated it across the area. "Look for yourself. There is nothing here but plants, trees, vines, and all that shit a jungle brings with it. You can't see a damn thing. If you hadn't been moaning, I might never have found you."

"You mean you might never have come hunting."

MacGammon dropped his arm. "That's not what I mean and it's not what I said." He returned to his chore of rolling the saturated parachute. "Sure, it's wet—pretty wet, if you ask me, but if we leave it here, we may need it, and then where will we be if we can't find it."

Rockdale started to object but then thought better of it. They were both shook up over the bailout and regardless of what happened, the two of them had to stay together until rescue arrived tomorrow.

Rockdale unzipped his survival vest and pulled out his small pint of water.

MacGammon looked up as he was double-folding the parachute. "I wouldn't do that, Rocky," he said, looking back at what he was doing and away from Rockdale.

Rockdale looked up.

"If you have a concussion, which you do by the way, all that water is going to do is make you puke." MacGammon tucked the folded parachute under his left arm, reached inside his right flight-suit pocket, and pulled out a handful of cords. "Didn't they teach you anything at survival school? First twenty-four hours, you don't drink your water." MacGammon put the ends of the cords in his mouth, taking one out and quickly tying it around the folding parachute.

Rockdale screwed the top back down on the water. MacGammon was right, as much as he hated to admit it. He thought he preferred the griping, whining-malcontent, nincompoop MacGammon than someone who might actually know something.

"There," MacGammon said, holding up the parachute.

How did he manage to compact a wet parachute into a tightly wound roll?

"We can go look for Carson. But why don't we try the radio before we do." MacGammon held up his left arm, pushed the watchstrap around, so the watch face was rightside up. "It's twenty after the hour, but what the hell. If Carson is awake and thinking, he'll have his radio on listening."

Rockdale pulled his radio out and made several calls. The two of them waited anxiously for several minutes before accepting the fact that either: one, Carson was unable to answer; or two, Carson's radio was turned off.

"Was Carson to our left or right when we were coming down?" MacGammon asked.

"He was to our right. I was directly in front of you and he was off to our right."

"Then we need to search at a ninety-degree angle to our trees."

Rockdale's eyes brightened. "I see what you mean. If I landed in front of you in that tree," he turned facing the tree from where he had fallen and pointed. "And you landed in this one." Rockdale jerked his thumb toward the one where MacGammon landed. "Then he must have come down in that direction," Rockdale pointed right.

"Wow, Rocky. You're not as dumb you pretend to be."

"And, you're not so dumb yourself, for a nobody from New Jersey."

MacGammon grinned. "Don't push your luck, you Southerners are all alike. Still fighting the Civil War and making fun of those who won it."

"I'm from Maryland."

"Maryland—Georgia—Kentucky. It don't matter. They're all south of Jersey City. Well, should we go do this and see if we can find Carson before he goes crazy with worrying about us?"

Rockdale nodded.

MacGammon pulled out his compass and took a reading. "Let's go."

A moment later, Rockdale fell into step behind MacGammon as the man from New Jersey tromped off, glancing down once more at the compass as he pushed aside the bush blocking their path. Hopefully, they were correct, and somewhere in this direction Stetson had landed. Rockdale followed three or four feet behind MacGammon, who treated each bush, vine, limb, and decaying obstacle as minor inconveniences. He marched forward as if he was on a stroll through a city park. Even Rockdale knew that jungles, much like the woods of western Maryland, were filled with wild beasts. With the exception of bears, wolves, and the occasional panther, Maryland was safe, and you always had "pound 77" to raise the police. Here there was neither a "pound 77" nor 911. All they had was what they had. And MacGammon walked as if there were no one or nothing around except the two of them, protected by the magical cloak of the rain and a compass showing them where to head.

MacGammon was right. Taking everything with them rather than creating a base camp was the right way to do it.

Seconds turned into minutes which turned into more minutes. Rockdale glanced back once during their movement to discover their path had disappeared behind the jungle bushes and vines. If MacGammon had listened to him and left the parachute behind, it would have been lost forever, and he'd have had to put up with MacGammon's bitching. For that alone, he was glad MacGammon had taken it.

MacGammon stopped, causing Rockdale to nearly bump into him.

"What?"

"Shhh," MacGammon said, raising his finger to his lips. "Listen."

Rockdale turned his head from side to side. "Listen for what?"

"It sounded like moaning—"

"Moaning?"

MacGammon motioned downward with his hand. "Just listen for a moment. It sounds like you did when I found you."

Rockdale listened, but try as he might he couldn't seem to separate the sound from the returning noises of the jungle. They rode and rolled over each other, intermixed with the hot, humid breeze that wafted through the leaves. Small patches of fog, from evaporating moisture, had begun to fill the spaces between the bushes. Africa was a beautiful, dangerous place. If you didn't like the weather, wait a minute, it would change.

A cry came from their right, and in the next instant, Rockdale followed after MacGammon, who was bolting through the bushes, slapping them aside, as he hurried in the direction from where the cry came.

CHAPTER 9

"HE'S STILL ALIVE," MACGAMMON SAID, LOOKING UP AT Carson.

Rockdale pulled a handkerchief from a pocket and wiped the sweat away from his eyes. Carson hung by his harness straps from the parachute. Thick bushes and bramble stopped the two sailors from approaching Carson any closer from below.

"If he hadn't moaned, we would never have found him," Rockdale said, stuffing the handkerchief back into the pocket. "Now how in the hell are we going to get him down?"

"But he isn't moaning now. All he's doing is swaying a little in the wind. Maybe he's dead?"

"And maybe he's not. Even if he's dead— Stop it, Mac! We've got to get him down, whether he's dead or alive."

"I don't see how we're going to get him down,"

MacGammon protested. "He's at least forty feet off the ground, and nowhere near anything we can climb out—"

"Stop it, Mac. Just stop it."

"And to get under him, we're going to have to chop our way through this mess."

"You know. Everything with you is no. Everything is too hard. Everything is so fucked up. Just stop it."

"Rocky, you're one fucked up mother, you know," MacGammon replied, shaking his head. "You know what you need?—"

Without thinking, Rockdale pushed the smaller man, causing MacGammon to stumble.

"Hey, man! This ain't the time and place for you to start a fight with me." MacGammon took two steps forward, slammed both hands against Rockdale's chest, and shoved the larger man. "Just don't fuck with me!"

Rockdale stumbled backward a couple of steps, the anger leaving him as easily as it had taken hold. "Sorry, Mac. You're right. I don't know what came over me." Rockdale tossed his helmet onto the jungle floor and ran a hand through his thick black hair. "Must be—"

"Must be the heat? The rain? How about us realizing we're alone in the middle of a motherfucking jungle with no McDonald's or even a Wal-Mart nearby. Man, you couldn't ask for a clearer sign of being lost." MacGammon laughed, stepped forward, and slapped Rockdale on the arms. "You da man here, Rocky. Just keep your cool. Last thing I want to do is to have to carry both you and Stetson on my shoulders out of this mess."

"Whadaya mean carry both of us?" Rockdale asked, slapping MacGammon on the shoulder. "Any carrying to do, I'll probably have to do it."

MacGammon pointed up at Carson. "Him, I'd have to carry because he's medical, and you, because if I have to beat your ass, you're going to be medical, too," he said in a dry voice.

"So how do we get him down?" Rockdale asked, his hands braced on his hips, watching their shipmate swinging above them as if some giant had hung him up out of reach.

MacGammon took a deep breath. "You're right, we're going to have to figure out how to get him down. It looks as if he's unconscious, so it ain't gonna be easy. Maybe we should circle him and see what the terrain is like." MacGammon tossed his flight helmet near Rockdale's.

Rockdale's eyebrows bunched. "Why? You think maybe we'll find a better way into him?"

MacGammon shrugged. "I don't know. Maybe we'll think of something if we're doing something, even if whatever we're doing doesn't make sense. My dad always said it was better to be doing something than doing nothing."

Rockdale nodded. "Okay, I'll go this way, and you go that way," he said, pointing to the left. "You are right about one thing. Anything is better than standing here watching him."

A few moments later MacGammon shouted, "Hey, Rocky, can you see me?"

Rockdale stopped. He figured he was at a ninety-degree angle to Carson from where he and MacGammon started. "Raise your hand!"

A hand broke above the brush on the other side of Carson and nearly exactly opposite to where Rockdale stood. "Yeah, I see you, Mac. Keeping walking and keep Carson positioned off your right shoulder. That should keep you in a circle."

"What're you talking about, Rocky? I can barely see him because of this jungle crap. I ain't tall like you and him."

Rockdale ignored the comment and continued to circle. *How are we going to get Carson down?* The moaning was what drew them to their lost shipmate, and, so far, he hadn't seen anything that would convince him MacGammon was wrong about Carson being dead. *Maybe the moans were his death rattle. Maybe Carson was in such pain, he cycled between consciousness and unconsciousness.* He looked up at Carson. The crewman's hands hung limply down the sides of his flight suit; fingers limp too. The flight boots drooped, the steel toes pointing down. Rockdale stopped, wiped the sweat away from his eyes again, and pulled the matted, wet flight suit away from his body for a moment. Small patches of isolated fog hung beneath the bushes where the earlier rain continued to evaporate from the wave of hot, humid air rolling across the jungle. He pulled the left sleeve away, feeling a slight coolness as the fabric lifted off his arm. Maybe he and MacGammon—and Carson—would never be dry again. Maybe God, or whoever the supreme being is, had decided this was their hell. Never dry again. Maybe when the rain evaporated, perspiration replaced it, and when the morning and afternoon rains came, they washed the sweat away for a while. He released the sleeve, watching as it quickly settled back onto his arm. The survival vest trapped the water and sweat beneath it.

He turned his attention away from his flight suit and back to Carson. Squinting, he eyed the harness straps between Carson's legs. If they didn't rescue the man soon, those straps would act like a tourniquet, if they weren't already, and stop the blood flowing to the legs. The legs and feet would start to die without blood. Carson's fingers looked as if they moved. He leaned forward, concentrating on the fingers. They moved again.

The bushes looked more accessible here. Rockdale

pushed them aside and started working himself closer to where Carson was hanging. Ten feet closer, he stopped and stared, his hand over his eyes. Yes, he was right. The man's fingers were moving. Not fast or often, but they were moving.

"Mac! He's alive!" Rockdale shouted. He jumped around, elated over seeing Carson move. In the back of his mind there had been this moronic thought of what they would do if Carson was dead. You couldn't keep a dead body with you in this heat. They would have had to bury him. Out here. With no headstone, and little chance of ever returning to find the body.

"Well, what'd you expect him to be? It ain't as if he's hit anything other than the trees when he came down. It ain't as if we found him because he was quiet!"

"No! But, you said—"

"I said he might be dead. I didn't say he was dead, and don't you go putting words into my mouth."

"His fingers are moving." Rockdale's head moved side to side as he tried to spot MacGammon.

"That's good news, Rocky. Tell him to reach up and un-snap his harness and quit fiddling around!"

"I don't think he's conscious."

Rockdale continued to stare at his dangling shipmate. After a few minutes, Rockdale cupped his mouth and shouted, "We'll get you down, Stetson! It'll take a few minutes, but be patient. We're here, and we'll get you down."

Nearby, bushes rustled, startling Rockdale, and causing him to jump back. The bushes parted and MacGammon emerged. "To hell with walking around him. Who's idea was that? And how in the hell are we going to get him down?" MacGammon cupped his mouth and turned toward Carson. "Carson, you asshole, you'd better not be goofing off and making us worry for nothing. If you ain't, then be patient for more than a bit while we figure out how to get you down!"

"Yours."

"Yours what?"

"Your idea to walk around him."

"Next time I come up with something that doesn't make sense, do what you always do and tell me it's a sucky idea."

"His fingers are moving," Rockdale said, pointing up.

"I see them. That doesn't mean shit, Rocky. Means he's alive, or those fingers could be moving with the wind."

"What wind? Damn, Mac, you are one dispassionate mother!"

"Yeah, yeah, yeah. You keep throwing those big words at me and one of these days, I'm gonna recognize one of them." MacGammon shrugged. "Okay, he's alive. You win. But, either he regains consciousness, or we're going to have to cut—"

The two aircrewmen looked at each other and together said, "Cut!"

"A long stick," Rockdale offered. "That's what we need. Something—" He stopped, bent down, and started shoving the bushes apart.

"To tie a survival knife on the end of it, and we can use it—" MacGammon started looking in the other direction.

"Like we use a tree trimmer back home." Rockdale retraced his steps toward the nearest tree.

Five minutes later Rockdale held up a long, crooked limb nearly twenty feet long. "I've got one!" he shouted.

MacGammon dashed through the bushes until he reached Rockdale. Rockdale held the limb out. "What'd you think?"

"It would never sell at Home Depot," MacGammon replied, reaching out and taking the limb. "But, you're right," he said with a smile. "It'll suit our purpose."

Rockdale dropped to his knees and pulled his survival knife out. He aligned it alongside the narrow end of the limb. "Here, hold it while I tie it."

With MacGammon holding the knife steady, Rockdale wrapped cord around the handle, binding it to the limb.

"It's not going to be long enough, you know?"

"I know," Rockdale answered. He looked at the tree. "I think one of us is going to have to climb the tree and shimmy out close enough to the parachute to cut the lines."

"Let me see if I have this right. One of us is going to climb the tree and slide out there on one of those limbs so we can cut him free."

Rockdale stood and hefted the makeshift tree trimmer. He pushed it up and down a few times.

"Rocky, that someone has to be me. I'm the lightest of us two."

Rockdale stopped hoisting the tree trimmer and looked at MacGammon. "No, I'll do it," he said quietly.

"Man, you're so full of bullshit, you're eyes are brown. Ain't no way you're gonna climb that tree. It wasn't four hours ago, you were coasting in and out of dreamland. Be just my luck to let you do this and I find myself squatting here going 'tsk tsk' while looking at what used to be you, splattered all over the ground, and Carson still up there playing swingman." MacGammon reached over and jerked the tree trimmer from Rockdale. "I'm the only goddamn healthy one of us," he said and then quickly mumbled, "And I'm not feeling too good myself."

Rockdale reached over and wrapped a hand around the makeshift trimmer. MacGammon jerked it. "No!" Rockdale held his hand out, motioning downward. "You can do it, Mac. I'm not trying to take it away from you, but you can't climb the tree and hold onto this thing at the same time. I'll stand—"

"See! I told you so. I knew you wanted me to go." MacGammon grinned. He reached over and pushed Rockdale's mouth closed. "Shut your mouth before one of those African flies that put you asleep flies in it."

"But—"

"I'm just kidding, Rocky. It only makes sense for me to go." MacGammon let go of the trimmer, turned, and put his hands on his hips. He scrutinized the tree, his eyes traveling upward as if mapping out his climb.

"I can hoist you to that low limb."

"You're going to have to. Otherwise, I'm going to have to make like one of those cartoon characters and run up the side of it. I don't think I can do that."

The two stood at the base of the tree. Rockdale watched quietly as MacGammon took his survival vest off, folding it beside the tree. Rockdale noticed the flight suit was a darker, wetter green where the survival vest had been.

MacGammon nodded. "Don't forget where we left our helmets. We'll need them tonight."

MacGammon took his gloves off and tucked them into the leg pockets of his flight suit. "Can climb better without them on."

"You ready?"

"I'm as ready as I'll ever be."

Rockdale cupped his hands, the fingers interlaced. Just as MacGammon stuck his left foot into the hand cradle, moans brought them up short. MacGammon brought his foot down and both men looked, staring quietly at Carson. The swaying airman's head came up slowly. The visor was still down on the dangling sailor's helmet, hiding the face from the nose up.

"Carson! Carson! You okay?" Rockdale shouted, his hands cupped around his mouth. Moans answered him.

"Stetson! You son of a bitch! Wake up and answer us! If you can't answer us, then at least unlatch your chest strap."

Carson's head rose and turned several times. It seemed to wobble on his neck. Rockdale pulled his handkerchief out and wiped his forehead and face. Carson must have hit his head coming through the trees. For him to be out this long, his concussion had to be worse than the one he suffered falling out of the tree.

Rockdale and MacGammon waved their arms over their heads, both shouting at Carson, "Over here. We're over here."

Carson's head swiveled until he looked in their direction. Rockdale saw Carson's lips moving, but neither man could hear what he was saying. "You hear anything?"

"His lips are moving."

"Listen."

Rockdale shut his eyes, concentrating on listening.

"We should move closer."

Rockdale raised his hand, motioning for MacGammon to be quiet.

Carson was saying something. He could barely hear the man. He needed to be closer, but Rockdale was afraid if he took the time to move, Carson might lapse back into unconsciousness. Whatever the man was saying, it was one word, and Carson was repeating the same word over and over.

"What's he saying?" MacGammon asked.

"I'm not sure. It sounds like 'wa.' "

"Water! That's what he's saying. Stetson wants water." MacGammon cupped his hands to his lips. "Stetson, you bastard. We're coming. You just hang in there, buddy." He turned to Rockdale. "Okay, give me a hand.

A moment later, the smaller man hung by his arms from

the lowest limb. MacGammon swung his legs, bringing them
up and through his arms. His legs wrapped across the top
of the limb. A second more, and he was lying prone on top
of the limb.

"Hand me the cutter."

Rockdale lifted the makeshift cutter and held it until
MacGammon grabbed it and pulled it up. "I'm going to go
stand near Stetson."

"Yeah, you go do that, but when I cut him down, don't
try to catch him or do anything heroic."

Rockdale was surprised. He had thought of grabbing
Carson when he was cut free, knowing it would knock him
down, but that it might also save his buddy from any further injuries. He opened his mouth to say something.

"Don't even try to deny it, Rocky. You're the hero type;
not the survival type." MacGammon pushed himself up
into a near-squatting position, his body pointing away from
the base of the tree. "This may be a jungle, but there's not
much difference between the rules for this jungle and the
rules of the jungle in Newark, where I grew up."

"Newark? Isn't that in Georgia?"

" 'Newark? Isn't that in Georgia,' " MacGammon mim-
iced. "Remind me to kick your ass when I get back down."
He stood up and grabbed the tree limb above him. "On second thought, Rocky, the way you're going, just keep a
record of how many times I'm gonna have to kick it. I'm
losing track."

Rockdale watched as MacGammon worked his way
along the second limb. After MacGammon climbed several
more limbs, the man started easing his way out toward Carson. Rockdale turned and made his way toward where Carson would fall when MacGammon cut him free. He wished
he'd used MacGammon's survival knife. Here he was forcing himself through intertwined brambles of vines, limbs,

and leaves with his hands, while above him MacGammon climbed toward Carson with both knives.

"Are you near him yet?"

Rockdale stopped and looked up. He didn't see MacGammon.

"Up here, Rocky. You blind or something?"

A motion caught his attention. There was MacGammon astraddle a small limb. The parachute was only a few feet from MacGammon.

"I see you. I'm nearly there."

"Take your time." MacGammon pulled the cutter forward and pushed it toward the nylon lines running from the parachute to the harness holding Carson.

"He should be down by the time you get to where he's going to fall."

"Wait a minute! Let me get there!"

"Ain't a snowball's chance in hell, I'm going to do that. I told you, don't do anything heroic. You can't catch him—"

Rockdale cupped his hands to shout. MacGammon had the knife—*his knife*—sawing back and forth against a tangle of nylon lines. "Wait! Wait!"

"Rocky, I know you better than you know yourself. We just need him down. The fall ain't gonna kill him. You can't see what I can up here. The bushes are gonna break his fall. Worse that could happen is he gets a few bruises—a cut or two maybe—and some scratches."

Rockdale turned and started hurrying through the bushes. Pushing the limbs apart and ignoring the blows as they whipped back against him. He had to reach Carson's position before MacGammon cut him down. He might be unable to see what Mac could way up there on the limb, but down here, he knew those bushes weren't going to break his fall. If anything, they'd be like spears cutting into and through Carson.

"Mac, don't cut him down yet. We don't want him to die when he falls."

MacGammon quit his cutting. "Rocky, you bleeding-heart liberal asshole. He ain't gonna die. He will die if I don't cut him down." MacGammon raised the cutter again and returned to his sawing.

Rockdale glanced every few seconds to see how MacGammon was doing. He had to get there before the man fell. Carson wasn't dead yet, and he'd be damned if he stood by and watched MacGammon kill him because Mac wouldn't listen to him. It might be the only way to get the man down, but it was useless if it killed him at the same time. *Hi, Stetson. You're down, but you're dead. Better luck next time.*

A sharp *twang* caused Rockdale to slow for a moment and look up at Carson.

"Hey, did you hear that?" MacGammon asked. "He's half-way down. Hey, Stetson, you bastard. You better bend those knees."

Rockdale leaned back slightly so he could see MacGammon. What he saw was Carson spinning around slowly, clockwise. Nylon cords holding the right side of the harness were drooped over the injured man. Only the left nylon straps held Carson to the parachute.

"Rocky, a couple of more cuts and he's gonna be one grateful son of a bitch."

Rockdale pushed aside the bushes, and ignoring the occasional thorns and backswings from the limbs, the aircrewman shoved and fought his way through the heavy growth. Another *twang* drew his attention.

"One more to go, and he's on a fast track down!"

MacGammon sounded almost giddy as if looking forward to Carson's fall with anticipation. Rockdale's lungs ached from the exertion, but he couldn't stop. If he wasn't there to soften Carson's fall, the man could die.

"Nearly there!"

Suddenly, he burst through a tangled row to find himself directly beneath Carson. A louder *twang* filled the jungle quiet.

"Anchors aweigh!"

Rockdale ran beneath the dangling Carson, trying to position himself where he could cushion his shipmate's fall. As he stepped left, the knife cut forward, catching the strap and pushing it farther to the right at the same moment that the blade finished its job. Rockdale turned quickly, looking up as Carson came free from twenty feet above him, hurtling toward the ground, feet first. Though he had the best of intentions, Rockdale startled himself as he jumped back, letting Carson tumble feet-first into the bushes only a few feet from where he stood. The man's head came back, his mouth opened, and Carson's screams filled the jungle as he disappeared into the bushes.

HOLMAN HEARD THE SCREEN DOOR SLAM SHUT BUT didn't turn to see who it was. He knew and waited until Upmann walked up beside him. "Sounds to me like this African National Army isn't a U.S. friend as they say," Holman said, reaching in his pocket for a Cubana.

"Could have been Abu Alhaul and his group. Mary said they knew for sure they had SAMs, but it was only speculation about the ANA having them."

Holman shrugged. "Seen one terrorist bunch, you've seen them all. Kill as many innocent people as you can and call them the enemy. Never face true warriors on the battlefield. Hide behind nationalism, religion, or just pure meanness. If ever there was an evil in this world, it's the modern terrorist with his penchant to hide murder, mayhem, and torture under some sort of acceptable banner. Kill the lot of them, I say."

"Here comes our Air Force colonel," Upmann said, pointing to Holman's left.

Holman let out a deep sigh. "Now, be nice, Leo."

"I'm always nice."

The colonel saluted as he approached the two men. "Jeff, how does it look?" Admiral Holman asked, returning the salute.

"We'll have two helicopters ready for liftoff at first light, Admiral." The colonel pointed at the horizon. "We won't have the helicopters reconfigured from special ops to search-and-rescue for another couple of hours. Even so, Admiral, wouldn't be enough daylight left for us to make it there and back before nightfall."

"I guess I'm kind of thick, Colonel," Leo Upmann said. "I don't understand why you can just take off and use the helicopters as they're currently configured."

Hightower smiled. "It's a matter of Air Force policy, Captain. When dealing with Special Forces types, we don't have to have the same equipment nor do we have the same worries." He held his right hand up and made a downward motion with it. "We just fly right in, hover for a moment, and they jump out. How they get back is usually their worry." Hightower clasped his hands behind his back and rolled back and forth on his heels as he continued, "For a SAR mission, we assume the worse, and that is the survivors won't be able to help themselves, and we won't be able to land. We'll have to blast through the jungle canopy with a specially designed seat and hoist them out one at a time. If necessary, we'll drop a heavy wire-mesh stretcher, strap the injured into it and hoist him or her up through the same opening."

"You have a take-off time yet?" Holman interrupted.

The roar of an aircraft touching down, tires squealing as they slammed against the runway, brought the conversation to a halt.

"Damn," Holman said. "Does that pilot want to land the aircraft or submerge it?"

"That would be our skipper," a voice behind the three men offered. "Wasn't due until tomorrow, but the Ranger was already loaded so he took off this morning. He's uncanny about how—"

Holman turned. Lieutenant Commander Peeters, the mission commander of the damaged Ranger 20, stood there. "Didn't hear you come up, Commander."

"Sorry, Admiral." He pointed at the EP-3E rolling down the runway, puffs of smoke coming from the tires where the aircraft brakes worked to slow the four-engine turbo-prop airplane. "When Craz— Sorry, when Commander Greensburg lands an aircraft, he expects that aircraft to stay on the ground."

Holman turned back to the runway, watching the aircraft continue down it toward the ramp. "Well, it definitely will stay on the runway if he keeps landing it like that. It'll stay on the runway, it'll stay on the tarmac, and it'll stay in the hanger until it's repaired."

"Admiral, I'm on my way to the tower to file our flight plan for tomorrow morning," Colonel Jeff Hightower said. "We intend an o-four-hundred show for an o-six-hundred launch. Should be a quick in and out, if they've found the missing aircrewman, and he's able to ride out himself."

"One thing we don't know, Colonel," Peeters offered. "We don't know if our chief has hooked up with the three aircrewmen who bailed out. The chief is the one who was told to work his way to the sailors. Hopefully, he's done that. If not, then there's a chance you may have to do a double retrieval."

Hightower reached up, pulled his light-blue hat off, and ran the back of his flight-suit sleeve across his forehead. He nodded. "Roger, Commander. I understand one of your chiefs bailed out after you ceased the bailout," Hightower said, his statement more of a question.

Peeters nodded. "That's true. Surprised all of us. By the time we realized the engine fire was under control, we had three out the door. The chief was reluctant to let them go alone." Holman saw Peeters eyes gaze off toward the horizon. "He is a very brave man. I doubt I could or would have done what the chief did."

Hightower smiled. "I don't know whether I should admire the man, berate him, or write him up for disobeying an order."

Holman removed the cigar from between his lips. "You have to admire him for what he did. Heart's in the right place and all that, though you are right. He should never have bailed out."

"I meant no disrespect, Admiral. But because of this brave chief petty officer, we may have to make two rescue retrievals instead of one. Plus, with the chief on the move, if he isn't with the three sailors who were told to remain where they are, we may have to set up a search pattern and start hunting for him."

Holman nodded. "I know. It may make your mission a little more complicated. But in this day and age of international terrorism, you want to admire something such as this for its heroism even as you question why in the hell he did it in the first place." He stuck the cigar back in his mouth. "I think I'll admire him for a while," he said softly, smoke filtering out with the words.

"Chief Razi is one of our best," Peeters offered.

The four turboprops of the taxiing EP-3E drowned out

any reply. Colonel Jeff Hightower saluted and sauntered off toward the tower.

Holman dropped the cigar onto the damp ground and ground it out with the heel of his shoe. Thoughts whirled through his mind about this upcoming rescue operation. He should have asked Hightower how much experience the man's crew had in SAR missions, but a full Air Force colonel would be well trained. The Air Force left little to chance when it came to safety. A simple in-and-out rescue is never that. If you're going to bring someone out, and you have to call it a rescue, then it is never simple. Special Forces missions on the other hand were planned well in advance, and everyone knew his mission and where to be for pickup. Search-and-rescue missions never have advanced planning. They were by-the-seat operations designed to get the fallen combatants out of the war zone and off to wherever medical attention could be provided. He slapped a mosquito on his neck. He hoped the worst the four endured was a little loss of blood to the mosquitoes.

The engines of the EP-3E wound down as the pilot cut power. Three of the engines were quickly feathered, coming to a stop as the pilot locked them down. The outer one continued to turn, driving the onboard generators until the ground crew could hook up a ground unit. The thing about these old birds, Holman said to himself, is that they are self-sustaining. Not like the Air Force, who fly in ground crews, ground equipment, and test the runway before one of their beefy reconnaissance aircraft lands. With the EP-3E variant of the maritime reconnaissance P-3, all the crew had to do was crawl on board, take off, and they could land nearly anywhere. The aircraft had onboard-generator power, and the crew was trained to repair the aircraft. Holman pushed his sunglasses back on his nose. On the far side of the aircraft, a ladder emerged from the rear and moments later aircrew members started disembarking. The first ones were hurrying around the aircraft checking safety lines. One of those, Holman knew, would be the static electricity wire running from the aircraft to the ground.

Everything about Africa was bright, hot, humid, and dangerous. The sun baked everything beneath it; the heat even lined peoples' faces. The humidity drenched them continuously and when it wasn't causing everything to remain wet, it changed to rain to make sure it didn't miss anything. And danger; danger was everywhere in Africa. It lurked in little microscopic things that could eat away your flesh, to insects that viewed the human body as its home, to reptiles whose bites killed instantly, to animals who viewed everyone as walking groceries, and to humans who knew no other way to deal with each other than through violence. Violence stirred up the population. How anyone could want— How? Why anyone would want to emigrate to Liberia and leave the land of coast-to-coast air conditioning was beyond Holman. This was his fourth visit in two years. Each visit came with a self-made promise it would be his last. This time the promise would be kept.

The faint wind stirred the palm trees lining the walk where Holman, Upmann, and Peeters stood watching the action on the tarmac.

The ground crew pulled and pushed the yellow, ground generator near the aircraft and with a flip of a cover, the supervisor connected the electrical feed to the aircraft. Holman saw the ground crew shouting at each other, but their words were drowned out by the single engine keeping power to the aircraft. The young man stepped back after making the connection and gave the copilot a thumbs-up. Holman saw the copilot turn and a moment later the last engine wound down, coming to a halt.

"Admiral!"

Holman turned. It was Colonel Hightower returning.

"Sir, we have our flight plan filed, but the Liberian colonel in the tower has denied it."

"Denied it?"

"Yes, sir," Hightower answered as he walked up. "Said we aren't allowed to violate the border between Liberia and Guinea."

"That's bullshit," Upmann added.

"Not to worry, my fine Navy captain. I filed a flight plan toward the border to conduct some flight training. He accepted that."

"But—"

Hightower smiled. "I think he was just going through the formalities of denying us overflight permission. This way he can tell his superiors he never approved us violating Guinea airspace."

Holman nodded. "Did you have to change your launch time?"

"No, sir. We'll still launch at o-six-hundred, around false dawn. Same time. May be a little sooner, but not much. All I want is to be able to see the ground without ground-terrain radar and lights. The four of us will be heading toward your downed airmen."

"The sooner the better, Colonel."

The Air Force colonel reached up, straightened his hat, and shrugged. "Sir, we Air Force have never allowed regulations to stop us from doing what we have to do."

"Are you sure you're Air Force?"

"Leo," Holman interrupted, reaching over, and touching Captain Upmann's arm briefly. "Colonel, that's good news. We'll be here when you launch."

"Sir, we will have both Pave Hawks reconfigured tonight, though we only intend to take one. The other is a backup in the event the SAR requires longer than we hope." Hightower paused a moment and then said, "Would the Admiral like to see our Pave Hawk helicopter?"

"Colonel, I would be honored," Holman replied. "Come on, Leo. Lieutenant Commander Pecters, would you like to join us?"

"Admiral, I'd love to, but I'd better stay here to greet my skipper. He's going to want to know what happened; where it happened; and what we are doing about it."

Holman nodded. "Tell the skipper I'll speak with him shortly."

"THIS IS THE PAVE HAWK HELICOPTER, ADMIRAL," HIGH-tower said, patting the side of the jungle-green helicopter. "The primary mission of the Pave Hawk is to conduct day and night operations into hostile territory, transporting the services' Special Forces team." He removed his hand and walked to the side door opening into the rear of the Pave Hawk. "The Pave Hawk is also known as the HH-60, a heavily modified version of the Army's Black Hawk helicopter. Difference is we have more sophisticated communications and navigational suites."

"Nice ship, Colonel," Holman said.

"It is, isn't it, Admiral," Hightower replied, patting the floor a couple of times where passengers would ride. "By tomorrow morning, my team will have installed a .50 caliber machine gun. I know your intelligence officer said it should be a noncombat rescue, but it wasn't noncombat action that caused your crewmembers to be down."

"*Touché,*" Upmann added.

"Good planning, Colonel," Holman said.

Hightower pointed toward the rotors. "The Pave Hawk

has two General Electric engines that give us a four-hundred-mile-plus range without air-to-air refueling, though we do have that capability. Reliability is outstanding."

The sound of wheels screeching, metal against metal, drew their attention. Approaching them were a group of airmen in light-gray flight suits, wearing the patches of the Air Force's Air Combat command, pulling and pushing a trolley with gray metal boxes on them.

Hightower pointed. "That's our ground crew, Admiral. That will be the rescue equipment we will need tomorrow to bring your crewmen up and out of the jungle."

About twenty feet from the helicopter, one of the airmen recognized the stars on Holman's hat and collars, and shouted, "Attention!"

"Stand at ease," Holman said.

The team quickly returned to the task of manhandling the heavy load to the helicopter. A man wearing the stripes of a senior master sergeant approached Holman, saluted, and addressed Colonel Hightower, "Sir, we need to get in here and modify the doorway for rescue."

"And the fifty-cal?"

The senior master sergeant nodded. "After we put the rescue pod in, sir. Shouldn't take long, Colonel."

"Rescue pod?" Holman asked.

"Something new, Admiral. It allows us to modify the Pave Hawk for the mission at hand. As you probably know, the most important piece of rescue gear for a helicopter is the winch, and we have a permanently mounted winch that is three hundred feet long—don't think we'll need that much—and has a payload capacity of a ton. Hopefully, we won't have to lift that much because the Pave Hawk can only lift about six hundred pounds and that's going downhill."

"Downhill?" Upmann asked.

"Sorry, Captain. That was an Air Force joke."

"I did have an opportunity to talk with the aircrew when they returned, Admiral, and they tell me the downed crewmen have survival radios with them. The sergeant and crew will be downloading the software into our personnel-locating-system so we can ensure that we're compatible with the survival radios your crewmembers are carrying. This will give us range and bearing to the crewmen, and let us locate them and get them home quicker."

"What's the flight duration for your helicopter, Colonel?"

"Admiral, with air-to-air refueling we could fly forever, but this time we're going with onboard fuel only. I estimate a maximum of four hours flight time. Figure one to one and a half hours to reach the vicinity of your crewmembers. Thirty to forty-five minutes to bring them on board, and then return by most direct route."

"Ergo, home for lunch."

"Captain, if everything goes well, we may have them back in time for a late breakfast."

"Sirs, would you mind moving back so my team can work on the chopper?"

Holman acknowledged the senior master sergeant's request and led them to the shade of a nearby palm tree. Here is another one of those wonderful places a pilot should be, near a runway, watching professionals doing the nation's work on aircraft. Personally, he wouldn't fly a helicopter. Why would anyone give up the throttle and yoke of a F/A-18 Hornet for the complicated, coordinated arms-and-leg movements needed to fly a helicopter? On the other hand, he would fight any budget-cutter's dream to save money by chopping out the helos. While it had never happened where he needed to be yanked out of some strange land, the *whup-whup* sounds of a helicopter settling in to bring you out has to be a tearjerking one for the pilot on the ground.

A tall, lanky figure wearing a khaki hat with the silver oak leaf of a Navy commander stepped into the shade with them and saluted. "Admiral, I'm Commander Charles T. Greensburg, sir; commanding officer of Fleet Air Reconnaissance Squadron Two."

"VQ-2 skipper?" Holman politely asked as the three of them returned the salute.

"Yes, sir. Just landed, Admiral, and according to my officer-in-charge here—"

"Lieutenant Commander Peeters?"

"Yes, sir, Captain. He's the deployed OIC. He told me a rescue attempt will commence tomorrow morning?"

Holman nodded at Colonel Hightower. "That's true, Skipper. Colonel Hightower and a crew from the Air Combat Command are going out first-light to bring them back."

"Sir, unless otherwise directed, we intend to launch tonight, locate them, and keep them company until Colonel Hightower brings them home." Greensburg said. The VQ-2 skipper clasped his hands behind his back and looked at Hightower. "Colonel, if we can exchange frequencies, then when you arrive tomorrow morning, we should be able to make your job easier."

Hightower nodded. "That *would* make our job easier."

"Skipper, you have my permission, but you may have a hard time getting flight-plan approval through the tower."

"No sweat, Admiral. We filed flight plans at the beginning of the month for twenty-five missions. Our flight plan was approved days ago. Lieutenant Commander Peeters told me the Liberians are being assholes about us flying into Guinea, but then again, I never intended to ask them. If they do, I'll tell them we're trying to see what altitude is best for the EP-3E to fly."

CHAPTER 10

RAZI STUMBLED FROM THE BUSHES, FALLING ONTO THE same path he had traveled more than an hour ago. His eyes widened as he pushed himself up, his smile growing for a moment before he burst into loud laughter, until after a couple of minutes, it decreased in intensity to a low, soft laughter that sounded more like an uncontrolled murmur. "Fuck you," he finally said, his voice low, not directing the expletive toward any one person but at everything that had tried to stop him, including his own imagination. "Fuck you," he said louder.

He squatted, unzipped his survival vest, and drank deeply from the plastic container of water. When he finished, he looked at the remaining water, sloshed it around a couple of times. "Will save you, but if I need water, what's a little monkey shit?" He patted his stomach and looked down at it. "Worm, you're dead meat when I get my hands on you. Just keep growing because it's not going to be a fair fight."

He picked the top of the plastic container up from the ground. "Got to tighten you or tight," he mumbled talking to the container as he screwed the top down. "Can't lose you, Mister Water. No, can't lose you." He shoved the pint container back into the survival vest and patted it a couple of times. He stretched his head and shoulders forward, his body tense. Razi raised himself slightly on his haunches like a lion waiting to pounce. *There be evil pirates in these woods, boys,* he thought. His slowly turned his head, his eyes narrowing as he looked both ways, unsure of what he would see or even what he was looking for, but deep within Razi a primal urge surged, desiring something, anything, to emerge onto the path with him. His hands opened and closed, one moment a palm with fingers spread wide and the next, knuckles showing white through a mud-caked fist. He stared transfixed at the sight of brown turning to red-white and back again. Seconds turned into minutes and nearly half-hour passed with him squatting, staring at his hand until a loud screech caused Razi to look up, breaking the trance.

Then, he stood, stepped to the side of faint path, unzipped, and marked his territory. His narrowed eyes searching for danger as he peed.

He had a mission. Ahead was his crew. Young, naïve, and unable to care for themselves. It was his job. The job of every chief petty officer—teach and protect. Razi zipped up, reached into his survival vest, and pulled out his compass. Yes, this was definitely the trail he had walked earlier. He looked down the path, as far as the overgrowth of the jungle permitted. Somewhere ahead were four, maybe five, armed African boy scouts whose idea of being prepared meant making sure the chamber had a bullet in it. He jammed the compass back into his pocket. His hand slipped over to the other side of the survival vest, patting the pocket for his knife, finding an empty scabbard, and he recalled losing it somewhere in the fall off the cliff. Raising his hands, Razi balled them into fists. *Knife? I don't need any frigging knife.*

Razi closed the survival vest and he marched off, covering the same territory he had covered a couple of hours ago. Thirty minutes later he came to the fallen tree that had caused him to stop—where he had worried about how to cross it, and what venomous snake might lie on the other side. This time, without hesitation, Razi jumped up onto the trunk of the fallen giant, dashed across it, and quickly jumped down. He didn't even bother to glance back or notice the African cobra that quickly slithered away from under the fallen tree into the bush.

Minutes later, Razi pushed huge leaves out of his way, only to have the water on the leaves soak his now jungle-heat-dried flight suit. He stopped. The leaves curled like natural saucers, trapping water from the earlier rainfall. Razi leaned down, tilted one leaf after the other, letting the tepid water flow into his open mouth, each leaf moving him forward along the path. Man-eating lions, African crocodiles, and monkey-shit worries had disappeared. Sure, the thoughts of jungle dangers flitted across his mind, but for some reason they no longer mattered nor did they worry him. No one, or thing, was going to stop him from saving his sailors. Not even the monster worm growing in his stomach. A day ago, he would have thought of those African boy warriors as kids. Now, deep inside, he knew if he encountered them, he'd wring their necks without a moments' hesitation. Civilization was only minutes deep in any man's soul, where one event could erase it and hurl you back into the primal jungle in which Razi now walked.

The seconds turned to minutes and into hours. Razi tripped on a vine growing across the path he followed.

He threw his hands out, stopping his body before it hit the ground. Razi pushed himself up. It felt good, and without thinking about it, Razi began to do push-ups—at ten he started counting aloud—and when he reached one hundred, he stopped in the upward position. Holding stable, staring at a column of ants swarming beneath him where his actions had disturbed their path.

He rolled over onto one hand and started doing one-armed push-ups, one after the other, silently counting, and each upward motion slower than the last until he reached thirty, and then he stopped again in the upward position. His arm and stomach ached. Razi dropped a knee and pushed himself upright, standing, breathing rapidly from the exertion.

Razi's eyes danced right and left as he tried to rationalize why he wasted time doing what he just did. While he stood quietly, growing uncomfortable with what had happened, he realized the light beneath the jungle canopy was fading. He looked up, his thoughts turning from the push-ups to his surroundings. The sun was setting. He wiped his hands against each other, knocking off decaying twigs and leaves. "Not much longer," he said to himself. He could hardly continue if he was unable to see where he was going. Still his hands were filthy. He wiped the mud and debris off the legs of his flight suit, pulled out his gloves, and slipped them on. He wiggled his fingers in front of his eyes. "Now you look clean."

Razi glanced at the compass, confirmed his direction, and started off. He pulled out his flashlight and flipped down the red lens over the lamp. The red light of the flashlight would show him the way, when what little daylight remained disappeared. It wouldn't light much of the trail, but it would be hard for anyone to see it unless they knew what to look for. Even aircraft carriers light their flight decks at night with red lights. You have to be looking for the soft diffused glow of red light to see it. He'd flown EC-2s when he was a petty officer—the small two-engine turboprop aircraft with the radar dome on top of them. Back when he was a young sailor, and before he switched ratings to cryptologic technician. Aircraft carriers look small when you're orbiting above them, waiting to land. At night, they're nothing more than faint red outlines with blackness between the lights. Some first-timers never returned for seconds.

He looked up in the direction he was heading. Rockdale, MacGammon, and Carson had to be within a mile. But between him and them were those boy warriors. Razi rubbed his chin, rough stubble scratching his palm. His beard grew fast, so if he was feeling stubble, it had to be nearing twenty-three hundred. Razi pulled the left sleeve back. His watch showed 10:50 on it. He wasn't far off. Over twelve hours they'd been out here? When did they bail out? They were airborne about 0800 hours: one hour flying time to get on track; and, about an hour later Razi was kicking his feet in open air. Something had to be wrong. They couldn't have been out here that long? He pulled the sleeve down and pulled the Velcro strip tight across his wrist. He did the same for the other one.

"Damn," he said, opening his legs wide, unzipping the bottom half of the flight suit. Razi reached inside, shoved his hands down into his khaki trousers, and tugged the boxer-short skivvies away from his skin. "Wet," he mumbled, thinking *crotch rot*. "But, that's why we have corpsman and medical miracles like crotch-rot cream."

He pulled his hand out, at the same time lifting his head. What in the hell was he doing talking to himself? He didn't know if those boy warriors were still moving or, maybe, they had gone to ground for the night. If still moving, then he'd stumble into them if he weren't careful. If gone to ground, Razi knew they'd be somewhere near the path, watching, ready to shoot his ass when he meandered by— not even caring that he might have crotch rot.

He closed the zipper. By tomorrow, he was going to be "one sore puppy" down there. But, by tomorrow night, he, Rockdale, MacGammon, and Carson would be back home. When he went to zip up the survival vest, his hand touched the survival radio. He hadn't used it since the EP-3E departed the area hours ago. What if they had mounted the rescue, already had his men, and he hadn't had his turned on to hear it all? He was surprised to discover that it didn't bother or worry him that something like that could have happened. What he did know was that his shipmates would never leave him behind, so if his three sailors were home drinking hot soup chased down by several six-packs, he'd be with them soon enough.

Razi pulled the radio out, reached to turn it on, and stopped. It was still on. He shook it and turned up the volume, relieved when he heard static come out of it. His head jerked up and Razi turned the radio down, but not off. Somewhere out there were armed boys. Even if he heard a rescue effort ongoing, there was no way they could rescue him before tomorrow morning. Too dark to see, and how in the hell would he find a rescue harness from a helicopter in the jungle? He couldn't even see his flight boots.

"HIS LEG IS BROKEN," ROCKDALE SAID FROM WHERE HE squatted over Carson. They were never going to get out of here, and Carson was going to die.

"He's unconscious, so he can't feel it," MacGammon said, walking up behind Rockdale.

Rockdale stood and pushed MacGammon, sending the

smaller, but stockier sailor falling backward. "Shut the fuck up!"

MacGammon pushed himself up with both hands, crouched, and ran at Rockdale. "I warned you, asshole!" He hit Rockdale with his shoulder, knocking the breath out of him. "I warned you."

The two men rolled against a bush, long, sharp briars ripping through their flight suits, drawing long streaks of blood where they pierced the skin. Pain sliced down Rockdale's cheeks as he rolled face-down through the briars. He slammed an elbow backward, striking MacGammon upside the head, and knocking the stouter sailor off of him.

"You could have killed him! I told you to wait!" Rockdale screamed as he flipped over onto his butt and sat up, the fight gone out of him.

MacGammon shook off his daze and jumped, knocking Rockdale over again. He pinned Rockdale with both knees, one on each shoulder of the taller sailor's arms. "And, he would have died if we hadn't gotten him down when we did," he said through clenched teeth.

MacGammon leaned forward and grabbed Rockdale's ears. "Listen to me, you little Maryland do-gooder. This ain't downtown Columbia or the tourist district of Annapolis. This is the mother fucking jungle. There ain't no one here but us, and we don't have time to hold group gropes and sing *Kumbaya*. All we have time for is to survive."

Rockdale felt the pressure from MacGammon's knees lessen. He twisted, freeing his right arm. Rockdale rolled to the left, throwing MacGammon off him. "You stupid fuck!" he shouted.

MacGammon pushed himself up. Rockdale stood.

MacGammon circled to the right, his legs never crossing, his arms held out to the side. In that split second of watching MacGammon move, Rockdale knew that here was a man who could or would kill him if necessary.

Rockdale dropped his arms. "You could have waited until I got positioned. We might have been able to get him down without breaking his leg."

MacGammon straightened. Rockdale could tell MacGammon was weighing whether to attack or stop. He should never have started this. Not against a person who's entire life had been one of survival.

"Stop, Mac," he said. "You were probably doing what—"

"Rocky, you're an asshole, you know. If you don't do it your way, then it's the highway." MacGammon dropped his arms and straightened. He shook his head. "We don't know if Stetson broke his leg when he came through the trees or when I cut him down. You just naturally assume if I'm involved, then worst case."

A moan broke through their argument.

"He's still alive and he's down. We got him down. It may not have been the most gracious way of exiting the trees, but he's down. Now, go look at that leg and at his head. You've had that Red Cross training shit; I slept through most of it. Besides, it ain't that leg what's keeping him unconscious. Take his helmet off."

"I guess you're right," Rockdale replied, turning toward Carson.

"Wow! There's something for the record books, 'Hey, guys, guess what I have to tell you. MacGammon was right about something. Amazing ain't it?' I want to be there when you say that."

Rockdale squatted beside Carson.

The man's eyes fluttered. "Water."

"He wants water," Rockdale said.

A hand came over his shoulder, holding a pint of water.

"Of course, he wants water. Here, give him mine. With the rain we get here, none of us are going to die of thirst."

"Here give me a hand."

MacGammon stepped around Rockdale and lifted Carson's head. Rockdale held the water bottle to the injured man's lips and tilted it slightly so water slipped into Carson's mouth.

"He's swallowing," Rockdale said, watching Carson's Adam's apple bob. Rockdale leaned closer, watching the water trickle into the man's mouth. He didn't want to pour too fast for fear of choking Carson.

"I wouldn't give him too much. Don't want him throwing up."

Rockdale drew the bottle away as MacGammon gently laid the man's head back down. "Let's get his helmet off."

"And let's find a better place to spend the night than here. I think a little higher ground would be better," MacGammon said, pointing toward the tree he had just climbed down. "Up there should be okay."

Rockdale unsnapped the flight helmet.

"On second thought, I'd leave that on until we get him moved."

Rockdale looked questioningly at MacGammon.

"If he's got something broke or out of line in his neck or head, then the helmet is kind of like a brace."

"Should we move him with this leg?"

MacGammon lower lip pushed against the upper. A few seconds passed before he spoke. "Guess you're right this time, Rocky. I guess we're going to have to cut the leg of his flight suit and check it."

"Let's hope the bone hasn't pierced the skin."

"Nope. I don't think it has. We'd see blood, wouldn't we?"

A few minutes later, the left leg of the flight suit had

been cut open from the ankle to only a few inches from the hip. Carson's left foot was turned awkwardly to one side. Above the ankle, a large raised bump showed where the bone had snapped. The skin had turned a dark blue where the bone poked upward from below. The knee faced straight up in an awkward direction from where Carson's left foot now pointed. Above the knee a second bump, the same size of the one near the ankle, identified a second break.

"I don't see where the bone has pierced the skin."

"Told you, didn't I, Rocky. No blood—no pierced skin. It's a little something you learn when you live in a neighborhood where bullets are a common neighbor." MacGammon dropped a small tube of anti-bacterial ointment beside Rockdale. "That's good for you. Your face is a mess. You'll need this."

All they had for cuts was anti-bacterial ointment, and Rockdale didn't think that would be too effective against a large wound. Rockdale rubbed the ointment over his face as the two sailors studied their shipmate. Carson's breathing seemed normal to Rockdale, but only two things could be keeping him unconscious—head injury or pain. Or both.

Rockdale screwed the top back on the tube and shoved it into one of his flight-suit pockets. He reached forward and touched the bump above Carson's knee. "What do you think?"

"I think—" MacGammon started, then suddenly stopping. "Christ! I don't know what I think. This leg of his is one busted piece of shit."

"Thank you, Doctor MacGammon," Rockdale said, his voice tight. They had better be rescued soon. He didn't think he could tolerate more than a night with this doofus.

"Don't try to be funny. You're going to have to straighten

it, and hope when you do that the bones inside the leg don't cut through an artery or a vein." MacGammon turned and started away. "I'll go find three or four limbs we can use for splints while you straighten it."

"What do you want me to do? I can't straighten this leg on my own. You're going to have to help."

MacGammon finally nodded and shrugged, "Okay, but let me find something for splints before you do it. I think you should stay here and make sure he doesn't decide he wants to turn over or something."

Rockdale agreed.

"The other thing you can do is decide how we are going to turn this leg to straighten it without doing more damage."

"Maybe we shouldn't straighten it," Rockdale said, his voice louder. "Maybe we should leave it as it is and strap it down that way."

MacGammon shook his head back and forth several times slowly. "Man, I don't know. You know, as long as Stetson is out cold like this, it don't matter which way his leg is pointed, but eventually he's going to surface and when he does, you can bet that leg is going to be one humongous pile of pain."

Rockdale sighed and took a deep breath. He looked up at MacGammon. "Go get some splints. I'm going to unlace his flight boots. We'll use his laces to hold the splints in place."

"We can use the straps from the parachute." MacGammon pulled his survival knife out. "I'll cut them off and bring them back with me. Leave his flight boots alone. At least they help hold some of his leg straight."

"We'll need to take off the one on the broken leg."

"I don't think so. He may have broken feet, also. I'd leave his helmet, his boots, and his gloves on until we move him and do a better check on him. The flight boots act like casts. Even if we don't take them off, we're going home tomorrow. Let the docs do it. That's why they get the big bucks and get to wear white uniforms."

Several minutes later MacGammon returned, carrying several long sticks. With the exception of one, the other five had been on the ground a long time. The two men sorted, argued, and measured each one against Carson's leg before cutting them, as near equal length as a survival knife would allow. Rockdale and MacGammon decided four sticks would be enough to hold the leg steady. After all, they kept telling each other when they agreed on a decision, tomorrow they'd be going home, and Navy doctors could have their shipmate. As long as Stetson was breathing, the two couldn't do anything wrong.

The two men sat back, wiped sweat from their eyes, and discussed the pros and cons on whether to set the leg or not. For thirty minutes, they weaved through the argument of either leaving it alone, or trying to set it, until finally they decided, with Carson still unconscious, that they'd follow the rules learned in Survival, Escape, Evasion, and Rescue school. They'd set it as best they could.

"We're going to have to turn on our flashlights, Rocky, to do it." MacGammon looked around the area where they sat around the prone Carson. "Another few minutes, and we ain't gonna be able to see anything."

Rockdale nodded. He had the task of turning the leg. The kneecap was upright, so the committee of two decided the upper leg break was okay. They'd leave it alone because it appeared properly aligned with the knee, but the break above the ankle was another story. The foot angled about forty-five degrees to the left. The only reason Rockdale could give for why the foot wasn't completely turned around and pointing backward was that the ground prevented it.

"You think it's a clean break?" he asked MacGammon.

"Man, any bone broken ain't clean. It's jagged. Ever seen a broken animal bone? They don't break even either. All we can do is try to line up the foot with the knee and hope when we get home tomorrow, we ain't screwed him up too much."

With MacGammon holding Carson by the shoulders, Rockdale settled down on his haunches, the toes of his boots digging into the ground under his buttocks. He grabbed the left flight boot.

"You know you're going to have to pull down and then turn, don't you?"

Rockdale nodded and released the boot. He licked his dry lips and wiped the sweaty palms on the knees of his flight suit.

"What's the matter?"

Rockdale pulled his handkerchief out and wiped his forehead. "I'm scared, Mac. What if I do something wrong?"

"If you do something wrong, then stop and do it right. Look, Rocky, grab the boot by the heel and toe. Stetson's unconscious. He ain't gonna know whether you did it right the first time. He ain't gonna know shit until he wakes up."

"But—"

"No buts. You grab that boot. One hand under the heel and the other grabbing the toe. Then, I'm gonna count to three. When I hit three, don't even think about it, you pull down and twist that boot to the left. When the toe of the boot is lined up with the knee, hold it there."

Their eyes locked in the faint light.

"Of course, you may have to push up on it for a moment so the bones connect again," MacGammon said, his voice low.

Rockdale leaned back on his legs. He took several deep

breaths, his eyes locking with MacGammon's, who winked at him. "You can do it."

Rockdale nodded, leaned forward, and grabbed the boot.

"One, two, three! Now!"

Rockdale jerked down and twisted. Carson screamed, knocking MacGammon aside as his upper torso rocketed up at the waist. Startled, Rockdale fell backward, releasing the flight boot. MacGammon, on all fours, scrambled back, grabbing Carson by the shoulders. When the breath ran out, the screaming stopped, and the injured man collapsed back into MacGammon's hands.

"Grab the foot!" MacGammon shouted as he eased Carson back to the ground. "I've got him!" MacGammon shouted, pressing down on Carson's shoulders.

"You got him?" Rockdale shouted, reaching forward and holding the boot steady.

"Check that leg. Make sure it's straight from the foot to the hip."

"It's straight," he said sharply. Keeping one hand on the boot toe, Rockdale crawled to Carson's left side. He ran his free hand up his friend's leg, rubbing it over every inch. He couldn't talk. His throat was constricted. At any moment, Rockdale was afraid he was going to cry. What if he'd killed him? What if twisting the leg, ripped an artery or vein in half? What if he killed Carson without meaning to? Maybe they should have left the leg alone.

MacGammon released Carson's shoulders and scrambled on all fours to the other side of the aircrewman. He moved alongside the leg, tossing a couple of parachute straps to Rockdale. "Come on. You can let go of the boot. That leg ain't gonna move. Let's get these splints set before Stetson plays Tarzan again."

Ten minutes later the splints were set and tied.

Rockdale fell over to the side, his right arm holding him up as his hip rested on the ground.

"Looks okay to me," MacGammon said, sitting back on his haunches.

Rockdale nodded. "I hope he's okay," he said, his voice low and trembling.

"Well, whatever you did, it's over with. Carson's back out of it again. Man, did that scare the shit out of us or what! One moment Stetson's out of it with only a moan here and a moan there, as if he wants to make sure we know he's alive, and the next he's screaming like a trapped bobcat. You should have seen your face."

Rockdale pushed himself upright. "I thought I had killed him."

"Naw, man. Dead men don't scream. Live ones do. And the less hurt they are, the more they scream." MacGammon stood, brushed off the seat of his flight suit, and walked to the tree he had climbed down earlier. "We can't rest, Rocky. While he's out we need to move him." He walked back to where Carson lay. "Come on, give me a hand. Help me clear away the debris over there near the tree, and then we'll roll out the parachute."

"Think that's the place?"

"Looks as good as anywhere else around here, and it is slightly higher ground. Looks to me as if we've found where we're gonna be when they show up tomorrow to rescue us."

More moans escaped from the injured Carson, drawing their attention again.

"I thought you said we were going to move farther away?"

"I did, but I think the less we move him the better his chance is that we didn't screw the pooch when we set his leg."

A low, drawn-out moan escaped from Carson.

"Leave him for a moment. He's probably moaning over having you stroke his leg for him."

"Not funny."

"Wasn't to him, either. A couple of times there, I thought maybe you were enjoying it too much." MacGammon laughed. "For the right amount of money, Rocky, I won't tell."

Rocky glared for a moment, unsure whether he should be angry. MacGammon was abrasive and wasn't someone Rockdale would even consider a friend, but they were stuck with each other so he had better make the most of it. The absurdity of the situation washed over him. Here they were in the middle of a jungle filled with people trying to kill them, and he was upset over being stranded with MacGammon. He shook his head and started laughing. He surprised himself. Laughter wasn't what he wanted. But it relieved his tension. It didn't make him feel a closer bond with the man with whom he was rolling and fighting through the African brush about an hour ago, but it put their situation in a better perspective. They needed each other.

MacGammon turned on his flashlight again and then slapped Rockdale on the shoulder. "Let's go. Night won't wait on us."

"Looks as if we finished Stetson while we could."

"Remind me to put you in for some sort of award, Rocky. Shit, man! What do you want—a band?"

The smile faded from Rockdale's face. They'd better be rescued soon.

MacGammon and Rockdale spent time clearing away the loose leaves, twigs, limbs, and such from the area. MacGammon piled the twigs to one side. "For a fire later," he explained.

Rockdale shook his head. "We might want to do without a fire. We're not the only ones around here."

MacGammon shrugged. "Okay with me, but don't come looking for protection when our flashlights burn out and the flesh-eaters come out for dinner."

"If we light a fire, we might attract attention."

"And, if we don't, we might attract attention. If we attract that type of attention, it isn't you or me who are going to make some wild animal's meal, it's our buddy, Stetson, here," MacGammon said, jerking his thumb toward the injured man.

It didn't take long to start a fire. To Rockdale's satisfaction, the smell of the burning fire was as much a comfort as the sight. Earlier, the place had been bright with eye-catching hues of greens and browns, and with nightfall, it was as if a curtain had fallen across the scene, changing everything to black and gray.

"Let's get the parachute laid out, so it doesn't catch fire, and then we'll move Stetson up here without killing him." Five minutes later Carson was on top of the parachute, his leg immobilized by the splints. They took Carson's helmet off gingerly and checked the unconscious sailor's head, discovering a huge bump stretching across the left side of it from near the left temple to where the spinal column joined the head.

"Don't feel good, does it?"

Rockdale shook his head. "No. Think we should put the helmet back on?"

The two discussed it a few minutes before deciding to leave it off. That way, if there was any more swelling, the head would have room to swell and not be constricted by the helmet. They didn't know if it was the right decision or not, but sometimes any decision is better than none.

Rockdale pulled his sleeve back and looked at his watch. "It's near midnight," he said.

"Sounds like time for dinner," MacGammon replied, opening his survival vest and pulling a chocolate energy bar out. "You ought to have one, Rocky. With your temper, you probably burned a lot more calories than me."

The two men sat silently as they nibbled on the survival bars, the jungle night sounds more apparent as the ability to see the surrounding area, which was small during daylight, had now shrunk to the area within which the small fire illuminated. Every so often, Carson's moans drew their attention. His moans came now and then, in differing tones, but they came—just enough to reassure them that he was still alive. When they failed to hear a moan for more than a few minutes, one of them would scurry the few feet to where he lay and check on him.

The two talked softly as if nightfall caused them to be wary of everything. The primary topics centered on Carson and the rescue that would surely come tomorrow. The two agreed Carson was to go first, even if it meant them having to wait for the helicopter to return. After a while, they decided one would sleep while the other stayed awake, keeping the fire burning, and ready to wake the other if something happened. They would trade places after a couple of hours. MacGammon insisted on taking the first watch. So, after the two dripped water into Carson's open mouth and watched him swallow it, Rockdale lay down on the parachute. He shut his eyes, expecting sleep to be elusive.

It seemed as if he had just shut his eyes when MacGammon shook him. "Rocky, your turn, shipmate."

Rockdale yawned. "Was I asleep?"

"If you weren't, then you put on a pretty good show."

"Anything happening?" Rockdale asked, propping himself up on his elbows.

"What? With your snoring? If there was anything with designs on making a dinner of us, your snoring scared it away." MacGammon patted him on the shoulder. "If you ever decide to get married, Rocky, pick a woman with bad hearing."

Rockdale moved to the tree where MacGammon had been and sat down. Another yawn escaped.

"You going to be alright?"

"If you mean, will I stay awake, of course I will. I've stood midwatches before. There's not much difference."

MacGammon laughed. "Rocky, you're one mixed up dude, you know. 'Ain't much difference' my ass. You fall asleep out here, no telling what'll wake you up."

Rockdale ignored him, drawing his knees up, and resting his arms on them for a moment before wiping the sweat from his brow. He was unsure whether his flight suit was damp from sweating or the earlier rain. A small compensation was that the fire was on the other side, so only the light reached him and not the heat.

MacGammon lay down. "By the way, it's three. I let you sleep a little longer than two hours. Too worked up to sleep myself," MacGammon pulled his helmet on and strapped it.

"You'll overheat with that on," Rockdale offered, "Damn." Why couldn't he just keep quiet and keep the conversation to a minimum with this taciturn sailor.

"Don't be stupid, Rocky. If I go to sleep without it on, those mosquitoes on your neck will be over here draining every ounce of blood from me."

Rockdale slapped the back of his neck and then looked at his hand. Several dead mosquitoes and a smear of blood marred his palm. How'd he know?

"Look at your face," MacGammon said, laughing.

The sailor had turned around to face Rockdale, propping

himself up on his elbow. MacGammon flipped around on his back and laid flat on the parachute. "I've already had my three hours of slapping the hell out of them. Your turn now."

Rockdale cleaned his hand on his flight suit. Then he took the other hand and ran it lightly over his face, feeling a slight burning sensation from where the briars had scratched him earlier. He didn't feel any mosquito bites, but the back of his neck itched. He turned up the small collar of his flight suit, covering most of his neck. Wasn't much he could do in this natural-wildlife sauna to stop everything that wanted some part of his life force.

Rockdale leaned against the tree, the back of his head touching the trunk. He rolled his shoulders a couple of times, trying to achieve just a little inch or two more of comfort. A crackle from the fire drew his attention. The edge of the parachute was several feet from the fire. Not much chance of a spark or ember setting it afire.

Moments later, he heard a soft snore coming from MacGammon.

Rockdale yawned. Small sounds from the jungle broke the silence around him, and the hot smell of decay rode the light wind. He hadn't slept well the previous night in the hotel in Monrovia, but then he never slept well when he wasn't in his own bed. His dad, who had spent years on the road as a Kodak representative, used to tell him that for a man to have a good night's sleep, he needed to be in his own home, in his own bed, and with his own wife. Rockdale didn't have a wife, but in Rota, where he shared an apartment with two other aircrewmen from VQ-2, he had his own bedroom. His stomach growled. And he had his own bathroom—the fourth element of comfort. He shut his eyes, concentrating on his stomach, willing away the tightening constrictions of his intestines. It wasn't as if they had toilet tissue in the middle of the jungle, and he wasn't going to wipe his ass with any of these leaves. Twenty-four more hours at the most. He shut his eyes for a moment.

His eyes shot open and for a moment Rockdale shivered slightly. Falling asleep on watch was a mortal sin in every one of the military services, but to fall asleep in the wild jungles of Africa was — On one side of them, a bunch of terrorists running loose, laughing and giggling over the prospects of killing Americans. Then, somewhere nearby, this ragtag African National Army wandering around the jungle like a bunch of wild locusts, destroying everything in their path. And on the final side— *Can there be more than two sides?* Rockdale wondered—there were the wild animals and things that truly owned the jungle.

He put his hands on the ground and pushed himself up, the wet underarms of the flight suit pulling away some hair with it. Walking across the top of the spread parachute, Rockdale moved to the fire. He squatted and grabbed some twigs from the pile MacGammon made. Then, one at a time, he placed the wood on top of the fire. What if he hadn't wakened? What if the fire had gone out while he was sleeping? He shuddered. He didn't want to think about it. The fire didn't go out, and he couldn't have been asleep that long. It was still dark. He tossed the last twig into the fire, brushed his hands off, and in the dim light Rockdale looked at his watch. An hour! He'd been asleep an hour? "Damn." It'd be dawn soon.

The bushes moved on his left, causing him to jump. His sleepiness vanished. His heartbeat pounded in his ears. After a minute of standing motionless and hearing no other sound from the bushes, Rockdale turned back to the tree, stopping along the way to squat beside Carson. The man's face looked black in the faint firelight and as he watched, it seemed the skin on Carson's face moved. He reached forward, and when he did a horde of mosquitoes flew away.

"Jesus Christ!" he said, drawing his hand back. He waved it back and forth across Carson's face, a face now covered in tight, white spots, marking where mosquitoes had feasted. What about him? He reached up and ran a hand across his own face, his vision clouding for a moment as mosquitoes flew away.

Rockdale glanced at MacGammon. The man had his visor down, the collar of his flight suit turned up and the Velcro snaps pulled tight. MacGammon had his gloves on. Mosquitoes hovered over the sleeping man, but most of his skin was covered.

Rockdale picked up Carson's helmet. He looked at the helmet and at the injured man, weighing whether to put it back on or not, wondering if the swelling had stopped. As he watched, mosquitoes covered Carson's face again. Wouldn't matter if the mosquitoes killed him, though he knew there was little chance of that. He gently lifted Carson's head, drawing a moan from the man. It took several minutes to wrap up Carson like MacGammon. Getting the helmet on the unconscious man had been the hardest. Carson's head dipped and bobbed like one of those bobble heads, Rockdale thought. Finally, finished with Carson, Rockdale found his own helmet, shook it to make sure nothing had crawled inside it, and then slipped it over his head, swinging the visor down. He pulled his gloves tight. By the time Rockdale sat back down at the tree, he was covered from his feet to the top of his head, and sweat poured down his head and neck, running under the flight suit onto an already saturated T-shirt. The helmet did keep the feasting mosquitoes off of Rockdale, but it muffled sounds and blinded his peripheral vision. If anything or anyone decided to approach the three stranded aircrewmen by any direction other than directly ahead, Rockdale would never see or hear them until it was too late.

Rockdale stared at the fire, his eyes locked onto the ebb and flow of the flames. He yawned. A few minutes later his head fell forward, and shortly his soft snore joined MacGammon's.

The bushes to his right moved. A frightened small creature of the night dashed out, jumped over MacGammon, and quickly disappeared into the thicket on the other side. Rockdale never saw the young lad who stepped into the clearing.

"SET CONDITION THREE," THE VOICE BLARED FROM THE IN-ternal Communication System speakers lining the fuselage of the EP-3E.

Senior Chief Pits Conar unstrapped himself. The aircraft was still climbing, so it was a good time to grab some of that fresh coffee brought aboard. He took his helmet off and laid it on the shelf behind the pilot. This time he was the extra flight engineer, so he had nothing to do in the cockpit while the pilot, copilot, and flight engineer manned the controls during the ascent. He pushed the curtains aside and stepped into the operating area of the aircraft.

Throughout the fuselage of the EP-3E, crewmen reached under their seats, pulled levers, and turned their seats forty-five degrees either right and left so that they faced the technical consoles lining the bulkheads of the aircraft. Some kept their flight gloves on, while most tucked them into the leg pockets of their flight suits. Fingers flew as operator attention focused on the sophisticated electronic equipment. A few unbuckled and headed to the galley in the aft section of the aircraft, to grab cups of coffee before they reached cruising altitude and turned toward the area where their shipmates waited for rescue. The white lights for takeoff had been switched off. Green computer consoles provided faint light. Each console had individual position lights, but the white light from these low-watt bulbs destroyed night vision as much as having the overhead lights turned—on so people used them sparingly.

Senior Chief Pits Conar walked carefully through the maze of activity and a minute later was sipping coffee from a paper cup. He didn't care one iota for Badass Razi, and him jumping out of a perfectly good aircraft was, as far as Pits was concerned, a bullshit display. Razi was good at that. Spotlights and brownnosing. For Razi to bail out *supposedly* over concern for his sailors conflicted against everything Pits had come to believe about Razi. Pits shuffled to the side, moving out of the way of others waiting to fill their cups. Holding on to the overhead railing, he took another sip, waiting for it to cool further. The coffee reached the lip of the cup, so he'd wait until he had drank a little of it before starting back up the crowded aisle to the cockpit.

He shook his head. Razi was a loud self-serving asshole who could conjugate any verb in the English language as long it was in the first-person singular. The man only worked to impress those around him, and then he goes and does something like this. Pits sighed, took a sip, and figured the coffee level was low enough to head back. He worked his way into the line again, poured a second cup, and started forward toward the cockpit, precariously balancing a cup in each hand.

Razi, if this is some sort of show-off, then I'm personally going to try to kick your muscle-bound piece of shit ass from here to Rota.

Pits weaved through the operators, taking care not to

trip over open boxes scattered along the aisle where they had been shoved for easy access. Everyone worked to turn-on, check-out, and step-off their position. Opposite the four passenger seats were the cryptologic technicians—CTs, everyone called them. The five operators were hunched forward, watching numbers and symbols zoom across panoramic displays. Everyone of the spooks had their mouthpiece shoved against their lips, and Pits noticed all of them seemed to be speaking at once. How in the hell they were able to keep track of the multiple data they received on their gear was beyond him. He had long ago given up trying to figure out what in the hell CTs were. Maybe you had to have some sort of glitch in your psyche to do the memory games they did. He recognized three of the CTs. Usually every mission had a CT trainee flying with them. Pits's lower lip bunched against his upper and his brow wrinkled causing the ball cap, slapped over his balding head immediately after removing his flight helmet, to slip forward. For this mission, the mission commander should have insisted that the spooks bring five qualified operators. Two of the CTs that Pits recognized were gifted musicians. Free beer and friendly women seemed to migrate to these two when they got their guitars going. Musicians and mathematicians—most CTs were good in either one or both of those fields, and Pits could never figure out the relationship between those hobbies and their profession. How Razi became a CT was beyond him. The man couldn't even whistle—*unless it was to draw attention to himself*.

An aviation technician operator, with her back to Pits, bumped him as he stepped around her. Neither apologized; it was too common of an incident to even bother acknowledging.

Maybe he was wrong about Razi. Maybe it was just a

personality thing, and Razi was truly a great chief—a warm human being with a soft spot in his heart for his men—a great patriot and wonderful American. Pits smiled; then again, maybe—*just maybe*—Razi believed his own bullshit so much that during the stress of bailout, he bailed out before his mind caught up to his bullshit. He laughed at the idea of Razi's shock when the man realized he was hurtling earthward without meaning to. *Serves you right,* Pits laughed.

Pits looked over the shoulder of the navigator as he neared the cockpit. The young officer was hunched over his charts, drawing lines from one point of reference to the next, while above him a geopositional satellite displayed their true position.

The smile left him as he reached for the curtain separating the cockpit from the operations area. The idea conformed to Pits's idea of Razi, but when they rescued Razi and the three others tomorrow, he could visualize the rooster strutting back and forth, crowing about how he saved those poor, unfortunate crewmen. *Damn, life's not only unfair, it sure is a bitch sometimes.*

Pits shook his head. In his head, that fake smile of Razi blinded his consideration of the man. No way Razi did this for those sailors. He was going to have to watch this self-serving—*Look, don't you think my biceps are firmer*—chief petty officer stick a star above his anchor device and call himself senior chief. He sighed.

Pits parted the curtains and ducked inside the dark cockpit. A small red overhead light lit up the flight engineer's seat.

"Here's your coffee," he said to the flight engineer. This time Pits was the second flight engineer. The one coming down with the skipper insisted he go with the boss.

"Thanks, Pits," Chief Petty Officer Roberts said, still

wearing his flight gloves, as he took the paper cup from the senior chief.

Pits shoved aside the flight folders the cockpit crew had thrown on his perch in the short time he had been away. The small uncomfortable shelves running along both sides of the cockpit behind the pilot and copilot also served as seats for the extra pilots and flight engineers when they flew. Pits sipped his coffee and kept quiet. They were still ascending and from the looks of things above them, clouds were moving into the area. One moment he could see the stars and the next they disappeared. Without moonlight, it was hard to tell what was below them. It wasn't as if they were flying over the United States or Europe where lights on the ground reassured everyone above that below them civilization existed. Here in Africa, there was none of that. Electricity lit up the major cities. Even a few miles from the major population centers, the lights gave way to black-ness as poverty and jungle showed a face of darkness to everyone who flew over.

"Skipper, we're passing one-two-zero," Lieutenant Evans said.

"Only a third of the way up."

"Roger, Skipper."

The only thing worse than flying with Razi was the anx-iety of flying with the skipper. The skipper's flights, for the most part, were calm, easy trips broken by moments of butt-tightening intensity. It wasn't as if the skipper was a self-serving sycophant like Razi, but the squadron's goat locker had reached the conclusion that the skipper was im-mortal. Even if they hadn't reached that conclusion, the skipper believed he was immortal. There were few immor-tals in the Navy. Most were admirals and master chiefs. All the others were pilots. What was it his sister said about dat-ing pilots after he and his wife lined her up with one from the squadron during her visit last summer? "I knew the date was half-over when he said, 'Enough about me; now let's talk about flying.'"

"What are you smiling about, Senior Chief?" Commander Charles Tidbody Greensburg, better known as Crazy Harry to the troops, asked, staring at him in the reflection cast on the cockpit window by the green and red console lights.

"Nothing, sir. Just thinking how great it is to be up here."

"I know what you mean, Senior Chief. I truly do." The skipper shook his head. "Just wish it was for some other reason than—"

"Yes, sir. I know."

It would not have surprised Pits to walk up the aisle at the Rota Chapel some Sunday and find the skipper standing alongside the chaplain handing out wafers, chugging the wine, and exchanging details on their last conversation with God. Anyone else, and Pits would have long ago convinced the detailers to ship him out of VQ-2, but there was something about flying with someone so confident that he was convinced he could put a four-engine air-breathing turboprop into orbit.

Therefore, as long as the skipper was at the yoke and throttle, wrapped in this cloak of immortality, nothing bad would ever happen.

Pits gently shook the coffee in the cup, watching the liquid swirl clockwise, stirring up the cheap military instant creamer from the bottom. The problem with the skipper's cloak of immorality was Pits's increasing doubts as to whether the cloak was large enough to encompass everyone who followed the man.

"About an hour to track. Another hour to first light after that," Chief Roberts said.

"We're going to find them," the skipper said. "When we

do, we're going to orbit over them until the Air Force finishes its crew rest and takes their leisurely time to fly out here and haul their asses up."

"They're scheduled for an o-six-hundred hours launch," the copilot said. "Three hours from now."

"When they arrive, we'll be there. Once I'm sure they have our four aircrewmen aboard, then we'll turn tail toward home plate, and call it a night."

"Passing two-zero-zero," the copilot said.

"What do you think?"

"About what, sir?"

"Here, nearer the equator."

Lieutenant Evans glanced at Chief Roberts and Pits. Both shrugged their shoulders.

"Nearer the equator what, Skipper?"

Crazy Harry let go of the yoke. "You know what! We can have some fun here."

Evans tightened his grip on the yoke, feeling the control of the huge EP-3E reconnaissance aircraft shift to him.

The skipper didn't care for automatic pilot and he seldom let others know when he was going to release the yoke, leave his seat, or doze off. Pits crossed his legs. It was that cloak of immortality.

"Nearer the equator the air is thicker. Means you can fly higher. I was thinking . . . I was thinking that we might be able to break the altitude record we set over Marbella, Spain."

"Skipper, we nearly crashed—"

"Oh, don't be stupid, Dell. We never 'nearly' crashed. Sure, we lost power for a few moments—"

"Power to all four engines!" Evans exclaimed.

"It wasn't as if aircraft don't lose power every now and again. The thing to remember is we reached thirty-six thousand feet before the engines sputtered."

"Skipper, they didn't sputter! They stopped. Kaput! Ceased to operate!"

Crazy Harry pulled his flight gloves tighter and wiggled his fingers. "All of the engines didn't stop. You make it sound worse than it was. Here, we should easily beat that record. It'll be fun and educational."

"Skipper, if you want fun, then let's put you and Colonel Hightower the helicopter pilot in the club when we return, and you and him can argue who flies faster," the copilot offered.

"Skipper, we only reached thirty-two thousand and some odd feet," Chief Roberts added.

Crazy Harry motioned downward with his hand, looking up at the reflections in the cockpit windshield. "Chief, the altimeter was screwed up. When you adjust for the altimeter error, we passed thirty-five thousand feet. I would say we were nearer thirty-six thousand. So what if our brethren and sisters who wrote the Naval Air Training and Operating Procedures—"

"Standardization," the other three said in unison.

"Okay, NATOPS it is. I'll call it NATOPS, but I thought it important for training purposes that you recognize what the acronym stands for. As I was saying, so what if NATOPS says the max altitude is twenty-eight thousand, three hundred feet?" He reached out and patted the top of the flight controls. "What the hell do they know? This baby can make forty-thousand feet. Who in the hell decided that odd three-hundred-feet-portion of NATOPS max altitude? That's like selling something for three-ninety-nine instead of four dollars; or, telling someone the distance is three point two miles instead of three miles. Do you realize somewhere we—*us taxpayers*—are paying someone megadollars to be that specific. Why didn't they just say, 'The max altitude for the EP-3E Aries II aircraft is a little over twenty-eight thousand feet, so be careful if you exceed it'?" He looked at the copilot. "The EP-3E flies faster than some goddamn helicopter."

"We agree," the three of them said in unison.

"Agree with what?"

"Agree with what you said about NATOPS, Skipper, and that we can outfly a helicopter," Chief Roberts answered.

Crazy Harry shook his head. "Oh, ye of little faith. I was just using that as an example of how they should have written it. Not an example of a fact. Don't believe that everything written down and approved by a bunch of engineers is a fact. Why, I've never—"

"—seen a project ever completed by an engineer," the other three said in unison.

"—seen a project ever completed by an engineer," Greensburg continued, "Because engineers always believe there is a much, *more,* better thing they can do to it."

"Sir, we've been lucky, so far, in this—"

"Listen, Lieutenant, let's don't trade skill for luck in this endeavor to prove the orbital powers of the EP-3E."

"Sir, I would never trade luck for skill."

"Good. Luck is always the better friend when you're losing power, hydraulics are gone, and you can't see the ground."

"But you'll still have enough power to reach the scene of the crash."

"You guys are beginning to get on my nerves," Commander Greensburg said. "I have a perfect aviation record—I've never left an aircraft in the air."

Pits leaned back, his head touching the bulkhead. He opened his mouth to join the banter, but instead tossed back the few remaining drops of lukewarm coffee. He'd heard this conversation on too many flights. The skipper arguing how wherever they were flying, the air was thicker;

the chief correcting him; the copilot counterarguing to talk him out of it, and the skipper rebutting with his theory that no one really analyzed the max altitudes of aircraft—commercial or military. If there were actual people who did that, then they wouldn't be so specific because they'd know that pilots believe NATOPS to be more like guidelines than restrictions. Most times he succeeded and beat the copilot and flight engineer down. Sometimes he didn't. When he didn't, then he invoked the fallback position of the God-given right of the skipper, and off they'd go, butt-cheeks tight, heading for the heavens.

"Skipper, you want another cup of coffee before we start searching for our men?" Pits asked.

Crazy Harry glanced up at the windscreen, his eyes meeting the reflected eyes of Pits. Finally, he nodded. "Okay, Senior Chief. Too many of you against me this time, so I will take the coffee, but I'll get it myself. But once they're safe, depending on fuel constraints, we're going to check the thickness of this African air. Dell Evans, level us off at twenty-four thousand and we'll cruise at that altitude. The skipper slid his seat back, unbuckled, and stepped out. "Why anyone would want to fly a fighter plane and stay strapped in one position throughout the flight is something that beggars the mind of us normal pilots."

"I think it's the piss tube," Lieutenant Evans offered. "I've heard it has suction on it."

Pits smiled as Crazy Harry shook his head. "That's just typical. Fighter pilots always get the better amenities. Probably explains the glazed look in their eyes when they land."

They waited until the curtains closed behind Crazy Harry before they spoke.

"Avoided another one," Chief Roberts said.

"Don't count on it," Evans replied. "Once our aircrewmen

have been rescued, he'll be thinking about it again as we head home."

"Lieutenant Evans, do you mind me asking if Dell is really your first name?" Pits asked as he started to follow the skipper.

The copilot shook his head. "No, it's Daniel, but the—"

"I gave him that handle," Crazy Harry said, sticking his head back through the curtains. "Dell is the masculine form of Dale and I didn't want to hurt his masculinity by spelling it *D-A-L-E,* which is why I keep the young lieutenant with me—the only reason I keep him with me. He reminds me of cowboys with white hats and the tales my father told about Roy Rogers and his lovely wife, Dale." The skipper reached over and punched Pits lightly on the shoulder. "Senior Chief, I thought we were going for coffee."

"Can do, will do, glad to, Skipper." Pits followed as they worked their way aft.

Crazy Harry stopped just before the galley and twisted the knob on the door leading to the small compartment where a metal canister about four foot high served as a urinal. There was a seated position—honey pot—that anyone could use, but the first person to use it had to clean it once they landed. So, like wolves, aircrew watched the head while they flew waiting for someone, who could no longer control it, to use the honey pot. Then, it was fair game for everyone.

Pits was drawing the second cup when the skipper stepped up, grabbed one, thanked Pits, and headed back to the cockpit. The only time anyone saw the skipper during a flight was when he made a quick head call. Otherwise, he lived in the cockpit, sitting up there, sometimes quiet, his thoughts to himself, and just when you relaxed, he'd voice his thoughts such as the one last month, wondering whether an EP-3E could do a roll.

Pits had been on that flight. It was a check-ride for one of the senior pilots. No one laughed. The skipper never joked about his flying. Pits had immediately tightened his seat belt and held on, because the skipper was also known to talk about trying something while in the middle of executing it. The skipper might be immortal, but at times such as that one, Pits believed the cloak had been left on the runway.

Other times, he believed the Navy was shielding a great leader from greatness. Crazy Harry was a phenomenal mix of great leadership and dangerous ideas. The key was to respect him from afar, but that was hard to do when you were crammed with twenty-two other aircrew on the same aircraft with a genius for a madman. Luckily, Crazy Harry didn't try to do a victory roll in the EP-3E, and he hadn't voiced the idea since.

"Well, Senior Chief, looks as if we're earning our flight pay today," Lieutenant Commander Peeters said, stepping up beside Pits.

"Yes, sir. We hear anything yet, Commander?" Pits tossed the plastic spoon into the trash and took a sip.

"Not yet, but if they keep to their SEER training, they'll be transmitting every fifteen minutes."

Pits nodded. "Yes, sir, but yesterday when we left them, we told them to expect rescue either late yesterday or early this morning. I don't think they'll be transmitting—"

"Chief Razi is with them. If anyone is sharp enough to know what to do, it's him. By now, he's got those three junior sailors standing watch, policing the area, and going over the details for a helo rescue."

I'm going to be sick, Pits thought. *The man is unbelievable! It's one BS after another and every one of these officers believe him.* "Yes, sir," he replied. "No doubt in my mind that if anyone can turn this into a good-news story, it'll be Chief Razi." Pits edged by Lieutenant Commander Peeters and walked back toward the cockpit, unaware of Peeters staring after him. Nor did he see Peeters eventually scratch his head with a questioning look on his face as Pits passed from view into the shadows of the aisle.

CHAPTER 11

RAZI SHINED THE RED LIGHT ON THE GROUND AHEAD OF him, waving the flashlight back and forth, raking the huge tangle of bushes blocking his way. He ran his free hand over his face, feeling the tattered cloth of his glove move through the mud and dirt caking his features. Razi reached out and pushed the leaves of the nearest bush, watching them move easily aside. Just one more obstacle to overcome, but—he took a deep breath and raised his head—none of the others stopped him, and neither would this one. He dropped his hand. The leaves sprung back to their original position. Razi straightened. He was a goddamn chief petty officer, and chief petty officers never let obstacles stop them—and they always fell so that their rank insignia was hidden.

He tucked the flashlight under his arm, the light pointing down, and pulled the compass from his survival vest. The survival vest hung loosely from Razi's shoulders.

Sometime during the night, he didn't recall when, he must have unzipped it down the center to allow the night air to dry the dampness from the sweat-soaked trunk of the flight suit. He touched the zipper halves with both hands for a moment as if to zip the survival vest back together, but a rustle to his right drew his attention, and he dropped his hands away.

After several seconds, Razi freed his compass, lifted the flashlight, and illuminated it. Squinting, he assured himself he was on the right course before jamming it back into the vest. Razi fought an urge to howl at the barrier in front of him. He'd done that a couple of times at earlier barriers only to discover the barriers fought harder. He knew his fellow chiefs would laugh at the idea of plants fighting you, but he had learned a lot in the jungle. Things no one else knew. Things he would never tell anyone. He touched the leaves for a moment. He snickered at the idea of him knowing these secrets and keeping them to himself.

It was better to go ahead without the fanfare of his howl. He nodded and grinned. His war cry, as he thought of it, was getting better. Razi reached forward, shoved the limbs aside, and stepped into the edge of the thicket. The red light barely showed a foot away in this mess, but he was on the right course toward his sailors, and nothing was going to stop him.

Razi had long quit wondering if the noise he made alerted those ahead. He wanted them to know he was coming. In his misguided reasoning, Razi had convinced himself that if those boy soldiers heard him coming, they would give up their pursuit and run in fear. He smiled at the thought of their wide-eyed fear as they scattered pell-mell into the surrounding jungle, running to momma. It never dawned on Razi, as it wouldn't on most Americans, that the children soldiers of Africa had long since seen and heard worse things in the night than an unarmed, dirty chief petty officer lost in the turbid jungles of their land. Most of Africa's children soldiers had no parents, and those few who did had little idea where their parents were, much less where they themselves were.

It took Razi two hours to penetrate the thick maze of jungle growth before he suddenly emerged into a semblance of a clearing that stretched off in the direction he needed to go. Razi didn't stop to congratulate himself on working through the jungle bramble. He stepped off, hurrying forward. Not sure why he was hurrying, but knowing he had to find his sailors before sunlight. Tomorrow the— What would come tomorrow? He checked his watch and his compass. Fifteen minutes before four. He bit his lower lip and shook his head in disbelief. Rescue! That's what would come. A helicopter swooping down, snatching them from the jungle, and by this time tomorrow, he'd be on his second case of beer.

If his watch was right, he'd been on the ground for over seventeen hours. He hadn't been that far from his sailors. Maybe he had walked past them? What if he had missed them, and when morning came he discovered he was miles away on the other side of them. Razi kept walking. He couldn't have made that much trail in that time. The fall off the cliff added a couple or three hours to his trek. It wasn't as if the jungle let you walk straight and didn't fight you all the way. *Oh, yes, he knew. Chief Petty Officer Razi was smarter than my other chiefs.* He patted himself on the chest. "I know things you'll never know."

Rockdale, MacGammon, and Carson were ahead. He shook his head. *Focus.* He had to be alert because the three sailors were near. He giggled. They had to be near, he'd walked too long for them not to be near. A wave of ecstatic relief washed over him as he envisioned their gratitude when he walked out of the jungle to join them. Rockdale, MacGammon, and Carson were probably curled up in fetal positions, holding on to each other against the jungle night. They'd be safe soon. He'd be there. No sailor was safe without a chief petty officer nearby.

He stopped and squatted in the middle of the faint trail, taking another swig of water. Razi shut his eyes. His legs ached. He rotated his right shoulder and wondered why it hurt. He thought maybe a few minutes nap while resting on his haunches would help. He shut his eyes.

Minutes later he opened his eyes, unable to sleep. He was too pumped up on reaching Rockdale, MacGammon, and Carson, hearing their accolades and feeling the slaps on his back when they see him. Somewhere ahead—and it couldn't be too far—his sailors waited. For Razi, the mere act of him walking into the middle of the three other aircrew was sufficient to mark it as a rescue. After all, he was a designated NATOPS instructor. What more could a bunch of young sailors lost in the woods want? The children soldiers could have their mothers, but sailors needed their chiefs, and he was these sailors' chief petty officer.

He squatted patiently, telling himself he should be up and moving, but the sense of urgency he felt earlier seemed to have evaporated because he had convinced himself his goal was only minutes away. He started to stand; rising halfway, before something—he didn't know quite what—caused him to sink back down onto his haunches.

He lifted his head, drawing air through his nose, smelling the jungle night. There was a new odor riding the humid breeze. He had waited patiently when hunting in the hills of North Carolina. A good hunter waited. This wasn't exactly a blind, but—He switched off the flashlight. The dark of the jungle immediately enveloped him. A sharp smell passed through his nostrils—a foul odor, almost like

urine. It took a few minutes for Razi to recognize the
ammonia-sharp odor for what it was—human sweat. He
lifted his arm, the soaked fabric pulling away, and took a
whiff. His nose wrinkled. It wasn't him, though his was
sharp. He raised his head and took several more whiffs. He
smiled, associating the odor with the children soldiers who
had earlier frightened him. His smile disappeared. Well, he
wasn't frightened now. He stood. The sooner he found
them, the sooner they could flee back to momma's arms.

The odor rode the wind. He turned his head until the
slight night wind hit him squarely in the face. It was at
that moment when Razi realized that the jungle sounds
were silenced. Everything had gone to ground. He had become so accustomed to the night sounds that they had
faded into the background, but with the light gone, the
odor assailed his nostrils, making the disappearance of
the sounds prominent.

Razi took several quiet steps forward, following the direction of the wind, hoping he recalled accurately his surroundings in the event he had to backtrack. He wanted a
little distance between him and where he squatted. Maybe
those boys with their pissant guns had decided to investigate. Something caught his attention slightly to his right.
He stopped, leaning against a nearby tree, blending into the
grays and blacks of the jungle night as they taught in survival school. He squinted in that direction, concentrating,
smelling the air. After several seconds, a flicker caught his
eye, and he smiled. It was a campfire. Not a large one, but
one nearly blocked by vegetation between him and it.
Maybe, just maybe, he'd stumbled onto the armed boys before they found him. He touched his flashlight, nearly turning it on before thinking better of it. He forced down a
giggle, thinking of the expression on those boy-soldiers'
faces when he dashed into the center of the campsite,

howling his war cry at the top of his lungs before beating the living shit out of them.

The longer he stared, the clearer the campfire became. After a while, Razi didn't know how long, he straightened. Then, he started toward the fire, stumbling over unseen vines as he moved, and several times grabbing trunks of young trees that made up this small grove through which he noisily approached the campsite. He heard voices talking and stopped, listening intently for a few seconds, until he realized it was his own voice.

Razi giggled again. *How stupid,* he told himself. "At least I'm not answering myself," Razi said aloud.

Razi took several deep breaths, one step forward, and squatted again, his head turning slowly from side to side. Bushes in front of him hid the campfire. Those boy soldiers waited ahead. He leaned forward on both hands and eased himself to the ground, sharp sticks poking him the length of his body. "They won't see me now," he mumbled quietly. Mustn't talk to myself. Must keep quiet until I wring their scrawny necks. Theirs were thin reeds of a neck, he recalled. He raised his right hand and made a fist, looking at the silhouette against the night foliage, and shook it several times. Just like that, wring their necks, and watch their puny heads flop forty-five degrees to the side. He twisted his fist back and forth, visualizing their heads flopping from side to side, bouncing off their thin shoulders. Razi giggled. *This is going to be fun,* he thought.

Razi dropped his fist and started crawling forward. He couldn't see the fire now, but he didn't need to see it. As long as he was crawling forward, they couldn't see him. Farther into the bushes, his survival vest, no longer strapped firmly to his body, caught on something, slowing his forward movement for a second. Razi wriggled out of it, continuing forward, his mind so focused on the boy soldiers ahead of him. Behind him, the limbs sprung back to their natural position, lifting the vest off the jungle floor into the lower reaches of the main bushes. The pouch flap holding the PRC-90 radio came open.

His mind was only slightly aware of the loss of the survival vest. He heard the muffled crackle of the radio behind him and a voice calling from it. A low voice called his name along with the other three, but it was behind him and his mind told him they weren't real, just another obstacle trying to stop him. His forward motion never stopped, Razi kept crawling forward, and in a few feet the voices from the radio could no longer be heard.

A half-hour later, Razi rolled onto his back, and raised his arms above his chest, stretching out the cramps racing through each arm. Dehydration caused camps, he recalled from SEER training. He patted his chest, searching for the water bottle. Both hands patted his chest. His survival vest was gone and with it the radio, the compass, the water, and what little food he had. For some reason, it didn't bother him. He raised his arms, twisting his hands back and forth, amazed that he could see them. Moisture dripped off his hands onto his chest. Dawn was coming. He giggled again. *I walked all night, killed some terrorists, and even crawled to rescue my sailors.* That story line should be worth a few free beers and maybe even a groping session with that new flight engineer. *What was her name?* He stopped for a moment, trying to recall the flight engineer's name who had swiped her finger through the peanut butter on his flight boot. "Damn, it'll come later," he said after a couple of minutes.

He sat up and brought his hands close to his face. Strands of torn cloth rippled the fire-retardant cloth of the gloves, leaving strips hanging by threads to the wrist portion. His hands picked at the tattered gloves, ripping apart the few remaining strands that held the fingers of the gloves together. His knuckles were red. Razi blew on them, watching blood pool where cuts and deep abrasions had torn the skin. He curled his fingers into his palms. *How did I do this?* he wondered.

Suddenly, shouts drew his attention. He quickly rolled over onto his stomach and raised his head. Gunfire ripped through the jungle, causing Razi to rise to his knees. The next moment he was standing up, tearing through the bushes. He could see the campfire to his right. He turned slightly and ran directly toward the campfire, ignoring the thrashing noises he was making as he tore through the jungle growth. The smell of gunpowder surrounded him. Someone in the back of his mind was screaming for him to stop. *"What are you doing, you stupid shit?"* the voice shouted. For a second, he was aware of the stupidity of running toward gunfire. He didn't even have a knife. Marines did this type of stuff. Not sailors. And definitely not Razi. This wasn't something he'd do, he told himself, but he kept charging. The fleeting moment of rational thought was lost in a primal urge to kill. He pushed the last bushes apart and stumbled into the circle of the campfire, his motion carrying him forward as he regained his balance.

A few feet from where he emerged stood Rockdale and MacGammon, their arms raised above their heads. To the right, lay a third body, wearing a flight suit, the head hidden by a flight helmet. That would be Carson. Standing over Carson was the malnourished African Razi had first seen in the downpour. The boy had the barrel of his gun pressed against the flight helmet. Two other boy soldiers stood between Razi and Rockdale.

Most would have paused, but in Razi's clouded mind, time slowed. He laughed as he changed direction slightly. Razi reached the two boy soldiers, slamming both fists against their heads at the same time. The young lad standing over Carson raised his gun, swinging it toward Razi, who had changed direction and was charging the remaining boy soldier. Razi howled, his war cry shocking the young soldier, causing him to pull the trigger before the automatic weapon was fully aimed. A fleeting thought of what it was going to feel like when those bullets hit crossed his mind, but Razi continued running—his cry filling the jungle. The weapon swung a few more inches and Razi's howling grew in intensity as he closed the space between them, a calm thought crossing his mind wondering if this time the boy's aim would be more accurate.

From the right, MacGammon hit the young African lad, causing the weapon to spray a pattern of bullets around Razi, barely missing the chief. MacGammon landed on top of the boy and started slamming his fists into the young lad's head, continuing to pound even when the boy was unconscious.

Razi stopped and looked down at MacGammon beating the boy. He turned. Rockdale had grabbed one of the weapons and was picking up the other from the two boys Razi had slam-dunked.

"A fourth," Razi said. "There's four of them."

Rockdale shrugged, hurried over to MacGammon, and grabbed his arm in midswing. "I think he's out of it."

Razi grabbed a weapon from Rockdale. "There's another one out there. Stay here. I'll be back." And he dashed into the bushes, disappearing quickly from view. Behind him, Rockdale shouted for him to come back, but he couldn't. Unfinished business was here somewhere. He glanced at the weapon. AK-47, he surmised. He wasn't sure because he wasn't a Marine, but he recalled the intelligence specialist saying AK-47s were the automatic weapon of choice for poorly paid terrorists. Besides, he would never ask a Marine what it was; they'd bask too much in the pleasure of having a chief petty officer ask them about something they believed every Navy person ought to know. No, he'd never ask a Marine. A limb swung back and slapped him across his face. Where was his helmet, he wondered as he kept charging.

MACGAMMON STOOD UP, HIS EYES NEVER LEAVING THE unconscious boy beneath him. Morning filtered through the trees, bringing faint light to the men. "You all right?" he asked, his breathing short and rapid.

Rockdale nodded. "I'm fine. Let's check Stetson."

A moan from Carson told them he was still alive. MacGammon laughed. "He'd gonna be one sorry mother-fucker, isn't he?"

Rockdale's brow wrinkled. "What do you mean?"

"Well, when we get out of here today, everyone—even *Reader's Digest*—are gonna want to know what happened, and only you and I will know."

"The chief will know."

MacGammon looked around the area. "Are we sure what we just saw was real? One moment we're about to be shot, and the next, we got Badass running through our campsite, screaming at the top of his lungs, slapping Africans about."

"Then he grabs a gun and disappears back into the bushes," Rockdale added. "Not the Chief Razi I know."

"You bet it wasn't. I didn't see a single officer to watch him. You know what, Rocky? I bet ya he's nuts."

"How can we tell? I've always thought he was nuts."

Gunfire from nearby sent the two men diving for the ground.

"I hope he gets whatever he's shooting at."

"He said something about there being four of them."

The sound of movement drew their attention. They saw the feet of the boy soldiers the chief had knocked down disappear into the brush. Rockdale raised the automatic weapon and pointed toward where they disappeared.

"I wouldn't do it," MacGammon said. "The chief is out there somewhere. You might hit him."

Rockdale didn't reply, but he lowered the weapon.

Carson moaned.

"Let's get his helmet off. Did you put it on him last night?"

"Yeah, I did," Rockdale replied. "You should have seen the mosquitoes covering him when I got up to throw more wood on the fire." He kept searching the surroundings, afraid any moment those Africans were going to return.

"Told you so," MacGammon said as he unstrapped the helmet and pulled it off Carson. Carson's hair was matted to his head, several streaks of hair falling across his eyes when the helmet came free. "See, Rocky. That's why the Navy makes us have short hair."

More gunfire came from a little farther out.

"He must be chasing him."

"Chasing his own shadows, more likely," MacGammon said.

They squatted beside Carson. "You want to hand me some bandages?"

"I gotta find our survival vests. They tossed them into the bushes when we took them off," MacGammon said as he stood. "You know something, Rocky?" He let a deep breath out. "That was as scared as I'd ever been."

Rockdale set the helmet aside. "I know," he said without looking up. He was afraid that if his eyes met MacGammon's, the slight hold he had on his emotions would let go. "I thought we were going to die," he continued, his voice trembling.

"Yeah, me, too."

"Be careful," Rockdale said.

MacGammon brushed off the seat of his flight suit as he walked across the parachute. "I doubt there are any others around here. What with the chief beating the shit out of two of them—"

"I thought you were going to kill the other one."

"I would have," he said softly, "if you hadn't stopped me." A few seconds later, he pushed into the bushes on the opposite side.

Rockdale listened to him searching. He raised the AK-47 and started scanning the surrounding bushes. The survival vests couldn't be too far. They weighed too much for the three lads who had the drop on them to toss them too far.

"I can't find them!"

More gunfire, even farther away, broke the morning noise of an awakening jungle.

Rockdale stood. "They've got to be out there," he said, stepping across the parachute toward the bushes, glancing back once at the unconscious Carson and African boy.

MacGammon stepped back into the campsite clearing just as Rockdale reached the edge. "They're gone," he said, tossing a couple of energy bars onto the parachute. "That's all I could find. The chief was right. There must have been a fourth one."

"Must have been more than four. If the fourth one was as small and tiny as the three we saw—"

"Speaking of the three," MacGammon said, pointing, "Where is the one I hit?"

Rockdale turned and looked. Only seconds ago, the third African boy lay sprawled out near the edge of the campsite. "Looks as if we've lost all three."

"At least we have their weapons."

"Weapons!" Rockdale shouted. "Without radios, how in the hell is the helicopter going to know where we are?"

MacGammon smiled. "The chief! We use Badass's radio."

"Shit! He didn't have a survival vest on when he crashed into here. He didn't have much of anything on. He didn't have his helmet, and his flight suit looked as if someone had taken a razor to it."

The smile left MacGammon's face. "You gotta be shitting me. Badass is a NATOPS instructor—*He's our NATOPS instructor*," MacGammon said, slapping his chest a couple of times. "The man wouldn't leave his survival vest." Then in a near whisper, MacGammon added, "Badass is too much of an asshole to violate an instruction!"

A wavering howl stopped Rockdale as he started to reply. "What the hell!" The howl reminded Rockdale of an old Tarzan movie that his parents enjoyed. "Where did Razi learn that?"

"I think Chief Razi's gone native," MacGammon said.

"THE HELICOPTER IS AIRBORNE, SKIPPER," LIEUTENANT Commander Peeters said, sticking his head through the curtains. "Should be on station in an hour."

"Wow!" Commander Greensburg replied. Nodding toward the east, he continued. "The sun has barely broken the horizon and the Air Force is airborne. Dell, write that down. It'll be a great quote someday."

"Aye, sir," Lieutenant Evans said, ignoring an order heard numerous times when flying with the skipper.

"Keep me informed on their progress, Chuck. I suspect we still haven't managed to raise our lads?"

"No, sir, but we're calling constantly," Peeters replied,

his voice trailing off. "Not sure why they haven't responded. We're in the right spot where they bailed out, and between the four of them, they have four PRC-90s. We thought about dropping a CRT-3, but it wouldn't do much good to give them a larger, more capable radio when we have no idea exactly where they are, so we'd only be throwing it away. We did drop the number-three life raft."

"Why'd you do that? There's no ocean around here except this jungle canopy."

"We thought they could use the food and water rations stored in it, as well as the radio."

Crazy Harry chuckled. "What we're going to find is the life raft in the top of one of these trees. Damn, best of intentions—"

Pits stood up and put his hand on Chief Roberts' shoulder. "You want to take a break?"

"I want to know as soon as we make contact."

Peeters acknowledged the order and pulled his head out of the cockpit, allowing the curtains to close.

"No, I'm okay, Pits. Besides, it'll be full daylight soon and this is the part of flying I enjoy most."

"Dell, let's take her down to treetop level."

"Roger, Skipper."

Pits grabbed ahold of the back of the flight engineer's seat as the EP-3E tilted forward.

"Ah, come on, Lieutenant! I said take her down, not drive around."

Pits put both hands on the back of the seat. In the next instant, the EP-3E's angle of descent increased past 45 degrees, as Crazy Harry grabbed the yoke and pulled back on the throttle.

"Set Condition Three," Chief Roberts announced on the internal communications system.

From the rear of the huge reconnaissance aircraft came

the sound of things falling, metal carrying cases toppling over, and curses from the aircrew as coffee and liquids joined the mess.

"Skipper," Chief Roberts said, "You know it would be best if we gave warning to the crew before we did one of your maneuvers."

Pits shifted his feet slightly to get a better position. Crazy Harry's face appeared in the reflection of the cockpit window.

"What do you mean, Chief, one of my maneuvers? Our aircraft and our crews are always ready for the unexpected. Did you hear any complaints from back there?"

"No, sir, no complaints, but it'll take a while to clean up the aisle."

"Gripe, gripe, gripe. Lieutenant Evans, take a note to remind me to write to the Master Chief Petty Officer of the Navy about the caliber of chief petty officers we're getting in the Navy today. Used to be, back in my time, a chief would never question a skipper's actions. Nowadays, everyone has a hotline but a skipper."

The aircraft eased up on its descent. Pits glanced at the altimeter and saw the dial slowing as they passed eight thousand feet.

"Chief, why don't you— No, you, Senior Chief. Take a walk through my aircraft and tell me who wasn't ready for us taking this bird down. You get their names and tell them their careers are shit."

Pits smiled. "Yes, sir, but you know something, Skipper. I'd be surprised if everyone wasn't ready. They know to be ready for the unexpected when you're the pilot."

"See, Chief Roberts! There's a senior chief who knows his people."

"But I will walk through the back, sir, and see how everyone is doing."

"Good, and while you're back there, bring me another cup of coffee."

The nose of the aircraft rose. The altimeter showed them at four thousand feet.

"Passing four thousand, Skipper."

"Okay, Dell, we're going to start circling here. Tell the navigator to mark this as Mark Zero. Then, we're going to increase our circle by three to five miles every 360-degree circuit. If we haven't heard from them by the time we're thirty miles out, then we'll start heading back toward Mark Zero."

Pits stepped out of the cockpit. All along the aisle, aircrewmen were shoving publications and loose items back into metal boxes. Several were wiping up spilled coffee. He saw no gaggle of people in any one area that would have been indicative of an injury, which was another sign of the skipper's immortality. For two years, the man had been leading one of the two Navy reconnaissance squadrons and during that time, not one crash; not one death; and not one major injury had occurred. Pits also knew that the cloak of immortality would disappear in an instant if any of those three things ever did occur. It may be the information age, but sailors' superstitions survived intact.

Ahead of him, Lieutenant Commander Peeters approached. "The helo is an hour out," he said to Pits as he eased past the senior chief and entered the cockpit.

Won't do much good if we don't know where they are or what happened to them, he thought as he started down the aisle toward the head and the mess. Flying a reconnaissance aircraft was lot like a day at work. You had a makeshift cubicle where you did your work; the bathroom was down the aisle; and, both a lounge and place to have coffee rounded out the workplace.

*   *   *

RAZI SLOWED FROM HIS RUN TO A WALK AS HE BLINKED
rapidly, trying to get his sight back after so many limbs had
whipped across his face. With his free hand, he wiped the
debris away, spitting out the bits of vegetation. His breathing was rapid and deep. It had been dawn when he charged
into the campfire, now morning light filtered through the
jungle canopy.

His brow rose up and down several times before his eyes
stopped blurring and he could see again. He turned his
head, searching the surrounding bush, spotting the telltale
signs to his left that someone or something had bent the
African bush back as it made a path. Razi started running
again, chasing whoever or whatever was heading in that direction. He raised the AK-47, his finger still on the trigger.
"No," he said aloud, thinking to save however many bullets
remained in the weapon. He laughed slightly. But when he
spotted this last child warrior, he was going to blow the little man's head off. A vision of a single bullet hole in the
center of the boy's forehead flashed across his thoughts.

Another sound intruded over his breathing, and several
seconds passed before Razi realized it was the sound of
distant gunfire off to his right. He must be running full circle and it was his sailors defending themselves. Without
pausing, Razi turned and started heading toward the gunfire, never thinking it might involve someone other that
Rockdale, MacGammon, and Carson.

He was making a new path through the jungle growth,
stepping aside heavier growth to crash through lighter barriers. Never stopping, though. His left foot sunk into a spot
of marsh, bringing a sucking sound as he pulled it out, but
he kept running. His lungs ached from the exertion, but Razi
was in great shape. His body mass from years of lifting

weights gave Razi the weight and stamina needed to move
through obstacles that a jogger would only have bounced
off. He was the Hulk. He was Tarzan. He was the entire
U.S. Marine Corps, though he would never give them the
joy of knowing it. No one and nothing could stop Chief
Razi—he was invincible and he was clearing the jungle of
those would kill him and his sailors.

An entangled barrier of thorn-ridden bushes appeared
in front of him. To his left, the barrier looked shorter and
weaker. He turned and drove into the bushes, the sharp,
thick thorns tearing the already torn flight suit and ripping
though the top layer his skin wherever the thorns touched.
His forward movement slowed, but his pile-driver legs
pushed his body through entwined limbs and vines, drawing more thorns toward him from the surrounding bushes.
The brush of a limb swiped across his brow. Razi continued forward, everything focused forward. Adrenaline racing through every muscle. Red clouded his left eye as
drops of blood flowed from where thorns had slashed the
skin across his brow. He wiped it away and kept moving.

Steady gunfire came from ahead. If Razi's thoughts had
been completely rational, he would have realized the distant gunfire was more than just a few weapons, but many
weapons blanketing the jungle sounds.

Several steps later he burst through the thorn barrier
into a small clearing. Standing ahead of him was a young
man holding an AK-47. Razi turned slightly and like a
bulldozer at full throttle plowed toward the African. Pain
slammed against his head, and a blaze of white light filled
his last moment of consciousness. His body took two—
then three more steps before Razi collapsed onto the jungle
floor. Above him stood several African men looking down
at the madman who had emerged from the thorns. One of
them turned his gun over, looked at the stock, and then

slammed it down on Razi's back—drawing a grunt from Razi. He then wiped the stock back and forth on Razi's flight suit, cleaning the blood off it.

THE SOLDIER RUNNING TOWARD GENERAL EZEJI CAUGHT Ojo's attention. He watched for a moment as the soldier stopped, saluted, and said something to General Ezeji, before turning around and racing back toward the sound of gunfire. Ezeji nodded at Ojo and hurried forward toward him. "Our soldiers have stopped Abu Alhaul, sir."

As if prophetic, the sound of distant gunfire reached their ears. "I would say they have engaged them, wouldn't you?"

"Yes, General Ojo. Seems we caught up with Abu Alhaul," Ezeji replied, his smile revealing blackened back teeth. "By this time tomorrow, Africa will be rid of another scourge—a plague to its humanity."

Ojo turned toward the sound of gunfire. "General, have the men advance, but tell them to stop when we see the enemy. Our soldiers in front should keep them occupied and block any escape. It would be good if we can involve as many of our warriors as we can in slaying Abu Alhaul."

"I have already sent my lieutenants to tell my soldiers, and I have dispatched runners to both Kabaka and Darin." He held his arms out as if wrapping them around a huge invisible barrel. "Like this we are. My right arm is General Kabaka's *trustworthy* forces and my left arm is General Darwin's forces. We are the center. We are advancing toward a line—a front opposite to our soldiers. When we reach the battle zone and connect with our soldiers on the other side, then we will have the foreigners surrounded. They can surrender—"

"No!" Ojo snapped. "No surrender. No martyrs, no

surrenders, no prisoners. Abu Alhaul will disappear into the jungle. Let those who worship his murderous ways believe him to have vanished from the face of the earth. The stories our soldiers will tell will be all that remains of Abu Alhaul."

He didn't mean to startle Ezeji; neither did he mean to embarrass his number-one general. "What was the gunfire to our north that we heard earlier?"

Ezeji shrugged. "I don't know. I sent a squad to investigate and they haven't returned."

The noise of the advancing soldiers of the African National Army tromping forward to the battle area, heading in the direction of gunfire, followed the dictum of modern combat to advance toward the sound of gunfire and turn the nose toward the smell of gunpowder. They couldn't be far away from where his men had Abu Alhaul surrounded. The smell of battle overrode the jumbled odor of decaying matter wrapped around the fresh smell of jungle vegetation. Ahead was the first of many goals Ojo had set for his vision of freeing Africa from the West. To him, it mattered little if the opponent was white or black. It only mattered that it wasn't African. This wasn't a war against any political or religious entity; it was a national war full of pride in country, in people, and its history. The hardest war would come next. The defeat of Abu Alhaul was a carrot to dangle in front of those countries whose might could wipe him from the face of the earth as easily as he would swap a fly. As long as the carrot hypnotized them against his national movement, he could consolidate further his gains in West Africa. The arena where political might and guile were preeminent was a much harder battlefield than the one they were engaged upon now.

The gunfire earlier from the north bothered him. Not the noise, but the fact that Kabaka's forces were on that side, and so was the Americans.

"General Ezeji, I would like you personally to check on the action to our north."

Ezeji nodded. "I understand, General. What if our loyal General Kabaka has taken the Americans? It would complicate—"

"It would severely complicate our survivability. If he has them, take them from him."

Ezeji saluted. "I understand, sir," and with those words the heavy Nigerian turned right and marched off, his retinue following.

Ojo watched until the jungle wrapped the soldiers from sight before turning back to face the direction where the tempo of gunfire was increasing. His concern for the Americans was not for them, but for his vision. While his army grew daily with new recruits, it would only take a slight miscalculation to cause the anxious Americans, French, and Nigerians to take action against him. He was no fool. Even though he called those who followed him soldiers, and his group an army, they were but a ragtag collection of individuals when compared to the professionals who made up real armies. Finishing Abu Alhaul would appease the nation states long enough for him to obtain some legitimacy, and for that he would turn to the scholars among his followers. He was a warrior, not a statesman; and when fighting the battle for world opinion, a pen and a steady voice were the best weapons, not a gun.

"THE CHIEF AIN'T GONNA COME BACK," MACGAMMON said, looking at his watch. "It's been nearly forty-five minutes and the aircraft is still orbiting."

Rockdale nodded. "We're going to have to find our survival vests."

MacGammon lifted a handkerchief and ran it across

Carson's head. "Maybe we should look for the chief's. He wasn't wearing his when he burst out of the bushes. Maybe he took it off so he could move faster."

Rockdale nodded. "Could be." He stood and walked along the bushes. "I think he came in through here."

MacGammon joined him. "You stay here with Stetson. I'm shorter and smaller. I can probably work my way through this maze better than you."

"No, I'll go," Rockdale objected. He was the senior petty officer, and he was the one who made Sailor of the Year last year while MacGammon was having his ass hauled before the skipper for some infraction or other. And since they'd been here, it had been MacGammon who had made the decisions. All this went through Rockdale's mind in seconds, recognizing MacGammon was truly the hero in this bailout.

Rockdale was surprised when MacGammon said, "Okay. But, be careful. We haven't heard the chief's piece firing in some time."

"Watch Stetson. If I'm not back soon, you're going to have to find some water or something for him. Like us, he's sweating, and none of us have any water to replace what we're losing."

Rockdale turned and pushed himself into the bushes where Chief Razi had appeared minutes before dawn. Seconds later, he wished he had listened to MacGammon—the other sailor was shorter and smaller, nearer the chief's size.

"Still no contact, Skipper," Lieutenant Commander Peeters said. "The Air Force is orbiting just south of the Liberian border, but he's only got about two hours of fuel remaining. If we don't locate Razi and the others in the next hour, we're going to have to release the helo."

Commander Greensburg grunted. "Damn it, why don't

they answer? We've been orbiting here since daylight. It's been over an hour since we started the search."

Pits shut his eyes and leaned back against the bulkhead of the cockpit. He didn't say what they were all beginning to believe, and that was that the four men were dead, captured, or worse, being tortured to death. Africans were no better known for their hospitality than the Jihadists. He took a deep breath. He should have been a better judge of character with regard to Razi, though deep down, Pits still wasn't fully convinced the man even knew what he was doing until after he bailed out. He had met others like Razi during his career. Those who became so enamored with their own self-made image that they began to believe it—act it—do it until circumstances called for them to rise to the occasion such as Razi did, and they did it before they realized they never really intended to do it. His eyebrows bunched. He tried to recall that thought, trying to figure out what it meant, unless it meant he'd been wrong about others during his career.

"Okay," Greensburg said, drawing everyone's attention. Several seconds passed before he continued. He glanced down at the fuel gauge. "We have fuel for another four hours. We aren't going off-station until only enough fumes are left in the tank to take us on the glide path to Monrovia. Chuck, you call homeplate and see what the status is on Ranger 20. Then, you tell the other crew to get their butts to the flight line. If that airplane can fly, then I want it to relieve us on-station two hours from now."

"Sir, I'll do that, but that aircraft lost an engine and—"

"Then tell them to leave some of the aircrew behind and fly on three engines."

Pits eyes opened. "Sir, that's against NATOPS. If they fly that aircraft—"

"Senior Chief, NATOPS is fine for peacetime flying, but I—you—we have four fellow aircrew out there somewhere and until someone senior to me orders us out of the air, we're going to fly. Chuck, you tell Lieutenant Gregory that if he thinks the aircraft is too dangerous to fly, then stay put, have a fuel truck standing by, and they can take this EP-3E backup."

"Yes, sir," Peeters replied, dashing out of the cockpit and heading toward the radio position.

Pits leaned forward. "Sir, you know this could cost you your job, if they fly that aircraft without a full maintenance inspection, engine replacement, and drop check."

Evans and Roberts looked at Greensburg, who didn't acknowledge Pits' words. Pits could see the man's face reflected in the cockpit window, while the other two looked directly at it. Crazy Harry loved flying. He loved the aircraft and he loved his crew. Only now did they realize the priority of the immortal they followed.

Something glistened in the windshield. Pits' brow wrinkled at what he thought were tears running down Greensburg's cheeks at the same time that the copilot and flight engineer looked away. He shook his head and thought, *No way. This is an immortal and immortals don't weep.*

"Never mind, Skipper. There are times when the best actions are not always the right actions, but they're the things we must do for a higher cause."

"Senior Chief," Crazy Harry said. "Bite me. Now, go get me a cup of coffee and quit this kid-glove thing."

Pits nodded, slid off the seat, and headed back to the galley. *You weren't going to get a sentimental comment from Crazy Harry.* Immortality carried certain morale requirements, and the three of them were witnessing an officer about to kill his career when the crewmembers he was doing it for may already be dead.

*   *   *

ROCKDALE PUSHED THE LIMBS OF THE BUSHES APART, jumping back when a spider the size of his fist fell onto the jungle humus and quickly scurried away. He glanced at his watch. Thirty minutes he'd been in the thicket, and he was sure he was following the chief's path because of how the humus was torn up. Plus, here and there, he could see where someone or something had broken a limb or torn off a bunch of new leaves. He squinted and leaned forward, concentrating on something hanging—it was part of a flight suit. Rockdale sighed for it confirmed he was on the right path.

He pushed forward, crawling on all fours as he back-tracked Razi's path. He glanced back several times, glad to see that his path remained marked along the ground by the disturbances that he and the chief had made. It shouldn't be too hard to find his way back to MacGammon and Stetson.

Several minutes later, Rockdale stopped and squatted back on his haunches. He raised his head to find it blocked by the entwined brush, so he slid sideways, resting on his hip, his upper torso braced by his right hand. Rockdale wiped the sweat from his forehead. His tongue was thick against his lips and his eyes burned from the salt of the perspiration. For the first time today, he believed there was a good chance they may die out here, their bodies food for the wild animals.

As he rested, the faint sound of gunfire reached his ears. He turned his head slightly trying to discern from which direction the gunfire was coming. He slid forward onto his chest before pushing himself off the ground with both hands so he could turn his head. Rockdale paused, trying to remain motionless as he listened to the gunfire. Wherever it was, it sounded far away, but here in the jungle, noises didn't travel far because of the natural insulation that abounded. Maybe it was closer than he thought. Above the thicket in which Rockdale moved, the wind shifted direction and with it, the sound of gunfire was carried away.

He waited for nearly two minutes, straining to hear it again. As he waited, he turned his attention to the path he was following. Here the chief had come from the left. A new sound caught his attention. The sound of radio static, and it was coming from somewhere nearby. He dropped to the jungle floor and started hurrying forward along the chief's path, ignoring the occasional thorn ripping his hands and head. The harsh vines and limbs tore at his flight suit, ripping it in places, creating fresh feeding grounds for the swarms of mosquitoes that seemed to appear from nowhere, drawn to Rockdale by his sweat and heat.

He could hear voices now and knew somewhere ahead was a PRC-90, but the green of the survival vest blended with the surrounding vegetation, so Rockdale moved as quickly as he could. His eyes marking the trail he was backtracking as his ears listened for the radio to broadcast again. Rockdale's hand hit a slick spot, slipping out from under him and causing him to fall, striking his chin on an upright stick. The stick slashed into his chin, enough to rip open the skin. Rockdale ignored the pain, jerking the stick out and continuing to scramble forward on all fours.

The ground here was torn up in several directions—probably from the animals that used it, but the mess camouflaged Razi's path. Rockdale waited on hands and knees, surveying what little distance he could see, trying to discern which way the chief had traveled. Unable to tell which way to go, Rockdale opted to continue in the direction he was traveling. As he started forward, the radio broadcast again. The garbled voice came from behind him. The entwined limbs and vines trapped him, holding him in the direction he was heading. Rockdale fought against them, bloodying himself in the process until he finally turned around. He scrambled back the way he had come. The sound of a voice broadcasting led him, his recklessness to find the radio causing him to slip and fall every few feet, earning him more cuts and abrasions.

Ten feet farther he heard the radio off to his left. Rockdale dove at the tangled vegetation, forcing the limbs apart, and like a treasure hidden from view, the chief's survival vest hung from limbs above his head. Rockdale had crawled by the survival vest hanging overhead without ever seeing it.

He reached up and pulled the vest down, jerking it free of jungle growth that fought to keep its won prize. The radio fell out and disappeared behind the thick trunk of the bush. Rockdale reached behind the vegetation, blindly swiping his hand back and forth, patting the area, searching for the radio. Finally, his fingers touched the metal and a second later, Rockdale had the radio pulled free. The voice kept repeating their names. He started crying. He wanted to stop, but he couldn't, his sobs came in long, drawn out moans as he blinked to clear his eyes so he could operate the radio.

Tears clouded his eyes. Here he was, the calm one, and he was crying like a baby. He was above this emotional bullshit, so why was he shaking? Rockdale started drawing slow, deep breaths. He held the PRC-90 tightly as if afraid he was going to drop it and lose it. This was their passport out of the jungle. This was the ticket home. His chest heaved as he concentrated on his breathing, bringing his emotions under control. The tears stopped, and he awkwardly wiped his eyes with a sleeve while both hands continued to hold the radio. A twenty-two-year-old sailor shouldn't be here in the middle of an African jungle.

Several more minutes passed before Rockdale regained his composure and his eyes cleared. He took a deep breath and said a few words aloud, ensuring himself he wouldn't choke up on the radio.

He released the radio from the death grip he had on it and raised it near his face. Rockdale checked to ensure the radio switch was on VOICE before he pushed the button and spoke, knowing that overhead were friends and fellow sailors with no other mission in mind than finding them. At that moment, he wanted nothing more than to hug each and every one of them.

"WE GOT THEM!" PEETERS SHOUTED AS HE DASHED INTO the cockpit. "The spooks have the signal DF'ed. We're about five miles south of their location."

Pits placed his hands on both sides of his perch as Commander Greensburg put the EP-3E into a left-hand turn.

"Let's go get them," Crazy Harry said. "Dell, let's get some altitude so we don't interfere with the helo. Chuck, Air Force inbound?"

"We're passing the location to Colonel Hightower now."

"Everyone okay?" Pits asked.

"We're still getting information, Senior Chief. Most important thing was to get their location. Jonathan is taking the data," Peeters said, referring to Lieutenant Jonathan Reed who was the mission commander on the earlier EP-3E mission when the four men bailed out.

Reed stuck his head through the curtain. "Boss," he said to both the skipper and Peeters. "Carson is injured. We've passed that information on to Hightower. Looks as if they will have to crash the canopy and hoist Carson out via stretcher. Razi is missing. According to Rockdale, Chief Razi routed some armed men who were holding them at gunpoint and the last they saw of him he was chasing them through the jungle."

Pits shook his head. Will this nightmare ever end? Razi was a pain in the ass before he bailed out. Now, there would be no living with him. "I'll go back and see what I can do to help."

"Like what?" Chief Roberts asked.

Pits shrugged. "Maybe call the helo and see how wide their doors are."

"I'm sure the doors are wide enough for the stretcher."

"I'm sure they are, too, but I don't think they're going to be wide enough for Razi's head when we do find him."

RAZI RAISED HIS HEAD, BLINKING HIS EYES, AND SLOWLY turning it as he took in the sight in front of him. A ring of armed Africans surrounded him. A rough tree pressed against his back and when he tried to step forward, he discovered his hands and legs were tied firmly. He was naked except for his skivvy shorts. He looked down and saw where the rope was tied just above his ankles. He could move his knees a little, but not enough to pull his ankles free. But he pulled, and as he fought the constraints the Africans laughed. His flight suit was gone. The flight suit lay wadded up against a nearby bush. The pockets had been pulled inside out, revealing that whatever he had in those pockets were now in someone else's.

"Let me go, you assholes!"

A tall, slender man, dressed in khaki shorts with a sleeveless shirt, stepped forward. "Welcome back, American," he said. "Seems you have tried to kill Ojo too many times, and too many times you have failed."

"What the hell is an Ojo, and who the hell are you?" Razi asked. Where were those man-eating lions when he needed them? How about those crocodiles? They'd be good right now.

The man pulled a long, slender knife from his belt. "I am General Kabaka, the future leader of the African National Army, and you're going to help me rid our movement of Ojo."

"I'd be more than happy to help you get rid of Ojo," Razi said. He twisted his hands back and forth, feeling the rope slide slightly forward, off his wrist. Raze glanced to both sides and saw the audience were in front of him, unable to see his hands behind the tree.

The one called Kabaka stepped closer, within range of Razi's hands, if he freed them. The African lifted the knife and with the backside of it, ran it down Razi's chest. "You are a good specimen for a belt. But, this skin is spotted, ripped, and cut in so many places that to find a single length is going to be very hard." He lifted the knife, turned his back to Razi, and spoke to the men watching.

Razi didn't understand what Kabaka was saying. It wasn't English. He pushed with his right hand and pulled with his left. The rope around his legs was going to be a problem. Even if he broke free, he'd fall forward onto his face. He took a deep breath. Twenty-four hours ago he would have been afraid. His eyes narrowed. Somewhere in the depths of his mind was a screaming ego shouting for him to beg, plead, do anything to live. The idea was appealing, but this man had no intention of letting him live. He was going to skin him alive. He'd read the intelligence reports enough to know this torture had been discovered in some of the villages razed by the African National Army.

Kabaka turned back to Razi. "Maybe your back is in better shape for a belt. You think I should try there?" He laughed.

"I wouldn't," Razi said, aware his voice had dropped as he became aware of what awaited him. "You wouldn't be able to see my face and my screams would be muffled."

Kabaka nodded a salute at Razi. "You are brave man, American. If you are so brave, then where are the others of your team so we may see if this bravery is something that runs through the veins of your special forces."

"I'm not Special Forces, and I'm not a Navy SEAL."

"Then why would someone dressed in jungle camouflage parachute into our area? Do you think we are stupid?"

"To answer the first question; that is a flight suit. We who fly aircraft wear them. As for the second question, I think you've already answered that yourself."

Kabaka's false smile dropped. He raised the knife quickly and slid the sharp blade down Razi's chest, barely breaking the skin. "The top skin lasts a long time if separated from the fat directly beneath it."

Pain raced through Razi, blinding him with its intensity, causing him to bite his lower lip, and shut his eyes. His breathing became deep and rapid.

"Go ahead, American, scream. It is good for the soul, and it makes great music for my ears."

No way Razi was going to give the man the pleasure of hearing him scream. He changed the direction of his hands, pulling now with the left and pushing with the right. He pulled his wrists apart, trying to stretch the rope. All he wanted was to get his hands around Kabaka's neck.

The knife was pulled away. Razi opened his eyes. Kabaka's face was inches from his.

"I wanted to smell your fear, American. Fear is very odorous, you know." Kabaka stepped back and glanced down at Razi's underwear. "Most would have urinated by now."

Suddenly, more Africans entered the clearing, their weapons raised. A stout, heavyset man, shorter than the lithe torturer standing in front of Razi walked into the center of the clearing.

"General Kabaka, what are you doing?"

Razi pulled his hands apart again and felt the tension give. He changed the movements of his hands.

"I have captured one of the Americans who is here to kill our leader, General Ojo."

"General Ojo said the Americans were not to be harmed."

Kabaka shrugged. "General Ojo did say that, but he is less concerned with his safety than we are. Is that not true, General Ezeji?"

Kabaka took a step forward. Ezeji raised his AK-47.

Razi watched with slight satisfaction that he recognized the weapon as an AK-47. He continued to work his bindings, feeling them loosen. He'd fall forward, but the man with the knife was still within striking distance. He was going to die here, but he was going to take this man with him. He shut his eyes for a moment and thought of his wife, Virginia, and his three children. They may never know what happened to him, but that would be good because they'd draw his entire paycheck for many years before the Navy decided he was no longer missing, but dead. And throughout the aviation community, the chiefs' messes would speak of Chief Razi, who disappeared in the jungle trying to rescue his sailors. Somewhere they would name a chief's club after him—The Chief Razi Chiefs' Club.

"Why are you holding your weapons on me and my men? We are on the same side."

Razi heard the click of the safety being released and opened his eyes. They were going to shoot him. He tugged on his hands. *Of course, I'd prefer to read the sign on the club myself.*

"We are truly alone out here, Kabaka," Ezeji said, dropping the title of general.

"What does that mean?"

"It means—"

The bindings came loose quicker than Razi was prepared. As he fell forward, he hollered his war cry, stretched his hands out and grabbed his torturer around the neck, taking Kabaka to the ground beneath him. The ropes around his ankles torn into his skin, sending fresh pain through his body, but he had the lesser weight of Kabaka beneath him, his hands tightening on the struggling man's neck.

Ezeji raised his hand. "Stay where you are. Do not interfere," he said in the native dialect of Kabaka's tribe. His men pushed the barrels of their guns into the backs of Kabaka's men, who dropped their Ak-47s onto the jungle floor.

Razi continued his war cry, screaming it at the top of his lungs. His meaty hands, strong from years of weightlifting, squeezed the man's neck, shutting off his air. The struggling lessened, but Razi squeezed tighter, waiting for the bullets that would snuff out his life. At least this one man would never survive to torture someone else.

Kabaka's right hand freed itself, the knife still in it. But, face down in the humus, Kabaka had little dexterity, so he brought the knife back and stabbed at Razi, but the knife only penetrated a couple of inches into Razi's side before the African lost consciousness and the knife fell harmlessly onto the jungle floor.

Razi jerked the man's head to the side and a loud snap caused Razi to stop his war cry. Beneath him the body shook uncontrollably as the nerve endings between the brain and the rest of the body released their hold on the man's bodily functions. The odor of urine and feces filled the air.

"Cut him free," Ezeji said, motioning one of Kabaka's men forward.

Razi felt the ropes around his ankles let go. He pushed himself off the dead African, falling backward on his butt, waiting for the firing squad surrounding him to fire. After several seconds, he realized many of the Africans' weapons lay on the ground and the stout fellow in front of him had his pointing down. Razi reached down and rubbed the numbness around his ankles. The painful tingling of the returning blood caused him to rub harder.

One of the Africans picked up the flight suit and tossed it to Razi, who watched it land at his knees, but he made no attempt to pick it up. Let them dress his body after they shot him, he thought.

"Looks to me, American, as if you need some medical attention."

His flight boots followed, landing jumbled on top of the flight suit.

"We have at least a kilometer to walk before our doctor can see to you," Ezeji said. "You would travel better with your clothes and boots on."

"Why don't you kill me here?"

Ezeji smiled. "No one is going to kill you, American." He pointed at Kabaka's body. "Whatever your mission was, you have succeeded. You have killed General Ojo, the leader of the African National Army."

Razi stared at the dead man for a while as he rubbed his ankles, then he looked up at the overweight African watching him, and said, "He said he wanted my help to rid Africa of Ojo. So, I did what he asked."

CHAPTER 12

ADMIRAL HOLMAN HELD DOWN HIS KHAKI HAT AS THE MArine Humvee rounded the curve. "Where did they find him?" he shouted to his chief of staff, Captain Leo Upmann, riding in the back of the open vehicle.

"He turned up at a Liberian border post last night. General Thomaston had a Liberian Army helicopter airlift him immediately to the hospital."

The Humvee hit a pothole, bouncing everyone, and causing Holman to bite his tongue. "Damn, son," Holman said to the driver. "This isn't an emergency. Why don't you slow this thing down before you kill us?"

"Sorry, Admiral," the Marine corporal replied. "The colonel said to get you to the hospital ASAP, sir." The Humvee slowed slightly.

"The colonel is right, Corporal, but I want to visit someone there, not be a new admission."

"Admiral, don't be too hard on the corporal. I told him to hurry, also."

The Humvee picked up speed again, then hit another pothole, throwing Holman to the right. "You sure you slowed down?"

"Admiral, I'm—"

Upmann leaned forward and slapped the driver on the shoulder. "You're doing fine, son."

"Leo—"

"Admiral, the chief is in surgery for his wounds. Mary said—"

"Two weeks ago, Leo, when those other three returned, everything pointed to Chief Razi being dead. The last any-one saw of him he was disappearing into the jungle, chasing a bunch of terrorists. Even his squadron has returned to Rota."

"Yes, sir. The aircraft damaged by the surface-to-air-missile departed the same day we set sail."

"Two days ago?"

"Yes, sir. VQ-2 still has a ground detachment here cleaning up loose ends and packing spares."

"One measly near-miss and European Command decides the information from the reconnaissance missions aren't worth the danger," Holman said, his voice raised over the noise of the Humvee. "Would have been nice if they had asked us for our opinion before they made the decision."

"Mary Davidson is at the hospital, Admiral. She had an opportunity to talk with Chief Razi before he went into surgery this morning. We should get some insight as to where he's been—" The Humvee swerved to avoid several Liberians pushing and shoving an obstinate donkey that had stopped in the middle of a bridge. Holman grabbed the dashboard.

"Damn, we're going to follow the chief into surgery at

this rate. Corporal, where did you get your license?"

"License? License, Admiral? Damn, sir, I'm a United States Marine. I don't need a license, sir. The colonel though—"

Holman looked over his shoulder at Upmann. "Remind me to have a word with the colonel when I see him."

"I think he must have taken offense when you ordered him to cease and desist from having their toys following you around the ship."

"Those things are like Georgia mosquitoes, buzzing around you, shooting past you, and then blocking your vision so you trip and fall."

"Admiral, VQ-2 left a senior chief in charge of the ground detail. It's my understanding that the man is a friend and shipmate of Chief Razi's."

The Humvee barreled through an intersection, took a curve leaning to the right; wheels squealing as the weight of the vehicle shifted.

"I think that was a stop sign we went through," Holman said.

"Don't know, Admiral. We were going too fast to tell."

"Corporal!"

"Sir, I have slowed down; it's just that this is straight stick, and I'm used to an automatic."

"We don't have automatic transmissions in military vehicles."

The corporal turned his head, facing Holman. "Sir, I know, and I explained that to the colonel, but he said this was a great time to learn."

"Watch the road!"

Holman turned to Upmann, who was laughing in the back seat. "Sure, go ahead and laugh. You're back there. Sometimes I think the Marines go to great lengths to figure out how to scare their Navy counterparts."

"The colonel says as soon as we Marines learn to walk on water, we won't need a navy anymore."

Holman shook his head. "Leo, how serious are the chief's injuries?"

"There's the hospital, sir," the driver said, looking at Holman and pointing forward.

"Son, do us all a favor and watch the road."

"He has a cut down the left side of his chest that has become infected, along with smaller injuries from the bailout and his sojourn through jungle."

"Broken bones, internal injuries?"

"Don't know, sir."

The driver whipped the steering wheel to the left, and slid into the driveway leading to the front entrance of the hospital. Gravel spun out to the side, ricocheting off the wooden sign with the hospital's name. The small one-story building glared in the bright morning sunlight from freshly applied whitewash. Screens covering the windows had specks and blobs of white paint splattered on them. The driver slammed on the brakes, stopping the Humvee right in front of the entrance. The engine coughed a couple of times and stalled. "Here we are, Admiral. I'll park over there," the corporal said, pointing at the parking lot, "and wait for you." The young Marine's head was down and bobbing back and forth as he stared at his feet.

The dust from their entrance caught up with the Humvee, covering the three men with fine red dirt.

Holman clamped his mouth shut, squinted his eyes from the dust cloud, unbuckled, and slid out of the opened door onto the graveled driveway, quickly heading up the few steps toward the doors of the hospital. A couple of white-clad male nurses stood to one side smoking cigarettes. Upmann shoved the seat forward.

"Corporal, stick shifts need the clutch pushed down when you're stopping."

Upmann quickly caught up to Holman as the admiral stepped inside the breezeway. Overhead fans turned slowly, shifting the humid air to keep the African heat moving. The sharp odor of ammonia assailed their nostrils for a moment, attesting to the Liberian effort to keep this newest hospital sterilized. Holman wiped the dust and sweat from his face.

Captain Mary Davidson, Holman's intelligence officer, saw the two men and hurried toward the admiral.

"Mary, what's the story?" Holman asked as she neared.

"Morning, Admiral," she said. A senior chief petty officer walked up beside her. Holman gave the man a short nod and returned his attention to his intelligence officer.

"Chief Razi will be coming out of surgery shortly, Admiral. Basically he's okay, but he has some infections—especially a deep one on his chest. They're in the middle of cleaning out the infection and packing the wounds to kill any reoccurrence." She nodded to the senior chief. "This is Senior Chief Conar. He's from VQ-2 and head of the squadron's ground detachment. He was also the flight engineer on Ranger 20, the aircraft the missile damaged. Same one the chief and the others bailed out of."

"Senior Chief," Holman nodded. "What do you know?"

"Not much more than Captain Davidson, sir. I have been in contact with Captain Greensburg."

"And the squadron is launching a bird to fly down today to pick up Chief Razi and fly him back to Rota. His wife and children have been notified. Needless to say, Admiral, there's a lot of happy people there."

"Will he be able to fly this soon after surgery?"

She shrugged. "Not sure, Admiral. The doctor said he'd

know for sure later, but he didn't see any reason that surgery would stop the chief from leaving."

"So, what happened? How did he get here and where's
he been?"

"Our chief has had one of those Navy adventures we
keep advertising about, Admiral. He bailed out and fought
his way to the sailors, just as Petty Officers Rockdale and
MacGammon said. He rescued them from being taken
prisoner by either the terrorists or the ANA, and then he
disappeared into the jungle pursuing their captors."

Noise from the front of the hospital drew their attention. Walking through the entrance was Thomaston. To his
left was a person Holman had never seen—young, dark-
skinned. The gait and haircut made Holman believe that
the man was military.

"Dick," Thomaston said, reaching forward and shaking
his hand. "I see you've heard about the rescue of your chief
petty officer." Thomaston turned to the man beside him and
then nodded at Holman. "This is Stephen Darin. Until a
few days ago, he was a general in the African National
Army. He was also our inside-man into the workings of
this growing national movement. Stephen has been a great
asset to Liberia and to the United States."

Holman shook his hand.

"He brought your chief back."

"Our thanks. Don't have to guess that bringing him
back means you can never go back."

"Not quite," Thomaston answered. "He may go back.
Darin has the loyalty and trust of the other generals inside
the African National Army, and it was him they sent out
with the chief. Seems our secrets aren't as secret as we
thought. The Nigerian intelligence also has someone even
closer to the new head of the ANA, someone named Mumar

Kabir, who has assumed General Ojo's role as the head of this rabble of an army."

"So, is it true? Ojo is dead? Killed by his own people?" Davidson asked.

"Yes," Darin replied, his eyes darting to the left as he broke eye contact with Holman. "Ojo was a malevolent leader, and with the demise of Abu Alhaul, the ANA believed it was time to switch from a pure military role to one that combined politics. Ojo wasn't the person to lead."

"So they killed him," Davidson said.

"No," Darin replied, shaking his head. A smile spread across his face, white teeth brightening across the man's dark complexion. He looked at Thomaston.

"Go ahead, Stephen, tell them. The chief will anyway."

"Your American Chief Razi killed him with his own hands." Darin stretched his hands out and made as if he was choking someone. "He grabbed Ojo around the neck and strangled him until he died." He dropped his hands. "Everyone was very happy over what the American did, and we buried Ojo near where we killed Abu Alhaul. Then, our forces completed the destruction of the remainder of Abu Alhaul's terrorists. America should be pleased."

"And no one tried to kill the chief?"

"No, Admiral, but one of our generals—General Kabaka, in protest, took his own life."

That sounded strange, Holman thought. It was also out of character. He looked at Mary Davidson. In her expression, he recognized a similar concern. It didn't sound quite right, but until he got more information, he would accept what Darin told them.

"And America will be pleased, Mr. Darin. The ANA has killed someone I would have enjoyed having the pleasure of removing from this earth; Abu Alhaul," Thomaston added. "Abu Alhaul and his followers are no more, and we can thank the African National Army—"

"African National Alliance, General," Darin corrected.

"Oh, yes. With the death of Ojo and this politician Mumar Kabir in charge, it seems that the African National Army changed its name to Alliance," Thomaston explained to Holman.

"We buried Abu Alhaul along with his followers. Then we swept the spot so no one would ever find it. They will fade from memory, which is what Mumar Kabir wants."

"We'll need a team in there to confirm it," Davidson offered.

Thomaston shook his head. "No. We—Liberia—think it is best to let Abu Alhaul just disappear. Neither make him a martyr nor make him alive. Let him just fade from memory."

"But we need to confirm that he is dead."

"Mary," Holman said. "We'll leave that decision to people higher up than us." He turned to Thomaston. "Thanks, Mr. President. We'll pass the information along and if others want to pursue it, we'll let them discuss it with you."

The doors leading to the operating rooms opened and a gurney emerged.

"That's him," Pits Conar said aloud. "That's Chief Razi. He's lost weight."

"Have you talked with him?" Holman asked.

"No, sir. I got here only a few minutes before you did."

The sound of a vehicle crashing outside the hospital interrupted their conversation. Liberian English erupted outside. Holman didn't speak the dialect, but he'd been in Liberia often enough throughout his three years as Commander, Amphibious Group Two, that he understood the gist, and it wasn't something he could repeat.

The gurney reached the group, who parted to allow it to

pass. Chief Razi's eyes were shut. His slow breathing moved the sheet up and down. Behind the gurney came two doctors, still in scrubs, removing their gloves and green caps. One was tall and thin, while the other was shorter and much heavier. Both were Africans.

"How is he, Doctor?" Holman asked.

"He's fine. We didn't put him under. We used a local on him, and he went off to sleep while we were taking out the stitches someone used on him. And he snored while we turned back the skin and wiped the infection away. I am surely impressed with a man who can sleep through what had to be very painful."

"We were impressed with the chief, also," Darin said. He looked at Holman. "The man has done so much in your military. The stories of his . . ." Darin snapped his fingers as he searched for the right word. "Adventures. I can only say that the man has had so many great adventures. My young warriors were enthralled night after night listening to him. We would have kept him longer, but a few days ago we recognized the red creeping along the edges of his wound and knew he needed proper medical attention, otherwise he would have died."

"He should be okay now," the doctor said. "He's going to have a quite a scar to add to his adventures."

" 'Adventures' is a little strong," Pits Conar said testily. "Chief Razi is known—" his voice trailed off when he saw everyone looking at him. He shrugged. "I just know Razi." He turned and sauntered over to a nearby water fountain, leaving the others to their talk.

An African wearing an off-white suit entered, carrying a plastic bag. He walked over to Thomaston, whispered something to the retired lieutenant general, and handed him the bag before turning and leaving.

Thomaston looked into the bag, smiled, and handed it to

Holman. "Dick, I appreciate the cigars, but I'm afraid my cigar days are over."

"Cigars?" Holman asked. *What in the hell is Thomaston talking about?* he thought as he took the bag. He opened and peered inside. It was a box of cigars—the kind Holman smoked. He looked up at Thomaston. "Where did you get these?"

Thomaston shrugged. "One of your officers dropped them off. Told my officer who took them that they were compliments of you. I was distinctly honored knowing how much you enjoyed them, how hard they are to find, and how well you protect them. But I could never enjoy them as much as you, and they're way too expensive for my taste."

Holman looked at Upmann. "My cryptologic officer," he said.

"Admiral, we don't know that."

"Leo, I have never allowed facts and common sense to cloud my judgment, and I don't intend to now." He turned his attention back to Thomaston. "Thanks, Mr. President. I will tell my protocol officer that the idea was appreciated, but the gift was returned."

"Now, if you have some Napa Valley wine, I doubt you'll get that returned."

"If I had a bottle of Napa Valley, General, I know where I would put it right now."

AN HOUR LATER, HOLMAN WALKED INTO OF CHIEF RAZI'S room. Over another hour later, he walked out, turning to Upmann. "Did you believe all of that?"

Upmann shook his head slowly. "I don't know of any reason why we shouldn't, but if half of it is accurate, the chief is a mix of John Wayne and Tarzan."

"Or Walter Mitty. Reminds me of that chief—yeoman,

I think—who convinced everyone that he was a security expert and got his ass shot off during the Albanian riots."

"Along with the group of VIPs he was assigned to escort."

"It does help to know what you're talking about and to recognize your own limitations. Few do, you know."

The two walked out of the hospital.

"Admiral!" Captain Davidson shouted from the steps as Holman and Upmann reached the walkway.

They stopped.

"Admiral, with your permission, I want to stay and do some snooping."

Holman stepped back up the stairs. "Mary, the *Boxer* is already heading east. This is probably the last helicopter out. If you stay, you're going to have to make your own way back."

"Yeah," Upmann added. "Instead of sailing back with us, ten days across the Atlantic, most likely you're going to have to take a ten-hour flight and meet us."

She smiled. "Damn, Leo. The sacrifices I make sometimes. Admiral, not everything this Darin told us, and what my human intelligence network tells me, adds up. This General Ojo didn't have a negative reputation with the populace. He didn't have a negative reputation with the intelligence community. And, he was believed to be someone we could talk to and reason with. This General Kabaka, on the other hand, was a sadist known for torturing his victims, skinning them alive. Chief Razi tells me the slash along his chest was done by someone who told him he was going to take his skin and make a belt out of it. That resonates better with Kabaka than Ojo." She shook her head. "There are some loose ends to tie up, and the most important ones are: Who did Chief Razi kill, and is Abu Alhaul really dead?"

Upmann and Holman exchanged glances.

"Admiral," Davidson continued, her voice firm. "Darin is either lying or Chief Razi is confused. Chief Razi doesn't strike me as someone who is confused. I think he may have an inclination to exaggerate his role in all of this, but I don't think he's lying or confused. He told me he didn't know the name of the person he killed, but apparently, one group of armed men held guns on the original group that captured him while he choked to death the man who cut him."

"Never heard of this Kabaka—that how you say his name?"

Davidson nodded.

"—until today."

"Well, I have, sir. He was one of Ojo's generals, he was known for his cruelty. The people feared him. Tales say he wore belts made from the skins of his victims. Razi wouldn't know this, but he said the man who cut him bragged about having a white belt. This sounds like Kabaka, not Ojo."

"Then why would Darin lie?" Holman asked.

Davidson shrugged. "I don't know yet, sir, but if he is lying, then Thomaston's spy is a turncoat. And the other question is why would they want everyone to think Ojo is dead?"

"He's Liberian," Upmann protested.

"What does that mean?"

Davidson answered, "He's native Liberian and native Liberians have an historic hatred for Americo-Liberians, and it would be easy to see that hatred carry over to the American expatriates who took advantage of the Liberian offer of citizenship and moved here. Such a movement as the ANA would appeal to the nationalism of such a person who may feel he and his ancestors are being further denied their rightful place within Liberia."

"And Ojo?" Holman asked.

"It could be that they believe this new person—Mumar Kabir—may be more acceptable to the larger picture," She paused for a second. "to the larger world audience, maybe. Instead of a general leading them, maybe Ojo has changed his name to become more acceptable."

"I would think that would be hard to hide."

Davidson smiled. "It may not be too hard, sir. We have no photographs of this Ojo—"

"We have photographs of Kabaka?"

"No, sir," she replied, shaking her head. "We do have photographs of a General Ezeji, who we know is with Nigerian intelligence. But our Nigerian counterparts believe that the man may have turned on them. Trust no one and you won't be disappointed seems to be their mantra."

PITS WAITED UNTIL THE DOOR SHUT BEHIND THE OFFICERS before walking up to the bed.

Razi looked up at him and smiled. "Well, well, well. If it isn't my best friend, the senior chief."

Pits cleared his throat. "Badass, I owe you an apology. I have always thought you were an arrogant, grandstanding, egotistical braggart whose every word was designed to promote yourself."

"Don't hold back, Pits. Tell me what you really think."

"What I really think is that I was wrong in some of those thoughts. Maybe there was some true unselfishness in your words."

Razi's eyes widened and he tilted his head forward. After a few seconds, he said, "Well?"

"Well, what?"

"All those other things about me being arrogant, grandstanding, and something egotistical—what about them?" He leaned his head back onto the pillow.

"Oh—those are still true, and it wouldn't surprise me to discover half of what you told the admiral and the other officers were bald-faced lies."

Razi shook his head. "You know, Pits? When I get well, I think I may have to stomp your ass."

"Like how you took that crocodile by the tail and shoved him off the cliff? Or how you raced through the jungle, slashing your way toward the men, only to have to fight the terrorists hand-to-hand to save our sailors. Or how you broke your bonds to kill the leader of the African National Army?"

Razi nodded, a confused look on his face. "Yeah, what about them? They're all true."

Pits sighed, walked over to the window, turned a chair around, and straddled it, resting his hands on the back of it. "Chief Razi, it doesn't matter whether I believe you or not. What I do believe is that what you did was brave—foolish—but brave. It was what a good chief petty officer should and would do." He slapped the chair. "And, I'm not sure I could have bailed out of that aircraft like you did for no reason other than taking care of your sailors." He stood, placing his hands on his hips. "Damn! I can't believe I said that." He pointed at Razi. "You are a real pain in the ass and even as much as you piss me off, I can't help but admire what you did."

Razi smiled. "And well you should, Pits. What I did was what any good chief petty officer would have done. You think it was hard for me to bail out like that." He nodded once. "Damn straight, it was. I knew I shouldn't bail out, but out there—over that jungle full of things that can eat, shoot, sting, or fang you—were my sailors." He shook his head. "Pits, I just couldn't think of anything else except being there for them. That being said, I think you deserve some sort of reward for recognizing what a great and wonderful human being I am. So, get me out of here and let's go have a few beers." He pushed himself up off the bed and threw his feet over the side. "Do you know how long it's been since I've had a drink? And to show you that I hold no hard feelings about you being an asshole; you can buy."

Pits laughed. "I might be having a few beers tonight; but for you, my fine modest friend, you'll be on an EP-3E heading back to Rota. A plane is on its way to ferry you back to mommy-san and the kids. Since the rules are no drinking twelve hours before a flight, there's no alcohol for you."

Razi lay back down. "Look, Pits. That aircraft can't possibly get here for six or seven hours followed by at least a two- to four-hour turnaround. I could have several beers and sleep it off before they take off."

Pits pulled his cap from his belt, put it on his head, looked in the mirror, and exaggeratingly straightened it. "Damn, damn, damn. Looks as if the hero will have to wait until tomorrow, or possibly next week, for that cold beer."

"No way. Virginia will meet me at the aircraft with a cooler."

"She'll meet you in the hospital, and without a cooler. You're being transferred to the hospital for recuperation, Badass. Rockdale and MacGammon have been released, but Carson is still recovering."

"How is Carson? I only caught a glimpse of him when I was fighting those ten or twelve terrorists." He smiled. "It's hard to keep count when they keep coming at you."

"He had a concussion and multiple broken bones in his left leg, but he's regained consciousness and on the road to recovery. Don't think he'll fly again, but doctors say he'll be fit for shore duty."

"What a horrible thought!"

Pits opened the door. "I hate to tell you this, but you're going to find out anyway."

"What?"

"They have put you in for the Bronze Star for your actions."

Razi grinned. His head moved sharply from side to side as if he was silently thanking a crowd. "With a combat 'V,' I hope."

Pits turned and jabbed his finger into his open mouth several times. "That's why I didn't want to tell you, but I figured if I told you, you'd have some time to get the strutting-rooster bit out of your system before the crew arrives."

Razi leaned his head back again onto the pillow. "Hey, Pits. Thanks, shipmate."

Pits walked to the door, turning at the last moment. "What else are shipmates for? Oh, by the way, I told the squadron to send the aircraft with the widest hatch."

"They're not going to make me use a stretcher to fly back, are they?"

Pits smiled. "No, I doubt it. But there is concern that your head won't fit through the entrance."

Razi smiled. "I think I can handle it."

The springs on the door pulled it closed behind Conar. Razi watched the door for moment. It moved again and one of the doctors entered, carrying a brown paper bag under his arm. "Here you are, Chief Razi," he said, handing it to him.

Razi pulled out a warm bottle of beer. "Oh, what a great day this is, Doc. Nectar of the gods. Remind me to name my first born after you."

"It is Liberia's own."

Razi twisted the cap. "Ouch, Doc." He shook his hand a couple of times, flexing his fist. "That hurt."

"Sorry," the doctor said, pulling an opener from his smock's pocket. A quick movement and the cap flew off, bouncing onto the wooden floor. He handed the open beer to Razi, who stared at it with open admiration. "You promised to tell me about the crocodiles?"

Razi nodded, looking at the young African. "And I will, Doc. It's just that it's a long story and this is only one beer."